SHADOW HUNTERS

It was there. It really had been there. Now it was out of sight inside the cloud, where they could never follow it with the naked eye in the pitch blackness of absolute night. It really had been there, but the radar couldn't find it. What kind of airplane did the Russians have that you couldn't spot at twenty miles on the radar carried by an F-15?

"No contact on pulse mode. Heavy interference. Trying long-range search."

The Russian Bear was still too close, flooding their radar receiver with random mush even though they'd turned tail on him. But just the same, with a clear target like that? And the night milk cloud wall was leaning right up over them. With a clear target like that, the set should have picked it out instantly. What kind of airplane pulling what kind of trick?

The cloud wall tumbled on top of them and the faint phantom of light went out. Nothing left but the stopped-down glows of the cockpit instruments. Not even a silhouette of the pilot's ejector seat. Nothing but purest night.

Also by the same author, and available from Hodder and Stoughton Paperbacks:

The Highest Ground
Frankenstein's Children
Chasing the Sun

About the author

David Mace was born in Sheffield. He is the author of six internationally published novels: DEMON-4, NIGHTRIDER, FIRE LANCE, and the highly-acclaimed THE HIGHEST GROUND, FRANKENSTEIN'S CHILDREN and SHADOW HUNTERS. His most recent novel is CHASING THE SUN. He and his wife and son live in North Lancashire.

DAVID MACE

SHADOW HUNTERS

CORONET BOOKS
Hodder and Stoughton

Copyright © David Mace 1991

First published in Great Britain in 1991 by New English Library Ltd.

New English Library paperback edition 1992

Coronet edition 1993

The right of David Mace to be identified as the author of this work has been asserted by him in accordance with the Copyright, Designs and Patents Act 1988.

Printed and bound in Great Britain for Hodder and Stoughton Paperbacks, a division of Hodder and Stoughton Ltd., Mill Road, Dunton Green, Sevenoaks, Kent TN13 2YA. (Editorial Office: 47 Bedford Square, London WC1B 3DP) by Clays Ltd., St Ives plc. Photoset by Rowland Phototypesetting Ltd., Bury St Edmunds, Suffolk.

British Library C.I.P.

Mace, David, *1951–*
    Shadow hunters.
    I. Title
    823.914[F]

ISBN 0 340 60148 5

For Philip, my son

Contents

PROLOGUE

Kola Bear

New Year 1989

Once upon a time it would have been a UFO. It would have been a cluster of unconfirmed sightings on the official list. But those kooky days were over. The Air Force had gotten real.

Colonel Oliver Eliot Lutwidge sat under a canopy of stretched acrylic. He sat in a dome of static night. It was smeared overhead with milk vapour as the faint light of the approaching moon breathed on a skin of stratospheric ice. The moon wasn't due up for almost an hour, but it had already banished most of the stars. Only the brightest still shone through the haze layer. At twelve o'clock and higher than Luzzi's head, higher even than the hoop of the midframe on the canopy, was the pole star. They were headed north through the motionless night. They were headed north at a sedate four hundred knots, four hundred and sixty miles per hour. Not very fast for an Eagle.

Down below were clouds painted dark, with valley sides brushed by that same milky smear. Coming up west of track, to the left, were the piled-up ramparts of a weather front. Under all that cloud, in the pitch blackness of a winter night, it was storm warnings for shipping on the Norwegian Sea. Up here, twenty-five thousand feet away, it was vanguard ghosts of moonlight in smooth air in the first half hour of the year. It was an easy airborne stroll for two Eagles and a Bear.

"By the way, sir." Luzzi's helmet turned to the right, and showed a three-quarter profile of face and oxygen mask past the high back of the pilot's ejector seat. But Luzzi wasn't speaking over his shoulder. He was keeping close watch on the other Eagle and the Bear. "By the way, sir. I clean forgot to wish you a happy New Year."

Lutwidge also looked to the right. Automatic reflex. Eighteen years ago and four ranks lower, he'd survived the skies over Vietnam – by always looking everywhere. In air combat you only got careless the once, and you could be dead. The worst possible piece of carelessness was to let the other guy see you first. It would kill you most every time. "Guess I forgot, too, Luzzi. Take as read." Without lights, a black silhouette at two o'clock and slightly high, McGee's F-15 rode like a special effect mask against the stratosphere haze. Twice as far away, on their beam at three o'clock and level, was the Tu-142, the Bear. "Ease off some. Double our spread."

"Easing off."

The stick between his knees nudged a shade to the left as the back seat controls shadowed the pilot's moves. This was an F-15D, a two-seat trainer. Lutwidge kept his hands and feet off the controls. Don't interfere with Luzzi. The boy was good, while Lutwidge himself was rusty and old enough at forty-four for his reflexes to be slowing – and his presence as unit commander in the back seat of a trainer on a real live intercept mission was a flagrant disregard of the rules. The colonel should be on the ground at Bitburg. He sure as hell shouldn't be here.

The Bear, big and ugly and three times the length of the intervening Eagle, saw them moving away. On came all its navigation lights, red on the wingtip, white on the tail fin, flashing eyes under its belly at front and rear. It thought the intercept was over, so it was saying goodbye. Or Happy New Year. Or who the hell cared. In daylight the Russian aircrew waved from windows and observation blisters, cheeky, taunting, deceitful friends. His own boys never waved. Lutwidge made sure of that. You don't go waving at people who might one day kill you.

With a real opponent around, you don't need UFOs.

In the black well below the repeater instruments, the stick nudged into the center again between his knees. Luzzi had them flying parallel to McGee's F-15, but now at twice the distance. In the dark you can't use even a fraction of full combat spread – a mile or more apart and three, four, maybe five thousand feet difference in altitude. In the dark you can't see each other unless you're close together. But it never feels too good to be cramped up in a close pair. Vietnam again, and avoiding getting killed.

The Bear kept his navigation lights burning. Deceitful friends. The huge Tu-142, the Bear-F Mod 3, had crawled its propeller-driven way right around Norway from its base on the Kola Peninsula. Basically a submarine hunter, it was running a maritime reconnaissance and electronic intelligence mission. It was watching Nato's shipping movements and it was eavesdropping on every radio and radar signal it could hear. The Russians came from the Kola just about every day, with their Bears or Badgers, their Coots or Mays – always probing, challenging, playing the Nato and Warpac game of perfect readiness that had lasted forty years.

Well the Americans, ever vigilant, were here.

"Sir, do you reckon there really is something going on?" In the front seat, Luzzi's helmet was turning regularly left and right, ceaselessly back and forth. Out over the starboard wing he had McGee's F-15 Eagle to watch, and next to it the Tu-142 Bear. And beyond those two aircraft, above them, below them, in front of them and behind them – everywhere around – he had the empty night sky. Most important of all, Luzzi watched the blind zone under Cole McGee's tail, just as McGee regularly checked the same unsighted wedge of air back of his partner's machine. Without help, if someone got low on your tail and came in fast before you made a precautionary turn – well you wouldn't know it until they killed you. "I wanted to ask, sir. Are we just here to scotch the rumours?"

"We're here to see for ourselves, Luzzi." Lutwidge patted the camera with its massive magnifying lens that was propped in his lap. "Just to see. Is the Bear still jamming?"

"Yes, sir. X-band radar, UHF, the IFF. He's swamping everything. Makes no sense as an elint mission."

It made no sense at all. To do electronic intelligence you sneaked around and you *listened*. You didn't drown out every channel the people you were spying on might want to use. But that peaceful-looking night out there was a screeching chaos on all of their radar and communication frequencies. Until they moved away from the Bear they wouldn't even be able to talk with McGee through the cacophony that would flood into their earphones. The Bear didn't want *them* to do any listening. Or the Bear was just being troublesome, for the sheer hell of it.

That – almost – was the whole problem. Maybe everything had a simple explanation, each little peculiarity by itself. Maybe the faint suspicion of some kind of overall reason was just a wild idea someone dreamed up on a night out in the bar, and because it was a rumour, it stuck. Rumours work like that. But they worked hardly at all higher up the Air Force command structure. The Ramstein headquarters of the US Air Force in Europe didn't want to listen. The Pentagon wasn't interested at all. So there were unconfirmed reports of unidentified aircraft interfering during routine intercepts of Soviet intruders? So some RAF guys had made a couple of sightings on moonless nights? So a pair of F-15s from the 32nd Tactical Fighter Squadron based up at Camp New Amsterdam claimed something followed them between two cloud banks? So what? There were no radar tracks and no visual confirmations – not from the interceptors and not from any ground station and not from the all-seeing Awacs aircraft patrolling Nato's north flank. It was just the spook at the end of eighty-eight.

Except that a week ago it was two of his own boys from the 36th Tactical Fighter Wing at Bitburg. They were escorting another Bear back up the Norwegian Sea, when *something* dived out of the night right between them and went vertically down into cloud which was shedding a rainstorm onto the ocean below. One F-15 stayed with the Bear, the other dived after the already invisible bogey. No radar lock-up, no gun camera shot, no description, no nothing.

But Lutwidge was inclined to believe his own boys. So here he was, with about the two best pilots he had, parked as a passenger in the back seat of a trainer on a four-hour mission that spanned the turning of the year. If you're going to break the rules just a little, best do it when the generals are all busy elsewhere. But break the rules when you feel you have to. Over Vietnam, the tactical advice they started out with from the armchair geniuses was to stand off and use your missiles. Don't close, and only use your gun as a last resort. So while they were trying to stand off in the trusting belief it would help them stay alive, the MiG-21s kept coming right on in and shooting the shit out of them. So Lutwidge had broken the rules, and shot back.

Now he searched the circle of night, an extra pair of eyes, an extra chance to see anything that might, just possibly, be sneaking around, some player of games intercepting the interceptors. He searched systematically, routinely, attentively. He looked over his left shoulder so that he could see the leftside tail fin like a black knife-blade against the night. Looking high, he swept the circle of faintly milky sky, clean around over Luzzi's head and the canopy frame, all the featureless way to the rightside tail fin which sliced the stratosphere behind them. Then he lowered his eyes to the horizon line, just above the dogtoothed tailplane, and swept around forward. He passed the wingtip, he passed the Bear and McGee's Eagle, he skipped past the back of Luzzi's ejector seat. He step-searched the faint horizon above that approaching bank of cloud. He came back around to the left fin and tailplane.

He couldn't look back and *down* because of the tailplane and the wing. He had to start only half over his shoulder, looking over the air intake and down in front of the swept-back leading edge. Over night-topped weather caps, his eyes stepped along that barely illuminated wall of cloud –

A tiny kernel of darkness, right out on their beam. A speck, a smudge of black in the midst of night, a hint, a *something*.

A very distant something pacing close to the cloud wall.

"Bogey," he said, voice flat with years of training and hours of real combat-flying from way back then. "Nine o'clock low at five miles plus," he added, with his mind jumping because someone was *there*, and that someone hadn't advertised himself, which meant bad intent.

"Looking for the bogey." Luzzi's head had turned. Lutwidge didn't need to take his eyes off the speck to know what Luzzi was doing in the front seat. The voice that came to his earphones was stretched, came out of a twisted windpipe. "Say angels." Luzzi, the pilot in command of the bird, was giving orders to his backseater, even if that backseater was a colonel. And damned right, too.

"Maybe angels twenty." Without being able to assess the range of that speck in the night, he couldn't estimate its altitude. It might be five thousand feet lower. It might be more. "It's around fifteen degrees down, slap against that cloud wall." It was the merest pinpoint of a speck backed by the vast escarpment of cloud lit – just – by faintly reflected moonlight. He got the camera off his lap and raised it to his face. With his helmet visor up, there was nothing but the clumsy muzzle of the oxygen mask to stop him getting the eyepiece comfortably close. He could get enough of a view through the telephoto lens. All he could see was a formless speck. Had to be much more than five miles away. A miracle he saw it at all. He presssed the trigger and the camera auto-wound.

"Tally one bogey."

So Luzzi had seen the speck. Confirmation. But they'd have to close to get anything useful on it at all. Once upon a time it would have been a UFO. Nowadays you knew it was a Russian changing the rules.

"Can't talk to wingman or control, sir. The Bear is still jamming."

The thing shifting on the edge of undetectability in the dark viewfinder was a shapeless point. They'd have to chop the range, even if that scared the bogey away. Once in the cloud they'd catch him on the radar, or they'd never catch him at all. But the Bear was wiping the radar clean . . . "Go right at him."

Luzzi didn't answer. The night just flipped on its side and something huge crushed him into the seat. At maximum the F-15 could pull nine gee. He managed to cushion the suddenly leaden camera as it plummeted into his lap.

The cloud rampart with its cruising speck scrolled down into the back of the pilot's seat. And then it flipped just as suddenly to the horizontal again, and the speck slipped out of sight behind Luzzi's shoulder. Nose down and power on. The push came from the back of the seat as Luzzi piled on airspeed. Leaning left, he found the pinpoint aircraft again out above the man's shoulder. He got the camera up, he found the minute thing in the grainy eyepiece, he clamped the trigger and let the autowind fire off a stream of frames. The magnified bogey strobed on and off as the reflex mirror flicked in time with the shutter.

Then it wasn't there . . .

Starting parallel, Luzzi was closing the lateral and vertical gap by making a shallow dive at a huge off-angle, keeping the bogey just to the left of the Eagle's nose. The intersect point was tracking forward through space at the speed the bogey flew. If it dived or turned away, it would seem to drop suddenly left. So he swung the clicking camera a little left . . .

And saw the spark of the bogey's tailpipe glow.

And saw it fade abruptly into that wall of cloud.

"Radar on!" he said. "Lock him up."

"Radar is on, sir. Gun mode. No contact."

"Use MRM." Medium range missile mode had a forty-mile range – the bogey *couldn't* be further away than that. Those clouds were at barely twenty, and rushing nearer.

"MRM mode. No contact. Also fuzz interference from

the Bear, sir. Trying supersearch. No contact. Fuzz interference. Still no contact. Trying pulse mode."

It was there. It really had been there. Now it was out of
sight inside the cloud, where they could never follow it
with the naked eye in the pitch blackness of absolute night.
It really had been there, but the radar couldn't find it. What
kind of airplane did the Russians have that you couldn't
spot at twenty miles on the radar carried by an F-15?

"No contact on pulse mode. Heavy interference. Trying
long-range search."

The Russian Bear was still too close, flooding their radar
receiver with random mush even though they'd turned tail
on him. But just the same, with a clear target like that?
And the night milk cloud wall was leaning right up over
them. With a clear target like that, the set should have
picked it out instantly. What kind of airplane pulling what
kind of trick?

The cloud wall tumbled on top of them and the faint
phantom of light went out. Nothing left but the stopped-
down glows of the cockpit instruments. Not even a silhouette of the pilot's ejector seat. Nothing but purest night.

"I have a contact on three-three-zero at one-forty miles,
angels thirty-two. Looks like a civilian airliner, sir. Nothing
else. No other contact. Interrogating IFF."

The IFF would check the identity of the contact, if it was
a friendly military or a suitably equipped civil aircraft. It
wouldn't find any intruder who could totally evade the
radar's net.

"Contact's transponder came on. Confirm it's a civilian,
sir. Still no other contact. There's nothing there, sir."
Luzzi's breath went in and out in sharp, displeased steps.
"But I did see it, sir. Did we get a photograph?"

"I hope so, Luzzi." Because now he was sure, now he
was convinced. An elusive ghost was playing around during their routine intercepts. No doubt of it.

Someone was playing footsie with them up here.

PART 1

Special Team

1

February 1st

Once upon a time there was a real war, and the US 8th Army Air Force stationed a wing of bombers at RAF Mondrum in Cheshire. The real war ended, but there was still the Cold War, and then there was Nato, and the United States Air Force just sort of stayed. Nominally the place remained RAF Mondrum, but in effect it became Mondrum Air Base, sovereign US territory, an enclave of the American Way hidden in the depths of little old England. It was a major facility too important to make the Pentagon's shortlist of possible closures for the early nineties. Mondrum served as a base for Military Airlift Command, and could provide wartime dispersal for the F-111s at Upper Heyford in Oxfordshire.

Once upon a time there had been a real war. Now there was just the long and patient wait.

In the winter of 1989, on Wednesday February 1st, Captain Ware of the United States Air Force drove through the Cheshire countryside towards Mondrum. Elsewhere in the world, things were moving. The Earth had moved in Soviet Armenia, and again in Tajikistan. The Red Army was beginning its move out of Kabul. The political landscape of Eastern Europe was quietly getting ready for a convulsion that no one would predict. There was cautious talk of a rundown of the Cold War, and peace, some day, being made between the superpowers. Ron and Nancy had moved out of the White House, and a new president and commander-in-chief had moved in. Captain Ware was moving to Mondrum.

Most of the previous year had been taken up with a secondment to Molesworth in Cambridgeshire. The 550th Tactical Missile Wing had begun moving into Molesworth, and the big worry was that the local British peace protesters would move in, too, just the way they'd tried to besiege Greenham Common. The real fear had been attacks by mad women peaceniks, leaping the wire by night and getting tangled up in the base security measures on Air Force leased and Air Force controlled territory. An *incident* was what the Generals feared – that one of the women, once they turned up, would go and get herself hurt.

Inevitably, female protesters were going to get arrested. So Captain Ware, who had just commenced a tour at the huge Alconbury base, was seconded as special security adviser to the nearby Molesworth annex. Not that Captain Ware possessed any unique skills in dealing with foreign civilian agitators – nor experience in the particularly tricky area of arresting, detaining and interrogating female prisoners, who might otherwise come up with all kinds of hysterical charges to the local press after being taken at gunpoint into a male-dominated military world. It was just that Captain Ware was available – and was a woman.

Life's like that a lot, if you're female.

And then the Tomahawk missiles of the 550th were negotiated away, and Molesworth was formally closed at the inactivation ceremony on January 30th. Captain Eileen Ware was free to return to duties at Alconbury for the rest of her tour. But no one really needed her there, and the Air Force was looking for someone to fill a new secondment . . .

Captain Eileen Ann Ware, thirty-two, black, born in Detroit, drove her USAF-lease car, a Ford Sierra with right-hand drive and stick shift, past Kettering and Northampton to the M1, then took the M6 north. She left the motorway and dived into fast little country lanes between Cheshire

trees. At Church Minshull she turned south towards Nant-
wich. She started down a long, flat stretch of road lined
with woodland. Winter-shallow afternoon sun fenced at
her eyes through the ranks of bare branches hemming the
far side of the route. It stabbed, it whipped her with
shadow, it stabbed again. A dark-and-dazzle tangle wove
the empty tarmac into the fabric of the wood. For a
moment the world was old, cyclic, self-contained with its
own intrinsic magic of purpose – a place where human
beings, with their tortuous motives and tricksy technology,
were just a transient little annoyance. For a moment. It
must have been the mesmerism. Nothing more than
tiredness after the long drive.

The entry between the trees appeared up ahead on the
right. She slowed and got ready to make the turn. There
was nothing to mark it at all. It looked like any little side
road, with grass verges backed by dark laurel which glistened in the shredded sun. The sign at the turning
announced it was no through road, a route to nowhere
real. She changed down, pulled the wheel, and cruised into
the trees. The tarmac was rutted by the scuff marks of huge
tires.

The little roadside sign at the second curve, isolated in
woodland, said *Ministry of Defence, trespassers will be
prosecuted*. At the next curve was a faded board on a pole
declaring *Ministry of Defence, RAF Mondrum*. Then the
road swung back between the sun-trapping trees, doubled
in width, and headed straight for a checkpoint with a
guardhouse in the middle, electronic gates, and floodlights
on tall poles. Left and right, a double fence disappeared
into the trees. The sign over the guardhouse said simply
Halt and declare your business. If you didn't know it
already, from back on the road you wouldn't even realise
that Mondrum Air Base was there.

The outer gates were wide open. She rolled through,
pulled over beside the guardhouse, and wound her window
down. Cold country air poured in around her.

The man in drab field dress behind the guardhouse

window looked down at her. Black woman in identikit jeans and a checkered wind blouse with a fake fur collar: Air Force plates on the car, but who could tell what inside. So she held up her ID at arm's length.

He came a little bit to attention in his seat. Then he turned away and said something to the interior of the guardhouse. Another Air Force soldier appeared at the window, a man with stripes on his sleeve and a clipboard in his hand.

"Afternoon, sergeant," she said.

"Afternoon, Captain Ware." The sergeant checked his clipboard. "We have a request here for you to report directly to security. Seems Colonel Wolford wants to brief you right away."

"So I've been told. How do I get to the security building?"

"Right along this way." Behind the glass, he waved his clipboard at the road that extended from the checkpoint. "Stay on Gateway Boulevard. Ignore the first couple of roads each side after you get through the trees. At the first big intersection, make a right. That sets you heading north on Enola Gay. When you come to the dog's leg where the avenue starts to swing left, there on the righthand side is security."

She nodded, and started to wind her window closed.

The inner gate beyond the checkpoint began to roll aside. She shifted into first gear.

"Remember it's drive on the right on the base," the sergeant called through her closing window. "And welcome to Mondrum, captain."

She followed Gateway Boulevard out of the trees and past the buildings and the parking lot of the education center. Late afternoon with the sunset colouring the sky in front of her, she ran into a slow stream of base wives driving base children back home from school. Most of them were turning north on Enola Gay Avenue. Next came sheds on the left of the avenue and ranks of residence blocks on the right. Cars full of kids peeled off between the blocks at each intersection. The cavalcade thinned out. It was the bigger cars that kept going, heading through the heart of the base towards officer country.

Enola Gay was straight as an arrow until the shunt to the left in the adminstration zone. The security headquarters was slap on the outside of the leftward curve. She turned out of the traffic and pulled up on the asphalt in front of the canopied door. *Do not park*, it said on the ground, without saying where she should go instead. She turned off the engine and got out of the car. The air was chilly and damp, but the sky overhead was clear. It didn't feel too much like rain. Frost by morning, maybe.

Colonel Wolford had an office on the second floor with a view west onto Enola Gay Avenue. He also had a visitor who sported a major general's tabs and hat trim. The colonel and the general wore their Air Force blue uniforms. Eileen Ware stood in the sunset pink that was coming through the windows, and felt caught out in her off-duty clothes. It would have been so much better to have had the time to drive to her assigned quarters and change into uniform before calling on her temporary boss. But then life's full of things that could have been so much better.

Both men rose from their seats. Wolford came over and shook her hand. His handshake was too weak, as if trying to make allowance for a woman's lesser strength. He smiled. His mid-forties face crinkled up in little wrinkles focused on his eyes. "Glad to see you, Captain Ware. The name's Dave Wolford." Then he turned towards the major general. "Allow me to introduce General Dodgson, Mondrum's CO."

Dodgson took her by the hand. He was a decade older than the colonel, and far less unsure of female officers. His grip was like a trap set to hold her fast. "Elias Abrams Dodgson. Welcome to Mondrum, Captain Ware."

"Thank you, sir." She squeezed back at his hand as hard as she could. "It's a pleasure to be here."

"I hope so, captain." He released her hand and she felt

the bones moving back into place. "You'll find it interesting. I'm sure of that."

"That's my anticipation, sir." She paused. They stood in a trio in the middle of the office. Her superiors waited for her, and she waited for them. Yesterday, at Alconbury, she received the new order: temporary secondment to special duty at Mondrum. This morning she got her things together, this afternoon she drove across half of England to get here. Well if they weren't going to tell her, she'd have to ask. "My duties here, sir." She switched her glance from Dodgson back to Wolford, who as chief security officer was going to be her direct boss. "I haven't exactly been put in the picture."

Wolford nodded. He folded his arms across his chest, and all traces of lingering smiles vanished. His principal mood seemed to be deliberate seriousness. "We have a new outfit forming in order to pursue a specific task, and the outfit needs a security officer attached to it full time."

"I know that much, sir." She nodded confirmation for him. "I was told to anticipate a stay of six to eight weeks."

Wolford considered that one. "Sounds about right. Think so, sir?" He looked at Dodgson.

General Dodgson shrugged. "Eight weeks, tops. After that the flying conditions won't be right, I'd say."

"So," Wolford repeated, "sounds about right. Your job, captain, won't be concerned with *physical* security as such – the base itself provides all of that. Your primary task will be to keep tabs on things to prevent *information* leaking out. Be around the unit, listen, make sure people keep in line. Besides that – and it will help with the primary task, because it should keep you up to date with everything that's going on – besides that, you can generally make yourself useful with personnel-related problems. You know the kind of thing – accommodation, transport, what's where on the base, and so on. Except for the unlikely event that we're going to have a spy in the unit, basically it's just a baby-sitting job."

"I see, sir." Security officer, she thought, attached to a

special unit being formed at Mondrum to conduct some sort of secret operation. Sounded like a responsible, demanding, interesting assignment. But it wasn't going to be like that, and as the 3rd Air Force's supernumerary and apparently superfluous female officer, she should have known it. Someone somewhere had decided the job was suitably straightforward for a woman to be able to handle okay, besides being too irritating to inflict on a man. She'd been in the Air Force ten years and it still wasn't taking her seriously.

"Needs a fine feeling for persuasion, Captain Ware," Dodgson said, qualifying the situation as though he'd read her mind. "And the ability to apply gentle admonition to keep all of those involved aware that they have to keep their mouths shut."

"I see, sir." A job needing a woman's touch, and damned all else.

"The outfit is small," Wolford said. "A non-flying CO with one of the Pentagon's intelligence officers to assist him, plus six pilots and six modified F-15s. There's a special equipment set for each aircraft, and there's an expert coming over from the States to look after that equipment. The stuff also requires security, incidentally. It's new, state of the art, and absolutely top secret. Ground crew for both air maintenance and aircrew support is being drawn from our own personnel here at Mondrum. The whole team is going to add up to around sixty men and women – plus families, of course. When we're dealing with informational security, families are a part of the picture, too."

"People talk," Dodgson said. "Word gets around. Eventually someone hears who goes and tells exactly the people we don't want to have knowing about this."

"Yes sir. Excuse me, sir." If they still weren't going to get around to telling her what the posting was about, what the *sense* of the job was supposed to be, well she'd have to ask directly. "What will the special unit be doing that requires secrecy beyond normal security precautions?"

Wolford looked at his commanding general. The pale

pink of a clear sky sunset was stripping years off his face by the minute. He seemed deeply aware that the imported security officer would have to know the secret she was supposed to be safeguarding, even if she was nothing much more than an elevated military policewoman. He was youthfully – innocently – concerned that his superior should appreciate the fact.

Major General Dodgson just nodded.

Wolford seemed relieved. "The cover is that the unit is testing special sensor equipment. The stuff has been evaluated in ideal conditions, but now it has to be tried out in the kind of bad weather you'd get in the European theater in winter. This ties in neatly with the fact that the aircraft will be fitted with special sensor equipment – in fact two sets of equipment, which just happen to be rival systems currently undergoing real evaluation in a race to land a major procurement contract. You follow?'

"I follow, sir."

"That's fine." Wolford bit his lip, looked at Dodgson for approval, then proceeded. "To give plausibility to the cover, which is sure to be blown at some time, we have a *deep* cover." He paused. He gave her an elaborate stare to make sure she realised just how important all of this was. "The deep cover is that the unit F-15s are in fact testing out the sensors by covertly intercepting and pursuing patsy air targets – civilian machines, plus other US and Nato aircraft. The high commands know about it, but secrecy has to be complete as far as all and any units and aircrew are concerned, otherwise the true capabilities of the sensors on test couldn't be evaluated adequately. The evaluation is worth the fuss because the contract – the *real* contract, I might add – is going to be worth something near a billion. Make sense?"

"It makes sense, sir." She waited. Wolford waited. Dodgson, she thought, might conceivably be amusing himself by watching them wait. "And the actual truth, sir? The operation the unit is running? I have to know what it is, or I won't be able to tell if someone starts blabbing about it."

"Ah," Wolford said. "Yes. Well now, that's one *very* sensitive matter, captain." He looked around at his office. Maybe he was checking on the number of chairs. "I guess you'd better sit down, Captain Ware. We'll give you a full briefing right away." He glanced at Dodgson. "You have the time now, sir?"

Dodgson just nodded. "Let's get on, Dave."

2

February 2nd

"Special Team," announced the man at the front of the room. "That's our designation. We're a small élite force, and the job we have to do is going to be one hell of a problem." Colonel Oliver Eliot Lutwidge paused. He was sizing them up the way a commanding officer superman does in the movies. He had the blue blouse of his uniform buttoned closed, he had his fists planted firmly on his hips. Rolled up tight in his left fist was his cap. His uncovered hair was cropped brown with eagle wings of grey extending from his temples. It looked as though just a little more length would have allowed the hair to curl.

"In fact," he said eventually, "it's impossible. But we're going to do it anyway."

His little audience didn't say a word.

If Enola Gay Avenue was the administrative, shopping

and social spine of Mondrum, Manhattan Avenue, which
ran parallel to it just half a mile to the west, was the working gut. For two miles, along both sides of the broad route,
were all of the hands-on facilities a major air base needs in
order to support a transport wing together with staging
reconnaissance aircraft. There were depots, store sheds,
workshops, maintenance hangars and service areas. In the
middle of it, on the western side with a view out over the
north-south runways, was the tower built above the flight
operations and control center.

Most of the structures and the facilities they housed were
relatively new, updated as the aircraft they served got
bigger and the support demands became ever more complex; but hidden away in secluded corners were a few remnants of earlier days. Down near the south end of
Manhattan, between the road axis and the periphery of the
taxiway, right next to the first bunch of dispersal shelters
awaiting redeployed combat aircraft if hostilities ever
broke out, was a disused leftover from the last war. Out
of the way and overlooked by nothing but the bare backsides of giant storage sheds, that's where they put Special
Team.

The unit's little empire was a short strip of apron crisscrossed by ankle-high hedges of grass and weeds growing
up between the ancient concrete squares. Along the one
side were low sheds, and on the other was a one-storey
structure with brick walls and a flat roof hidden behind
brick parapets. Lead-lined drain holes poked through the
parapet along the front of the building. The heads of dor-
mant winter weeds peered over the top. The windows in
the tired façade were assemblies of little panes set in metal
frames. Paint flakes still stuck to the metal.

The inside was no kind of palace. Board floors, plaster
walls painted in some colour which had mellowed to a
variable buff, ceilings stained brown in the wartime days
when everybody smoked. The doors were plywood on
warped frames, and every one of them squeaked. The light
switches and power sockets were in metal boxes screwed

to the walls, with exposed cables running down from the ceiling or up from the floor. The cables had been sparingly stapled in place, and then bonded fast with repeated applications of paint. The heating system belonged in some museum of industrial relics. There was a boiler room at one end of the building. The burner ran on oil. The water it eventually heated circulated on a gravity loop through vast iron pipes laid along the outside walls a couple of inches above the floor. In a very mild winter, it managed to make the place tolerable.

The furniture, though, wasn't so bad. It was scavenged from the rest of Mondrum, and it was the most basic available, but at least it was up-to-date. The chairs in the briefing room had writing rests like you'd find in any college classroom. The table at the front had a top finished in pine veneer. But the two chalk boards screwed to the wall were painted green – and what you had to use on them was real chalk, with a sponge in a bucket to wipe them clean, and a towel on a hook to dry the chalk slurry off your hands before it ended up all over your uniform.

Lutwidge wasn't using the chalk boards. He was standing in front of the table like a lecturer at ease. In front of him, filling half of the chairs, were just six pilots and one security officer. Behind him, seated beside the table, was Lieutenant Colonel Ernest Jameson Charles, the intelligence expert flown in by the Pentagon.

Eileen Ware wanted to study the pilots, but her attention was a prisoner of Lutwidge's act. Just by standing there he told you he was a leader. He demanded everything, he got everything – or he got you out of his sight. He was an ideal frontline commander made flesh. His pilot days were over, but he knew combat flying as well as anyone possibly could. In America's last war, in Vietnam, he survived a string of encounters with MiGs, and gunned and missiled his way through enough confirmed kills to become an official double ace. When the Aggressors were set up to rival the Navy's Top Gun air combat school, Oliver Lutwidge was one of the experts they pulled in to put together the training program. Now his regular job was commander of a unit of F-15s at Bitburg in West Germany. He was a fighter pilot's chief, a man of action who'd moved behind a desk, but who possessed a presence and a certitude which *inspired* his boys. He was a man's man in a man's world.

His face, she thought, looked as though it was built on a steel frame, an action man armature clothed in lean flesh. The interior lighting was neon, a single concession by the building to the postwar passage of time, and the strips were burning as the dull day darkened outside. Neon casts a shadowless light. But his cheeks were shaded and his eyes were bright inside guarded pools. Lutwidge wore a hard and dark charisma, and it suited him well.

The man represented most of what made Eileen Ware uneasy about the human male.

"First task," he said. "Let's introduce ourselves. Most of us have never met before."

He surveyed his pilots. Four of them wore day uniforms in Air Force blue, but two were in green flying gear. Thorndike and Pinkett had only just arrived, ferrying in their aircraft from the States. They'd had time to get out of their cockpit kit and strip down to their overalls, time to down a cup of coffee and a hamburger organised by Eileen Ware – because no one else thought of it and everyone seemed to assume she should – and then Lutwidge called the unit briefing almost before they'd even signed their aircraft over to the ground crew officer.

"Guess we'll start at the top." Lutwidge turned towards his immediate junior, the lieutenant colonel. "This is Ernest J. Charles. He's the man with all the information we think we need for this operation, and access to all of the stuff we're likely to find out we need before we're through. But what he's *really* here for is to pick up every shred of information we find out for ourselves along the way. Because, gentlemen –" His eyes swept his audience and rested on Thorndike, the female pilot. His eyes never came anywhere near Eileen Ware. "We're going on a hunting expedition. That right, Ernest?"

Ernest Charles nodded, a small smile enlivening his face. He seemed to be enjoying the last moments of the joke: we know, but some of them still don't.

But Charles surprised Eileen Ware. Charles looked right at her. Intelligence expert assesses security watchdog, and anticipates inadequacy. She looked back. Black woman encounters white male two ranks senior, and wants him to believe she believes in herself.

"You people have been picked for this number," Lutwidge said, "because you each have exactly the expertise we need, you have the experience on the F-15, and nobody beats you on points anywhere in the Air Force. Cole McGee and Donald Luzzi know each other." He pointed to the captain and the first lieutenant over on the side opposite Ware. "They're both from my outfit in Bitburg, and they're the only pilots I got to pick for myself. They don't have the fancy backgrounds of the rest of you, but they're the best. And if you want to know anything about me, I guess you'd better ask them."

McGee, quietly, was preening himself. His CO said he was as good as the best, and his CO had to be the guy who knew. Luzzi just looked awed, but with a serious determination not to lose out to anyone. He was the most junior rank by one, and the youngest by four years. And he worshipped his colonel – a man that a young fighter pilot could look up to with pride.

"Okay, now." Lutwidge fixed his gaze on one of the two majors sitting in front of him. "Clyde Lincoln Talley."

Major Talley returned the gaze. He looked, it seemed to Eileen Ware, uncomfortable. He didn't like too much eye contact, or he didn't like Lutwidge so much – or the situation he was in. Talley's right hand lay open on the writing rest of his chair. The hand wasn't relaxed. The man was carefully holding his hand still.

"Clyde Talley isn't wearing the ribbon right now, but he holds a decoration won on active service. That right, Major Talley?"

Talley shrugged, just barely.

Lutwidge still had the man transfixed with his eyes. "Out of all of you, he's the only one who ever flew a combat mission. He used to fly F-111s. He was stationed here in the UK. In nineteen eighty-six he took part in the Libya raid. He had the toughest job of all, namely flying the EF-111A Raven for the electronic countermeasures mission escorting the bombers. He was decorated for the mission, and he won a citation for an incident on that mission. That right, major?"

Again, Talley shrugged. He looked left and right, but he contrived to avoid everyone's eyes.

Modesty, or embarrassment at being pointed out a hero. Colonel Lutwidge didn't seem to be aware that such a state of mind could exist. He just went on staring at the man, waiting for him to take a bow, expecting him to perform. Show the others that there's something here to show. Score a point. Open the competition. Get on with the rivalry for who's going to be the best of the bunch.

Talley was looking at his hand as it lay flat on the chair's writing rest. He'd given up on the possibility of outstaring Lutwidge. But he wasn't going to be beaten – he wasn't going to tell, wasn't going to be made to tell.

Eileen Ware knew. Bare career details on all the unit pilots had already arrived at Mondrum, and it was part of her job to keep copies in her drawer. On the Libya raid, the adventure in the night that missed Kaddafi but wasted an awful lot of other people, he scored the one and only air-to-air kill. In his F-111, armed with heat seeking missiles for its own protection, and uniquely vulnerable because of the electronic racket it was making to cover the movements of the bombers it was escorting – in his EF-111A Raven he shot down a MiG which tried to do the same to him. All the cards should have been with the MiG. In a much quieter way than Lutwidge, Clyde Lincoln Talley was also the stuff of which heroes are made.

Abruptly, Lutwidge snapped his head up. A cryptic gesture – did it mean disapproval, acceptance, or unadorned impatience? The fist that held his rolled up cap moved

down from his hip and tapped his thigh, twice. Then he
near enough shrugged. He addressed the rest of his team.
"Clyde Talley had experience on the F-15 before he moved
to the F-111, and he's been flying F-15s again for the last
couple of years. He's over here from Wright-Patterson
AFB. He's been working there on stress evaluation for
the eyeballs-only tactics they're developing. At Wright-
Patterson they want to know how well a pilot can cope
with the overload, when he has to fly a mission without
radar or communicational support – which he's going to
have to do, if he's going to survive in an era when the
enemy might be circling around and waiting for him in an
aircraft that itself is stealthed, that can see him coming if
he uses his radar or talks all the time, but which itself isn't
going to show up on his radar so *he* can see *it* coming.
And believe me –" Lutwidge looked around at Lieutenant
Colonel Charles. "That's going to be relevant for this
mission."

Charles nodded. Charles smiled.

"Okay, now." Lutwidge fixed his gaze on the second of
the two majors sitting in front of him. "Craig James Bellman is one of our test pilots. He's the cream *de la* cream.
Right, major?"

"People tell me," Bellman said. He was looking back at
Lutwidge, but he said it to everyone else.

Lutwidge liked it. His fist went back to his hip and nested
itself there. Bellman might be a guy who didn't hide his light.
Lutwidge, quite unmistakably, approved of that. "Craig
Bellman can fly most anything, but just lately he's been
taking it easy and sticking with the F-15. Except for this
posting, he's at Kirtland AFB. At Kirtland they're evalu-
ating the kind of sensors our stealth aircraft are going to
need in order to find their targets, and which regular aircraft
are going to have to use to do the same – or to go up and fight
back against a stealthed opponent. Once again, the name of
the game is radar avoidance. If there's a stealth aircraft
around, a radar transmitter is a beacon which is going to
get you blown out of the air. Is that right, Ernest?"

Ernest J. Charles nodded. "That's right. The advent of stealth will totally change battle area procedures. Radar – your own or anyone else's – will light up as if you were out in the middle of a floodlit stage. But it won't confer any advantage on the regular aircraft caught in the light, if it's up against a fully stealthed opponent. The stealth aircraft will move through the light as if it didn't exist, as if everything was totally dark. It will maneuver into missile range – and then the regular aircraft has gotten itself into trouble. You can't make use of radar if a stealth is around."

Lutwidge was nodding his head – a little too much, as if he didn't quite want such a lengthy contribution this early in his act. He turned to the two remaining pilots, the pair in khaki flying gear.

Both of them had captain's rank. The man was black. You didn't see so many blacks who made pilot, never mind made it into the élite. Black faces were rare among aircrew, infrequent among officers, and only really heavily represented down among the noncommissioned ranks. Eileen Ware herself wasn't all that far away from being in the vanguard of encroaching equality within the world of the US Air Force. In some respects – but not in others.

The white captain was a woman. A female Air Force officer was pretty much a commonplace. But a female fighter pilot was as exotic as aliens from outer space. To penetrate that clique, that last great bastion of the macho male, she had to be tough as steel. To be *here*, assigned to Special Team, she had to be better than just about anyone else allowed in the air.

The question would be, if Lutwidge appreciated that.

Lutwidge picked out the man. "Dwight Hardy Pinkett. He has Aggressor training and plenty of experience on the F-15. These days he flies with the Thunderbirds."

They sat up. They all of them sat up and noticed – all except Bellman, that is. Donald Luzzi, the junior man, let his eyes go wide, and had to make an effort to get his expression back under control. Was it the fact that Pinkett flew with the Thunderbirds air display fleet – or that a *black* flew with the Air Force's ultimate glamour boys?

"That means he's an absolute expert on tight position flying – which is something we're really going to need on this operation. Of course –" Lutwidge addressed Pinkett directly. "It also means you're all set up for F-16s right now. Think you can handle the move back to the F-15?"

"I just flew one clear across the Atlantic," Dwight Pinkett said slowly. "I didn't get wet, sir."

Lutwidge just stared at him for a little while, and Pinkett stared back. Lutwidge shouldn't have missed that. Lutwidge knew damned well Pinkett had just arrived from the States in the cockpit of an F-15 Eagle – the man was sitting there in front of him wearing a flying suit. If Lutwidge had momentarily overlooked it, an assumption had to have caused the oversight. Pinkett might be going to have problems making the adjustment? Because why?

Eileen Ware knew. She met it head on just as soon as she educated herself out of the ghetto in Detroit. And it had been hitting on her ever since. So Lutwidge, provisionally, had to be placed into that particular category. You met them all over.

Pinkett didn't let it show. He just sat it out. He was here, and that was victory enough.

"Sandra Lee Thorndike," Lutwidge said, turning to the last of the group. He had his steel composure intact. There was no telling where he'd decided to hover on his scale of respect graded to contempt. "Let me tell you she has test and assessment scores I've never seen before, so don't go thinking she got this far just by being friendly." He grinned.

Eileen Ware couldn't see Thorndike's face, couldn't see how she decided to react. Nothing in Lutwidge's expression suggested he might have realised how near he'd come to delivering an archetypal insult. Maybe that wasn't his intention at all.

"Thorndike joins us direct from Nellis AFB. She's completed Aggressor training there, and is due to go as an instructor to the 527th TFT Aggressor Squadron at Alconbury here in the UK. Right, Captain Thorndike?'

Thorndike nodded. She had dark hair, cut short at the front and as long as the nape of her neck at the back. Right now it was flattened to her head by hours under a flying helmet. The effect lent no glamour at all — but then the contest Lutwidge had instigated was one of competence. "That's right. Sometime in the summer, sir. The posting's been delayed on account of the new training program at Nellis."

"The people at Nellis are putting together a program aimed at teaching eyeballs-only tactics for both day and night interception missions." Lutwidge talked to the rest of them on Thorndike's behalf. "If there are stealth aircraft up against our forces, their main mission is going to be to shoot up our own pilots in the air. The stealth would have to be aggressively countered, but the number of stealth aircraft our side is likely to have available isn't going to be enough, and their main mission will be to cut apart the other side's regular combat aircraft anyway. So for anti-stealth operations we're going to need pilots trained in appropriately safe and effective tactics. Once again, that means no radar — just two eyes helped out by sensors in the visual and infrared bands. The Nellis program complements the work at Wright-Patterson and at Kirtland." He paused, and took time to check every individual pilot. "So, I figure you're beginning to guess how it hangs together. Am I right?"

Silence.

Lutwidge reaped the reward of playing the up-front dominant commander. When he shut up, no one else was quite ready to start speaking. Obviously, he was entirely used to the phenomenon. He turned away. He moved around to the side of the table opposite Charles, and sat down on the table's edge. He sat with one leg raised so his thigh rested along the table, and so that his body was half turned towards his pilots. He looked at them calmly, he folded his arms — just a teacher waiting for the class to catch up.

But Eileen had seen his face while he was turned away.

No one else would have been able to see, and Lutwidge probably didn't register the fact that she caught a glimpse of the attitude he'd installed behind his action man mask. She saw, for a moment, a little of what he was thinking while he took in hand the strings of his puppet personnel.

Lutwidge, sourly, had smiled.

So she watched the puppets. McGee and Luzzi, the colonel's boys from Bitburg, would be fully aware of what this was all about. The go-for-a-good-mark question had been addressed at the four specialists. Thorndike she couldn't see properly. Pinkett was keeping his face impassive. Talley wasn't going to change his tactic of reactive silence. But Bellman was ready.

Bellman was blond. He was bronzed. He wasn't especially tall, because pilots never are, but he had a body which looked to be neatly muscled and aesthetically trimmed, as far as you could tell through his clothes. His clothes — his uniform — had that extra special something you usually only saw on senior officers with stars on their shoulders and hats. His *day* uniform, blouse and pants, was hand tailored. Which meant Bellman had money, too.

"I guess," he said slowly, "we could just be here to take a first shot at pulling all those anti-stealth elements together. See what kind of problems surface the moment we try working in realistic field conditions. Seeing as it's stealth-related, that would explain the fuss they made telling us not to go around talking to anyone about this assignment. Only problem with that would be — I guess they'd have told *us* what was going on." He smiled, a flash of perfect white within bronze. "But they didn't."

"Special sensors," Thorndike said. She'd inclined her head briefly towards Bellman. Now she waved her hand back and forth to indicate Talley and herself. "Eyeballs-only tactics for survival in environments within which stealth aircraft are thought to be operating. Well, the F-117 is already flying. They have some at Nellis. It would deploy forward to the European battle area in a real war. So —

are we going to be flying test missions against the aircraft here?"

Lutwidge waited. But once the wait didn't seem about to end, he shrugged. "Any advance on that idea?"

"Hope we don't have to fly the F-117." Pinkett shook his head. "It might be hard to see, but it sure isn't agile."

Thorndike laughed. "A streamlined brick, the guys at Nellis say."

Lutwidge unfolded his arms. He spread his hands, a catcher waiting for another ball to be pitched. Nothing came. So he placed his fists on his hips again. "You're close enough, but you're not going to get there." He looked over his shoulder at Charles, who smiled. Then he turned back to Thorndike, Pinkett, Bellman, and finished up looking at Talley. "We're going looking for a stealth aircraft."

Talley looked up at Lutwidge, and didn't take his eyes off the man's face. He still didn't say a thing. But imperceptibly, as if he'd seen the inevitable sense of it, he nodded.

Lutwidge smiled at the rest of them. "A *Russian* stealth aircraft."

Lieutenant Colonel Ernest Jameson Charles had the floor for the moment. Oliver Lutwidge had taken the chair by the side of the front table. He listened attentively, motionlessly. An intelligence expert from the Pentagon deserves full and obvious respect. But Lutwidge was also displaying *approval* of his rank junior, and thus declaring himself to be in a position to judge the man. Lutwidge thought a lot of himself.

"We'll save the details for a later briefing," Charles declared. "Right now you need the basic picture. So first of all, the background."

He perched on the front of the table, his hands down by his sides. The heels of his hands rested on the table top, his fingers tapped at the metal tube running beneath the edge. He leaned forward a little in a pose of relaxed eagerness. At one of the wartime briefings this room must have seen, he'd most likely have had a pipe in his mouth. Instead he was a non-smoker. The modern Air Force is a healthy bunch.

"Fundamentally, we're technologically more advanced than the Soviets. But that doesn't make them boys from the backwoods. They near as damn it have a real space station up there, they have advanced materials, and the MiG-29 is a good candidate for being the most dangerous thing in the air. In our context, this means that if we can build a stealth aircraft, so can they – even if they have to stretch themselves to the limit to do it. That's the reasoning behind these programs at Kirtland, Nellis and Wright-Patterson. We want to be prepared for when it happens. Well –" He shrugged. "Maybe it has happened. We have the F-117 getting ready to go operational, and the B-2 looking for Congressional money so it can get off the ground. And it's beginning to look as though the other side also has a stealth aircraft in the air. And if so, they're awful confident about what it can do."

"Beginning to look." Talley had decided to speak at last. He had a soft voice, very quiet but very clear. "On what evidence?"

"Last spring we identified a new type of aircraft. Our satellite got a picture of it parked in front of a hangar at their Ramenskoye flight test center. We obtained two confirmation pictures, then they stopped getting careless and remembered when our birds would be orbiting overhead. All the pictures were taken before sunrise or after sunset, so there are no shadows to help elicit the shape. In fact we deduce they were only flying the machine at night. It appears to be a broad delta, with twin tail fins canted outboard, and a comparatively long nose. It was painted dark, most likely in black camouflage. New aircraft observed at Ramenskoye are allocated the provisional *Ram* designation. Our list has been growing over the years. This latest we call Ram W, until the Soviets decide to announce its real name." Charles smiled faintly. "We're in danger of running out of letters. Fortunately, our intelligence assessments say they've run clean out of money and there won't be any more new aircraft."

"Why," Thorndike asked, "does that wind up with us sitting right here at an air base in England?"

Charles nodded happily. Intelligent question, suitable for addressing to an intelligence officer. "Since the fall there have been some unusual sightings reported on Nato's north flank. The British RAF were the first to pass questions up the line, which figures since they handle a disproportionate share of the air intercepts over the Norwegian Sea. The Norwegians have also made one report. US Air Force pilots from Iceland and from the European mainland have filed reports. The last sighting was made by Colonel Lutwidge here, and First Lieutenant Luzzi. Captain McGee followed when he saw their machine turn towards the new contact, but by then it had disappeared from view."

All eyes on Luzzi, McGee and Lutwidge. McGee and Luzzi made modest, and turned their gazes to their colonel. Loyalty, Eileen Ware thought, can tip right over into the sentimental.

"All sightings," Charles continued, "have been fleeting and unconfirmed. On every one but the last two occasions, only one man in fact saw anything at all, and no radar track has been registered. Colonel Lutwidge managed the only set of air-to-air photographs we've obtained, and all they show is a speck at extreme range in faint and indirect moonlight. The thing on the photographs could be just about anything so long as it was no bigger than, say, an F-15. The point about the double visual by the colonel and by Luzzi, plus the photographs, is that we have proof that it's more than just suggestion or spots before the eyes. That proof is relevant, because once again, we have no radar tracks. On that particular occasion the Bear they'd intercepted was jamming radar frequencies, but at the apparent range from the Bear, their own AI radar on the F-15 should have registered something. However, the unidentified aircraft evaded their radar even while slap in the middle of its scanning field."

"Stealthy," Bellman said. "Nice and stealthy. So this has been happening often?"

Charles shook his head. "By no means. If the Soviets really are flying a stealth fighter around our flank over the Norwegian Sea, and if they're doing it frequently, then most of the time we never know — which must be very heartening to them. Once in a while they get a little unlucky with the light. Or maybe their pilots get just that little bit too sure of themselves. That's understandable, I guess. Being able to fly around right under our noses in a near enough invisible aircraft must be quite some thrill."

"I'll say." Bellman liked the story a lot. He relaxed in his chair and folded his hands behind his head. "Do the Brits and the Norwegians agree there might be a stealth out there?"

"They don't know. We haven't told them. Let them wonder if it might be one of our own aircraft playing around." Charles shrugged. "We haven't yet told them about the identification of a Ram W at Ramenskoye."

"Is it a Ram W?" Pinkett asked. "Do the pictures indicate it's one and the same aircraft?"

"No." Charles shook his head. "But at the Pentagon we think that's just what it might be. We can't use that designation, just in case the association is false, but we've given the bogey we're looking for right now a name based on the same initials. I kind of like the name, myself." He paused, he smiled. "For this operation we're calling it Red Wraith."

Bellman laughed. "A commie aircraft that's rumoured to exist. Like it. Red Wraith. What's our operation going to be called? The hunt for Red Wraith."

"Blind Date," Lutwidge said. And Bellman didn't comment on that. Lutwidge would be a comfortable number too big for Bellman. "Operation Blind Date."

Charles waited to be sure Lutwidge had finished, then continued. "We believe it's a stealth aircraft. We believe the Soviets have gone for the third main application for such an aircraft type. The point here is that fully stealthing an aircraft brings both advantages and penalties. You smooth its outside to get rid of all the sharp angles and big side surfaces, so it reflects the absolute minimum radar energy back to anyone who's scanning the area looking for targets. This changes the aerodynamics of the machine, and it puts constraints on the control surfaces. It just isn't going to be as maneuverable as a conventional aircraft. Not only that, but having smoothed up the outside to make it nice and clean, you don't want to go hanging a whole load of munitions under the body and wings and turning it back into a noisy radar target. So you carry your bombs or missiles recessed on fewer weapon stations, or maybe even inboard. The weapons load is lower."

"And it's slower," Thorndike said. "The compressor and turbine blades of the engines make highly reflective radar targets, and you can't coat them with absorbent materials because of the engine's working temperature. So to minimise the chance of a radar system seeing the aircraft from directly ahead or directly astern, you bury the engines inside long inlet and exhaust tunnels. Right? So you lose some power. So you're not going to be supersonic. The F-117 isn't. Nor the B-2."

Charles nodded. "That's correct. What you end up with is definitely not an air combat machine like the F-16 or MiG-29. But you get high survivability. You can use it for ground attack missions, where it can go back again and again at targets in relative safety. Or you use it as a deep penetration strategic bomber, where it should survive layers of air defenses and hit targets right in the enemy's heartland. In neither case does the stealth aircraft need to use its own radar, which would give it away as surely as if it lit up a searchlight on its nose."

"And the third option?" Talley asked. "That would be deep zone air superiority, right? In the air superiority role, a stealth aircraft loiters over a battle area — or maybe slap on reinforcement routes across the Atlantic from the States. It can't be seen itself, but it can see everyone else at extreme range because they're lit up by each other's radars. It picks its targets, has plenty of time to maneuver into attack position despite its speed disadvantage, and it launches a missile. Because you don't know it's even there, every attack is a surprise."

"Right," Charles said. "Absolutely right." He nodded happily, satisfied with the logic of the guessing game. "Air superiority requires good endurance, and it's precisely this role that we think the other side has gone for. We think Red Wraith represents a threat to our own aircraft in the air."

"So," Thorndike said, "what are they doing flying the thing over the Norwegian Sea? Seeing if we can see it?"

"Yes. That's about it. The big question is, what might their motive be for testing it against us?"

"And why," Bellman asked, "would they want to go flying their Red Wraith in company with reconnaissance or elint aircraft? So it doesn't get lost?"

"So it gets targets," Talley said quietly. "So that it gets to latch on the tails of our interceptors when they come up to look at the big intruder. That way it gets enough aircraft to test itself against. It tries following them without getting detected itself. They're letting us provide them with realistic targets."

"Yes," Charles said again. "That's how it looks. It's damned cheeky, but they've as good as gotten clean away with it."

"What's their mission profile?" Thorndike asked. "And when do they fly?"

Charles rocked forward a little on the edge of his table. He pursed his lips. "What we have on the mission profile is circumstantial, obviously. There's a pattern we can elicit from our tracks of Soviet air movements over the past four months. One of their reconnaissance or elint aircraft comes around from the Kola Peninsula on a night probe against our defenses. At the same time, they fly a tanker aircraft out over the northern Norwegian Sea. It keeps station for a while, then it returns to base. Our radar tracks show no other aircraft coming up to the tanker for replenishment.

Of course, we wouldn't expect to see any Red Wraith that
turned up. Now, the tanker *could* be on some kind of
independent exercise, because that's right where it would
have to be to replenish attack aircraft moving against Nato
naval forces in the northeastern Atlantic. But it turns up
neatly on time to service any Red Wraith, if that Red
Wraith was planning to meet up with the big aircraft that's
on its way down the Norwegian Sea to draw out our interceptors. Sometimes a second tanker turns up just nicely on
time to perform the same service on the way home."

"Has this mission profile coincided with every reported
sighting?" Pinkett wanted to know. "It isn't just one of
these probable fits?"

"Every time there's been a sighting," Charles answered,
"it turns out they were flying one of these coincidental
tanker missions. However, it doesn't follow the other way
around. By no means every time they fly one of these mission patterns do we see what might be a Red Wraith sneaking up on our interceptors."

"So." Thorndike had her arms folded. She was getting
into the business of working the task through. "What
about the timing. Just when do they fly their missions?"

Charles smiled at her. He smiled satisfaction, appreciation of coherent logic. He smiled at the neat poetic fit.
"Red Wraith flies on long, dark winter nights — when
there's no moon."

"Yup," Bellman said. "Guess he would, at that." He
stretched his arms up in the air. Not impressed by it all, he
was signalling — amused enough, but not impressed. "So
he's maybe not even there — always assuming he in fact
exists. And if he is there on any one possible mission, he
doesn't hardly show on radar, he's painted black and
there's nothing but starlight, and the best we can say is he's
somewhere near where the big reconnaissance aircraft is
lumbering around the sky. How in the heck are we supposed to find him?"

Charles shrugged. He looked over his shoulder at
Lutwidge.

Lutwidge stood up and came around to the front of the table. Charles stayed where he was, perched on its edge. Lutwidge placed himself beside Charles, but he stayed upright in his at-ease posture, fists on his hips. He nodded thoughtfully, and everyone waited.

"The Russians," he said finally, "appear to be setting a neat little trap for us. They set up a bait aircraft, we take the bait, and Red Wraith sneaks up on our tail. The principle seems to be that you have to be able to predict where your target is going to show. That's how Red Wraith finds aircraft to follow. We're going to use the same principle."

They waited.

After a while Lutwidge smiled. It wasn't the sour, self-satisfied smile Eileen Ware had seen the first time. This smile was friendly, for public consumption. "We're still putting the details together. We'll let you know."

There was a disappointed pause.

"Well I guess," Bellman said lazily, "the easy way would be to use our lovely Captain Thorndike as bait. We dangle her there where the Red Wraith pilot can't possibly miss her. He sticks on her tail with his tongue hanging out. At the same time someone sneaks up behind and catches him by the balls." Bellman pointed at Pinkett. "He's just the man for that job, wouldn't you say? His face has inbuilt night camouflage. Pinkie locks up Red Wraith, then he calls the rest of us in for the fun. How about that?"

Lutwidge grinned. "I'll put it on my list of fallbacks."

Pinkett didn't grin. He didn't even smile. All he did was stare at Bellman half as if he couldn't believe in the guy.

Thorndike's tactic was to get right back to the serious business and ignore the jibe from Bellman. "Why are we flying the F-15 for this operation?"

"It has long range and long endurance," Lutwidge said. "We're going to need that if we want to find a Red Wraith. Also, the F-15 has the speed and agility we're going to need to trap Red Wraith once we've found him."

"And once we get a Red Wraith locked up," Talley

asked, "what do we do then? What's the aim of the operation?"

"Pictures," Charles said immediately. "So many we can build our own Red Wraith. But we don't want to do anything to jeopardise the improving relations between Washington and Moscow."

"Pictures," Lutwidge repeated. "I guess pictures will do to start us off with." He wanted more. It was the action man armature showing through the mean flesh. Lutwidge, the fire-eater, the combat ace from once upon a time, wanted a piece of the phantom Russian aircraft.

"Why the F-15C?" Thorndike asked. "Why not the F-15E — or the trainer, the F-15D? Those are two-seater aircraft with the same performance. With someone in the back seat we'd have twice as many eyes to look for our needle in a haystack at night."

"Time constraint," Lutwidge replied. "The only F-15s presently fitted with the sensor sets we'll be using just happen to be Cs. You and Pinkett flew two of them in today, Bellman flew a third in yesterday, and the only other three in existence are being ferried out from the States tomorrow. There isn't time to install the stuff we need into other aircraft. If we didn't have to take time to familiarise with the tactics we'll be using, I'd want us to be ready to go day after tomorrow." He moved his eyes to include all of his pilots once again. "Gentlemen, we are in a hurry. We have six, or at the outside only eight weeks. By the end of March the northern sky will be too bright for the Russians to fly their Red Wraith undetected, moon or no moon. If we haven't found him by then we'll have missed the opportunity. He'll have completed his proving missions, and the odds are good he won't be back again next winter. We'll be getting no second chance."

Charles nodded in support. "If the Soviets really have an operational Red Wraith, then we are in deep trouble. The only way to minimise that trouble is to find out everything we can about the aircraft. In fact, the top brass are very exercised about Red Wraith. The real problem is the Soviet motive. In view of the reforms introduced in Moscow, and especially the relaxation they're showing in their foreign policy, why would they want to fly covert penetration missions against our air defenses? If they catch a Nato aircraft unprepared – an aircraft which *sees* Red Wraith, that is – they risk panicking the pilot and winding up with a shooting engagement. One interpretation is that some hardline Red Army generals actually want to provoke an incident in order to compromise the present leadership. The alternative I prefer is the economic angle. The Soviet Union is flat on its back and just cannot afford major new defense programs. A stealth aircraft has to be an obvious candidate for cancellation. In this view, the generals are taking a high risk to prove Red Wraith is both effective and immensely valuable in the hope of forestalling any such move. At intelligence, we believe a cancellation of *all* new Soviet aviation projects may be imminent."

"There's also a second constraint," Lutwidge continued. He wasn't interested in Soviet politics, just practical matters. "That is to say, security. Special Team is a secret. Our mission is ultra-secret. The existence of Red Wraith is even more secret than that. Nothing – I repeat, *nothing* – is to be said to anyone outside of us here in this room, plus the other officers on Special Team. We have to talk with each other, we have to talk with the expert who's coming over from Kirtland to look after the sensor sets, and we have to talk with the ground crew officers. But that's it. That is *all* of it. We cannot take the chance that something leaks out. Because somehow, around I don't know what kind of corners, it might come to the attention of some guy out there in the big bad world who's working for the Russians. And if they get to hear we know about Red Wraith, they cancel the missions immediately – and we've gone fishing." Lutwidge stopped for a moment and licked his lips. "And I do not like wasting my time."

Lutwidge paused. He shook his head for emphasis. "I do not propose to waste my time. Do we all of us understand that? Right now you are answerable to me, and I am

answerable to General Famula in the Pentagon, and that's
the limit of it. We need Mondrum in order to function, but
we have operational autonomy. We need the Air Force's
UK operations center at Mildenhall, so that whenever we
want they can clear everything else out of our way. And I
do mean *everything* – US aircraft, Awacs, the British, just
all and everyone who could spoil things for us. But Mildenhall doesn't call missions – we do. *I* do. It's my minimum
price for being asked to do the impossible."

And then Lutwidge smiled. It wasn't in the slightest
degree friendly. It was the sharpened smile of a man who,
under different circumstances, would have no problem
sending others to their deaths. "Let me repeat, I do not
propose to waste my time. I'm going to tell you how to do
the impossible. And you are going to go out there and do
it for me, gentlemen. You *are* going to do it."

3

February 7th

The F-15 Eagles screamed out of the night like two angels
of death. Their tires shrieked on contact with the runway.
The ground bound them, the earth glued them to its skin
and slowed them down. It put a stop to their fury, their
freedom, their flight of power. It waited all around with a
rolling quiet as their defeated engines succumbed to sleep.
It called them back. It ended their games. It won once
more.

Until next time.

The aircraft were towed from the taxiway past hangars and store sheds. If they'd made the journey under their own power, their exhaust plumes would have set fire to the buildings alongside the roadway. Special Team's location wasn't too convenient. But it was secluded.

The huge metal birds were parked side by side at the end of the apron, midway between Special Team's equipment sheds and the dispersal shelters which had been assigned to the unit's machines. They glinted in the floodlights rigged along the rooftops. The F-15 Eagle, sixty-four feet long, is an enormous aircraft for a single human being to fly. It possesses a consummate ugliness – but it exudes an aura of murderous perfection. It is the ideal of air superiority made incarnate in metal, acrylic and computer silicon. It is a devil of the skies.

The devil riders stayed in their cockpits long enough to complete the immediate post-flights, then they climbed down the ladders brought to the aircraft by the ground crew. They signed over the machines to Erin Heller, the unit's air maintenance officer, and walked beneath the floodlights towards the crew building. They had the slovenly walk of tired people. It was two in the morning, and they'd been in the air for over three hours. One of them – Thorndike – lifted off her helmet and tugged at the hair plastered to the back of her neck.

Eileen Ware was watching. Eileen Ware saw her shiver. It couldn't be the cold. Forty-five degrees, Mondrum's radio station kept announcing. It was a mild night for February, with heavy cloud and damp air. What had made Thorndike shiver would be the breath of the night against the sweat drying on her neck.

The pilots went through to the locker room to change and shower. The process took a little while. There was no segregation in the crew facilities: Thorndike and McGee would have to take turns. Eileen waited in the corridor leading to the briefing room. Lutwidge passed her by on his way to the debrief. He nodded, but he didn't say a word.

Captain Eileen Ware, a security officer sitting around in her camouflage blouse and pants and her soldier's boots, was redundant except as an errand girl and a driver to help out with transporting the visiting personnel. She could have made Rodeck, her newly assigned assistant, do this detail, but she sent him home mid-evening after they'd brought the pilots in for the pre-flight training briefing. Why should he suffer the indignity, too?

McGee and Thorndike came along the corridor and followed Lutwidge into the briefing room. They nodded, but they didn't say a word. Their own excuses for silence were pretty good. They'd been flying a box around Ireland, up above the clouds over empty expanses of ocean. They'd been flying a close pair — without lights, without radar, without the luxury of radio communication between the two of them. Some of the time they were allowed to use the infrared or the night vision TV systems fitted to the aircraft, sensors that helped them avoid losing each other or else colliding at five hundred miles an hour. The rest of the time they had nothing but starlight and their own unaided eyes. The drain on mental and physical energy during that kind of flying just wasn't imaginable.

Lutwidge, presumably, knew what he was doing. He sent his pilots out every night, now there was no moon. The Blind Date mission was going to call for close pairs flying for up to five hours in total darkness and without using radar or radio, so that was what they were going to learn to do.

The debrief was little more than a formality. Lutwidge would go through the experiences of all six pilots during the coming afternoon. He'd also call the pairs for the following night's flying. He was mixing them around, testing out who trusted who and which of them hated each other's guts. But along the way he recognised the need for them to sleep. At two thirty he emerged from the briefing room and walked back to his office. Thorndike and McGee came out into the corridor. They were ready for the ride home.

Eileen led the way out into the floodlit night, where

ground crew still worked on the illuminated aircraft. On overlapping stars of shadow, they walked along the front of the crew building to where Eileen's car was parked with the remaining vehicles. Thorndike took the front passenger seat, McGee got in the back. Eileen started the Sierra and reversed out of the row. As she circled around to leave Special Team, she saw Lutwidge emerging from the building on his way home. He had a car of his own. His rank was high enough to jump the base's queue for leased vehicles.

They drove out of the floods and into night alleys between vast storage sheds, with only the headlights to shoulder shadows aside. It was a dreamy, disorienting, deserted maze.

"Nice of you to wait up for us," said the disembodied voice of Cole McGee from the back seat. "Everybody else home safely?"

"Home safe," Eileen said. "The Lolite failed on Luzzi's aircraft." Lolite was the experimental night-vision TV system. It seemed far less reliable than the rival Iris, the infrared sensor set. Lolite, maybe, was losing the contest.

"It did? Another computer overload? Last night it crapped out on Talley."

"Bugs in the program," Thorndike said, "and faults in the hardware. The fucking thing isn't operational."

"If the colonel says we need it," said the voice in the back.

Up ahead between the sheds were the lights of Manhattan. Eileen put the headlights on dip, then made a right onto the deserted avenue. Manhattan was bright enough so that she could see things inside the car. She saw Thorndike's feet move uneasily during the turn. The woman wasn't yet used to sitting on the left side of a righthand drive car while cruising down the right side of the road. She was still trying to hit the pedals.

"What do you make of Colonel Lutwidge?" Eileen asked. "How does he rate as the CO of an air unit?"

"He knows what he wants," Thorndike said.

"I guess," said the voice from the back, "they couldn't

come any better. I mean, he sleeps if we sleep, he doesn't when we don't. He's like that in every detail. He gives one hundred absolute percent. All he expects is the same."

Go easy, Eileen thought, on opinions about Lutwidge when a boy from Bitburg is around. She drove past the intersection where Gateway Boulevard came in from the east, and headed south along the last quarter mile of Manhattan. Night-time sheds on the right and shadowy fuel bunkers on the left, and nothing else to see. Try another conversation opener. "How about Bellman?"

"Got to be the best," said the voice. "Just look at the way the colonel rates him. Craig Bellman is tops."

Thorndike didn't say anything. Funny, but she'd have thought that Thorndike would.

At the south end of Manhattan, where the road swung around to the left and became Arlington Avenue, was the entrance to the trailer park. Mondrum had to have an overspill for the excess personnel who flooded in during the big exercises, and Arlington was it. McGee was housed down here, and so were Pinkett and Luzzi. Eileen cruised along the sparsely lit rows of numbered trailers until she came to McGee's anonymous home from home. He got out and said goodnight. Eileen turned around at the end of the row and headed back for the road.

She turned east on Arlington Avenue and followed it around past the parade ground, past the turnings on the right to the sports center and the Arlington Hospital, and came up to the intersection with Gateway Boulevard. She waited while an MP patrol drove through, then crossed Gateway and started north on Enola Gay. Nothing and no one was moving in the middle of the night on Mondrum's main artery. They got right along to the Officers' Club before they saw anyone at all, and that was just one of the staff locking the backlit doors.

Opposite the medical center she made a right on Thunderbolt Drive. They passed the rear of the administration blocks and got into the residential zone. Sandra Lee Thorndike still hadn't said a word.

At the end of Thunderbolt, where there was just an empty field of night straight ahead, she followed the road around left and headed north on Hiroshima Boulevard. After a silent quarter mile they passed the end of Fortress Drive on the left. Bellman had been housed on Fortress. And Thorndike, briefly, had turned her head to look into the empty street.

"So," Eileen said. "How about Bellman?"

"Never in this or any other lifetime." Thorndike reached out and planted both hands on the dash. Maybe it was to cure the lingering itch to have a steering wheel in her grip while the car drove. "You want him, you got him."

"Me?" Eileen laughed. Bellman would only sneer at her. Most likely he wouldn't touch a black woman. He probably had the same incidental contempt for her that she had for him. "What would I want with Bellman?"

They passed Mitchell Drive on the left. Next but one was Thorndike's.

"The fuck of the century," Thorndike said. "That's what he thinks he is."

"He does?" It had an interesting ring to it. "And is he?"

"I don't intend to find out."

They passed the end of Liberator Drive on the left. On the right, the empty night gave way to duplex houses.

Thorndike sniffed. "What is it now? Tuesday the seventh, right? So this is going to be my sixth day here. He's tried it four times already. Won't take no for an answer. Every proposition gets less pleasant than the last."

"That's not so nice, I guess." Eileen slowed and made the left into Mustang Drive. "Want to complain about harassment?"

"Complain? A complaint goes first to the unit CO, right? So what does Lutwidge do if I tell him Bellman can't wait to stick his dick in me? He gives the man a citation and gives me a reprimand for undermining pilot morale."

"I guess he might at that. You don't like Lutwidge, do you?"

Thorndike didn't answer.

Mustang was lined with low-rise apartment blocks. At the second block before the end, Eileen pulled over to the kerb and stopped the car. Thorndike opened the door and got out.

"Thanks for the ride," she said. "I appreciate not having to walk clear across the base." Then she leaned down, one arm on the roof, one hand on the top of the open door. "You should try pulling some strings. Is there really no movement on getting cars for us?"

Eileen shook her head. "Motor pool tells me there's a waiting list. That's it. Colonels and above get preferential placement, the rest of us wait for a vehicle to turn up."

"You have this car."

"I brought it with me from Alconbury. Besides, I have to be mobile to do my job. Don't I?"

Thorndike seemed more or less convinced, but she gave a little shrug. "Bellman has a car."

"I saw that, too." Maybe Bellman had strings he could pull. Maybe he bounced a motor pool secretary until she promised him anything in the world. Maybe blond and bronzed test pilots always get whatever they might want.

Thorndike's face had closed to a mask again. "Look — nice of you to concern yourself, Ware. Okay? But I can survive Bellman. And Lutwidge." She straightened up and shut the door.

Eileen made a right at the end of Mustang, then a left on Yokohama Boulevard. That took her back to Enola Gay Avenue. She drove up to the north end of Enola Gay, turned left on Nagasaki Boulevard, then made the first right at Sabre. All she passed on the way was another MP patrol. She took the first left off Sabre into Starfighter Drive West, and pulled up right at the end. That was where accommodation had found a one-room apartment for her. It wasn't the worst part of the base, but it wasn't the best. Less than a mile away was the north end of number one runway, and that was where half the aircraft at Mondrum howled up and down.

4

February 8th

Kathrin had one of her books out again. This one was an old paperback with a dull yellow cover and the edges of the pages dirtied by daylight. It lay on the kitchen table between her cup and the coffee pot. Folded into the pages was a bookmark made of tooled leather. On top of the book lay a freshly sharpened pencil for writing in the margins. Kathrin still hadn't lost the habit she learned on the way to getting her degree. The repeatedly re-read book must be more margin notes than text by now. It was *Nineteen Eighty-four*, the one where England was called Airstrip One and was ruled by a totalitarian regime based across the Atlantic on the North American continent. The author was British, dead, and about as anti-American as you could probably get.

Clyde Lincoln Talley had no time for books like that.

Kathrin was looking at him. She was standing in the kitchen doorway and just looking at him. She was dressed now, she had her hair dried and disciplined into a blonde mane swept back from her ears. All that was missing was the makeup.

These days he caught her looking at him more and more. "Something wrong?"

She shook her head, a small movement without a shift in her features. The look was always hard. Or remote. Or closed off. Something like that. Sometimes, if it wasn't for the self-control, it would have made him weep.

He reached for the coffee pot. The black liquid rippled around like bitter ink. The glass needed scrubbing on the inside. There was a tide-mark up at the level where it was usually filled. The coffee pot – like the cups, the furniture, the carpets – came with the house. Anywhere they moved in, Kathrin would always go through every single thing and rub, scrub and near enough disinfect it. For a short duration posting, when the place they got was furnished and fitted out, and all they brought was their clothes, she would wash all the crockery and cutlery until it was sterile. It wasn't like her to accept stains inside a coffee pot.

Or maybe she had cleaned it off. Maybe he'd been drinking that much coffee for the past week. Slowly, so the coffee ran in a thin stream and cooled some more, he filled his cup again.

Kathrin Yvonne Talley came over to the table and pulled out her chair. He poured coffee into her cup. Civilised. Whatever else went wrong, step by step down the staircase slope, they stayed very civilised. That was where the hope still lay. It survived because they didn't accuse each other. Bad, and still getting worse, but it was a joint failure, no individual's fault. On account of that hope he'd brought her with him on his crazy posting, which shouldn't last even a couple of months. The kids stayed behind – it wasn't worth interrupting their schooling for such a short time. The excuse was too good to miss. He brought her with him so they could escape the people who knew them at Wright-Patterson, could get away from the social pressures and the buzz of the kids – be *together* again for a while. It had to be a good idea.

So far, Kathrin seemed to hate it.

He pushed the grapefruit shell aside, and turned his attention to the toast. He picked the slice with the burned corners so she didn't have to eat it, or openly refuse it. No need to let avoidable fights happen. "Planning on getting out today?" He went for the butter. To hell with health conscious margarine.

"It's fog outside. It's eleven in the morning and we have the lights burning because it's fog outside. This is an English winter, Clyde. We've seen them before. They're all like this."

He spread butter across the toast, and the knife scraped with a bright little sound as if the slice was hollow. The toast was toasted to perfection. "It's going to brighten up later. So — are you planning on getting out today?"

"I'll stay in the house. It's warm."

It was warm, it was nice. It was a very nice house. It was right out on Dresden Drive, inside the Tokyo Avenue circuit. Tokyo Avenue was at the extreme northeastern corner of the residential zone of Mondrum, out where Nagasaki and Hiroshima joined up, and as far away from the airfield, the heavy traffic and the air movements as you could get. Outside of the Tokyo circuit were just fields, then the belt of trees, and somewhere behind those was the perimeter road and the double fence. After that came England. Inside the circuit were the select houses for senior officers — generals and full colonels in high-ranking seclusion. And Clyde Talley and his wife were here, and Clyde Talley was just a major.

But it would have been a general who got them the house. Maybe General Everett of Strategic Air Command. He was Kathrin's father. Or General Ames. He was her uncle in the Pentagon. Every step he took, their shadows fell in front of him. Every rung he climbed was a place they'd already been.

"It's two and a half miles from here into the center, Clyde."

He nodded. He reached for the honey jar.

"So how's it going with getting us a car, Clyde?"

He opened the honey jar. The lid let go with a sticky reluctance. "I told you. I asked Ware again. There's a waiting list. On every base there's a waiting list." He took the spoon and dipped it into the honey. Kathrin insisted on a spoon. "She's put us on the list. She's put me at the top of the unit names because she knows you're stuck out here. Okay?"

Kathrin shrugged. "And how *long* is the list?"

"I don't know." He held the spoon over the toast and let the honey flow down onto the melted butter like translucent smoky gold.

"What kind of contacts does this Captain Ware have?"

"None, I guess." He looked up at her face.

She was nodding to herself, and looking over to the kitchen window, where the blank fog brooded dimly outside. "Guess I'll try a couple of phone calls."

He stood the spoon back in the honey jar and let it sink slowly into the resistant syrup. No sense in getting angry. He watched the spoon's imperfect little hydrofoil glide its way downwards to the bottom. The phone calls were inevitable. What was remarkable was the patience she'd displayed, the length of time she waited while he tried to get somewhere himself. That might be a good sign. So there was no sense in getting angry.

"Clyde?"

She was looking at him, Kathrin Yvonne Talley, born Kathrin Yvonne Everett. She was looking at him with something that went back to the days when they met. She was looking at him with the eyes of Kye, the Harvard graduate who was so delighted to be in the company once again of a man who really *did* things.

"Clyde, that's four straight nights he's had you flying these training missions. Is he planning another one for tonight?"

"I guess so."

She frowned. "You haven't done this much night flying in more than two years. Reckon you're going to be okay?"

He hesitated on that, because it was worrying him sick. It was the ghost in the back of his mind. But he put on a smile. "I'll be just fine, Kye. Don't worry."

"Taking the tablets?" She said it like it didn't interest her at all.

He nodded.

5

February 9th

A sunny afternoon with a light wind, fifty-two degrees under a bright sky with little floating clouds. All winters should be this warm. Pity you couldn't see anything from the window except the shadow of the building enveloping the parking lot out back.

She got an office on the ground floor with no view, which was all that an evidently unnecessary officer could expect. On the other hand it was nice of them to find her a room here in the security building instead of over at Special Team. It got her out from under Lutwidge's eyes.

"Nice day, sir."

She turned her head and looked at Master Sergeant Rodeck. Seated at the desk in the corner by the door, he'd twisted around in his chair and caught her staring out the window. Dammit, but she wasn't going to get herself taken seriously by daydreaming.

"The boys have football practice in school today, sir. Nice that it isn't raining. Jolene hates it when they come home with mud all over everything."

Eileen Ware nodded. Think of *something* intelligent to say . . .

Then there was a knock on the door. And it was Major Villers who came in. He stalled in the open doorway.

"Afternoon, sergeant," he said to Rodeck. The Mondrum team greeted each other before they concerned themselves with visitors. Then Villers looked her way. "Captain Ware, I just spoke with Colonel Wolford."

She nodded. She folded her hands on her desk. That was real nice, that Major Robert Villers had gotten to speak with Colonel David Wolford. Let's hope it made the major's day.

Villers decided he should proceed. "He just got a call from the motor pool, and asked me to pass it on."

Eileen raised a single eyebrow.

Villers' hand shifted uneasily on the door handle. Finally he gave up waiting for her to say something. "Seems they have a car ready for Mrs Talley. Major Talley's wife."

Eileen nodded. Down came the eyebrow. This morning she'd checked with the pool. No cars available, and no one from Special Team nearer than twenty places from the top of the list.

"Seems they've informed Mrs Talley. Seems they told her someone will be over this afternoon to bring her into the center, so she can pick up the car. It's a Mercedes, by the way."

Eileen nodded again. Things had been moving, obviously, and had been passing her by. Yet another of life's little encounters was fading into defeat.

"Their people are all tied up." Villers paused, then let loose the live round at last. "Colonel Wolford asked if you might go and collect Mrs Talley."

She'd had almost enough warning to duck the bullet. It didn't hit her right between the eyes, but it nicked her self-esteem, and it *hurt*. She managed not to look at Rodeck, nor let him see how shaken she was. She kept her eyes on Villers. "I'm busy," she said.

Villers inspected her desk. Papers — yes. But piles of papers? No.

"And in a few minutes I'm due over at Special Team." She went for a smile. "I'm checking up on the security requirements for the special sensor equipment they're using. It's state of the art and, well, secret."

"Oh," Villers said. Resistance clearly hadn't been expected.

"So I don't really have time to run errands for the motor pool right now."

"Ah," Major Villers said. "I guess that's kind of awkward."

For whom is it awkward, she thought. For the motor pool? For high and mighty Mrs Talley? For Colonel Wolford? Or for you, Major Robert Villers, because now you're going to have to order me, a captain, to go run an errand that shouldn't be worth anyone higher than an airman basic?

"I can make time right now."

Eileen looked at Sergeant Rodeck. She tried to conceal the surprise.

Rodeck was putting the cap on his pen. "Guess I'll go fetch Mrs Talley, sir." He was looking at her, not Villers. He put the pen on his desk. "I can still get this stuff finished today. And we don't want anyone getting his underpants all twisted." Rodeck shrugged. "Figure of speech."

Figure of speech. Aimed at Villers?

She smiled at Villers. "Does that solve your problem, Major Villers?" And she thought, dammit, now I have to make a real visit to Special Team.

Cloud was creeping up from the south and obscuring the pinks left behind in the sky. There was no one in sight anywhere along the quarter mile of access roadway leading to the airfield's taxi strip. On the right, the blank backsides of store sheds picked up a pale salmon sheen from the sunset. It breathed a superficial softness over asbestos, iron sheeting and cement slabs. Ranged along the left side, flanks of shadow getting ready for the dusk, were the long embankments of the blast-protection mounds shielding the first row of dispersal shelters. Grassed over and with precisely bulldozed sides, they looked like a nose-to-tail alignment of rectilinear long barrows. Who would be buried there? The unremembered souls of the uncountable dead, if a new war, an escalating nuclear war, ever came?

"KC-135." Erin Heller gestured with her plastic coffee cup towards the end of the roadway. Out on the blank flatness of the airfield, a jet-engined tanker was rolling along the runway. It was so far away they couldn't hear its roar. "Regular rotation for Strategic Air Command. Comes in every Thursday afternoon at five fifteen." She turned around and looked up at the nose of the F-15. "And I used to long for a change of routine."

Roy Sellert, still fresh from sunny Kirtland and still feeling the cold, pushed his hands into the side pockets of his coat. Sliding against itself, the nylon outer fabric of the garment swished softly. "But now you long for the routine?"

Erin Heller shrugged. She had dirty green fatigues over the top of her overalls, and a baseball cap perched on her head. She had dirt under her fingernails and grease smeared on the backs of her hands. With chocolate coloured skin and African features, with no rank insignia visible, she could have been any junior grade on the Mondrum ground crew. In fact she was Captain Heller, Special Team's air maintenance officer.

Eileen finished up her own coffee. It came from the automat, and it was already cold. It was also pretty foul. But Erin Heller had offered the drink, and we black girls in the officer corps have to stick together. She licked the taste off her lips. "Lutwidge making demands?"

"I'll say he is."

Roy Sellert, the captain from Kirtland, adjusted his glasses. "Seems like the guy goes for broke."

"Hundred percent mission capability," Erin said. "There is *no such thing* as one hundred percent mission capability. Every single one of all the tens of thousands of parts in every single machine cannot possibly be working perfectly *all* of the time. If you want to be totally sure you can put six machines in the air absolutely any time you want, you need at the very least *eight* machines on the strength. We have six machines." She finished up her coffee. The look of distaste could have been for the dregs, or the CO.

"But Lutwidge wants one hundred percent," Eileen said.

Erin Heller took Eileen's empty cup and stuffed it inside her own. "Lutwidge wants one hundred percent."

"So?" Eileen put her hands in the pockets of her parka and pulled the open garment closer around her hips. The chill made itself felt as soon as the sun was gone. "Tried telling him?"

Erin made enormous eyes. "Do I *look* that crazy? No way. I just cancel sleep. Six days of this and we haven't even started the real missions yet, and I would *kill* to get more than four hours a night. Roy, would *you* try complaining to Lutwidge?"

Sellert shook his head. "I wouldn't. But then I don't have so much to do."

"You have the problems with Lolite," Eileen said.

"Well – that's not so bad."

"New equipment," Erin said, "means new shit for the poor folks from air maintenance." She looked around at the F-15 again. With its nose above the level of their heads, with its gaping square intakes and the outspread sweep of its wings, it seemed like some nightmare bird that was ready to pounce. "Well, this Eagle is all set for tonight. Guess I'll see how my girls and boys are making out with the next one. Nice talking to you." She turned away and headed for the people busy around the next aircraft. From down among the dispersal shelters where another machine was rolled out for attention, the breeze brought the smell of JP-4. A tank truck was feeding that Eagle.

"Tell me," Eileen said to Sellert, "what makes the Lolite system less reliable than Iris. I mean, the two systems are in competition for this huge contract, aren't they? But it's Lolite that seems to have the problems. Last night it failed on Pinkett's aircraft."

"The rightside pointing mirror failed," Sellert said. He blinked at her for a while through his glasses. If she's the *security* officer, he might have been thinking, maybe she should in fact know what it was needed protecting. "Sophistication. That's the big difference." He turned around and pointed at the F-15 looming over them. It was fitted with a pair of equipment pods which protruded forward like spurs from the tanks strapped outside the engine ducts. "Maybe you should take a look at the test set."

He led her under the nose towards the gaping wedge of the air intake on the right side. For a moment she was staring straight up into the maw of the engine. Along the outside of the duct, like half a boat welded into the long angle under the wing root, was the conformal fuel tank. The conformal tanks came in right and left pairs. They fitted so snugly to the body of the aircraft that they didn't change its aerodynamics or reduce its performance; they were toughened so that the F-15 could throw itself around the sky as wildly with them fitted as without. The three auxiliary tanks the aircraft could also carry created extra drag, and had to be released if anything exciting happened during a mission. An F-15 needed those drop tanks as well as the conformals to make its maximum range of three and a half thousand miles – but the conformals were the secret of its combat endurance.

In more ways than just range and performance. The auxiliary tanks tied up weapon stations and reduced the total warload. But each of the conformal tanks had two additional weapon stations, one behind the other, along its lower outboard edge. Fitting conformals had no effect on killing power.

Roy Sellert patted the long spindle mounted on the forward station of the conformal tank. It was at Eileen's eye level. There were four little windows set in its side, and sheltering inside the transparent nosecap was a lens. Modern machines can look at you.

"This is the test set configured for the F-15. At Kirtland

we also have them for other aircraft types, but all six that fit the F-15 are right here."

"They're for the evaluation program," she said. "You're comparing the performance of the two systems. Right?"

"That's right. And the winner gets to take home a contract worth millions." Sellert nodded at the stream-lined pod. "Worth getting on for a *billion*, once the Air Force and the Navy start equipping all of their air combat units."

"The evaluation program is an exacting business?"

"Oh it sure is. With that kind of money involved, you can't take the manufacturer's word for anything at all. With the profits they can see – and the income they need to secure – the rival manufacturers are *enemies*. Believe me."

"And you test them both the same way?"

"Oh we sure do. That's why the test set is like it is – we can operate Lolite and Iris in exactly the same situations. Most important of all, the pilots can switch from one to the other any time they choose and make an immediate comparison. Talk with Craig Bellman, if you like. He's one of our lead pilots on the program."

Eileen nodded. "Maybe I will." And maybe, she thought, I won't. "Both systems are night-vision aids, aren't they?"

"Yep. Iris is the infrared imaging system developed by Aerosensor, Lolite is the low light television from Datadyne Avionics." Sellert spread out his hands as if he was describ-ing a cinerama process. "They cover right around from the aircraft's left side to its right side – nine o'clock to three o'clock, yes? They divide it up into seven fields of view, at nine, ten and eleven o'clock, at twelve o'clock – that's dead ahead – and then at one, two and three o'clock. Iris does it with seven separate cameras, pointed one in each direction. Lolite does it with one camera aligned straight ahead, and then a camera for each side of the aircraft. The side cameras have a rotating mirror to switch the field of view. It was one of the mirrors that failed on Pinkett's aircraft last night.

Kind of ironic. Lolite is *so* sophisticated – and about the simplest component in the system fails and takes out three fields of view."

Eileen pointed at the windows in the sensor pod. "The cameras are mounted behind these?"

"That's right. Well, when I say *cameras* I mean imaging units. Each one contains the optics, the electronics, and so on. Each unit comes from the respective manufacturer sealed and certified. All we do is mount them in the pods and use them." He pointed back at the tail end of the pod. "Support systems are in the tail compartment. Then in the main section we have the cameras. There's the Lolite unit with its three-position mirror, then three Iris imagers aligned on independent directions, and right here in the nose is a Lolite unit pointing dead ahead. The pod on the left side contains a corresponding arrangement of units. The only difference is that there it's an Iris imager mounted in the nose to cover the twelve o'clock direction."

"And the pilot can call up the view along any of those directions?"

"That's right. But we've had to fit modified instruments in the cockpit. You're aware that the instrumentation for the original F-15 was old fashioned dials and switches? Well this version here is as up-to-date as they come. The dials and switches are replaced with cathode ray tubes and boards with push-button keys. The head down displays – you understand head down? The pilot has to move his eyes down inside the cockpit to look at the instrument board."

Here we go again, she thought. I'm a woman, I'm black, and I don't play every day with their ultimate phallic toys. "I've been in the Air Force ten years, Roy."

"Um – sure." He stared at the pod for a moment. "No offence, huh? Well, the head down displays carry radar information, navigation data, weapon states and so on. The pilot calls up whichever he wants. But to juggle with both Lolite and Iris as well, we have to fit an additional control board to run the systems and to call up images. With the HUD – the head up display –"

"I know what a head up display is, too." She decided to smile for him. With people like Lutwidge, Bellman and Charles around, she didn't need to go making enemies as well. "There's a combining glass mounted over the top of the instrument panel, right on the pilot's eyeline. The pilot can see straight through it at the sky ahead. But there's a television screen – a cathode ray tube – mounted down below it and pointing upwards. The pilot sees whatever's displayed on the tube, reflected in the glass of the head up display. Over the HUD he can call up most kinds of information, and see it at the same time as he watches the sky. It means he doesn't have to take his eyes off a target even for a second. Am I right?"

"Absolutely. And the field of view directly ahead from either Lolite or Iris can be combined on the HUD without any trouble. The pilot gets a picture aligned exactly with his naked eye view. Basically, Lolite lights up the box of sky dead ahead for him. Iris shows him what it looks like in infrared."

"And what he's looking for on this operation," Eileen said, "is an aircraft – either the heat image of it on the Iris system, or a brightened-up version of what it looks like in near darkness. That's right, isn't it? Lolite is an image intensifier."

"That's it." Sellert radiated enthusiasm. "Basically Lolite is just that. The computation, though, is really sophisticated. Lolite will scan all seven fields for you. It will register any new element in the image and alert you. In other words, it searches for possible targets by itself. Also, it will track targets for you while you get on and do something that's more urgent right at the moment. In fact, what Datadyne want to do with Lolite is produce a system that does exactly the same job as radar – but without sending out any kind of signal that advertises the user's presence. Lolite is breaking entirely new ground. Of course, you get a few problems. What we're doing at

Kirtland is essentially asking whether the problems are acceptable in light of what Lolite can do but Iris can't, or whether Iris in practice works out just as useful for the pilot as Lolite."

"I guess that's quite a difficult equation to solve," she said. "And — I guess this operation provides a unique opportunity to test both systems against the real thing."

"Yep." Sellert patted the sensor pod again. "You got it. The way each system performs on this operation is going to settle the contract, I expect. If Red Wraith exists, that is. And if they happen to run into it."

If Red Wraith existed. And if they found it. What would happen then? Eileen lifted her eyes. What she wanted to see was the sky over the aircraft's wing. How were the clouds coming on? Was it going to be overcast or might there be a frost in the night? How dark was the world as dusk came down?

What she saw was the conical port right over her head, a hole set in the leading edge of the wing's shoulder, just back of the engine air intake.

It was the port through which the gun fired.

"Maybe they will run into it," Sellert said. "Maybe Red Wraith really does exist. I guess personally I don't believe it, though." He was adjusting his glasses again. They hadn't slipped, but he reseated them on his nose as if they had. "We're pushing right at the edge of our technology to build stealth aircraft and the sensors you have to use with them. Look at the problems with Lolite, or the sheer cost of Lolite and Iris. Who knows if the Russians can do it at all? I guess you heard the news."

You guess I heard what news, she thought. Why would anyone on Special Team tell *me* anything? I'm spare. I seem to be the wrong side of everyone's conceptual horizon. "What news?"

"Nobody told you?" He looked with concern at the pod of the test set, which looked back through its inscrutable windows. "With this stuff around, they should take the security aspect a hell of a sight more seriously."

"What news, Roy?"

"Tonight will be the last time they do any of this familiarisation flying. From tomorrow we're going on standby for the real thing."

PART 2

Quiet Sky

6

February 11th

Eileen Ware watched the tablets make the rounds. The
mission would run for a planned four hours. If they found
a Red Wraith and chased it, they could extend to fully five
hours. By the time they got near the intercept position the
sliver of new moon would have set, and they'd be flying in
total darkness. They would be flying in close pairs, without
any communication between aircraft or with Mondrum
control, and they would be alert the entire time for a near
enough invisible ghost stalking through the vast audi-
torium of night. It was one hell of a way to end a Saturday.
They might really need the tablets.

United States Air Force policy allowed for what was
called pharmaceutical assistance on long-duration night
missions, especially solo and over ocean. In such conditions
pilots had a triad of problems. At night both body and
brain would have preferred to be asleep; alone in your
aircraft, there was no one to talk to and no one to check
on your alertness; in the dark there wasn't much to see to
provide orientation for a tired mind – and over open ocean
there was next to nothing at all. The danger was fatigue,
inattention – and sleep. For a lone pilot, even in peacetime,
sleep was a fatal luxury.

So the Air Force let them take tablets. It gave them
amphetamine for alertness during a mission, and barbiturate to help them catch up on sleep afterwards. The practice

was closely controlled to avoid abuse. Prescribing for individual pilots was restricted and the doses had to stay small. Dexamphetamine sulphate and quinalbarbitone sodium were controlled drugs. In a very different context they were known respectively as uppers and downers.

In another context, Eileen would have been so uneasy she'd have complained. Coming from military police work into security, she knew about the threat of drug abuse. Locked up inside those self-sufficient ghettos known as bases, if peacetime service personnel weren't prime targets for illicit kicks, then no one was. The routine and the boredom were the problem. If people were going to get amphetamine and barbiturate, they had to be watched with the eyes of a hawk. Normally she'd have expected the medical officer assigned to the unit to check the pilots over before they took off – and to check them over again when they returned from the mission, middle of the night or not.

But Dyson just wrote a prescription for more than enough to cover the requirement, and had it sent over. All Eileen was expected to do was check that the total of tablets in each box tallied with the number on the prescription form, to be sure the orderly hadn't diverted any on the way over from the hospital. The pilots would take what they needed and the remainder would be flushed into the sewer and out of all corrupting reach. The pilots flying for Special Team were the best the Air Force could assemble. They were people you could trust.

So Eileen watched the two little boxes pass from hand to hand. Neither Dwight Pinkett nor Sandra Thorndike took a tablet. The others took two dexamphetamine each, and a quinalbarbitone. Talley was the last in line. He pocketed his own tablets, then snapped the plastic lids back on the boxes. Without even glancing her way, he went out in the direction of the locker room. When he returned, he handed her the empty boxes. The excess tablets would be nothing more than a wet sludge on the wrong side of the lavatory pan, inaccessible and neutralised.

"Before we proceed, gentlemen." Lutwidge let them have

his nice-man smile. He'd snapped up everyone's full attention in less than two syllables, and that was how he expected it to be. "Allow me to introduce Major Susan Wizer." He pointed to the visitor seated at one end of the arc of chairs.

Major Wizer was in her late thirties – she would be as old as, or older than anyone else except Lutwidge, and possibly Charles. She had auburn hair which flared out in a brim of upturned, back-turned waves from under her cap. She gave an impression of fierce competence, as if she'd met legions of Lutwidges through the years of her service career, and had convinced every one of them that she could do her job to perfection. She looked like a winner should.

"Major Wizer is one of Mondrum's air control officers. She's going to be assigned to us for the duration. Major Wizer will be our dedicated link into US Air Force Europe's control network. With her expertise we'll be able to run our missions and call Quiet Sky when we need it. Right, major?"

Wizer nodded, a polite but slow gesture. The colonel might condescend, but it wasn't going to flatter her.

"And obviously –" Lutwidge indulged himself in a dramatic pause. "We're calling Quiet Sky tonight."

No murmurs of eager anticipation from the pilots. Lutwidge had them firmly schooled into respectful, wide awake waiting: the four specialists had picked it up from the Bitburg boys. Eileen shifted in her seat. She had a chair right over on the side opposite Wizer, in front of one of the metal-framed windows which reflected the briefing room in rectangular fragments floating in night. She picked the place because of the iron heating pipe running along the outside wall, but the heating wasn't so hot at Special Team, and what she got was a draught across her neck from the wartime window. She couldn't change her place now Lutwidge had started. If the man would just get on.

Oliver Lutwidge planted his fists on his hips, the sign of real business beginning. "The Russians have initiated what looks to be a possible Red Wraith mission. They have an Ilyushin Il-38 May coming south over the Norwegian Sea, and what we assume to be a tanker variant of the Tu-16 Badger closing on the hold position we associate with Red Wraith sightings. It could really be that the May is playing bait to draw up our interceptors, and the Badger is going to refuel a Red Wraith which is on its way to join the bait. The May – the suspected bait – is due at its presumed turn position at oh-one-hundred hours." He turned towards Charles. "Check?"

Lieutenant Colonel Charles nodded.

"Oh-one-ten," Wizer said. "On the latest plot."

Lutwidge accepted the correction without comment. Charles seemed mildly amused. Wizer stayed impassive.

"The moon is down," Lutwidge said, "at oh-oh-forty-eight. Any Red Wraith will then close on the bait. That's when our intercept pair will also move in and set up the Draw Play. We've gone through it in detail, so right now I'll just summarise the Draw Play profile. Let me emphasise, gentlemen, that this is the real thing. This is a full scale Blind Date mission. There may be no Red Wraith present at all this time around, but we don't assume that until we've missed him."

Another pause, while his pilots waited. McGee and Luzzi radiated Bitburg eagerness. Thorndike and Pinkett seemed unaffected by the threshold of possible action. Bellman sat with his legs stretched out, as if he flew off to look for possibly non-existent needles in pitch darkness every night of his life. Talley looked tense.

Lutwidge had transferred to the unfriendly version of himself. He was doing the demanding and they were doing the fulfilling, and that was all of it. "Draw Play goes like this. We fly a pair of interceptors right at the Russian bait. They talk with each other, they talk with control, they use their radars – it looks just like a routine interception. The interceptors are *our* bait for Red Wraith. They stay with the Russian bait aircraft and give Red Wraith plenty of time to come in. If he really wants to play his stealth advan-

tage, he's going to sneak right up on the tail of the interceptors and follow them around the sky – for intelligence data,
and for the sheer hell of it. I guess there's no one here who
doesn't appreciate what a kick it's got to give those Russian
pilots, being able to do that to our aircraft. We'd do it to
them, orders or no orders. In fact –" He shook his head
slightly, with a smile that said, gee, this is quite a thought,
you guys. "On solo missions in an aircraft that's damned
invisible except right up close, they can do just *whatever*
they like, and their generals never have to know about it."

Some toy, Eileen thought. A stealth aircraft, to Lutwidge,
would be just about the ultimate gift, a big boy's best ever
plaything. He was *envious* of his enemy.

"Draw Play is a trap for Red Wraith. He creeps up on
the tail of our interceptors, and our hunters slide in on *his*
tail. To double our chances we fly two hunter pairs, which
operate independently until fully closed up on our interceptors. While the interceptors stay high on the way to the
bait, the hunters fly a high-low-high pattern. They start
high for fuel economy, but once they're about to come up
over the horizon of the bait and the presumed Red Wraith,
we tell them to go right down on the deck. The hunters
do not acknowledge. They maintain rigorous radio silence
until they trap a Red Wraith. If the mission doesn't pan
out, the hunters still don't say a word until they're accepted
for landing approach back here at Mondrum. The Russians
listen the entire time on Nato frequencies, and we absolutely do not want them to know the hunters were ever in
the air. We don't want to spook Red Wraith. That right,
Ernest?"

"We want to photograph him." Ernest Charles added.
"We don't want to frighten him off before then."

"Once our interceptors report they've taken up station
with the bait, and before the hunters come up over the
ocean horizon where the bait and the Red Wraith can see
them, we call Quiet Sky. This cuts out all – I repeat, *all* –
friendly radars which in any way illuminate the area of
operations. This means our on-station Awacs aircraft,

ground-based surveillance radars, and air-traffic control radars belonging to both the military and civilian authorities. General Famula at the Pentagon has looked after this for us. Quiet Sky is set up, and all we have to do is call it. I don't know what stories they've given to the rest of the Air Force, never mind to the other people in Nato and the entire civilian sector – and believe me, I do not care. All that concerns me is ensuring that *not one single radar* points at our hunters and lights them up for the Russian aircraft. The bait will be on a regular elint mission, and will be scanning passively to pick up everything it can about our radar systems. It would see any airplane lit up by secondary illumination from a third party's radar. And Red Wraith would see it, too. They see our hunters *once* – and Blind Date is over."

He put in another pause for emphasis. He looked along his line of faithful pilots. He got to Sandra Thorndike.

"Sir, I'm concerned about the Quiet Sky concept."

Lutwidge lifted his head slightly. Interjections from lesser team members were not expected.

"At Nellis we use the term to describe a battle environment where neither side is using radar because of the presence of stealth aircraft." Thorndike turned towards Talley. "I believe that's how it's used at Wright-Patterson."

Talley nodded.

"Conditions," she continued, "where it's also to the enemy's advantage not to use radar. That doesn't apply here. When we call Quiet Sky, the bait aircraft will lose sight of anything it may have been tracking with the benefit of secondary illumination. It might then turn on its own radar. That would blow the operation."

Lutwidge lifted his head a little more. "One. The bait is engaged in electronic intelligence. The sense of an elint mission is you listen to the other side. You don't stream out your own electronic emissions for the other side to listen to." He looked emphatically *down* at her. "Two. If the bait's radar lights up targets from nice and close – like our pair of interceptors – it makes the entire task of closing and tracking too goddam easy for Red Wraith. That's no way at all to prove the aircraft's capability. Three, and as a precautionary consideration. If the bait is on an elint mission, it makes sense if we turn our radars off just as soon as our interceptors have acquired it visually. That will merely look as though we're denying it elint data. It will not give rise to suspicion that we're up to anything more elaborate. Does that answer your problem, captain?"

Thorndike shrugged. "I guess."

"Good." Lutwidge relaxed – like a snake deciding it wasn't hungry. "The hunter pairs will hear when Quiet Sky is called. They will then climb up towards the bait. They will circle beyond visual range and listen to the interceptors talking with control. The entire time they will search for Red Wraith. When the interceptors are instructed to leave the bait, the hunters will follow behind and gradually close up on the interceptors. The mission ends in two ways. Nothing is caught, the hunters draw level with the interceptors, and everyone heads for home. Alternatively, the hunters trap a Red Wraith and lock on his tail. The nearest hunter then breaks radio silence and calls the fact, and all six aircraft join in the task of boxing in and photographing the Russian plane. Once we have him, we don't let go until fuel state compels our last F-15 to head for home. So – any questions on the basic mission profile?"

"Fuel," Pinkett said immediately. "Do we go with a full load?"

Lutwidge nodded. "Full internal, conformal tanks, and three auxiliary tanks. Five thousand four hundred gallons."

"Weapons?" Bellman said.

Lutwidge smiled. "Each aircraft goes with its gun charged with a full drum of twenty millimetre. In addition, each aircraft will carry two AIM-9L Sidewinders. A radar homing missile would be useless against a stealth aircraft, and you're not going to see your target at long range anyway. The Sidewinder is limited to close range, but its infrared capability is exactly what we want."

"When we've photographed Red Wraith," Bellman asked, "do we shoot his ass off?"

"No." Lieutenant Colonel Charles jumped in like a referee seeing a clinch. He might be number two to Lutwidge, but he was also the Pentagon's overseer. "Blind Date is an intelligence gathering operation. Nothing more than that."

"But," Lutwidge said, "we don't miss out on self-defense. It could just be that the Red Wraith pilot has orders to shoot down any aircraft that looks like getting too close. They might want to keep their baby secret. With a stealth doing the killing, they'd get away with it – our ground radars just wouldn't see what actually occurred. We'd assume the missing plane merely went and crashed into the sea. It happens."

"What are the pair allocations, sir?" McGee asked. "Who's flying what position?"

"You and Luzzi are flying the interceptors. You've flown pairs plenty of times, so I'd like to keep you together. The hunters will be Talley with Thorndike in trail, and Bellman with Pinkett. And if the Red Wraith *is* there this time around, I'm going to be extremely interested to see who gets to him first. The interceptors are in with a chance of winning – you might see him on your tail before the hunters get in close. Okay now." Lutwidge relaxed, a superman re-adopting merely human stature. "We'll take a break, then Major Wizer will give us the navigation data."

Lutwidge left the briefing room and Charles followed after him. The pilots sat and looked at each other. Here came the first full mission on their ghostbusting operation. What chance, Eileen thought, that Red Wraith is even real?

Bellman stretched his arms up in the air. "Real thing, huh?" He beamed at Talley. "Reckon you can beat me and Pinkie to a Red Wraith, Talley Boy?"

Talley didn't answer. He stood up and headed for the door at the back.

"Draw Play." Thorndike got up and pushed her chair aside with her foot. The chair rumbled over the board floor. "Does the guy think this is a football game? Are we in college or something?"

McGee was standing up as well. So was Luzzi. "It's a good game," McGee said. "Develops personality. A draw play is a good analogy for the tactic we're using."

"Sure is," Bellman agreed. "Never played college football, Thorndike?"

She glared at him.

"Well then."

Sandra Thorndike shook her head. "Look, Craig Bellman — aside from being fit, you don't need muscles and meat to fly an F-15. You need brains. You have the brains, I have the brains. All you need is fucking brains."

"How about just fucking, Thorndike?"

Thorndike simply turned her back and walked after Talley towards the door.

"Captain Ware?"

It was Major Susan Wizer. She'd crossed the room and come right up to Eileen's shoulder. She was very close, opening a private exchange. Her eyes were brown, pupils dilated in the interior light. They gazed without blinking.

Eileen started to turn. "Major Wizer?"

"You have to wait around until the birds come home, don't you?"

"I do."

"Well why not sit in with us at operations?" There was no smile to accompany the invitation, just the steady close-up inspection. "That way, at least you'll be up-to-date on anything that's happening. If they ever do catch a Red Wraith, you'll want to know before the pilots land and start blabbing to the ground crew. Even Colonel Lutwidge will buy that argument."

Eileen nodded. "I guess he will, at that."

7

February 12th

No sleep, no moon, no incident, nothing at all. No Red Wraith. You couldn't expect to get lucky the first time.

Clyde Lincoln Talley hauled himself out of the seat and up over the rim of the cockpit. At thirty-seven you get stiff after four hours glued to your ass. The cockpit had been cosy, while the night was cold with a thin rain falling. The perforated treads on the ladder glistened in the crosslighting from the halide floods around the roofs of Special Team. He took his time descending the ten feet to the ground.

The warrant officer shielded the clipboard from the rain for him while he signed over the machine. In the remarks column he added *Lolite system failure*. The thing had crapped out just as he came up within sight of the interceptors, the location where a Red Wraith might have been. He watched while the warrant officer hugged the clipboard up high against her shoulder with its blind side to the breeze, and entered the time. She wrote 0250.

Kathrin left for London early the previous day. She took the car – her car. She'd have been back hours ago. She'd be tucked up in bed and the car would be standing in the driveway on Dresden right at the other end of the base. He'd be needing a ride home in the rain.

He walked across the apron towards the crew building.

The concrete slabs didn't drain properly: his shoes splashed through thin puddles. Tiny cold raindrops pricked at his ears, his forehead and his cheekbones. In a different mood they'd have been refreshing, but the mild euphoria from the amphetamine was fading. When you come down to earth, depression tends to follow.

Thorndike fell in beside him. Her feet scuffed through the skim of puddles. "Operation Blind Date," she said. "Fucking needle in a haystack. If, that is, Red Wraith even exists. And if the Russians would do something as crazy as fly it at us — just when they want us to believe they're really nice little good guys. Fortunately for the Free World, Lutwidge knows all commies are bad. So he *knows* they have to be flying a Red Wraith. Is Lutwidge nuts or is it me?" Thorndike kicked an arc of water ahead of her shoe. The drops sparkled like diamonds disappearing into dark. "Find Red Wraith, photograph him, frighten him off, and get Lutwidge a pat on the back. What do you think of our chances, Clyde?"

"Luck," he said. "Either we run into him, or we don't. After that we have a chance, if our skill is up to it." But the luck stays in the equation, he thought. The sheer treacherous luck.

They went inside to the warmth and light of the building.

Lutwidge wanted a debrief on the no-luck mission, just a check on the feasibility of the Draw Play profile. A detailed debrief could wait until the next afternoon, but even a limited session meant there was little time to waste on other niceties if they wanted to get home to bed. The problem was the shower.

The facility adjoined the locker room. It was fully tiled, with a row of shower heads down each side and a drain in the center of the floor. No segregation, of course. After four hours strapped in their seats for a mission, no one was in a hurry to rush back out of the shower. So Thorndike would just have to bide her time until the guys were finished. But taking a separate turn in the shower would

make her last out of the locker room. Lutwidge and his
little debriefing would have to wait for her. Women aren't
punctual. They always come late. It's a truth in the male
mythology.

But the hot water had taken the stiffness away, and the
steam was starting to get to him anyhow. He could afford
to finish with the shower now, and maybe his move would
get the other guys around to leaving as well. Clyde Talley
squeezed water out of his hair and got ready to go find his
towel. Getting his hands down to the back of his neck, he
opened his eyes.

Sandra Thorndike came into the noise and the steam.
Naked, she passed by the glistening male bodies and sought
the one free shower head in the back corner. There were
whoops and whistles amid the clatter of water spattering
on tiles. She walked through it all with a striding kind of
dignity. She couldn't afford to wait any longer, and with
an automatic, unthinking conspiracy they'd forced her to
choose between little evils.

She closed them all out, let the hot water wash their eyes
off her back. She stood facing the wall, her hands splayed
up on the tiles, her eyelids closed. The shimmering water
cascaded down her skin. After a while she soaped herself,
then did a slow pirouette to rinse the lather away.

Bellman punched him lightly on the shoulder. Moving up
sideways, he leaned very close in a buddy-buddy approach.
Special rules allow naked heterosexual males to touch each
other.

"Tits a little small." Bellman grinned, his face awash
with suntanned droplets. "But nice and pert and pointy,
huh? In fact from top to toe a neat piece of work." Then
the punch on the shoulder again. "I'll be there before you
are, Talley Boy. After all — you're a married man. You've
got it at home ready any time you want it."

Sandra Thorndike decided to leave. She went head up,
pacing out through the spray and steam and the water
flooding the tiles. Talley watched her disappear between a
clutch of male bodies. If Bellman had been right, it

wouldn't be so bad. Kathrin was at home, sure enough, but that part of the marriage had been dead for a long time.

Bellman brushed blond strands off his forehead. "Had more trouble with the Lolite, I hear."

"Yes." Talley lifted his soap out of the ceramic holder on the wall and got ready to leave. "I was coming close up behind Cole and Don and moving out sideways." He would have been closing the trap, if a Red Wraith had been inside it. The pair Bellman was leading didn't join up with Cole McGee and Donald Luzzi until three minutes later. Clyde Talley would have won. "The images of both aircraft coincided in the field of view. The computer reset and then crashed." He turned the soap over in his hand, like a slippery worry bead. "Does that happen often with Lolite?"

Craig Bellman shrugged. "Not to me, anyhow. The system is a delicate baby. You have to use it right, Talley Boy. I never have problems."

Dwight Pinkett was passing in front of them on his way out of the shower. He landed a backhanded slap right in the middle of Bellman's chest. "*We* never have problems, Mister Test Pilot. With this tight-up nose-to-tail position flying we have no problems at all. Do we?" He grinned brilliantly at Bellman, then went on his way.

"What was that about?" Talley asked.

"Oh, you know how it is." Bellman was arranging for fresh water to flow over his chest. "He gets assigned as my tail man. The entire mission, all he has to do is stare right up my ass. You know the way that gets a nigger excited."

Talley didn't know. Unless it was the excited urge to split Bellman's ass wide open with a burst of twenty millimetre cannon fire. Bellman encouraged that kind of response.

"And there goes Pinkie, first out of the shower after our own private white woman. Chasing ass again." Bellman shook his head. "Anyone would think he had an equal right to it. These niggers are all the same." He ducked his head under the stream of water.

Talley got away from the man then. What stung was the

way he'd caught himself immediately thinking: I don't want Pinkett to get her any more than Bellman. If anyone's going to, if she's going to get it together with anyone at all, I'd want it to be . . . I'd want it to be . . . But he was married to Kathrin and he still loved her – or at least, still wanted to. Thorndike – any woman but Kathrin – would just be a way of getting the sexual pressure out. A fling. A release valve. Making more time for the marriage to get healthy again. That was it.

At three thirty-five Lutwidge sent them home. They'd be on standby the coming night. Maybe he'd be calling a mission – it all depended on what the Russians did. His pilots had to get a full slice of sleep. Main debriefing would be at fourteen hundred. By then, with luck, Captain Roy Sellert should have sorted out the glitch in the Lolite on Talley's machine.

Bellman was in a generous mood. Cole McGee, Don Luzzi and Dwight Pinkett were all accommodated on the Arlington trailer park, and he made a detour to drive all three of them home. Nothing nice, Talley thought – just another chance to show off his goddam car. The man owned a BMW, a 735 in midnight grey. It was big, heavy, mean and low. It was dark and dangerous. It was Bellman's private stealth machine.

Sandra Thorndike was housed a couple of streets away from Bellman's eventual destination, but she was taking a ride home with Ware. Clyde Talley lined up for a ride with the same driver. Ware was a harmless kind of a woman: nice enough, a mix of pretty and plain – and very insecure, he thought. The kind of unassertive black that even the likes of Bellman ought to tolerate. Ware and Thorndike were near enough the same age and were the same rank, but they were total opposites. Ware was an Air Force foot soldier, quiet, compliant, and she didn't interest him at all. But Thorndike was a top pilot, aggressively assertive . . . And she interested him. Jesus, he could even put one over on Bellman.

And Jesus, he was some kind of a chauvinistic fool.

They didn't talk at all. Ware drove them away from Special Team, where the ground crew were dismounting sensors and draining tanks, and headed north on Manhattan. Halfway along, around level with operations control, she made a right on the only road from one end to the other of Manhattan that crossed through the workshops zone to Enola Gay. They came out in the middle of the dog's leg on Enola Gay, somewhere between the medical center and the last of the shopping malls, and headed north past recreation halls and the movie theater. The only people they saw in the dead-of-night base were a pair of MPs in a jeep parked at the corner where they turned into Yokohama Boulevard.

Ware detoured around one block to let Thorndike out on Mustang Drive, then headed out to Hiroshima and turned north again. Talley sat in the passenger seat, on the left, looking at the line straight down the middle of the mesmeric run of road. In deep night, with headlights and streetlights, there was nothing else to see. Except that the tarmac darkness glistened after the rain. He watched Ware's driving. First I fly for hours at near the speed of sound, then we cruise at speed-limit twenty along a totally deserted road. Damn her policewoman's obedience of the rules. Sleep! Get me home and get me to sleep.

Irritability was the lingering goodbye of the dexamphetamine, and it meant he wasn't quite ready for sleep. The edges of his tongue still carried the bitterness of the quinalbarbitone, but it was slow taking effect. Zombie tiredness, yes, but no trace of drowsiness just yet. Maybe he needed another.

They cruised around the circuit of Tokyo Avenue and turned inwards on Dresden. Ware let the Sierra roll to a halt at the grass kerb. No lights in the house, but the car was parked right there in the dark driveway, blistered bead-bright by the night's rain. It was a two-door Mercedes coupé.

"Your wife's safely home, Major Talley."

He nodded, looking past her at the car, a motionless little galaxy of hard gleams in dim streetlight. It was the right kind of vehicle for a general's wife. Or a general's daughter. "Thanks for arranging the car for us, by the way."

"I didn't arrange it," Ware said. She turned towards him, a dark face in dark shadow concealing dark eyes. "You should know that."

"I do." He felt himself teetering on the edge of leaning forward. So he turned and tugged the catch of the door. "I was just being polite. My wife pulled strings. She does that kind of thing." He pushed the door slightly and the courtesy light came on over their foreheads.

She was studying his eyes: dexamphetamine dilated the pupils. She was checking his face: dexamphetamine causes vasoconstriction, it squeezes the blood out of your skin and makes you pale. But so did the night, and tiredness. "Go easy on the tablets, major. I guess that's general advice, not specifically for you."

"Sure." He opened the door wide.

The house was warm. It still smelled of other people's carpets, but it also smelled of Kathrin's Chanel. Four in the morning, and the perfume still lingered like — love left over in the air.

In the kitchen he took a second quinalbarbitone and washed it down with buttermilk. So the combined dose of barbiturate might make him dozy through the afternoon? So who would complain about that after tonight's mission? By evening, when they might be flying, he'd be wide awake again. He went to the bathroom, across the hallway of the chalet house, to brush his teeth.

Cotton wool discards smeared with makeup still sat in a little pile on the back shelf of the washbowl. Kye always tidied up, unless it was late and she was tired. And her towel was wet. And large amoeba-like lozenges of water still sat in the bottom of the shower. The shower head wasn't quite cold. The soap was awash.

Going to London, she said. Be gone all day. Be back in the evening. If Lutwidge calls a mission, take care. See you at home if he doesn't, see you whenever you get back if he does. Going to spend the day in *London*, she'd said. Back in the *evening*.

She couldn't have been back more than an hour.

So where had she been? And why take a shower at night, instead of in the morning?

He climbed the stairs to the upper floor bedroom. She was asleep. In the echoed light from the stairs, he opened the bottom drawer of the tall chest. He pulled aside the tracksuit he didn't need and the swimming shorts he wasn't going to use, and exposed the pill containers in the rear corner. He took the excess pills from the Special Team prescription and added them to his little horde.

When he slid into bed Kathrin rolled away from him. That was all she did.

8

February 15th, night

Sunday and Monday on standby for nothing, then a mission called late Tuesday evening and confirmed at midnight. The Russians had another May, an Ilyushin Il-38, trundling around the north of Norway, plus another Tupolev tanker moving out to that hold position over Arctic ice floes west of Bear Island. Colonel Ollie Eliot Lutwidge sent them looking for his Red Wraith again.

Sandra Thorndike gripped the stick tight in her right fist and clamped the twin throttles in her left. Hotas — hands on throttle and stick. The original F-15 pioneered the concept. You had so many buttons for your fingers and thumbs added to the grips of the joystick and the throttles, that once you were set up you could fly without taking your hands off the two primary controls. With not having to glance down at instrument panel switches, with vital data presented by the transparent head up display right in your forward line of sight, you could chase and fight and kill an enemy and never have to take your eyes off of him nor all the rest of the dangerous sky. Technology could be a wonderful thing.

But it had limitations.

At four hundred and sixty knots, at Mach 0.85, and just a hundred feet over the sea, you got a rough ride. The Eagle bounced up and down as if it was smashing across the ridges of factory roofs. Just vertical gusts in turbulent low-level air, but it jarred her bones into the seat every second or two, bounced the helmet on her head, and was progressively shaking her eyes out of her face. Vision kept disappearing like she was watching a TV with the vertical hold gone mad.

At four hundred and sixty knots, and just a hundred feet over the sea. A momentary mistake, a tiny touch of nose-down angle, and she was dead. In the HUD, glowing against night and dithering every time the aircraft really kicked her, she watched the arrow marker on the altitude scale. If it wanted to rise she'd know she was starting to climb. And she watched the W-symbol of the aircraft waterline in the artificial horizon's central gap. If the symbol started to drift down from the artificial horizon, pull up the nose or hit the sea.

On the deck, under cloud, in intermittent seconds-at-a-time rain, there was nothing else to see at all. Just her instrument board if she took the time to look, the symbology of the head up display suspended in black — and Bellman.

He was a double focus of white heat, fifteen degrees high and out in front of her, like binoculars looking back at you with laser light in some stupid science fiction film. He led the pair and she followed him in trail. She chased after his balls of fire through the night, desperate not to lose them. Maybe the idea amused Colonel Ollie. Maybe that was why he switched the hunter pairs around this time out, Pinkett trailing Talley and Bellman leading her. Bellman was leading her a merry dance.

The nose-to-tail flying for Blind Date was something else. It tied two aircraft together as if they were on a string. The lead pilot followed the course and watched the sky – ahead, above, left and right. The lead pilot didn't have to waste a thought on keeping the pair together – just watch where they were going and look out for Red Wraith. The trail pilot had exclusive responsibility for keeping up behind the lead aircraft. It took near enough full concentration. You couldn't drop back or drift out of line, because if you lost sight of the lead man you lost him for good. There'd be no calling him up and asking where he was, no using your radar to locate him in the night. All of that was taboo in a quiet sky. The pilot in trail just stuck to the tail of the other machine, and when there was time would throw glances left and right and over the shoulder, just in case a Red Wraith was there.

Flying this kind of pair formation was crazy, but it fitted the mission concept – you had to give Colonel Ollie that much. They could have flown four individual hunters, but that would have multiplied enormously the chances of them mis-identifying each other as a Red Wraith during the critical Draw Play phase. And it would have upped the prospects of a collision, too. Flying two hunter pairs kept the sky tidy. It also had an advantage if they did by some miracle really run into a Red Wraith. They'd instantly out-number it two to one. A pair of fast and agile F-15s should be able to box up a slow and sedate stealth aircraft immediately, and hold it long enough for the rest of Special Team to move in for the photography and the fun. By then, of course, radio silence would no longer be needed, and they'd be jabbering to each other like monkeys on a picnic.

Bellman wasn't on a picnic. He seemed to be out here on a thrills mission of his own. He was off course. All she could do was follow him faithfully. He should be twenty miles to the west, well clear of Norwegian oil production platforms. He should be at least two hundred feet higher, where the ride was slightly smoother and the risk of diving into the sea in pitch darkness nowhere near as great. So what was the bastard doing? Trying to test her nerve, hoping to shake her off his tail and make her blow the mission? He could do what he liked as surely as if their own F-15s were invisible stealth machines. There was no incident radar at all hitting them, the radar warning receiver was silent. No one was watching. Their IFF senders were switched off, so the aircraft weren't squawking out their presence and identity to anyone who was listening – the *orthodox* wartime precaution that prevented your friends from shooting you down. So no one knew they were there. Bellman could do whatever he liked, and it would be her unsupported word against his.

No prizes for guessing who Lutwidge would listen to.

She flew with both Lolite and Iris switched off. Lolite she was beginning not to trust. In the bare two weeks since they started this flying, the system had failed on her and on everyone else – except Bellman, of course. It had crashed for Talley twice. Too damned fucking sophisticated to work right, a technological step too far in pursuit of a billion dollar contract. Iris was reliable. She'd have liked to put the Iris forward view, the twelve o'clock field, on the head up display in combination with the flight path data. It would have let her see the waves she was racing over. But Bellman's machine was in the field, and was so close that the heat emissions from its tailpipes would overload the camera. The same problem would have hit the image intensifying Lolite – the sheer brightness of the jet exhausts would have blinded it to everything else. That was why neither system came with a rearward looking camera: the exhaust stream from the carrying aircraft would have wrecked the picture. Such a shame, because Jesus God Almighty, the miracle a combat pilot needed most of all to help stay alive would be an eye scanning the sky under his or her own tail.

Bellman put a gentle jig to the right, and she followed precisely. The heading nudged over a couple of degrees. She took her eyes off the HUD and glanced down at the illuminated screen of the horizontal situation display. They were further from the course Wizer had given them – twenty-two, maybe twenty-three miles to the east. The Magnavox receiver was on and there was no light burning on the caution panel, so she hadn't inadvertently deafened herself and missed a course modifying instruction from control. If the bait they were going to meet changed its heading, Mondrum would have to tell them through the device of talking openly about it to the Bitburg Boys, the highly visible interceptor pair. Otherwise they'd just arrive in the wrong place and –

Bellman broke hard left –

Patterns of lights appeared everywhere in front –

Bellman's twin suns tipped one over the other and whipped out of sight to the left –

Oil platforms. Ships. Something. At one hundred feet and more than five hundred miles an hour and no warning at all, she was tearing straight through the middle of suspended cities. A huge block of lights right. A little thing dead ahead. A vast Christmas tree with cantilevered flare stacks left. North Sea oil stencilled in night and faster than you can think –

It was a little ship ahead. Green light, starboard side, must be on the wheelhouse. Double white on the masthead – *left* of that? But it could be a tender with its superstructure right on the bow and a derrick on the stern. Get *up* over it –

She pulled the stick and pushed the throttles. It went under out of sight, wheelhouse below the right wingtip, stern derrick below the left. An F-15 roaring *that* low like an explosion out of the night. They'd never know what it was. They'd have empty bowels and cardiac arrests —

She eased the throttle but kept the nose high. Get a safer altitude, get a margin for error. Two hundred feet. She took her left hand off the throttle and poked buttons on the supplementary test set control panel. Three hundred feet. Iris on, twelve o'clock field selected dead ahead, combined up on the head up display. Four hundred feet. She leaned the stick a little left and push-pulled the rudder bar with her feet. Iris's infrared horizon of lukewarm sea tipped left side up in the HUD, exactly matching the artificial horizon under the waterline mark. Five hundred feet. Lolite on, eleven o'clock field selected, called on the redundant radar display screen at upper left of the instrument board. Its horizon tipped in faint distance beyond a monochrome corrugated sea. Five hundred feet. The waterline mark was starting to slip through the gap in the artificial horizon as the turn took away airspeed and lift and the nose came down. More throttle. Five hundred feet. Tipped gently in a level turn, with an infrared view dead ahead, plus an image intensified low light TV picture of what was coming around the turn. Safe enough. Time to look for Bellman.

She turned and looked out left, a little high because the world was canted over. Far away were the bunches of suspended lights — the accommodation platform, the production platform with warning glows at the top of its tower and ferocious flames at the end of its flare stacks, and the little ship in the middle. She hadn't seen them because Bellman's dazzling tailpipes were in the way.

The indescribable bastard had aimed right at the complex and broken clear in the last second.

He hadn't tried to kill her. He was just having fun.

He was proving she wasn't good enough. She couldn't cut it. She didn't belong in a world of macho men.

He'd had to play dirty to do it. But in the real heat that the Air Force trained for, dirty would be the only way to play.

So he'd proved it.

She started around in a long circle looking for him. But she already knew he'd raced over the horizon and disappeared.

Clyde Lincoln Talley didn't trust Lolite. He didn't trust anything any more. His religion used to be a belief in no one and nothing but himself. That was how he got so good. Then Libya happened and the church caved in.

He had the Iris twelve o'clock view combined on the head up display. It added almost nothing to the transparent blankness. The moonless sky was pitch dark by natural light, and the cold stratosphere produced no infrared glow. The cloud ridges were silvered very faintly by starlight, and lit from inside with the barest touch of relative warmth. Iris added nothing he couldn't have seen with his bare eyes. At the moment, at 0520 and almost forty minutes since the moon went down, there was just nothing at all to see.

He had Lolite's twelve o'clock field called up on the screen at upper right of his board, the multifunctional display. Inside the little glows of the push-buttons around the edge of the screen, it showed a miniaturised version of the world ahead, a stratosphere sky hazed with enhanced starlit ice clouds, plus half-bright mountain ridges of weather clouds coming right up to his flight level. The electronically brightened view was as monochrome as deepest night.

Deepest, darkest natural night, empty as the dome of heaven belonging to a dead god, surrounded him outside the acrylic canopy of his flying machine. He could be alone in all existence.

Except that Pinkett was no more than three hundred feet behind him, low on his tail and out of sight. Cole McGee and Don Luzzi were two thousand feet higher and a few miles ahead. One hundred and fifty miles behind and probably headed back home was the Il-38 May, the bait. Somewhere, round about level and closing up on McGee and Luzzi, was Bellman with Thorndike on his tail. And somewhere, maybe, in the radar-blank and radio-silent limbo of quiet sky, was the black painted delta of a Red Wraith.

He listened to McGee and Luzzi chattering with each other and talking back and forth to control. Every time they transmitted, his UHF transceiver lit up and told him the relative heading – almost dead ahead, right where he was going. Every time they spoke to control they confirmed their airspeed and their altitude. He kept his airspeed higher so that the gap closed. He kept two thousand feet lower so that the trap stayed exactly set. If Red Wraith was stalking the interceptors, it would stay well down below their tails so it could track them easily against the naked sky, and so that they would have the least possible chance of seeing their sneaking shadow. If Talley came in lower still, he had the best chance of seeing Red Wraith up there in the night. And by staying down among the cloud tops, he ensured that no Red Wraith moving in from an even greater distance could get a clear view up at him from below.

Bellman, if he knew what he was doing, should be using the same tactic, flying cautiously through the night with Thorndike chasing his tail. Sandra Thorndike had a nice tail. But it was going to be Bellman who got his hands on it, if anyone did. That would please Lutwidge, too. In the colonel's world view, real men had active balls and real women always went for them. That was the natural order. That was God's good thinking.

Concentrate. He had to concentrate. No sleep all night, and now it was 0522 and he'd been flying this damned machine for over three hours without a break in his hundred percent attention. With nothing to see, in fact, but hypnotic night. The problem with dexamphetamine sulphate was that once you were used to it, the stuff didn't help so much. He'd taken his second little tablet as they left the bait and began to close the trap. If his concentration was starting to slide, maybe he should unhitch his mask long enough to swallow a third. But then when you took more, the side effects started to surface. He already had a headache, and there was a nauseous little wave crest poised in his stomach. Maybe he should, or maybe he shouldn't take some more.

But the big problem, really, faced him on a different front.

Kathrin went to Wales for the day. If she was stuck in this God forsaken hole of a country she might as well see some of the prettier bits, she said. Drive right over to the coast and the romantic castle ruins. She said. Well the day had started sunny, but the weather coming out of the west – from Wales – brought cloud and rain, and the sun went down at twelve after five anyway, and it was dark by six. Kathrin still wasn't back when the pilots were called to Special Team at ten in the evening. She wasn't back when he phoned home to tell her – if she was interested – that the mission had been confirmed and would last the whole night. By then it was past midnight – and Wales was only a couple of hours away from Mondrum. He didn't even have any means of checking if she'd in fact left the base at all. Nor did he have private transport. He couldn't cruise around looking for whose house or apartment Kathrin's car was parked outside. He should have noted the mileage before she left.

Or possibly he shouldn't give a damn.

Lolite beeped.

Down on its little screen was a flashing box, halfway up from the field center to the top edge.

Lolite beeped again.

Lolite had found a new element in its field of view, a little speck of *something* that had emerged from the bland background.

Lolite beeped again. He poked the test set control button, and the box stopped flashing. In the center of the box was a tiny lateral smudge on the artificially grey night sky. The center of the smudge was faintly brighter. An aircraft with fuselage mounted engines, seen from behind. In the corner of the box was NID – no identification. With a closer view of something already stored in its computer, the system would even be able to match the image and tell him what it was. This image, though, was too small. He poked the button again and the box disappeared.

Gently, so he didn't throw Pinkett from his tail, he eased the throttles forward and added another twenty knots.

It was there in the head up display. When he blanked out the Iris view, there was nothing to see. But when he restored Iris, he had a bright little speck of converted heat image, dead ahead and around ten degrees high.

The little standing wave of nausea in his stomach started to curl over in a crest. The headache slipped right in behind his eyes.

He pulled up the nose and added more power to keep the airspeed of the Eagle constant. Readouts from both engines moved in unison on the engine systems panel. He put the F-15 into a very shallow climb.

The thing was miles ahead, but close enough to see on Iris. In fact it was so bright on Iris that he should have seen it himself before the Lolite system managed the trick. He should *concentrate*, for God's sake. Above all, *now* he should concentrate.

It was just one single aircraft.

McGee and Luzzi were flying a pair, side by side, and their last report said they were a thousand feet apart. At that range, they'd appear as two little specks separated by less than a finger's width. Bellman and Thorndike were stuck nose to tail. They'd come up on the screen as a double image with two engine signatures. So possibly, just possibly . . .

The converted infrared view from Iris was too crude. He took his left hand off the throttles and punched keys on the supplementary panel fitted with the aircraft's test set. He swapped them around, put Iris on the multifunctional display on his instrument board, and put the Lolite picture on the head up display. Now he was looking through the HUD's flight path symbols at an electronically enhanced version of the real night which hovered out at infinity.

He pushed the throttles, eased the nose attitude, and maintained the angle of climb while increasing speed by another thirty knots. He twisted around and looked once behind him. He looked past the high back of his seat, out through the tapered rear of the canopy, over the invisible rump and between the twin blades of the tail fins. The two tail fins stood like black knives against a faint floor of starlit cloud. And right in the middle of the gap, just high enough to see, were the twin tips of the fins on Pinkett's aircraft. So he wasn't alone.

Because the thing he was chasing was a Red Wraith.

He unlocked the gun. The little cross marking the bore-sight line appeared on the HUD. He unlocked the gun camera, which was the only thing he hoped to be using. Little bits of acid spilled off the crest of his stomach wave.

Lolite beeped.

Two overlapping boxes flashed in the HUD, two new targets picked out by the system's computer. The new specks were below the Red Wraith in the field, but the field had an upward perspective, which put them ahead of it and at higher altitude. The first contact was included inside both new boxes.

He pushed the test set control button. The boxes stopped flashing and advertised NID. Lolite didn't know. But Talley could guess – the contacts were McGee and Luzzi. And they had a Red Wraith coming up on their tails.

The boresight mark sat in field center below all three targets. If he ever had to use the gun to protect himself, he'd have to aim with his eyes alone, the way they did it in the first war, the second war, and in Korea. The F-15 had some of the fanciest gun-aiming radar anywhere in the air. It tracked a target for you, predicted its shifting position if it was moving relative to your own aircraft, and told you where and just about when to shoot. But the radar wouldn't work reliably, or even at all, against a just about non-reflecting stealth target. So the eyes had it. No other way.

It was a sliding three-layer sandwich. McGee and Luzzi above and being overtaken by the Red Wraith below, and the Red Wraith being overtaken by himself and Pinkett as they climbed up towards it. He was closing the range fast while steadily reducing the vertical separation. Thousand feet, at a guess. Soon have to watch he didn't overshoot. Soon be so close he wouldn't lose it, and could call out that it was there.

The image of the intruder was a firm little shape – flat wing plane and two upright fins. What little was known about Red Wraith fitted well enough. The image of the intruder was so close to one of the more distant interceptors that it was going to interpose itself. The image of the intruder was going to touch. Last time that happened in his Lolite field, the system crashed. He should ease out sideways to change the relative viewing angle and keep the two images apart –

They touched. The view vanished from the HUD. It flashed on again as Lolite reset. It vanished. It stayed vanished.

He stared at total night.

The test set panel lit up with a Lolite error warning. Fuck the thing. He started to loosen his hand on the throttle so he could put the Iris image back on the HUD –

On the multifunctional screen, in the miniaturised Iris view, the brighter speck of the Red Wraith started to slide out sideways, breaking gently to its right. No damned time to juggle fancy systems. Find it dead ahead with your *eyes*, and call in help.

He thumbed the transmit switch on the throttle. "Talley. I see one Red Wraith. He's at around one mile behind the interceptors and five hundred feet lower. His angels twelve thousand. My angels eleven thousand. Climbing to get on his tail. Pinkett, you come up beside me."

He put on power and leaned the stick gently over to the right. Let Pinkett see his maneuver in time not to move up and slap into it. Down in the little Iris display, the faint specks that were McGee and Luzzi started to swing left and out of sight. The last he saw of them, they suddenly split apart. They'd be coming around on separate courses to turn the tables on their reported shadow.

Their shadow, a crude heat signature in the center of the screen, got bigger. In the chunky, poorly discriminated infrared view, all he could make out was a warm little tipped-up piece of wing with twin hotspots in the middle.

"Control," said the voice in his ears. "Anyone else see the bogey?" The voice was Lutwidge, far away in Mondrum.

"Pinkett. I'm moving up on Talley. I got his bogey."

"Thorndike. I'm right where Talley called the bogey. Is he on my tail?"

He was coming up on the curve. He should see the thing with his naked eyes through the empty HUD. It was against the sky, it would be a silhouette, it was less than half a mile. From the Iris view he knew right where it was — center field and slightly high. Dead ahead over his nose.

In the Iris view it jinked left, then flipped up and swept right. The movement was enough. Straight ahead with his own eyes, he saw it on the sky, a sharp little blackness under shadowed night. And turning to escape.

He pushed more power and tipped the stick right, kicked the rudder around. Over went the world and on came gee to squash him into his seat. Transmit switch. "Talley. Bogey is breaking right on two-two-zero. Two-three-zero. Steady turn."

"McGee. I'm coming in on two-seven-zero. I see three on Lolite."

Steady turn. He could *see* it against the sky. Delta wingform, twin engines, twin fins. Around fifteen hundred feet ahead. He pulled more gee into a tighter turn to catch it.

"Thorndike. I got a bogey on my tail. Close and cover me and he's sewn up."

"McGee. I see two F-15s. Assume Talley and Pinkett. Third aircraft assume bogey."

Something in the side of his eye. He looked right, and out over his wing was Pinkett's F-15 overhauling him inside the turn. Pinkett was out to snap the Red Wraith first. No way. Gun armed? Check gun armed.

It was armed and ready. He had the boresight leading on the Red Wraith now.

"Pinkett. I got the bogey on eyeball."

It snapped around and broke hard left.

He whipped the stick across and kicked the rudder hard over. He had to turn his head to follow it, through past the hoop of the canopy's bow frame and out left. Forget the Iris. It was way outside its field. His Eagle went over on its left side and the Red Wraith rolled up above his nose. He pulled the turn tighter and it started dropping down towards the peak of his bow frame. Where was Pinkett? A collision would be insane. Not left. Not right.

He twisted his head half off, and there was Pinkett up over his tail, coming round on the inside of his turn. *Tight* was how that man flew.

"Thorndike. I got two bogeys on my tail!"

It slipped down behind the bow frame.

"Pinkett. Hey, Talley, ain't that an F-15?"

"Thorndike. I can't shake them. Close and cover me!"

He got ready with the gun, slipped his finger over the trigger on the stick. He was still adding power to increase the rate of turn and bring the boresight pipper to the target. It came down under the bow frame. Too sedate. It should reverse. Or put its nose down and dive –

"McGee. I see three F-15s. No bogey."

"Thorndike. That's a fucking F-15 on my tail. That's two fucking F-15s!"

The bogey eased right off. The pipper swept over it and started to aim at the air where it was headed. Squeeze the trigger half closed as the shot came right –

"Pinkett to Talley. That's an F-15 you got there."

"You fucking shitheads!" No call sign, but Thorndike's voice. "You're tailing *me*!"

He let go of the trigger.

He started to roll out of the turn and take off the power.

A black shadow in the night, Pinkett's machine slid up on his left wing and levelled beside him.

Thorndike's F-15 was coasting out straight as an arrow

ahead. It sat neatly over the horizon, where near black nothing met the night-satin sheen of cloud tops in starlight.

The shot he'd set up was with the gun, not with the gun camera.

"Luzzi. I'm coming up behind. I have four F-15s on Iris. I have McGee, Talley, Pinkett, Thorndike. I guess I got all of you."

He was supposed to chase and photograph Red Wraith. Instead he got right to the point of killing Thorndike. The wave of nausea waiting in his stomach started to break . . .

"Bellman. I'm behind *you*, Luzzi. I'd have you, too. I have five F-15s and no Red Wraith. Nice one, guys. Nice one, Talley Boy."

He got right to the point of killing Thorndike. Oh Christ, he nearly did it. His religion used to be to believe in nothing and no one but himself. And then the church caved in. The roof came down over Libya. Now the walls were collapsing, too.

"Control. All aircraft nosedive." It was Lutwidge, an icy voice from hundreds of miles away. "Repeat nosedive. Get right down on the deck. The bait just switched on a radar on low power. Get down before he sees you."

The church had caved in and there was rubble on his altar.

He pushed the stick forward and put the nose right down. The waterline mark flipped clean off the HUD. The nose-down angle scrolled to sixty degrees before he pulled up in a steady dive. The altitude started coming off too fast to read. Nothing on the radar warning receiver. No incident radar, so the bait hadn't seen them yet. At least he hadn't done that ultimate damage to Lutwidge's operation.

And as he went over the top of the dive, the sickness in his stomach peaked in bitter vomit that erupted into his throat and got as far as his teeth. He swallowed it back, a sharp-edged gulp at a time. Keep it down, keep it down, and get down on the deck.

"Control. The bait must want to know what all the squawking was about. Get on the deck and off his horizon before he puts his radar on full power." A UHF transmission grates intonation into a raw evenness, but you could still feel the sheer anger in Lutwidge's voice. "And resume and maintain radio silence."

Talley dived into total blackness under cloud. He watched the velocity pile on and the altitude ripple towards zero. He swallowed down the bitter acid and plummeted into disgrace and disgust.

9

February 15th, day

They got back just before the sun rose. It took over the sky somewhere high above the clouds. Down at Mondrum Air Base they had a blustery wind with rain.

Lutwidge hauled them into the briefing room without time to change out of their flying suits, and he lashed them. Not even his number two, Charles, was allowed inside. Lutwidge turned it into an inescapably private affair. His pilots had fouled up, and it *hurt* him. With some the tactic might work very well. His own regular unit would be used to it, and anyone who didn't like the way things were done would have had time to transfer out. The ones who stayed would be suckers for the colonel's steel charisma. You could see it in the shamed responses of McGee and Luzzi. They were Bitburg Boys, they were the colonel's guys, and they were utterly sick at the way they'd let him down.

But the others were specialists. They commanded

unbeatable skills and earned unparalleled assessment scores. And they were perfectionists. When they made a mess, the most cruel and most constructive response was to let them take themselves apart. Perfectionists *worry* their way towards flawlessness. What doesn't work is telling them they don't know how to fly.

Clyde Talley watched it go hopelessly off the rails. Lutwidge couldn't do this right, and that was just fine. If he, Talley, the only authorised hero among the six pilots, the man who was credited with shooting down a Libyan MiG-23 – well if he had to suffer in a self-sustained agony of failure, it was nothing less than satisfying to watch the commanding officer dismantle any unit coherence in the process of haranguing the others. If Talley hadn't been so central in the little disaster, he'd almost have enjoyed watching the session collapse into a theater of recriminations.

"All right now," Lutwidge was saying. "Let's summarise this absolute *fiasco*. Thorndike fouled up twice. Talley fouled up once – and boy, did he do it good. And everyone else fell right in with it when Thorndike popped up in the dumbest possible place, and Talley called her as a possible Red Wraith."

"I don't see –" Thorndike started.

"*I'm* doing the summarising, captain."

"And I'm *answering*," Thorndike snapped at the man three ranks above her. "And I don't see what's supposed to be dumb about tailing in behind the interceptors and using my eyes to look for any fucking Red Wraith."

"What's so dumb, *captain*, is that after you went and *lost* Bellman, you failed to allow for the time you wasted looking for him. You came up right in the middle of the Draw Play pattern, and right where the hunters were expecting a Red Wraith to be. Continuing with the mission was not dumb. Having the sense, thank God, not to go calling for Bellman or looking for him with your radar – that was not dumb. Coming up into the middle of the trap – a single aircraft precisely where everyone was looking for a single aircraft, and no one had any reason to expect it was you – was as dumb as you could get. As is proved by what happened next."

Lutwidge's eyes came around to Talley.

But there's nothing, Talley thought, you can say to me that I don't already know. There's nothing you can tell the others. It can't hurt any worse. Because the one error you don't know about – that no one knows about – is the even worse way I got mixed up. I damned near fired my gun, instead of my camera, at Thorndike.

"You, major, saw Thorndike's F-15. You assumed it was a Red Wraith and you called it as a Red Wraith – *before* you'd moved in close enough to confirm. The goddam Russians *don't fly* F-15s, major. So? So what's the reason? Why did you break radio silence and set the whole thing in motion for an F-15?"

Talley thought: stay calm, don't show yourself up any more than the mission itself did. Don't be a hysteric. "My Lolite crapped out before I had an identification. The Iris image was too crude at that range to supply –"

"But I told you, Talley Boy." Bellman was grinning at him. "You have to treat Lolite right. That's three times the system's failed on your aircraft. What are you doing to it?"

Stay *calm*, he thought. For Christ's sake stay calm. "The Iris image couldn't supply an identification. I had no visual. I had a risk of losing the contact, so I called in help." And Lutwidge, of course, wasn't buying it. Lutwidge was staring back at him with sheer contempt. Which was too much. "It was dark. Yes? What was I supposed to do? Wave my hands? Shout? Sure – Pinkett was only three hundred feet behind me. But I had to break radio silence to tell even *him* to pop out sideways and take a good look."

"Hey, Talley," Pinkett said. "What's that mean? So now I'm to blame because you called a non-existent Red Wraith?"

"You fouled up, too," Lutwidge cut in. "Your Lolite didn't crap out, Pinkett. But you were dumb enough to accept Talley's identification instead of using your own eyes and then calling the error. And then the rest of you come crowding in for the fun." He turned his gaze on McGee and then on Luzzi. They flinched, they withered. "You split and came around to get behind the bogey Talley reported, which was good enough. But you failed to check your tails first, even though he told you it was right behind you. If it had been a Red Wraith, it would have been *following* one or both of you, for God's sake. Your maneuver could have thrown it off, spooked it that little bit too soon, or just made it move so fast across a dark sky that the guys on its tail lost it. That, too, was dumb. About the only one who comes out of this like a reasonably intelligent human being is Bellman."

Craig Bellman glowed with self-satisfaction.

"*Bellman?*"

Everyone looked at Sandra Thorndike. She was pantomiming disbelief. She hated Bellman.

Lutwidge's glare was scornful. "He put himself in sweeper position. He *thought* before he acted. He recognised a lot of machines would be crowding in on one place, so he waited where he could move up and see what was going on, and could pick up on a Red Wraith if it slipped clean out of the mess. That's good, Thorndike. It's called flying with your brains."

Thorndike had control of herself. Talley could see her doing it a step at a time. First her fists loosened, then her shoulders dropped a fraction of an inch. Finally the tendons in her throat relaxed. Her face stayed like stone.

"If Bellman is *so* good," she said slowly, "how come the wise guy was so far behind that he still came up on Luzzi's tail, even after Luzzi went right around the outside? Luzzi started out at the front, and went around so wide he came in behind McGee, who also started out at the front. Bellman here, who is flying the same initial course as the rest of us, comes in behind him. He doesn't overtake any of us while we maneuver. What was Bellman's machine doing up there? *Hovering?*"

Lutwidge just looked at Bellman.

Bellman shrugged. "I dropped back. Good anticipatory position flying, Sandra Lee."

"The hell it was!" The anger lashed out at Bellman. She'd set up her diversionary target, and could let rip without taking on the boss. "You were way out of position! Way back behind where you should have been. You're a law for yourself, Bellman. You're flying your own private missions out there for your own private glory."

Bellman just shook his head.

"We have no radar tracks," Lutwidge said softly. "In quiet sky conditions we can't see where anyone flies. The only record of an aircraft's flight path is the inertial calculations stored in its navigation computer. And since we're not dealing with a collision or an accidental shoot-down here, I do *not* propose to try piecing Bellman's flight pattern together from that source. Is that clear, Captain Thorndike? Is that quite clear?"

"Okay," she said. "Okay. Bellman isn't a pilot. He's an angel, and we don't touch him. Fine. So long as we know the rules we have to play by." She gave Lutwidge a smile, a very sour smile. "But now we've heard all about how we fouled up and blew the mission, how about some constructive suggestions?"

Lutwidge was almost quivering. He was fighting with his own self-control. In the world he set up, no one answered back. "Do you have any, Captain Thorndike?"

"I have one," she said. "In blowing the mission – which we surely did, however you see the blame – we fucking nearly blew the operation, too. The bait aircraft heard all the fuss, and decided to see what was happening. It turned a radar on. If it had turned the thing on at full power, it would have picked up the whole bunch of us. No more sneaky flying, and no more visits by any Red Wraith. And that's your error, Colonel Lutwidge, sir. Quiet Sky is no protection if the other side doesn't need to maintain it."

Lutwidge didn't answer. He didn't even move.

"Can it, Thorndike." Cole McGee leaned forward and

stabbed towards her with his finger. "You don't run Special Team, so just shut your lip."

"No, Cole." Lutwidge shook his head. "That's a fair one."

Cole McGee kind of shrugged.

Sandra Thorndike almost looked surprised.

"Captain Thorndike has the right to bring it up," Lutwidge went on, "seeing as how she's the one who mentioned the risk associated with Quiet Sky in the first place. I discounted it." He nodded slowly. He was looking over their heads towards the back wall of the room. It was costing him an effort to come down and admit he was a mortal and a fallible man. Or maybe, Talley thought, Lutwidge had realised how wrong things were going and was astute enough to play the penitent at the right moment in order to get things back on the rails.

Lutwidge went on nodding into space. "That was my mistake, and I guess we're going to have to take it on board. We're going to have to rethink the way the mission's configured. Okay, gentlemen." Suddenly he was back in his hierarchical place, the master of the store. "Let's all cool off and go get some sleep."

Lutwidge left them alone. He left them with a wasted night, and a miserable early morning with rain lashing the window. A wet wind was starting to leak in around the panes. Little bubbles were coming up through the bottom corners of the metal frame. It was cold in the room.

"Heating's out," Don Luzzi said after checking the pipe along the base of the wall. Someone had to say something.

"You see, Thorndike," Cole McGee started, "your attitude is all wrong. You come on strong with the balls-breaking stuff, and everyone's your enemy. But you just saw what a great CO the colonel is, admitting his own mistakes along with everyone else's."

"Balls," Thorndike said. She stood up and turned towards the door at the back of the room.

"C'mon, Sandra Lee." Bellman reached out and tugged

at a loose fold of her flying suit above her hip. "Don't you like a little messing around in private in the dark?"

Backhanded, she broke his grip so hard there was a slapping sound as her fist hit his wrist. "Not with a bastard like you! Not with a bastard who throws me off his tail just to louse up my act!"

Bellman just rubbed his wrist and smiled. "I didn't do anything, Sandra Lee. Prove I did. Can't you cut it? Aren't you as tough as the rest of us? Are the cracks in your makeup showing?"

"Bellman," Talley said, "just leave it alone." The man was getting to be a sickening jerk. Bellman wasn't funny, he wasn't witty, but he simply didn't know it.

Bellman seemed genuinely puzzled. "Are you some kind of a libber-lover, Talley Boy?"

Don Luzzi walked right between them, voting with his feet on the sense of the whole cat fight. "Hope there's still hot water for a shower," he said. "With the heating being out, that is."

"Let's go see," Cole McGee said. He followed Luzzi out of the room. That left Clyde Talley with Thorndike, Bellman and Pinkett.

Bellman stood up slowly and started past Thorndike. He leaned towards her and said soft enough for the others to hear: "Come on, give your foxy little body to me, and we'll make out and make up. Or don't you like sex with a guy?"

Talley thought she was going to spit. Bellman just swaggered out of the room. For him it had to be a simple equation: a woman who wouldn't have him certainly wouldn't waste time on any other male, therefore lesbianism was the only answer.

Now Dwight Pinkett was on his way out. He, too, paused in front of Thorndike. "I'm a filthy nigger and you're a sexual pervert. Welcome to Bellman's world."

"Huh," she said.

"By the way, I do know Bellman dumped you deliberately out there. On the last mission the jerk tried skipping all over the sea just to lose me. Didn't work, though. I have too much experience at tight formation flying."

"Meaning I don't?"

"No. Just meaning I know about Bellman."

"Well tell Lutwidge!"

"Pinkie!" It was Bellman again, looking in through the door and smiling as usual. "No sense in risking a shower here, so I'm heading home. I'm giving Cole and Don a ride down to Arlington. Want to come, too?"

"Sure, Mister Test Pilot." Pinkett headed for the door. He waved over his shoulder without turning. "Sleep tight, you guys."

That left Talley alone with Sandra Thorndike. They were sinners in the church of perfection, and Lutwidge was the high priest. The others, the faithful adherents and the temporary apostles, shunned them.

Thorndike went ahead to the locker room. By the time he got there she was already in the shower. He opened his locker. His uniform blouse was hanging from a peg on the back of the door, and he turned the jacket to get at the inside pocket. That was where he put the tablets. He picked a quinalbarbitone, popped it in his mouth, and swallowed it before the sugar coating dissolved. In an hour he'd be home in bed, and desperate to sleep. Wonder what time Kathrin had finally gotten home?

Thorndike stood facing the wall again, with water pouring over her skin. The water wasn't hot, but it was adequately warm. He showered. He watched Thorndike standing with her hands on the wall, her face upturned. Glistening water ran on her back, over her buttocks, trickled down between her thighs. They were alone in the shower, in the locker area, possibly in the entire building. He only had to step right up there behind her, and reach his hand around. She'd whisper "Talley?" and then she'd relax. Maybe he'd bend her a little forward . . .

The worst happened. He got an erection he wasn't going to be able to think down again. He turned his back, but it wouldn't fade. He started to edge his way around to the exit from the shower. Kathrin didn't do any of that with him any more. He was reduced to taking himself in hand every time the tension grew too great, otherwise it would be the humiliation of wet dreams and stained sheets at the age of thirty-seven. The whole business, every time, was a little ritual of defeat. Each time he flushed the tissues down the pan, more of his self-respect went with them.

He looked around as he reached the exit, hoping Sandra Thorndike hadn't seen. She was still standing in her private Niagara. She tipped her head forward into the stream of water. Then she turned her face around his way. He left in a hurry. He didn't see if she opened her eyes. But he thought she did.

Eileen Ware had fallen asleep in the driver's seat. They had to tap on the window to wake her up. As she drove away from Special Team she turned on the radio to keep herself alert. Mondrum's station had a morning show which was vile in its bright breeziness. Forty-three degrees and raining, with a wind from west-northwest, it told them cheerily. They were driving through it with metronome wipers, they were starved of sleep, they were defeated and cold. They had the weather in their bones.

Kathrin's car was there on the drive. Walking past it, he put his hand on the hood. The raindrops were cold. But the Mercedes was warm.

She came out of the shower while he was on his way to the kitchen. Her hair was tied in one towel, her body was wrapped in another from underarms to knees. "Morning, Clyde," she said, and turned to the foot of the stairs.

"Where were you?" He propped himself in the open kitchen doorway, back leaning on the hinge side, hand stemmed against the opposite frame. "Where *in hell* have you been?"

She took her time. One hand was holding the towel over her breasts. The other moved, a lightly clenched fist, and planted itself against her hip. She was his domestic Lutwidge, his other tyrant, another judge who'd found him wanting. Kathrin Yvonne Talley, born with the soaring expectations of an Everett, had closed the proceedings against him long ago.

"I didn't want to come on this posting, Clyde. You dragged me back to this piss-hole of a country in winter. If I try and find myself some fun, that's *my* business. I don't owe you any kind of explanation. I might still be married to you, Clyde, but it isn't my fault any more."

She went up the stairs.

In the kitchen he fixed himself a sandwich and a glass of buttermilk. He took another tablet of quinalbarbitone sodium. By the time he'd finished, she was back downstairs and installed in the living room to get on with her day. Out the whole of the night, and bare-faced about it. Unassailable.

He went up to the bedroom, opened the bottom drawer, and added the surplus tablets from the previous evening to his little horde. Dyson, the MO, was doing him a favour with the over-prescribing, but maybe not enough of a favour to be sure of meeting all possible needs. He should think of a way of improving his backup supply. But not just yet. With luck, Blind Date and the whole insane business of hunting for Red Wraith might already be over.

PART 3

Electric Fox

10

February 16th

The heating failed at Special Team. It came as no great surprise. Museum pieces are supposed to be looked at and dusted, not operated for twenty-four hours a day.

No one at Mondrum knew anything about the ancient installation hidden at the end of Special Team's crew building, but the terms of the lease on the base relieved the United States Air Force of all responsibility. The British looked after all buildings, plant and machinery that wasn't especially sensitive to US security needs. As at all US bases, routine maintenance and repair were managed by the British Government's Property Services Agency. Their friendly engineers were just a telephone call away.

Mondrum had two commanders. There was Major General Dodgson, who ran Mondrum Air Base — which had aircraft, equipment, related stores, over three thousand personnel and more than double that number of dependants. There was Squadron Leader Eric Blair, who was in charge of RAF Mondrum — which had several square miles of land, lots of buildings large and small, one office, one officer and one officer's wife. Squadron Leader Blair, who was in reality nothing more than a liaison officer, led an isolated life as the only British serviceman on the facility. The essence of his existence was to receive requests from the American administrators for assistance with repairs, and phone these through to the British Ministry of Defence, who then passed details to the Property Services Agency.

The heating system went down in the early hours of Wednesday, and a pair of PSA engineers sporting Ministry of Defence passes turned up at midday Thursday. It was exceedingly fast work.

Special Team, Blind Date and the Lolite and Iris equipment mounted in the air test sets were all highly secret. Either the two British engineers would have to be vetted, which could take months, or they had to be escorted. So Eileen Ware finally had something to do that fell within the scope of her specialty. Big deal.

At least it was a sunny afternoon, a crisp forty-three degrees with a chill westerly breeze. And next to no one was around – including Lutwidge.

Master Sergeant Charlie Rodeck shielded his eyes against the winter sun and looked towards the aircraft shelters on the south side of the unit area. Two of the F-15s had been rolled out under the open sky, and some of Erin Heller's staff were working on them. Nothing else seemed to be going on. Special Team was temporarily standing down from operational readiness.

Eileen Ware counted the vehicles parked on the apron in front of the crew building – just six, including her own car and the Transit the engineers arrived in. "I guess," she said, "it's all quiet on the Special Team front."

Rodeck giggled. He was a great big block of a man, an imposing military policeman turned security staffer. His laugh was an incongruous little thing. "Seems they really know how to bitch at each other, by all accounts."

"Keeps them busy. They don't have anything else to do right now." The conditions were wrong. It was bright moonlight most of the night, peaking with the full moon on Monday. No Red Wraith would be flying for at least another week.

"Gives the ground crew a bit of a break," Rodeck said. "I never heard of constant one hundred percent mission capability before. Nor has Captain Heller, nor any of her people."

"Colonel Lutwidge is pretty unique, sergeant."

"Seems he is. By the way, Captain Ware." He was looking down at her with the pale blue of the empty sky behind his head. "Seems you're kind of isolated here. Isn't that so?"

She was isolated. She had no real work most of the time, no professional involvement in Special Team, no significant contact with the rest of Mondrum's security force, and no social life at all. She had a one room apartment with furniture supplied, and nothing much to do there, either. She decided on a bare nod.

"I was talking to Jolene. We'd like to invite you over for supper – if that's not out of line?"

"Out of line?" Eileen shook her head. "I think that's a very nice idea."

"Be nothing special, mind. Just a regular family meal with an extra place at table. I mean, with three growing kids we don't get to do anything like a dinner party."

"Sergeant Rodeck, that sounds just fine. I'd be pleased to accept."

"Good. That's settled. How about tonight? Say six thirty? The kids are real eager to meet you. I've just about brainwashed them into realising security is even more important than glamorous things like flying airplanes, so when a security *officer* comes into the home, they're going to listen to every word. So is six thirty okay?"

"Six thirty it is. I hope I live up –"

"Captain Ware! Say, Captain Ware!"

Sellert, the equipment specialist, was coming across at marching speed from the row of sheds on the opposite side of the Special Team area. Over there, in one of the workshop bays, was where he kept his stockpile of Lolite and Iris units, plus the test set pods used to fly the systems on the aircraft. He came right up to them, looking upset.

"Captain Sellert?" she said.

Roy Sellert pointed back the way he'd come. "One of those heating engineers is working in my equipment store."

Eileen shrugged. "Yours is one of the workshops on the heating circuit. I guess they have to check all of the pipe they can get at. Let's just hope the fault isn't some kind of leak in the pipe where it goes from one building to the other under this concrete here. They'd have to dig the place over."

"That's not the point. That equipment over there is *important*. It's also absolutely state of the art and covered with any security order you can think of. Is it okay if — well, if one of them just messes around in there?"

"The guy has to do his job, Roy. Besides, they only got in here because they have valid Ministry of Defence passes. That's the way it works in the UK. A Ministry of Defence pass means the British security service vouches for them. Were you ever in the UK before?"

Sellert shook his head. He looked over his shoulder, and then turned back to Eileen. "Should be okay then, I guess. If you say so. But that stuff is just *so* sensitive — way ahead of anything else in the world. I get kind of jittery about it. Even when people say the Cold War is about over, we still have to maintain security." He gazed at her steadily to make his point. The way he was standing, the shallow sun reflected off the lenses of his glasses and right into her eyes.

She stepped sideways. He turned his head, and the twin suns moved a little way around the curved lenses. She gave up. She decided to needle him gently. "Lolite seems to make quite a few people jittery. It's failed three times on Talley, hasn't it?"

Sellert nodded. His face turned sad. "Yep. Some people claim it's over-ambitious, over-sophisticated and over-designed. It's certainly pushing image-processing technology to the absolute limit, and that just has to give rise to problems. Basically the Iris system is looking better — this is the way the feeling is going on the program at Kirtland. We want the best sensor we can get for stealth, but it has to be one you can rely on under real conditions. We'd like to get the wrinkles out of Lolite, seeing as it has much greater potential, but reliability is what counts. Though lately Iris was running into a set of hitches and glitches. Craig Bellman could tell you about that, since it picked him to play up on. I guess we've been lucky with Iris so far on this operation."

Eileen shrugged. Roy Sellert always suggested she ask Bellman for information. Everyone seemed to think Bellman was tops. Maybe it was the test pilot charisma. The man himself was pretty vile.

"Well," Sellert said, "my stuff won't be the only sensitive equipment around here in another couple of days."

"How come?" she said. And she thought: now what haven't they bothered to tell me?

"Lutwidge didn't say? He has a Raven coming in to join the team. An EF-111A. An Electric Fox." He caught up with the fact that she didn't yet understand. "An electronic warfare aircraft for escort duty. The thing is just *loaded* with secret bits and pieces. This guy Lutwidge is really something else. He only has to waggle that string he has connecting him up to General Famula in the Pentagon, and he gets anything he wants."

Eileen looked at Charlie Rodeck. "Sergeant. I think it's time I finally had a talk with your Colonel Wolford. It would really be a neat idea if *someone* would start telling me what's going on."

11

February 18th

By Saturday morning, the Special Team building was warmer than ever before. They came in from the rain and gathered in the briefing room – the six pilots, Lieutenant

Colonel Charles, Major Susan Wizer, and Lutwidge. Colonel Ollie Lutwidge had the new mission profile for them.

"As you'll know by now," he said, "we're getting the use of an EF-111A Raven. It's being loaned to us by the Forty-second Electronic Combat Squadron, which is with the Twentieth Tactical Fighter Wing at Upper Heyford. Clyde Talley served at Upper Heyford with the Twentieth a couple of years ago." Lutwidge turned the focus of his gaze on Talley. "In fact he was a pilot with the Forty-second ECS. He flew an EF-111A in the escort role on the Libya mission in nineteen eighty-six. Right, major?"

Talley nodded.

Talley looked tired. He looked rough. He looked as though he wasn't over his mistake on the last mission. Sandra Thorndike assumed he would be tougher. As one of the pair of higher ranking pilots, with only that asshole Bellman for a rival, by rights he should be back on the bounce. Bellman had all the self-generated charisma, but Talley had the genuine combat kill. The only person in the room who'd also been shot at in the air, who'd made any kills in combat, was Colonel Ollie. The rest of them were would-be heroes. Clyde Lincoln Talley was the real thing.

He should be, she thought, on top of this.

"The normal role for the EF-111A Raven," Lutwidge resumed, "is to jam an enemy's anti-air radars so as to protect ground attack aircraft. That's why the Raven is attached to an F-111 tactical wing. It's the role Major Talley's aircraft was flying when we bombed the shit out of the Libyans. Right, major?"

Talley nodded again.

Lutwidge nodded briefly in turn. At least Colonel Superman was responsive enough to have learned not to expect a more talkative reply from the man. "However, the aircraft carries about the most sophisticated suite of electronic countermeasures in the Air Force, so it fits our requirements exactly. We're going to use it to protect our hunters from the risk of being illuminated by a Russian radar, either from the bait aircraft, from other more distant air or ocean units, or even conceivably from the Red Wraith itself." He glanced at Sandra Thorndike. "We're abandoning Quiet Sky as too insecure."

Sandra Thorndike gazed right back at him. I was right, she thought. One up to me. And you, Colonel Ollie Superman, are plain lucky that the bait used a low-powered radar last time and didn't in fact catch us like a bunch of moths in a searchlight. You lose out when you don't listen just because it's a woman who's talking.

"The EF-111A Raven will follow our pair of interceptors out to the bait at high level. Once the interceptors have visual contact with the bait, the Raven will commence aggressive jamming on all radar and communication frequencies the Russians might conceivably use. In fact it will jam *everything* except the frequencies we need for our control channel and our ship-to-ship channel. The interceptors, the Raven and control need to be able to talk with each other, and the hunters have to hear everything that's going on, but we want those Russians both deaf and blind. The obvious justification for the tactic will be plain nastiness on our part. The bait is ostensibly on an elint mission to listen to Nato emissions, so we go up there and hound it by saturating the entire spectrum with raw noise, thereby wrecking its mission. We anticipate the Russians won't seek any deeper motive than that." He looked around to where Ernest Charles was sitting beside the front table.

Charles nodded. "At the Pentagon the feeling is the Soviets should buy it as just another variation on the standard game."

"The saturation jamming of the area right around the bait will wipe out the electronic sky, and provide a protective cloak for our hunters to approach and circle. When the interceptors leave the bait, the Raven will leave with them – and will continue jamming. The hunters will follow inside the protective cloak, and will slowly close up on the interceptors in the hope of trapping any Red Wraith that's decided to follow them. What we're doing, in other words, is retaining the Draw Play concept but using a different means to avoid detection of our hunters. We're rendering the Russian radars totally ineffective, and at the same time masking secondary illumination from our own radars on Awacs, ground stations and so on. We're calling this Dark Shroud, for self-evident reasons."

"Neat," Bellman said. Bellman would.

Colonel Superman, though, was pleased by the appreciation. He came out with one of his nice smiles. "We also need a call sign for the new aircraft. We can't just stick with the pilot's name, since either the pilot or his number two might be answering. We're going to call it Romulus." His smile broadened into something like true good humour. "I'm reliably informed that in *Star Trek* it was the Romulans who protected their spaceships with a cloak of invisibility of some kind. Ernest here suggested the name."

Lieutenant Colonel Charles beamed, and nodded his head in a token bow.

Boys, she thought. Everywhere I go, every unit I join, I end up confronted with overgrown little boys – with their Draw Plays and their stupid science fiction spaceships. Sometimes it almost seems they're right. Front line flying might be no place for an intelligent woman. Except I do it so damned good.

Colonel Superman was now thoroughly pleased. He was rubbing his hands together at the thought of the new toy he'd get to play with. "The aircraft is due here Monday. We'll have no trouble in accommodating it, since Mondrum is a designated dispersal base for Upper Heyford's F-111s in case of war. Because Blind Date is such a critical and difficult operation, we're getting the Forty-second ECS's best. The pilot is Lieutenant Colonel Todd Beamish. Know him, Major Talley?"

Talley shook his head. "He wasn't with the Forty-second during my time."

"No? Well I guess he'll be pleased to meet you, seeing as you're the unit's absent hero. However, I'm sure you'll know his electronic warfare officer."

Talley didn't say anything. He was waiting for Colonel Ollie Superman to pull his latest infernal rabbit out of the hat.

"His EWO is Captain Jacob Baker."

Talley's head turned sideways and back, as if in an elaborately slow shake of the head. Sandra Thorndike saw his face turned fully towards her for a moment. The expression of tense tiredness broke apart, and then reformed. In between she saw shock.

Baker seemed to be an unpleasant surprise.

Some kind of old enemy, she thought. A guy he just couldn't stand? A guy who once screwed his wife? Yet another dose of feuding would be exactly what Special Team needed.

"Captain Baker," Lutwidge went on, "flew with Clyde Talley as his EWO on the Libya mission."

She caught him in the corridor as he was coming out of the locker room. He was still settling his coat over the blouse of his uniform. He was going to walk right past her.

"Clyde?" She put her hand up against his shoulder. She had to push until outer fabric and inner lining were pressed to his collar bone. "You look kind of rough these days."

"I'm just fine." He was fastening the zip together.

"Still sick at the mess you and I made of the mission? It wasn't just us. And it wouldn't have happened at all if that asshole Bellman hadn't deliberately thrown me."

"I'm not still sick at it." He wouldn't look at her. He was staring down the corridor. "I'm kind of in a hurry. I have some shopping to do in the center."

"But you don't have your car." She looked over her shoulder to the grey daylight that was spilling into the middle of the corridor from the entrance door. "It keeps raining. And Ware isn't around this morning. Wait until someone can give you a ride, why not?"

"I feel like walking." He slipped past her hand. He walked down the corridor and turned the corner towards the door. His head was down.

Around the corner, the door banged at his back.

Pinkett came out of the locker room and stopped right next to her in the corridor.

"Dwight, does it seem to you as if Talley's under some kind of strain? He looks bad."

Pinkett shrugged. "I figure he just doesn't like being the only proven hero on the team *and* being the one who really fouled up a good mission we were flying. Makes him kind of unfriendly, though."

"He looks kind of — well, hung over. You don't suppose he might have a drink problem, maybe."

"Brought on by what?"

"Hell, I don't know. Marital, sexual, financial?"

Dwight Pinkett shook his head. "He's a top line pilot under constant appraisal. Hey, at Wright-Patterson they've been using him on their program to *evaluate* stress in relation to anti-stealth tactics, haven't they? No way does he have a drink problem without anyone knowing about it. But now *you* have a problem."

"I do?"

He nodded towards the door behind her. "Seen your locker lately?"

Eileen Ware wandered in to avoid another rain shower. Lutwidge's supply car was parked outside, but things were so quiet on the Saturday afternoon she was sure to hear him coming in time to get out of the way. She had the beginnings of a real problem with the animated action man: she was *afraid* of a one-on-one meeting. But he seemed to be in his office, and the door was closed. She went past to the end of the corridor, where the briefing room was located.

Sandra Thorndike was the only person there. She was seated on one of the chairs, facing the front table and the chalk board on the wall behind it. On the writing rest of her chair was a notepad with a pen discarded on top of it. Her elbow leaned on the writing rest, and her forehead was propped in her right hand. She seemed to be shading her eyes.

Eileen was just turning to leave.

"Need anything?"

Thorndike was looking at her with the impersonal irritation of someone just hauled out of their thoughts. So Eileen shook her head. "No. Sorry, I didn't intend to disturb you."

"No problem." Thorndike lowered her right hand and poked at the pen lying on her pad. "Can't concentrate, anyhow. I'm just here because it makes a change from my tiny little apartment, with its nice bare walls and none of my personal effects. Work here, work there — what's the difference?"

"I know what you mean." Eileen had an equally bare apartment up at the north end of the base on Starfighter Drive, she had the office in the security building, and anywhere she cared to wander at Special Team. For variety she could go sit in the car. "What work are you doing?"

"Maneuvers. I always like to go through air combat maneuvers." Thorndike tapped at the pad. "Then I check my intuitions by running through the math on turn rates, climb rates and so on. Trouble is, I know what an F-15 can do, but I don't know a darned thing about any alleged Red Wraith."

"Do you need to? I mean in terms of air combat. Is this talk of Red Wraith putting up a *fight* to keep itself secret really that realistic? Would the Russians actually do that?"

"Search me. But I know the absolute minimum that any Red Wraith we actually find *will* do. He's going to do his absolute best to throw anyone who finds him right off his tail again. That means tight and fast maneuvers. Combat maneuvers. Right?"

Eileen shrugged. It wasn't her specialty. "If you say so."

A flicker of impatience, replaced by a little bit of up-front teacher's tolerance. "The essence of air combat — at least, of close-up combat, once both pilots know the other guy's there – is to get on the enemy's tail and stay there. Sure, we have all-aspect missiles, and a gun attack is possible from just about any angle, but your best chances of a kill are to take him from behind. A heat missile is most likely to hit if it homes right in on his exhaust pipe, the brightest target he presents. The gun is best from behind, because you get the longest shot at the target coupled with the least complications with predicting his relative movement. If you don't predict, your shells are going to go through the air where he was, not where he is by the time they arrive, right? So you want to be on his tail, with as little angle-off as possible. This all means that air combat maneuvers are designed to force the other guy out in front, and then to keep him there. With me so far?"

Eileen nodded. "And while you're trying to keep the other guy out in front, he's trying to throw you off."

"Exactly. Whether he wants to get around behind you and kill you, or just wants to unload you and bug out fast as he can, he has to push you out in front so you can't stick like glue to him any more. Air combat maneuvers. That's what it's going to be about."

"So you rehearse them in your head."

"I try. In order to handle any encounter with Red Wraith, I need to be able to look up, down and sideways just as fast as I can turn my head. Neither Iris nor Lolite is going to help at that stage. They might make finding Red Wraith easier in the first place, but with a limited set of separate fields of view, they're useless for maneuvering. I'll have to rely on the Mark Two eyeball – the trained pilot's eye – and do so in near total darkness. I need to *anticipate* where he'll be and what he'll do from one second to the next." Thorndike picked the pen off the pad and slipped it into the inside pocket of her blouse. "Trouble is, we don't have the least real idea of what he can do. If in fact he exists."

"I guess not." Eileen watched as Thorndike closed the notepad. "What do the others think about the problem?"

"Hell, how should I know?"

"You don't discuss it?"

"Discuss it? Us? But we're rivals, aren't we? Can a woman cut it, can a black? Can a regular front line pilot beat the rest? Or will it be the test pilot or the genuine decorated hero? Watch this space."

Thorndike glowered somewhere at the wall. It's an opportunity, Eileen thought, to voice a cautious opinion on something and see what someone else might think. "The colonel doesn't seem too concerned with forging his pilots into a coherent team, does he?"

Sandra Thorndike looked up at her again. "No, he doesn't. His notion is that the best fighters are a sackful of quarrelling cats. He gets us quarrelling all right, so then we foul up. Why, in the final analysis, was the last mission a fiasco? Because Bellman threw me off his tail."

"You're sure he did it deliberately?"

"Look. You're in security and I don't question your competence. I'm a pilot and you don't question mine. Okay?"

"Okay," Eileen said. With the regard in which she was held by just about everyone else on Special Team, she didn't need to go antagonising a more or less natural ally like Thorndike. "So why would Bellman do that – throw over a mission for a personal kick? Does he hate you that much?"

"Bellman is an egotistical asshole who doesn't give a flying fuck for anything but his own glory. Also, he sure doesn't like me." Thorndike stood up. "Come and see."

The locker room was as uninviting as the rest of the crew building. A pair of back-to-back benches occupied the middle of the floor – just two wooden seats made of single planks, and a central backrest rail. A dozen dark green lockers lined one wall. Six had names newly stencilled in white. Up under the ceiling on the end wall were two slit windows which let in a little daylight. In a row under the windows were a set of coat hooks. Six of the hooks were obscured by flying helmets. Oxygen lines, oxygen masks and communication leads dangled beneath them. They looked like a catch of mysterious molluscs, disembowelled, with their entrails let out to dry. Off the other side of the room was the shower area and the toilet, and between the two doorways stood a wash basin with a wall mirror above it. The whole facility was basic.

Sandra Thorndike's locker was the last of those with stencilled names on the doors. She leaned against the next one in the row, and tapped the painted name on the front of her own.

The name had been defaced. The fresh white paint of two of the letters had been scratched clean away. The "o" had a gap in its circuit. A bar had been improvised across the letter by scraping the old green paint right down to the bright grey metal underneath. It was a piece of neat and careful negative graffiti.

The name now read *The dike*.

Eileen Ware couldn't, immediately, think of anything to say. A smear was vile. A sexual smear, in a world of the proudest heterosexuality, was worse. It was also a political smear. Any woman who flew combat aircraft in a man's world had to be a feminist, and a feminist would be a man-hating pervert. It was one of those allegedly logical things.

"Well?" Thorndike said. "Can't you get the perpetrator for sabotaging military property, or something?"

"Um – who is the perpetrator?"

"Bellman."

Just like that, caught and court-martialled. "Why should it be him?"

"Because he figures I should let him fuck me, and I don't intend to."

"Come on. He wouldn't really think like that. And he wouldn't react like that. A guy can get turned down."

"He's a woman-hating male supremacist. There really are some of those about, you know. And who in hell should it be otherwise? No one else has tried to get his metaphorical fingers inside my panties, so I haven't had the opportunity to turn anyone else down. Try talking with Bellman, why not? Try talking on anything remotely intelligent. He'll let you know women are for fucking or forgetting."

Probably, Eileen thought, he wouldn't even let me escape with that much recognition of my existence. On top of everything, Bellman seemed to be a racist, too. "Have you considered advising Lutwidge of the problem?"

"Lutwidge? I wouldn't expect anything but a patronising smile. Nor would I give Bellman the satisfaction of seeing me run for help. I can handle it myself. I believe I may have said that once before."

"But shouldn't Lutwidge know there's a war on between two of his pilots? Especially if it's throwing his operation."

"The hell with his operation. Who expects to catch an invisible airplane in the pitch dark, anyhow? At Nellis we've been working on anti-stealth tactics. As far as night operations are concerned, the interim conclusion is — there aren't any. It sums up this way: you can't see him — but he can kill you. The only thing you can do is stay quiet, and hope you don't meet up with him. He holds all of the cards. So what the hell." Thorndike turned, rolling her weight so that she leaned with her back against the locker next to her own. She stared at the opposite wall. "I'll handle this on my own. It's Talley should have people worried. He isn't holding up so well to the shit-slinging."

"Talley?"

"Didn't you notice how strained he's looking? Bet that suits Superman just fine."

"Superman?"

"Our colonel leader. Bet he'd dismiss it as good healthy self-criticism by a top line, top performance guy — ride anyone hard enough and he'll keep on his toes. But I think Talley's sitting on some sort of private thing which spoils his self-confidence, maybe. Could be that it makes him unable to take the sniping. What would you think?"

Eileen shook her head. "I don't know anything about the guy. You're supposed to be a team on a single operation. Isn't there any way you can talk to each other? Someone should try drawing him out."

"Well — I tried. In my own clumsy little way. I don't think even he likes me, though I can't think what I've done to him. Maybe that guy arriving Monday, Baker, knows something about him. Talley really sat up when he heard the name."

"Baker? The electronic warfare officer on the new aircraft?"

"The same. Seems he flew as Talley's EWO when Talley was with the Twentieth wing at Upper Heyford. He should know plenty about his former pilot."

"I guess he should." But getting entangled in any of the little fights and feuds bubbling up in Special Team seemed a particularly pointless idea. They all regarded her as an outsider, so the best Eileen could do was to stay outside until and unless something occurred which really did affect security. On the other hand, this amount of conversation with Thorndike was the closest contact she'd managed with any of the pilots. This tiny piece of progress was probably worth retaining. "If you can handle Bellman's tricks by yourself, what do you propose to do about it?"

Sandra Thorndike turned her head to look at her defaced name on the locker door. "Repair and ignore. Where do I get an itsy little bit of white paint?"

12

February 20th

Talley couldn't sleep. It was after three. He woke up at midnight, and just stayed that way. Too much to think about, and all of it too terrible.

Kathrin was asleep. Her breathing changed, she turned over now and then, but she slept on soundly. At least she was there beside him in the bed.

Clyde stared at the dark ceiling. In the upstairs bedroom of the chalet house, the ceiling over the bed sloped down towards the headboard. The darkness dissolved its perspective. It could be empty sky. It could be Thorndike's machine, sliding down past the bow frame and coming closer, ever closer, to the line of his boresight. The trigger should fire the camera. But he'd set up the gun instead. He set up the gun because he was so fast, so good, so automatically tough in the real situation. The likes of Bellman could strut and posture and proclaim any amount of potential brilliance. Clyde Lincoln Talley was a pilot who cut it when it counted. He was a real kind of killer.

So, excited and tired, he cleared the gun – even when he didn't need it.

In his empty, black, imagined sky Thorndike's machine slid forever down towards the boresight mark. And sometimes it was that other aircraft in the night over Libya.

Kye was asleep. So nice that she was there. He needed her more and more the worse it got. Trouble was, there wasn't any way left to say so.

She was at home, of course, because she had the decency not to do it unless a mission took him away. Kye always had style.

If only she wouldn't go out with other guys. If she wouldn't do it at all. They were here for another month at the outside, while the nights stayed long. Couldn't she hold off screwing around until then? Why did she start it after all this time? The marriage hadn't been good for years. It was outright bad for the last two. But adultery hadn't been the answer before.

It was so bad, the sandbagging that muffled any last vestige of communication was so thick, they couldn't even get close enough to fight about it. They sniped indirectly, not explicitly, not right out in clear bombardments and barrages. At times she acted as though she had no idea what he meant. Her ice cold refusal to acknowledge him, to *meet* him at all – that was the cruellest torture she could have devised.

So she'd wanted to *have some fun* while he was away on the England posting. So he'd *tried to ruin it* by dragging her here. Well his blackmail *wasn't going to work* any more and she wasn't going to keep up the *pretence* any more, Clyde Talley. *This marriage is dead* and I want out of it.

She wanted out of it.

But – it wasn't dead, and it wasn't necessary for anyone to know about the awful bad patch. The marriage *was not dead*.

But it would be if she went on the way she'd suddenly started, because eventually folks would notice and the rumours would begin. Then they'd all know he couldn't keep his wife happy so she went elsewhere for her fun. And it would be she who opened up the pain for everyone to point at, and that was so unfair and sick and cruel of her, and the marriage would be truly over and done.

And now Jake Baker's going to be here. The past is coming back.

Jake Baker, and the ominous – the omen-rich – error he nearly made with Thorndike's aircraft. All coming back.

Thorndike's F-15, and the boresight, and the aircraft in the Libyan night all coincided on the dark ceiling.

He got out of the bed. He needed sleep. He needed a sleeping pill. To hell with its eight hour effect. He'd be groggy until midday, but Beamish and Baker weren't due until the afternoon. By then he'd be bright and shiny – because he'd slept.

In the dark, he slowly slid open the bottom drawer of the big chest. Under the swimming shorts and the tracksuit in the back corner, he located the plastic pots of pills. He carried them down the stairs to the kitchen and the light. The dexamphetamine were little things, and the quinal-barbitone were bigger, but they were tricky to keep apart by touch alone. The little reserves were running low. The mix-up with Thorndike had shown what tiredness could do. Fatigue was a function of not being alert enough on a mission, and not sleeping well enough between times. He needed uppers and downers. He needed more of both.

He put a quinalbarbitone in his mouth and washed it down. He went to the bathroom. He went back upstairs. He closed the drawer so quietly, then slid back into the bed. Kye mumbled and turned, gently, away. He started to snuggle up to her. Half asleep, she used to like that so much.

"Clyde," she murmured. "Get your hands off me."

Lieutenant Colonel Todd Beamish arrived first. He was forty, he was married with three kids, and he was the senior EF-111A pilot at Upper Heyford. He flew his machine to Mondrum solo. The EF-111A Raven landed with its long wings stretched wide, then the wings were cranked back to maximum sweep before it was towed from the taxiway to Special Team and backed into the secure seclusion of one of the shelters down on the south side. The Raven was packed with sensors and jamming transmitters, plus all the computation required to run them: it had to be protected from unauthorised eyes.

Todd Beamish arrived solo, with the right seat in his Raven's cockpit empty. Captain Jacob Baker, aged thirty and single, moved to Mondrum more sedately. He drove up in Beamish's car. They wouldn't need two cars at Mondrum, and Baker's vehicle at their home base was an Air Force lease while Beamish's was his very own. His wife, apparently, had an Air Force lease vehicle for shopping and taking the kids to school. So Baker brought the car for Beamish, with their personal baggage in its trunk, while Beamish flew the aircraft over.

Beamish was polite and friendly. He didn't move in at Special Team with an air of intending to take over as senior rank pilot. He seemed routinely enthusiastic. He didn't get *happy* until his car arrived in one piece. It was an old and perfectly ordinary Chevrolet, a Caprice Classic, but it was re-sprayed and waxed and the chrome had been polished and the vehicle looked almost like new. For some quirky reason, he loved it.

Talley turned up barely in time for the general briefing. He looked washed out – like a man who'd been to an all-night party, and hadn't enjoyed it. He greeted Baker with a show of handshakes and shoulder slapping. It woke up a memory in Eileen Ware, a little detail from when she was seventeen – the insecure way Nixon used to pump hands and pat backs, shortly before he had to leave the White House. Secretly, she'd felt sorry for Nixon. Those were the innocent days.

Lutwidge had pulled everyone together for the briefing. He had his pilots there, plus Charles, their intelligence expert. He had Sellert present because of his equipment expertise, and Erin Heller because of her air maintenance responsibility, which would now extend to include the Raven. Susan Wizer, the team's dedicated air control officer, was in the room. Eileen was there because security was just a fact of life. Everyone ignored her except Susan Wizer. The woman's steady gaze, every time she caught it resting on her, made her uneasy: what might it be she wants from me?

Lutwidge introduced the new men, then he went through a résumé of Red Wraith and Operation Blind Date. The newcomers were impressed, the veterans of two unsuccessful missions were a little bit fired up once more. Lutwidge, she had to admit, didn't do too bad. Action Man seemed at his best when describing an impossible task and telling people how certain he was that they would do it.

After the briefing and after the talking broke up and Talley had already disappeared, Eileen took the new men to meet their temporary homes. She drove Baker in her Sierra, while Beamish followed in his Chevrolet. She came out of the alleys between store sheds and turned right to head south on Manhattan Avenue. Like half the rest of Special Team's aircrew, Baker and Beamish were installed in trailers in Arlington.

"You looked pleased," she said, "to meet Talley again. Did you enjoy flying with him?"

"I wouldn't know if *enjoy* was really the right word."

She took a glance around at Baker. He wore a moustache, and was stroking it with the knuckle of his index finger. His eyes were busy looking at everything he could get to see of Mondrum. Go for it gently, she thought. "Was there any kind of problem?"

"What? Problem? No way at all. I used to *admire* flying with Clyde. Everything he did – it just told you he was perfect. He brought experience on Phantoms and F-15s, and he put it all into the F-111. He didn't in any way resent the aircraft – which I've seen happen – even though it doesn't handle like a fighter. He went right ahead and learned everything he could about its strengths, and never asked too much of it. He was the *safest* pilot I ever heard of. And then when it mattered, he went and did the impossible."

"You mean the Libya thing?"

"That's right. The MiG that caught us as we were going back out over the coast." Baker paused to look left along Gateway Boulevard, the route he'd come in by and would recognise. The last piece of Manhattan would be new. "It isn't what you're reckoned to be able to do in any kind of F-111, never mind an EF-111A – survive a MiG on your tail, recognise it as a target of opportunity, come around tight on a one-chance snap turn. I mean, one minute we had our wings tucked back tight and were starting to run, the next we had them fully extended like one of the Navy's Tomcats in a dogfight. Speed off and a knife-edge turn, and then he puts a missile right up that MiG's tailpipe. The orthodox view is you don't carry even self-defence weapons on an EF-111A. Well Clyde proved the point on that one."

That would be what Baker meant by admiring Clyde Talley as a pilot: Talley had brought him back alive although he shouldn't have been able to. Another of the F-111s, a regular bomber, had been lost on the way back over the coast. Baker would be very grateful to Talley. So he could be the right person to talk to, so why not now or never? "Would you happen to know of anything that might be bugging Talley? Giving him sleepless nights, maybe?"

"Nope. Besides, I haven't even seen the guy for more than two years until today. Do you think he has some kind of problem?"

"I don't know." They were coming to the end of Manhattan, where Arlington Avenue joined from the left. She slowed and got ready for the curve, and then the turn for the trailer park on the right. "He might."

"Well, the only grey area would be his marriage, I guess. It wasn't really going so smooth."

Eileen took the Sierra around the curve, then put her light on early for the entry so Beamish behind her would have plenty of warning. "Did Talley tell you?"

"Nope. Never."

"So how do you know?" She changed down, then hauled the wheel around for the entry to Arlington trailer park.

"Well, when you fly in the seat next to a guy, you do just everything with that guy, the whole time. You talk, joke, you confide. But Clyde never talked problems from home. Never. Now everyone always has little problems from home. Most of the guys are married, and believe me, there are no exceptions. A guy only ever wouldn't mention the problems if they were *big* problems, and he kind of thought it wouldn't be right or polite to hit you with them. Do you get what I mean?"

Eileen nodded. She was cruising past the lines of trailers in search of the correct row.

"But all that must be over," Baker said, "or the marriage just wouldn't exist by now. Why do you ask, anyhow?"

"Oh – he seems a little troubled and unhappy." Here came the row. She slowed some more and pulled the wheel. "Also, he doesn't seem to have handled so well the fact that the foul-up on the last mission was largely his mistake."

"Ah yes, I already heard about that. Seems to me the mission requirements are kind of strenuous – plus it sounds like everyone else also fouled up good. The thing is, though,

Clyde's kind of a sensitive guy, really, and I can't imagine he'd like not doing something right." Baker pointed ahead at the last few trailers in the row. "Is this it, by the way?"

"This is it," she said, and let the car roll to a halt level with the last two trailer homes. She waved Beamish to drive around in front of her. "Home from home. This is yours, and the last in the line is for the lieutenant colonel. They've put you right down here so it's nice and quiet if you need to sleep through the day."

"Thoughtful of them. What's that over the fence?"

"Straight ahead? That's Mondrum's power facility. And over that way, behind the trailers, that's the sports center."

"Figures. Ah – do we have the keys?"

"Your boss has the keys." She nodded to where Beamish was parking his elderly Chevrolet. "Tell me something – what does he see in that old car?"

"Todd's Chevvy?" Baker grinned. "His kid – his first kid – was born on the back seat. They didn't start out for the hospital in time. He swears he's never going to sell it, just drive the car until it fades away."

"I guess it's a good enough reason to hang on to the car, at that." Just one item of information, Eileen thought, and a perfect stranger like Beamish is turned into a person possessing feelings you can understand. Talley stayed a stubborn mystery, a puzzle with all its key pieces missing. "About Talley still. I'd have expected a hero – which is what he is – to be a little more confident and, well, thick-skinned."

"Why?" Baker shook his head. "All of that's just mythology. And besides, I never had the idea that Clyde *liked* being a hero. He didn't like the attention and the fuss, or the expectations or the pressure. He didn't like that at all."

13

February 23rd

Thursday started with a frost, stayed crisp and sunny all day, and then a hail storm hit in the middle of the afternoon. It hit as Clyde Talley was crossing Enola Gay from the corner of Thunderbolt, right in the heart of the administration area. It was the first bite of the British winter. The hail stones bit his cheeks as he ran across the sidewalk and in the door of the medical center.

He waited his turn among base wives and off-duty service personnel. The medical center, located conveniently right in the middle of Mondrum's social and economic nucleus, offered surgeries and clinics for ante-natal mothers, the worried, and for the everyday walking wounded. Heavier calibre medical care was on offer at Arlington Hospital, down at the south end of town. Dyson, the MO who'd been saddled with the additional responsibility for Special Team, was in the psychology and neurology section at the hospital.

The appointments were running just about to time. He was sent to the room with *Capt J. Rosen* on the door.

Dr Rosen, behind the desk, was a woman in her early thirties, about the same age as Kye. She had a small frame, short black hair, dark eyes. Her left hand displayed no wedding ring. Funny how he was starting to check that out so efficiently. Bellman would have approved. Clyde Talley didn't.

Clyde Talley could get sick at himself.

"Sit down, Major Talley." Rosen's right hand was hovering over the keyboard of the computer terminal parked on the side of her desk. "We don't have a record on you. You're new at Mondrum, I assume?"

"I've been here three weeks. I'm with Special Team."

"Ah – the secret squad. The unit no one's supposed to know anything about." One of her fingers pointed elegantly at the screen he couldn't see. "That appears to extend to your medical records. Do you suppose they haven't been transferred to Mondrum?"

"I believe that's possible." He didn't like lying, but at least it was a little lie to begin with. He knew damned well about the medical records, otherwise there was no sense in being here. "We're at Mondrum on a short duration posting – another six weeks at the outside before we're reassigned to our regular jobs. I guess they might have decided to save on the office work."

"Apparently." Rosen folded her hands neatly on the empty blotter in front of her. No wedding ring, no engagement ring. Empty, delicate little fingers. "Well, Major Talley, what can I do for you?"

Leave her hands alone, he thought. You've met attractive female doctors before. You're a married man, and Kye – as everyone always tells you – is beautiful. Jump right in like an honest man with a silly little problem. "I'm having difficulty staying awake nights, and also difficulty sleeping. Fatigue coupled with insomnia, I guess." He left a pause just long enough for Rosen to get ready with a question, then pre-empted it. "It's interfering with my alertness and efficiency during operations. That is, we're running night operations."

"Almost the only thing Mondrum knows about Special Team is the fact that you're engaged in night operations." Her folded hands had tensed. Her fingers made little seesaw motions. "Isn't Major Dyson, over at the hospital, in charge of medical requirements for Special Team?"

"He's handling the pilots," Clyde said. "Pharmaceutical mission support." He watched as her fingers started to tap the quiet keyboard. She'd be checking, as a conscientious doctor should, on the records maintained at the hospital. In view of the temporary nature of the posting, Dyson wasn't even required to keep records of the drug regime he used for the pilots. Like every other doctor, Major Calvin Dyson was a very busy man who needed no additional case load. The self-serving laziness of the Air Force bureaucrats, who'd decided against transferring records on Special Team personnel, coincidentally made life much easier. There were no central records, no medical files, nothing to write reports into. Dyson just *had* to be too busy to have opened computer files he didn't need.

If she found his name at Arlington, he'd have landed himself up to his neck in trouble.

"There are no records at Arlington." Rosen tapped more queries into her keyboard. "I recall hearing that Major Dyson was specifically looking after the pilots." She lifted her head as something appeared on the hidden screen. "At least they've heard of you at personnel, Major Talley. You are officially here at Mondrum. Clyde Lincoln Talley, aged thirty-seven, married, seconded from Wright-Patterson AFB. Yes?"

He nodded.

Rosen glanced back at the screen. "Just the bare career record." Then down went her head, and her eyes looked at the screen, then at him, from under lowered brows. "But you are a pilot, Major Talley."

"Yes," he said. He was ready for that. Thank God he was. "But I'm not flying with Special Team. I'm a tactical adviser. If you don't mind my being very imprecise, our pilots are testing out some new sensors under realistic operational conditions, and my job is to help refine the tactics they're applying as we go along. It's actually a whole new area we're exploring."

"It's secret," she said, "and doubtless none of my business." She didn't sound particularly resentful. More than anything, she sounded slightly impatient. There were a dozen other hopeful patients outside, and up until now there'd been almost no slippage in the appointment timetable. "What exactly do your duties entail – in general terms, of course – and where does the problem with your sleep pattern arise?"

"Well, I sit in at operations control during the missions, and then we debrief in detail once the pilots have returned. Depending on when exactly the missions are called, that can take half the night or even the entire night. I think that's what I'm finding difficult. The irregularity, I mean – plus the fact that we don't fly a mission more than every third or fourth night, on average." He edged a little forward on his chair, acting ill at ease. "It's to do with the moon. We need moonless conditions. I think I've kind of lost my grip on my sleep pattern. I'm finding it very difficult to stay fully alert during a mission, and at the same time I'm just not sleeping properly between missions. It's – well, it's making me pretty washed out, and I'm anxious that the quality of my work is starting to suffer. And we can't just wait for me to catch up again. We're working on a very tight time constraint."

"You do look very tired." Dark-eyed, she was studying him closely. "I noticed as you came in."

Concession, he thought. Acceptance. And I'm sitting hunched forward on the chair, so I look a little tense and anxious, just like I should on the basis of what I say. And Jesus, am I tense for real. Doing this is new to me. I never stooped this low before. It's a bridging solution, that's all. Just a bridge across Operation Blind Date to help me skip back to firm ground on the other side. When Blind Date is over and Special Team is disbanded, I'm going to be coming out of it with a head that isn't in a knot and a marriage that's been rescued from the garbage can. It's going to be rescued *if* I keep on top of the flying. Because if I don't foul up and don't fall apart, then I can work with Kye on resolving our real problem.

"So, Major Talley, would I be right in deducing that you would like something to help you stay alert through the night when necessary, and to help you sleep at other times?"

"Yes," he said. He looked anywhere he could find on the empty parts of her desk. He found her hands, folded on the blotter again. No wedding ring, no engagement ring. If people would just wear a third grade of ring to declare when they had a steady partner in life. It would make things . . . so much easier for desperate husbands in search of relief.

Pathetic relief. He didn't want to cheat on Kye, no matter what she did, and cheating on her wouldn't help. He wanted her to love him again. Little word, turns you over inside. If he started to shake, it would blow open the whole charade with Dr Rosen.

Her hands, her neat little hands, were wrestling gently with themselves. "I see even from this record that you're a very experienced pilot, Major Talley. Decorated. Time on F-4s, F-15s and F-111s. I presume you're familiar with the use of dexamphetamine sulphate to enhance alertness during high-stress night flying?"

He nodded, thinking: she bit, she swallowed the story, she believes me, she believes I'm the perfect example of a dedicated and responsible officer. Basically it's the same as Dyson, cutting corners and failing to monitor the way the drugs he prescribes are used, because he knows beyond question that he can trust the pilots he's dealing with. In Rosen's case, she's using the trust factor to skip across a whole mess of decision steps.

"And quinalbarbitone sodium as a soporific to overcome sleep disruption?"

"Yes," he said, and risked looking at her again. She would think, quite simply, that he'd been embarrassed to ask for help. "In fact we employ the regime quite extensively on the stress evaluation program at Wright-

Patterson. The sensor equipment we're testing here is all
tied in with that."

"So I understand," she said, and smiled very briefly.
"From the rumours I've picked up." She turned her chair
slightly and pulled open a drawer in her desk. She brought
out a blank record card and then a pen. "If I'm going to
prescribe for you, major, I certainly need to keep a record
of my own, as long as you remain with us here at Mondrum." She started to fill in his name and details from her
screen. He'd expected this. It wasn't a problem. The Air
Force kept coherent records which followed a man around
during his professional life. If the medical file wasn't at
Mondrum, nothing medical from Mondrum would find its
way into the file. Rosen would tear up her record card the
day he left. "I'll put your unit as Special Team," she said.
"Is that all right?"

14

February 24th

Friday night was party night. In three entire weeks Lutwidge had done nothing to help his pilots get to know each
other or to feel even a little bit at home on the base. But
Major General Dodgson was a more socially aware commander. He had a unit guesting at his air base, the unit
was now fully operational, and even if their operation was
a rigorous secret they still deserved some kind of a celebration. So he ordered a mingle where the officers of Special

Team could meet and mix with a relevant selection of Mondrum's regulars, plus wives.

Kathrin came to the foot of the stairs as Clyde was twisting in front of the mirror in the entrance hall, checking the back of his blue full dress tunic. Kathrin wasn't wearing blue.

She'd dried her hair so it was swept back and flared out in curling waves of blonde. It exposed her ears and the long sides of her neck. In her ears were the pearl studs. Around the circuit of her throat lay a single string of milky oyster spheres. The necklace accentuated, by interruption, by its lustrous white sheen, the lecherous, warm-white satin sweep of her skin from neck to shoulders to arms, to her back, to the first roundness of her breasts. She wore the red silk dress, sleeveless, strapless, tucked bodice, gathered at the waist and flounced to the hem. It boasted no ornament to distract from its single carmine signal: this is wealth, this is beauty, this is splendid eroticism. This is the queen of the ball.

"No pointed remark, Clyde? No complaint?" Without checking her image, in a haze of Chanel, she slipped past the mirror. "Everyone will see I didn't buy this out of a major's salary."

She bought such things with the top-ups she received from a Mommy and a Daddy who knew his salary couldn't possibly keep her in the style she deserved. Thirty-three, a wife and a mother, and still taking from the parental home. On the other hand, why turn down the goodies when the result looked so good? She was showcasing *herself* for the evening, but it gave him the satisfaction of being seen in the company of his stunning wife, of being marked as the lucky, happy, successful participant in an enviably ideal marriage. It was good to go public with an assertion of harmony — an omen for a future they were going to get right.

So he beamed. "Kye, you look just great." And he thought: if you want me to, I'm content to play for time. I want to ask. I want to know who it is. I want you to promise that you won't do it again, so we can pass on by and let our marriage heal. All it needs is time. You always have to give things time. Organic things like a human relationship need a *lot* of time to grow over their wounds. "Just great! Tonight we're going to show them what a wonderful couple we really are." He turned to the coat rack and took her fox fur, already unpacked from its case, off the hanger. The coat had the weight, stiff and chill, of dead things. "Come on, let's get to your car, Kye."

She turned, she slid her bare arms into the cold lining. He lifted the coat and settled it on her naked shoulders. As he let go, the hairs of the pelt kissed goodbye to his fingertips – a luscious caress of perfect, cancelled life. Like the marriage.

"You're a little euphoric," she said, turning. "Don't let it affect your driving. It's going to freeze tonight."

He shrugged. "I can fly an F-111 at nine tenths the speed of sound at treetop height in a snowstorm at midnight. I know it because I did it. I can cope with your little old Mercedes and some ice skim on the asphalt."

"I'm sure you can." She put her hand on his shoulder, an unprecedented gesture these days. "Be sure you don't peak too early, Clyde."

So he followed her out to the car while wondering what she meant. Here she was, dressed to delight, and he was trying so hard because he'd given up the recriminations and the questions and decided to let her be. So maybe there was a chance, if the party mood mellowed them well, that when they came home they might begin the restoration of their relationship. Maybe there really was a chance.

When it's badly bruised hope hardly springs any more, but it still stumbles eternal.

At the officers' club on Enola Gay, the mingle was under way in the upstairs suite. They joined the little invitation-only throng and lined up their first maneuver. It was a piece of the old teamwork coming through.

General Elias Dodgson was the host, and he was automatically on hand to greet the guests as they entered the suite. With socialite ease, he just happened to be in the right place, chatting with his wife, Maybelle, and with Lutwidge. So real live hero and general's daughter, they homed in on the host while blithely bypassing the cloakroom table set up for the occasion. They shook hands, they said their good evenings, they let a moment of small talk begin ... Then Clyde stepped behind Kye and took the collar of her coat, and Kye pulled her shoulders back – and the silk-lined fur slid slowly from her naked shoulders.

Lutwidge's eyes widened. Dodgson's speech faltered. Maybelle Dodgson nodded softly at the sheer style. It was a one hundred percent delivery on target.

Clyde Talley took her coat and checked it with the civilian flunky, thinking what a great advertisement Kathrin made for his ideal image as the glorious and flawless top-grade pilot – what an unbeatable symbol of his *success* she was.

When he came back she'd moved on, and was chatting with Ernest Charles, the lieutenant colonel from the Pentagon, the man from Washington who maybe had all the right Air Force social contacts. He handed her the coat check and she put it in her purse. He steered her away from Charles with the excuse of reconnoitering the buffet, via the bar. Because Charles might be a danger, he might have those heavy calibre connections Kathrin craved. His ground fire might lead to Clyde losing his wonderwoman wingman.

They circulated. Clyde was lively and extrovert and he *liked* himself tonight. Kathrin basked in her own moving light, her crimson nimbus: the best dressed woman among the civilian wives, and a dazzling jewel beside the officer ladies in their blue tunics and blouses and full dress skirts.

Even Captain Ware was wearing blue for once, instead of her drab security garb. She was standing with her boss, Colonel Wolford, and being polite to his wife. Wolford, a genteel beast, drank Kathrin with his eyes while she glided by.

They made the rounds of the Special Team people, like lead players on the party stage. Thorndike, Luzzi, McGee, Sellert; and Pinkett who was staying side by side with Erin Heller; and Bellman who was sweeping his sights systematically across all the targets military and civilian. And Todd Beamish, who wanted to discuss sometime the finer points of flying Ravens. And Jake Baker, who was enjoying his beer and said he wanted to talk old times. Old times at Upper Heyford, working and flying together, old times like the Libya raid. And the MiG-23?

Clyde disengaged without looking where he was headed. Let Kye handle Jake Baker. Just let him get out. So he suddenly found himself passing right across the course of Captain Jessica Rosen, with Major Calvin Dyson and wife closing up on his tail. By the time he'd masked shock with friendly politeness, the two medical officers had him in the sandwich. If they wanted to shoot shop at him, if Dyson found out Rosen had prescribed or if Rosen realised he was flying one of Special Team's machines –

He started to mumble an excuse about refills, and waved his empty plate and the dregs in his glass –

Major Wizer intervened in a smooth maneuver. A five-way conversation is an unstable constellation. As the automatic pair, Dyson and his wife dropped out and drifted away. Susan Wizer was watching the men and women in the room. Susan Wizer, he realised, was an overt predator, checking who was with whom, who was separate and who was separable. Jessica Rosen, neat, petite, disadvantaged by lack of height, was covertly employing the same search and track routine. She seemed hardly a huntress, less aggressive, more patient. It was her short dark hair, her delicate hands, her contrast to Kathrin. He would have wanted her to pick on him – but now he'd made her his source of supply, and even the innocence of an extended conversation could give him clean away.

Wizer had mapped him, measured him, moved him off the list. It was her eyes, passionless brown eyes that didn't blink. She checked him out, categorised him, and turned her attention elsewhere. She did it with such detailed scrutiny, such instant intimate distance, that his unsuitability didn't even hurt. Instead, she watched Jake Baker. And Kathrin. Susan Wizer watched them both. Through a meaningless screen of momentary chitchat he saw, fascinated, how she measured each of them with equal care. She wasn't just checking if they were together, she was assessing the attitude, the availability, the value of each individual target. He didn't say, that's my wife by the way – he didn't say a word. Transfixed, he looked on while Wizer repainted the people in the room for him as focal features in a searing sexual landscape.

Then Bellman, busy with Beamish and his own self-importance, passed by.

He saw Susan Wizer acquire, lock on and track.

She looked at Rosen, and on her almost immobile face she raised a single eyebrow.

Rosen glanced around at Bellman – not at Beamish – then turned back and shook her head. "Not my type," she said.

But she watched as Wizer closed in for the kill.

Who might be making out with whom? Were the married couples really together? What invisible bonds stretched between them and the free individuals? During the subtle dance of merchandisers mingling in the reception suite, what threads were being untied, what new attachments woven? What did this segment of the human world look like through Wizer's steady eyes?

And who was it, who might it be *here* in these rooms – who was making out with Kathrin?

He didn't ask. She didn't answer. She drifted away.

Who could it be? None of the pilots, nor Lutwidge. They were all busy with the missions at the same time as he, her husband, was airborne and out of the way. Charles might be a target, but he was locked up with Lutwidge in the operations center every time Special Team went looking for its blind date. So who was Kathrin's illicit attachment, who had she found at Mondrum to tempt her into easy adultery? He'd caught her twice in the aftermath of a late homecoming, with no explanations nor answers nor excuses. Had it started with the missions, or did she begin during the preceding week while Lutwidge had his pilots tied up half of every night with training flights and debriefings? How did she find her way around so soon? Maybe it was a determined move, a pre-planned punishment for the crime of hauling her here from Wright-Patterson.

So who was eligible in Kathrin's eyes? All of the men looked at her, but could he detect any special something in the *way* one of them looked, or talked with her? Or was there anything in the way she talked with them, looked at them, stood beside them? Watching, he saw her taunt and flatter every man she met with the same expert cocktail, vermouth light, of cool come-on and calm keep off. In this public arena, with smiles and dance favours, words and little goodbye waves, she imposed an egalitarian rule upon all the males, an exactly equal absence of rights. She played her starring party role to perfection.

Her inattention picked one man out as different, as exceptional, as worthy of note. Kathrin's consistent avoidance marked him as being linked to her by a bond which could persist across intervening heads and additive pieces of time. Kathrin's careful distance tied her to Clyde.

Relaxed by a couple of beers, Kye's husband curled up in his thickening cocoon of self-criticism. He stood there and watched as he did it: the apotheosis of doubt has been attained when you no longer dare intervene in your own self-destruction. You see it develop, and it seems inevitable. It seems the right thing to do. Because he'd been a little snappy, a little less than charming in his self-satisfied euphoric glow. Inadvertently, he'd appeared to withdraw from her and resume the stand-off of their static fight. It all went wrong again when he moved away and left her with Jake Baker, because Jake had brought back the past.

He shouldn't have been afraid. He should have stayed

and talked, and systematically nailed the lid on things —
this is okay, these memories we can kick around, but *this*
we avoid and the subject stays closed. He should have met
it head on. Instead he ran away, and Kathrin knew, and
then he failed to be honest, to apologise — goddam it, even
to be nice. So sure of himself, he went and kicked her when
she might have wanted a caress. So she drifted away. So
he shouldn't be surprised and shouldn't blame her. So make
the best and don't compound the newest damage.

He moved on the periphery and observed the way she
talked and danced with other men. Kye was just *enjoying*
herself. In red and pearls and mane of blonde, she was a
moving center, a magnet for every eye. And it meant he
was doing just fine. Because everyone could see there was
no cause to worry for a perfect husband in a perfect marriage to a perfect wife. Everyone could see the foundation
of trust deep below the surface of their affair.

And somewhere in the throng was the other man. The
toy she'd taken to torture him with. From somewhere, here,
the other man was watching her — and him — right now.

He swept all of their eyes. No one looking at him. He
tracked back to Bellman, blond and bronzed and muscled
and wealthy Bellman. He flew the same missions, so it
couldn't be him.

Thank God that it wouldn't be him.

He was standing with his back to the crowd at the bar,
looking out into a main room, still surveying all the bit
players enrolled on Kathrin's stage.

"You seem a little out of it."

He looked around at Eileen Ware, who'd arrived by his
shoulder. "I do?" He shrugged. "Well I don't feel it."

"No matter," she said. "Guess I'm just one wallflower
projecting the problem onto others."

"What makes you a wallflower?" He didn't care, but
small talk helped pass the time.

"Oh — I don't belong to the Mondrum establishment,
but at the same time I'm basically an outsider at Special

Team. One way or another you're all about flying. Roy Sellert, Erin Heller, Charles — they're not that far away from you pilots. Me? I'm a foot soldier."

"I guess," he said.

Ware nodded to herself. She looked out into the crowd. She couldn't miss the flash of red dancing with her own boss, a very circumspect Wolford. "Your wife is the star among the ladies. I'd have thought you'd be the center of some attention yourself."

"Why?"

"Well, this is a support base. Transport, tankers, that kind of thing. You're a combat flyer. In fact you flew a real combat mission. In fact, you brought down a real enemy aircraft that by rights should have taken you clean out of the air."

"Oh." So here came the MiG, he thought. The goddam Libyan MiG. The medal on his chest and the albatross around his neck. The cross laid over his back.

"I was talking with Jake Baker about that. He's still *really* impressed. I mean, I guess he would be, seeing as you certainly saved his life."

"If he sees it that way." He checked out her glass, and her glass was empty. An ideal evasion. "Can I get you a drink?"

"No thanks. I have a lot of driving to do when this is over. Tell me, how does that happen? I mean, how do you arrange to shoot down a MiG-23 when you're flying an F-111?"

Here goes, he thought. Trying to evade the direct question tends to make people mad. Heroes are allowed a measure of reticence, but once the patience is played out they're obliged to do their duty and deliver. He'd learned that over the last couple of years. "Our mission in the Raven was to protect the attack aircraft by jamming all the defender's transmissions, right? First in and last out. Well we were withdrawing back over the coast, still firing the ECM routines to protect the rest of the guys from radar-directed ground fire or missiles. It was pitch dark, and we were keeping low. Suddenly Jake tells me there's an infrared threat on our tail. I jink, we don't even have time to fire flares, and then this air-to-air missile goes by over the top of the canopy. Then it's tracer chasing the missile. The pilot of that MiG was good. He'd picked us, of course, because he could see us from the noise we were making. He'd gotten in close because the ground clutter kept our systems from seeing him. He almost had us with the missile, and he used his gun the second his missile missed. In fact, when we landed back at Upper Heyford, we found a chunk missing from the right stabiliser where a shell hit."

"It was that close?"

"That close." He nodded, remembering his act. "I broke left and throttled through so I could come around tight without losing altitude. The point is, though, we were still flying nice and slow so that we took longer to get out, while the attack aircraft could overhaul us and escape under the cover of our jamming. At that point in the mission, it was independent maneuvers and every man for himself while the Libyans were still trying to get their air defenses organised. Well, their one pilot who was organised had gotten to us, and I wanted to come around tighter than he'd believe. So to tighten the turn, since the Raven was still at low energy, I swung the wings right out. That about cuts the radius of turn to something less than a quarter, as well as dumping speed. The idea was to whip around so tight we'd snap clean out of the other guy's line of vision and he'd overshoot and lose us in the dark."

"He'd just fly right ahead," Ware embellished, "and not know where you'd gone."

"That's it. Anyhow, Jake looks up through my side of the canopy on the turn – which means out horizontal relative to the ground – and says he's seen a Flogger, in other words a MiG-23. We didn't have any corroboration from incident radar hitting us, but then we were jamming the bands he'd have wanted to use, anyway. I guess he came in on the noise we were making, and then closed on visual. Well, a MiG-23 is about the most dangerous thing the Libyans had to throw at us, so I pulled the turn right around to come out in the one place he couldn't possibly believe an F-111 could get, namely right in behind him. As I'm levelling off, Jake says the MiG is directly in front of us and in range. so I arm one of the Sidewinders we're carrying, I hold the little glow of the MiG's exhaust right on our nose until the missile tells me it's locked on. Then I release the missile and get the fuck out of there at a huge off-angle, in case my missile misses and the MiG comes back looking for us."

"But your missile didn't miss."

"No." It hit — every time he ran it through in his head, the missile hit. It couldn't possibly miss, not when homing right on the glowing tail of a straight running target at two, maybe three miles range. "Jake saw the explosion. That's not the same as actually seeing the MiG taking the hit. We didn't see that, we didn't see it go down, we didn't have gun camera confirmation for any part of the encounter. It counts as an unconfirmed. Just a target of opportunity."

Eileen Ware was looking up at him. Thank God, at least she wasn't doing it with admiring eyes. A black woman with insecurity and an ethnic chip on her shoulder, she might have been primed to tumble for the perverse attraction of a shining white hero. "Jake Baker says it was the tightness of your turn, plus the sheer speed with which you got the missile away before he was out of reach. An F-111 doesn't expect to shoot down a MiG-23, does it? The speed of your reaction is what got him."

"That's right. The speed of my reaction." My speed, he thought, my sheer breakneck haste brought that aircraft down. There wasn't time, so I didn't think. I performed automatically with excessive perfection. I did the real killing.

"You don't seem all that pleased about it."

He shrugged. "Nothing to it. No heroics." He held up his glass, which was as good as empty, and provided just the exit he needed. "Look, you might not want another drink right now, but I do. Excuse me."

When he got through the crowd to the bar and set down the glass on the polished surface, the glass rattled. His hand, his flawless pilot's hand, was shaking.

Libya did it every time.

The air was turning hazy with a glow all of its own. The bright lights and dimmer corners were pole and periphery of a motionless roulette wheel. Kathrin was playing the field, a red bet moving through the blue sectors. She was making them court her in admiring conversations – colonels Lutwidge and Wolford, lieutenant colonels Beamish and Charles. Why go for another mere major when you already had one tamed as your husband?

She was flirting.

And one of them, possibly one of those colonels, certainly one of the men here tonight, someone she'd had the chance and the reason to meet – one of them, when his back was turned, was fucking her.

She wouldn't do that with him any more. She was doing it to punish him for bringing her back to wet and wintry England. At Mondrum there wasn't enough warmth or glitter or social whirl. Wright-Patterson, with its research programs and resident high careerists, with its visiting top brass and sightseeing politicians, had suited her so much better, had showcased her on a much more appropriate stage.

Now she stood here, moved there, glided over the floor, simpered or scintillated in soft exchanges – an unbearable challenge to his success, telling him how small it was. She punished him. In this bright and busy public crowd, she flashed a constant silent signal to him, her husband, who she never touched any more and who no longer got to lay a hand, a finger, a fingertip or a tongue touch on her, who never breathed her perfume close like a flower, tasted her body, stroked her smoothness. A non-stop soundless signal came clear across the room along the private channel that only the two of them shared or even knew was there. Deliberately, and for him alone, she was being an implacable symbol of his failure.

Bellman and Wizer, same age, same height, same rank, same purpose but oppositely charged, were orbiting each other, reactive radicals bound in a short-lived compound of sexual chemistry. Wizer would be demanding, wouldn't tolerate the slightest hitch or glitch of imperfection in the performance. Well Bellman was the surest guy she could possibly pick to do it for her.

Dwight Pinkett was already as far as little touches and strokes with Erin Heller, the air maintenance officer. That would become a brown-skinned duet in the dead of night, an Afro-American party in some corner of a foreign land that is forever Uncle Sam's. For the freelances it was turning into a swinging singles scene, dispersed all over the base it was going to be a big bang of a night. Some of the marrieds might be making out with sideline partners, too. Roy Sellert appeared to be sorting the field, and he had a wife back at Kirtland. Todd Beamish was busily moving around. There seemed to be no one who wasn't already paired or else chasing tail.

Crazy, Clyde, you're crazy. You're just seasoning the scene with sexual frustration – seasoning it so liberally, it doesn't have any taste any more except to choke you. You're dropping bumpily down from a foolish man's flight, hope and euphoria faded and a rough landing ahead. You need more fuel to keep flying until there's time to make a soft touchdown. Need to stay smooth, stay smooth like every pilot should. Beer is too thin a mix. Need octane of a richer kind. Get a drink.

Get a good strong drink.

15

February 24th, night

Dodgson and his wife had left long ago, and now the mingle was looking a little meagre. Lutwidge, not a naturally social soul, had gone. Wolford and wife had gone. Charles had left. Beamish didn't seem to be anywhere.

Kathrin had vanished.

In the men's room he cornered Jake Baker. He waited by the washbowls, and while he waited a hard-eyed stranger wearing a worn face and a dazed halo looked out of the mirror at him with a slow but certain nod which said: look here, sucker, and see the real Clyde Talley.

Jake crossed back from the urinals and carefully washed his hands. In a slow motion moment, with water splashing the soap suds away, he studied the glass he'd left waiting on the shelf above the bowl. The level of the beer, he seemed to decide, was right where it ought to be. "That's real nice, Clyde. Standing guard over my beer." He beamed.

"Have you seen where Kathrin might be?"

"She left." Jake withdrew his hands from the flowing water. After a moment's consideration, he turned off the tap.

"Left?" That just wasn't possible. He had the key for the Mercedes in his pocket. And late on a cold night with a couple of miles to go, she wasn't going to walk.

Jake turned towards him, because the hand drier was a couple of bowls further along behind Clyde. "Said she was tired. But you were having a good time talking and that, and she didn't want to drag you away."

Clyde took a step back in the direction of the drier. Jake followed a step, then paused, turned, and reclaimed his beer with a wet hand. Then he came pacing Clyde.

"She left with Todd," Jake said.

"Todd Beamish?" Clyde kept walking backwards with uneasy steps, while events scrolled in reverse towards unreality.

"Yep, she left with Todd." The drier had come into sight past Clyde's shoulder. Jake placed his beer carefully on top of the machine, then pressed the button. Out came the hot air like an inexhaustible, cynical sigh. "That guy Wolford drove them home. He was taking his wife."

Clyde listened while the drier gasped its disbelief. So who was taking his own wife? "Wolford drove them home?"

"Yep. Real nice of him, too. Seems he lives at the north end, somewhere near where you are, and Todd has a trailer like the rest of us – down in the deepest south. Real nice of him."

"When?" He watched while Jake, slowly in the stream of air, washed his hands of the affair. "When was this?"

"Near enough an hour ago. Before midnight. Didn't she tell you?" Soberly observing how his hands dried themselves, Jake shrugged. "Guess she didn't want you feeling you had to leave."

Clyde shook his head. He looked at the shining tiles and glass and porcelain of the men's room, and there were no unlit corners where sense might be hiding. All evening watching, and yet he missed the main event? He was looking for her regular playboy, but Beamish couldn't be the one. Beamish only arrived Monday. So he missed the move of the moment, when his bitch of a wife went off to pull a fast little cracker with the new guy.

The motor in the drier died.

Jake reached up for his glass, then realised it was wet.

His stalled hand hovered for a while. In the meantime, the other hand hitched up the side of his tunic and disappeared into the pocket of his pants. Eventually it came out again, dragging a handkerchief behind it. Then with his hands arrested in disparate space, with the glass untouched and the handkerchief dangling, Jake turned his head. He looked unhappy. "Clyde, there's a problem I need to talk with you about. Guess I got to get drunk before I have the guts to say it."

What was it going to be — that his marriage was in the garbage can? That he knew. That he finally, reluctantly knew.

"Guess I got to get drunk." Jake's face was sinking into misery. His moustache, drooping with his mouth, emphasised the effect. "About Libya, Clyde."

Libya? *Jake* had a problem about Libya? Not *Libya*. Not *now*. Not Libya on top of the catastrophes of the moment!

"I have to go." He sidestepped and went past Jake's back.

Jake's head swivelled around. "Clyde? I need to talk."

But he kept walking forward, on towards a bleak new world that had vile people in it. In the mirror windows along the wall above the washbowls, that hard-eyed Talley kept pace with him. Sucker, sucker, sucker.

Pinkett and Heller were long gone: doubtless they were at it energetically in her apartment or his trailer. Bellman had left with Wizer: high demand had met high performer, and the encounters would continue all night.

Clyde Talley stayed.

Kye could have climbed out of the car when Wolford brought Beamish home. Some excuse like old friends, or comparing notes on Upper Heyford. Beamish would have offered coffee, and Kye could say her husband knew and would be calling by later to join the nostalgia before driving her home. Wolford and wife would leave, and right now they'd be rocking the trailer. Later, Beamish could drive her home with his own car. She wouldn't do it in her marriage bed, in case the unwanted husband arrived.

Whatever else, Kye understood the niceties of decent behaviour.

Clyde Talley started to get decently drunk. It was the sensible thing to do. He had to work with Beamish, he still had to live with Kye. He wasn't going to cry off because of private life disasters. They weren't going to turn him into Special Team's first failure. Professional pride could carry him anywhere.

Around one in the morning only the hard cases were left. In an irregular circle of seats beside the wreckage of the buffet, were Jake with McGee and Luzzi and Thorndike, and Sellert with Rosen. Dr Jessica Rosen had taken her pick, choosing the married man whose wife was far away but still provided an insurance against unwanted involvement. She had her arm wrapped around Sellert's, and her delicate hand stroked his wrist. Thorndike was watching them. The other three guys were drinking and leaning together in a loose little buddy-buddy group, happy and without a care in the world. Sellert and Rosen kept up with the conversation. Quietly, Thorndike was watching them.

Then she stood up and came over towards him. Her tunic was unbuttoned, her collar was open, her cravat was undone just like the men had their ties loose. Even in a full dress skirt, she was one of the guys.

"You look unhappy, Clyde."

"I do?" He checked his glass of whisky, and downed the dregs.

"You do. Since before your wife left. Had a fight?"

"None of your business."

"Okay – I only asked."

Now he was snapping at bystanders. He started preparing an apology.

"Might you two be leaving?" Ware stopped beside them. "I only ask because I'm stuck here until you people go, because it's me who has to make sure you get home safe." She pointed at the seated pilots. "There's too many to take in a single trip. So while I'm waiting for the rest to get around to leaving, I might as well take you."

Clyde shrugged. "I still have a car." But he didn't want to go home, in case Kye wasn't there. Give her more time to get back, so there's no need to fight.

"Fine." Ware turned to Thorndike. "One passenger isn't a full load. Would you like to stick around until I can persuade the others to leave?"

Thorndike shook her head. "Clyde's taking me home. My place is right on his route."

"Fine," Ware said. "That help I can use."

Clyde looked at Thorndike, and decided to nod.

Outside, the cold wrapped damp hands around them. Big flakes of white whirled down through the corona of light in front of the entrance. Hats on and shoulders hunched, they hurried past the remaining cars. Their shoes slithered on wet snow. It was an inverted night, shimmering blanket on the ground, blackness shedding crêpe crystal butterflies above.

At the car, under the light next to the entry from the road, he saw how she was looking at him as he unlocked the rightside door. He swung it open for her. "Problem?"

"You look dead beat, and kind of high on drink. Sure you're safe to drive?"

He started around the back of the coupé. "I can fly an F-111 at nine-tenths the speed of sound at treetop height in a snowstorm at midnight." He unlocked the driver's door. "I can cope with a Mercedes in a snow shower on a slow road." He took off his hat and swept wet snowflakes from its crown, then he opened the door and threw the hat into the back of the car. "So let's go."

The big blade of the single wiper scraped an arc across the windshield. The rear window was caked, so he reversed blind into empty space. He put the heater on boost, and hot air came out of the ducts right away. Neat kind of car, Kathrin had arranged for herself. He rolled out on Enola Gay and turned north. Nothing was moving along the avenue of streetlit snow. He took it nice and easy while the wiper swept slithering snow scales away. The Mercedes purred.

"Thunderbolt," Sandra Thorndike said. "You just missed Thunderbolt."

"Shit." He wasn't awake, he was on autopilot. "I'll take the next big one. What's it called?"

"Yokohama," she said. "They have some neat names here."

"I guess." The security building went past, and then they were turning through the dog's leg and entering the north shopping area. Some of the display windows, lighted to advertise the wares of franchised stores, illuminated the winter night. The white mall of snow was trackless.

"How about that great big baby Bellman?" she said. "I turn down the offer of sucking his nice little dick for him, so he defaces the name on my locker so it comes out as *The dike*. You saw that?"

"I saw that. You painted it out again."

"I painted it out. One day – *one* day – I'd like to get that asshole one-on-one and fly him clean into the ground. I could do it, you know. I could outfly any one of you Buck Rogerised airborne Tarzans. Believe me."

Watching descending snow swing in against his windshield, he nodded. Maybe she saw the gesture, maybe she didn't.

"Dwight's also been getting some dirty tricks from Bellman on the missions, right? But he just isn't interested in joining forces against the motherfucker. Maybe Dwight finds it useful to have me stuck one rung lower than he is on the Air Force's macho white social scale. This is Yokohama coming up, by the way."

"I see it." He hadn't, but now he did. He slowed gently over the snow and made the right without a hitch. Yokohama was residential blocks: unlit façades, sidewalks with verges, streetlight poles alternate sides – all of it unmarked white with snow coming down.

"Bellman isn't so nice to you, is he? Why don't we get together – mutual support against the asshole?"

He thought about that. He tripped a step beyond it. What if they got it together? Imagine the point he'd score against Kathrin if he, too, got it away from home. What she could do, maybe he should do. And Bellman had pointed to Thorndike and claimed he'd get to her first. Well think of the boost if Bellman couldn't, but he really did. Think of the boost.

"Hey! Here. We want to make the right."

He was overshooting the turn. He was too drunk and too tired. He touched the brake and hauled the wheel around. The nose, with its Mercedes gunsight star, started to swing right and into the opening. The tail started to slide left. He had to let the skid look after itself. If he corrected into it, he'd hit the building on the corner. The back wheels overtook the front, and hardly leaning sideways at all on the slippery ground, the car turned itself around in the snow. As the intersection passed him by, rotating, he ran through the right way to do it – slow, stop, reverse to the turn, and then take the corner with stately ease. It took a very long time before the car was sliding backwards, and by then he was looking diagonally into the intersection and the street he just came from. Gear out, brake on easy to stop the slide –

The Mercedes bounced over the kerb. Then it jolted again and the noise was brief but awful, and they stopped.

He switched off the ignition, and the purring turned to silence. Sandra Thorndike, who'd been looking backwards, now just stared at him.

He opened the door and got out into the cold. His shoe slipped on the buried kerb where it ran right under the body of the car. He looked at the beautiful swirl of the skid marks ploughed around the corner in fresh white snow. Oh fuck, he thought. He went to look at the back of the car. It had whacked into one of the little concrete posts of the picket fence fronting the building on the corner. The shock-absorbing fender was crushed and the trunk looked dented. Oh *fuck*.

Thorndike got out and stood on the other side, shaking

her head as snowflakes landed in her hair. "Do that with an F-111, Clyde, and you'll have rewritten the Air Force pilot's manual."

Then he heard the engine, very close in the silent night, and when he looked at the intersection, headlight pools were pushing wedges of scintillating snow moths around the corner under the dimmer streetlights. The headlights paused, pointing right at him, and the engine idled. Then the gear clanked home and the covered jeep rolled up and stopped in the white road so that it blocked any intention he might have of driving away. The engine of the jeep went on chugging to itself.

They wore sidearms and sticks, and warm coats to keep out the cold. Both the sergeant and the airman had helmets to keep their heads dry. The white helmets went well with the snow.

He stood there without his hat, wet snowflakes melting in his hair and sliding icily down his neck, and all he wanted to do was curl up and howl.

"Special Team," the sergeant said, and handed back their passes. "Been having a little party tonight, I'm told. Are you the driver, sir?"

Clyde nodded.

"Your car, sir?"

"My wife's."

The MP looked at the front plate. "Mondrum car. That'll make charging the repair simpler. With respect, sir." He leaned his head slightly to one side, incongruous under a heavy helmet. "With respect, you've had a deal more to drink than you should, driving a car. Do you have far to go?"

Thorndike pointed along the street. "Just a block."

The MP paused, watching snowflakes slowly pile up on the wiper, which had stalled diagonally across the windshield. A little piece of snow slithered free from the bottom end of the blade. "Best thing is if we take the car along to the pound, seeing as we can't leave it stuck across the sidewalk until morning. The two of you go on home now,

major, captain. We'll handle the car. You can check with
the pound about collecting it tomorrow, sir. Is the key still
in the ignition?"

Clyde nodded.

"Then you'd best get your hats out of the car before you
leave, sir."

Without coats in the miserable cold, with wet confetti
sticking to their tunics and three inches of snow starting to
soak through their shoes, they retreated along the street.
Muffled in the winter night, behind them the Mercedes
started up and then the car and the MP patrol drove out
of earshot around the corner on Yokohama. They walked
on through a dim little snow desert towards the intersection
with Mustang Drive.

He could howl, scream, weep. He could fall at God's
feet and pound them with his fists. Why did *this* have to
happen? He's outside on a winter night in the snow. He's
being a *good* husband. His wife is off fucking other men –
is probably fucking one right now – and all he's doing is
driving a colleague home. Then he makes one little mistake.
So while she's doing adultery and destroying his marriage,
his self-respect, his success and his social status – he gets
stuck with having to crawl to her with a confession about
a dumb little error he's gone and made. It's so *unfair*!

Without a word, they trudged around the corner into
Mustang.

First he fouls up on a mission and nearly shoots at
Thorndike's aircraft. Now he modestly crashes Kathrin's
car, and really impresses Thorndike with his driving skill.
He strands himself a mile or more from home in the middle
of a snow-bound night. Any sympathy he might have
gotten from Thorndike he just blew with the latest display
of sheer stupidity. It's so unfair.

"What is it, Clyde? You're reacting way out of pro-
portion here. The car has to be repaired, it costs some
money. So?"

They'd stopped on a sidewalk all of their own, claimed
by two furrow lines of footsteps that followed them from

the corner. Next to them was the entrance to a low-rise block. Over the door was a projecting slab to make a token porch, and under the slab burned a single light. The second step, right at the foot of the door, was almost free of snow. They stood beside the gap in a little picket fence, which was decorated along its top by an undulation of frozen cream. The snowflakes falling between them and the light were turned from clean white to sooty black. Everything turns dirty in the glow of unattainable goals.

She had her tunic clutched tight with folded arms. She was shivering. She had snow on her hat and her shoulders and sleeves. "What is it, Clyde?"

And he thought: just a little bit. Let out just a little bit. You can't keep it *all* pressured up inside. Let out just a piece of it, in this unreal nightscape so empty and alone in a stupor of tiredness and alcohol daze. Here it doesn't matter, and she won't remember anyway. "My wife and me. Our marriage is falling apart. Just coming completely to pieces."

Shivering, she nodded.

"We don't talk. We don't do anything together any more. Not anything at all. And now she's started doing it with other guys. Maybe she's been doing it at Wright-Patterson and I just never knew. Maybe that's why she hates me for bringing her here – because it ruined her fun. Now she's not even hiding it. And it just –" He was looking at her eyes, and they blinked back at him. "It just –" He was staring at her eyes, but they were sending him no signal at all. "Just cuts me up."

Silence.

Then she reached up and rested a hand on his shoulder, crushing miraculously crystalline fragments of snow. "I realise that, Clyde. Come on in. Sometimes just a little human warmth helps. Come on in, why don't you?"

At a quarter after two, Eileen Ware set out with Baker and McGee and Luzzi. She drove them down to Arlington and unloaded them one by one. Jake Baker was asleep. She had to nudge him awake, push him out, and wait while he unlocked the door of his temporary home. There were no lights in the windows of Beamish's neighbouring trailer, and his unused car stood at the side of the track, a Chevrolet cake coated in thick white marzipan. Wolford had brought Beamish home, of course.

Eileen started north on Manhattan, the direct way back to her apartment on Starfighter Drive. The snow fall had receded to nothing more than irresolute flakes. It had partly filled the older furrows and laid a white skin over the night traffic slush on Mondrum's working axis. She drove slow and easy, with the tires spluttering through the wet mush. Up ahead waited something big, like a black and white bridge drawn across the street.

She got to two hundred yards and had stopped before the thing acquired a proper shape. It was white over black, with people underneath. The white was the upper surface of wings, wide nose strakes and flattened fuselage, camouflaged with transitory snow. The black was its featureless underside. The people were ground crew and Air Force soldiers, busy and bustling or bunched up and waiting. For a moment, tired and taunted by the shadows from lights, caught in the stasis of a winter night, she wondered if this was a real stealth machine – one of their own on secret deployment, or a Red Wraith flown from its base on the Kola Peninsula by a defecting Russian hero.

But then the long airplane found its proper category. It was a Blackbird, an SR-71, a sly precursor of stealth. The few still in service staged at UK bases when reconnaissance missions brought them across from the States. This one must have developed a problem. They were towing it across Manhattan from the hangars to the specialist workshops. It was a night creature caught on the ground.

She waited. It took her long minutes to realise that the tractor towing the Blackbird had broken down.

It was two thirty and she wanted her bed. She wasn't prepared to drive all the way back to the south end of Mondrum, and then up the entire length of Enola Gay. She hauled the wheel and let the car rudder its way across the slush, and into the aircraft alleys between the hangars. She could weave north through the service areas, bypassing the road block and coming back on Manhattan about level with the operations control building.

Tire tracks crisscrossed continuously in front of her lights. She went carefully over the slippery ruts of compacted snow. She went past lighted hangars and through dark concrete chasms. She cruised a mysterious landscape of hidden, heartless magic.

She stopped the Sierra and let the engine mutter to itself, gently massaging the car. She looked at a single pair of fresh tracks which peeled off and vanished into alley shadows. Down that way was nothing but Special Team.

Who would want to go down there in the middle of the night? No mission, no aircraft emergency, no work to be done. What kind of head case couldn't keep away?

Lutwidge? Might Lutwidge sneak out to secret assignations with his killer machines? Stroke their noses, a lovesick former ace who didn't get to fly any more? A fetishist in secluded communion with his F-15s? Or maybe he went to sprinkle the aircraft with holy water and sanctify them in their search. Or to slip a solid silver shell into the gun magazine of each Eagle, thus ensuring they could kill the evil Red Wraith.

So who the hell actually cared?

She engaged the gear and drove on.

Sandra Thorndike used tissues to wipe the stranded cream of semen from her thighs. Then she shuffled up to the head of the unfolded convertible bed and sat in one of its sofa corners. She waited, legs crossed, arms leaning along the cloth upholstery. No need any more for modesty, no reason to cover herself.

He'd swallowed her with his eyes. He'd touched every little piece of her with hands and mouth. He had such a boundless, desperate, such an *urgent* hunger. Then she'd taken hold of him — and his hunger had exploded in a harmless little disaster. And he fled the bed. So she waited in the sidelight from the lamp on the table, where the unpackaged condom lay, still rolled up and getting no nearer to being used. A little waste of little money, no harm done at all.

Talley, naked, hid in the shadows of the room. He hugged himself in the armchair, feet drawn up in front of him on the seat, thighs squeezed together, arms wrapped around his shins, face pressed into his knees. He was an upright overgrown foetus without any warm womb to hide in, who'd just missed a fleeting foray back into that natal safety. He was an overgrown adult foetus, thirty-seven years old and finally admitting it would never have wanted to be born. He wouldn't talk, he wouldn't answer, he wouldn't be reached at all.

When he started to sob she realised she'd strayed right out of her emotional depth. The act of a girl scout helping out had gone totally wrong. The good deed for the night was a failure, not a favour. He'd only exploded in a little mishap over her thighs. Yet somehow she'd blown his head open for him. She'd gotten it so he was sitting there with all the tubes and wires and wheels and bits of his psyche hanging out in a bloodied tangle, and no way did she know how to cope with the mess.

When his sobbing didn't cease, she started to throw his clothes at him, gently. A little while after that, he threw himself out. She stripped the semen-sticky sheet from the bed and dumped it on the laundry pile. Then she took a shower.

Clyde Talley marched home through his silent night, his feet dragging disobediently in the crunchy icing of snow. Not a single flake fell in front of him. Mondrum was a soundless, breezeless, motionless wonderland sliding steadily past him. Silver sparkles winked from the white blanket beneath each streetlight. He was cold through his skin to his bones, but too numb to care.

Tonight God's universe decided to double over on itself,

and it was Major Clyde Lincoln Talley of the US Air Force who got the unenviable honour of disappearing into the fold. If his mind could have been that bit more exhausted and his body that bit more drunk, he'd never remember and it wouldn't matter. Except that everyone else watching the geek show would know. Be sure you don't peak too early, Kye had said. Well he did. Oh yes, he did.

Hope stumbles eternal into night.

When he got home, one of the few things his eyes still registered clearly was the time — only three thirty, and he was just alert enough to be surprised.

Kathrin was fast asleep. Her clothes were dumped around the bedroom, except for the dress which had been carefully hung on the front of the closet. There were no leftover signs of Beamish, or anyone else, being there, and no way to tell when she got back. No way to tell whether somewhere else, someone else helped her unpeel the dress, unroll the panty-hose, slide out of her panties and open her thighs.

Who cared? Who really cared?

For the first time in a very long while, he went to sleep without needing a tablet of quinalbarbitone. That was a precious helping of heavenly peace.

But he couldn't afford the price.

PART 4

Dark Shroud

16

February 25th, evening

Early Saturday evening, Action Man called a mission. The moon wasn't due to rise until a quarter after eleven, and in the meantime the Russians were creeping around from the Kola with what could be a Red Wraith pattern. So Special Team had to go and meet them. His pilots, after all, had enjoyed the entire day to get over their hangovers and any other side effects of the previous night's man-euvers. They were, in the can-do world of Colonel Oliver Eliot Lutwidge, fit.

Eileen Ware sat with Lutwidge, Charles and Wizer in the booth at operations. She watched the patient people at their desks down on the main floor, and waited out the creeping progress of the mission displayed on the big screens on the opposite wall. Everything went fine until the two interceptors had the bait on visual, and Lutwidge called Dark Shroud. Romulus, the EF-111A Raven, switched on its jamming suite and induced a dense and furious snowstorm on the display. Bait, interceptors, Romulus, the hunters who were getting ready to come up off the sea – they all vanished inside that obscuring veil.

Four minutes later a single contact emerged from the southern fringe of the mush on the screen. That wasn't in the plan.

It didn't transmit. It didn't answer any call-up. It

emerged climbing, and it went on up to twenty thousand feet. It kept coming south. It showed no IFF response to identify the machine, and used no radar which could have signalled the aircraft type. Neither the Awacs halfway to Iceland, nor the one orbiting the Netherlands, could tell what it was. Their radars, watching from hundreds of miles away, tracked the contact and discovered nothing.

It might have been a Red Wraith made mysteriously manifest as it flew down the Norwegian Sea.

It wasn't Romulus or McGee or Luzzi: they were talking all the time from the bait. The four hunters couldn't report in without breaking radio silence.

But it was an F-15. The Awacs worked that out from the contact's radar scatter characteristics when it was a hundred miles closer. It didn't transmit, didn't answer, it showed no IFF. It brought Lutwidge to a pitch of fury. One of the unspeakable fools was fucking his operation, and he'd pull the imbecile's ass right over his or her head.

When the F-15 crossed the Scottish coast, Susan Wizer sent up an aircraft to meet it. She had to use a reconnaissance Phantom from Alconbury. The people at Alconbury complained until 3rd Air Force HQ at Mildenhall cleared the decision: the only alternative would be to alert the British RAF, but Blind Date was an exclusive American party. So the Phantom went out to intercept the F-15 with lights blazing, and guide it back to a safe landing at Mondrum. The oncoming aircraft wouldn't even be able to talk to the tower. Without a pacer, the best it could possibly do in darkness would be to crash within earshot of the base.

At eleven twenty Eileen Ware drove from operations down to Special Team. She parked where heaps of dirty snow, ploughed off the apron, had been piled like clumsy blast protection along the front of the crew building. She waited in the floodlights of the freezing night, and watched from her car as the huge predator of an F-15 was towed into the service area. In a matrix of its own elaborate shadows, ıt was a demon of the night tied down by ground crew prayers.

She recognised the pilot in the open cockpit as soon as the helmet and oxygen mask were removed. The pilot was Thorndike.

Erin Heller was at the foot of the ladder. She'd been ready for an Eagle returning with pieces missing, an engine burned out, munitions exploded, any kind of catastrophe at all. What she got was an outwardly perfect aircraft. Thorndike climbed to the ground, signed over the Eagle and walked away. Erin Heller ran up the ladder and clambered into the cockpit.

Sandra Thorndike threw her helmet and equipment on the back seat, then she got in beside Eileen. She didn't even say hello.

In the booth at operations, while Susan Wizer watched over the aircraft returning on schedule from another unsuccessful mission, while Charles just listened, Lutwidge took Thorndike's report.

"First the Iris failed," Thorndike said. "I switched it on at thirty minutes into the mission, and at forty-two minutes it failed. I didn't break radio silence to report the fact."

Lutwidge nodded. He looked, Eileen thought, as though he was ready to lynch his pilot.

"I figured Lolite and my own eyes were good enough to go through with the mission."

Lutwidge nodded again.

"It went okay until you called Dark Shroud. I had Lolite operating when Romulus started the jamming. I got immediate interference that erased the picture. I checked the other fields, and they were the same. I noticed my horizontal situation display was going crazy – the navigation numbers were oscillating. I tried to switch Lolite off but it wouldn't respond. At two minutes after Romulus started Dark Shroud, my entire instrumentation wiped out."

Lutwidge blinked. "*What?*"

"Everything crashed." With her hands on her hips to

mirror her commanding officer, Thorndike was standing stubbornly at ease. "I lost Lolite. I also lost the head up display, every head down display, the backup vertical situation indicator – everything run by or slaved to the central computer. All I had was the backup dials for the engine systems, the barometric altimeter, and my wristwatch. The UHF was out, the radar was out, all the avionics were out. If anything was in fact working, I couldn't have done a thing with it because all the displays and keyboards were out."

Lutwidge blinked again. "Why?"

"Fuck only knows. Romulus started jamming, I got interference on the Lolite, then all of my avionics crashed."

"Interference?" Charles asked. "From Romulus?"

Lutwidge was shaking his head. He was still facing Thorndike, but he was looking into infinity. "Impossible. The avionics on an F-15 are too well shielded. F-15s are *designed* to fly with an aircraft like Romulus protecting them with ECM. Lolite is shielded." He turned around to Charles. "Isn't it?"

"Lolite has to be." Charles shrugged. "It *has* to be."

"Lolite was swamped by the ECM," Thorndike said. "Lolite is useless. Just solid gold garbage."

"Sellert," Lutwidge said. "Sellert has to make sense of any interference on Lolite. And of why the Iris system failed, for God's sake." He turned to glare at Eileen. "Drive Thorndike back to the team area so she can get out of her gear. We're tied here until the rest of the aircraft get in. Is Heller already working on Thorndike's machine?"

Eileen nodded. "Yes, sir."

"Right. Its avionics are her problem. Drive Thorndike back, then go get Sellert. I want him looking for answers before midnight. If he isn't at his own accommodation, try wherever that MO lives."

"Rosen, sir. I can get her address."

"Yes. That's the kind of job you're *here* for, Captain Ware."

"I know, sir."

"Excuse me." It was Wizer, still seated at the desk fronting the window of the booth. She had her chair turned away from the TV screens and telephones. "Captain Thorndike, you say you lost all your instrumentation. You lost navigation data, position data, compass." Wizer was in shadow in a booth lit softly so that the occupants could watch the screens of the main room. But Eileen could see that Wizer's eyes, unblinking, were fixed on Sandra Thorndike's face. "I just projected the return course you were following. It would have brought you to within thirty miles of Mondrum. How did you do that?"

Thorndike shrugged. "I knew where I started from before I lost the instruments, so I figured out the course in my head. Then I went up high so I could see the stars. Then I took it from there. Kept the pole star lined up relative to the tail fins."

"Without a starsight," Wizer said. "Without any navigation aid. What do you say to that, Colonel Lutwidge?"

Lutwidge looked around at Wizer. Then back at Thorndike. Two women officers had arranged to rub his nose in one of his own prejudices. What Thorndike had just done sounded equal to Lindbergh crossing the Atlantic. Lutwidge had the grace to show a flicker of a smile. "Neat flying, Thorndike."

17

February 26th, morning

By noon on Sunday, both Erin Heller and Roy Sellert were red-eyed and exhausted. They joined Lutwidge, Charles and the pilots for the mission debrief. The discussion fell into two parts. The first issue was the new mission profile with the EF-111A Raven. Did Dark Shroud do its screening job, how did the bait react, how did Beamish and Baker find the business of flying Romulus in trail behind the interceptors?

The bait hadn't acted upset or alarmed, and everyone on Special Team was happy with Dark Shroud. Aside from the fact that they'd found no Red Wraith, the mission was smooth.

Except for their first Iris failure, together with what the ECM from Romulus appeared to have done to Thorndike's aircraft.

Sandra Thorndike sat between Talley and Baker. Clyde Talley hadn't spoken an avoidable word to her since they started their abortive love-making on the night of the party. She'd have been hurt by his iciness, but she wasn't his only victim. Todd Beamish was learning not to try conversation with Talley. Beamish acted mildly confused, but Sandra wasn't going to enlighten him — or check out whether he was faking the confusion. She wasn't going to get involved for Clyde Talley any more. Either Beamish had in fact done it with Talley's wife, in which case he knew what it was all about, or he hadn't, in which event Talley was building up enemies he didn't do better than deserve.

What did matter was the way her own aircraft had done its best to kill her the previous night.

She went through it again in detail. Lutwidge grilled her for information, but for once Superman seemed aware that it wasn't her fault. His attitude kept Bellman off her back. All she got from anyone was professional questions. Superman had really surprised her. He'd started out the way it ended the night before, but this time he did it in front of the other pilots. He complimented her on her flying. Credit, for once, where it was due.

Neither Heller nor Sellert had any real answers.

"The Iris fault seems unconnected," Sellert said. He pushed his glasses back up his nose, and launched into the summary. "All seven imaging units failed for the same reason. The freon coolant in each unit vented clean away. I have no explanation for this. I've sent an enquiry through to Kirtland, and they have no answers. The freon cools the solid state components which convert the infrared image into an electrical signal for processing and presentation. The freon is designed to bleed away during operation, and the bleed rate is controlled by the Iris computer. I can't think of any reason why the computer bled off the whole of the coolant. And I *really* can't think why it should do it to all of the units at once. The only suggestion I have at present is a computer command error."

"This never happened on the Kirtland program?" Lutwidge asked.

Sellert shook his head. "Recently we had some individual imaging units overheating in connection with coolant loss, but nothing on this scale. Right, Craig?"

Bellman nodded. "That's what I remember, Roy."

"So Iris vented all its coolant," Lutwidge said. "That led to each camera unit overheating and failing. Am I right?"

Sellert nodded. "That's correct."

"So we have no answer. And until we do, we can't fly

Iris." Superman thought about it for a while, staring into space. "And until we have an answer about Lolite, and how it crapped the avionics on Thorndike's aircraft, we can't fly Lolite either. Which means we're grounded by the technology they've built our operation around. We can't find a stealth aircraft without one or other of those sensors. It's the job those things are *designed* for. So – do we have an answer on Lolite?"

"No." Sellert poked at his glasses. "Right at the moment, I have no idea what went wrong. Lolite's done some weird things at Kirtland, but it never picked up electronic interference like this. I mean – it's gone through all the standard shielding tests. And it never took an aircraft's instruments with it when it went down."

"You're sure that's what happened?"

"No, I'm not *sure*. I'm just guessing. The Lolite control computer is wrecked – and I mean physically wrecked. Circuit boards are burned through and switches fused. It must have had an overload, followed by power surges and massive shorting. It's what you see when a piece of equipment has been knocked out through being hit by extremely powerful interference. The source has to be the jamming coming from Romulus, but Lolite should have been shielded adequately against that."

"And you think the result of the Lolite overload was a surge that also took out the aircraft's avionics?"

"I think that could be what happened. The Lolite computer communicates with the aircraft's central computer. That's how the pilot can manage Lolite, and how the central computer can present Lolite's images on the cathode ray tubes in the cockpit. There's a physical connection and a continuous information exchange between the computers. Further, the Lolite computer is mounted inboard along with the aircraft's central computer. When the Lolite computer went wild, it would act like an antenna transmitting mush into the central computer right next to it. And once the computation was completely out, any signal from the pilot to cut power would be blocked. That's why the effect stayed on until Thorndike landed, I guess." Sellert turned to look at Erin Heller, and shrugged.

Captain Erin Heller took her cue with confidence. She was the same rank as the security woman, Ware, she was the same gender and she was equally black – but it didn't seem to worry her. Ware, maybe, wanted to be accepted in a white world. Heller, who pulled Pinkett at the party, might be entirely satisfied with her own ethnic pride. We're all of us, Sandra Thorndike thought, on every side of every racial and sexual divide entirely equal, but it doesn't mean we have to bust a gut bridging the difference. The alternative attitude, though, made Ware more interesting.

"Something hit the F-15's central computer," Heller said. "It seems to have burned some circuits, but mostly it just wiped software. I can't repair physical damage inside the modules because I don't have the equipment, and I can't diagnose or repair software failure because I don't have the expertise. All I can do is put modules on the test center, run the tests, and remove the defective ones. Probably I'm going to be taking out the central computer and most of the higher level avionics."

"The cause," Lutwidge said. "Is it interference from the Lolite system?"

"I can't think of anything else."

Lutwidge nodded. He seemed like a Superman who was running out of magic crystals. He had a Red Wraith in his head, but he looked like losing his chance to zoom around hunting shadows until he'd woven a real wraith out of thin air. "Can you get the F-15 mission capable again?"

"Yes, if I don't run out of spares. I have limited stores. We don't generally base F-15s here at Mondrum."

"I think," Charles said, "we should be able to get priority supply. That's the impression I picked up at the Pentagon."

Lutwidge nodded again. "Thanks, Ernest. At least that's a little bit of light in the picture. Captain Heller, how soon do you think you'll have the aircraft flyable?"

Heller shrugged. "Can't say, sir. With a task this size, I

even have a manpower problem. The other aircraft also need routine attention. I have good people, but I still have to oversee what they're doing. I was thinking of asking for some help." She turned her head and looked straight at Sandra. "I was going to ask Captain Thorndike if she could help out by looking after my people who're taking modules out of her aircraft."

Sandra nodded. "Sure. Whatever I can do."

"What about the Lolite and Iris problem?" Lutwidge said to Sellert. "Can you get around to checking over the other sets and the spares?"

"Well –" Sellert looked unhappy. "I'm by myself here. I don't have a single technician. I mean, I could really use some help, if there was someone with the right skills. Craig, you know these systems from Kirtland. Could you help out?"

Bellman shook his head. "Sorry, Roy, but what I know about is the pilot's side of the interface. I know what comes out of those systems, but I don't know what goes on inside of them." He smiled a radiant apology. "I am sorry, you know."

Bellman, Sandra thought, is the biggest asshole. He wouldn't even offer to hold a screwdriver for the man.

Beside her, Baker pulled himself upright in his chair. "Could I help out? I'm no kind of expert for Lolite and Iris, but I'm well up on electronics and infrared imaging systems." He paused to stroke his moustache with the knuckle of his index finger. "It's my job on the Raven, after all."

In the locker room they were getting their coats. Outside waited lunch for the lucky ones and work for the volunteers. Sandra Lee Thorndike opened her locker door, with its freshly repainted name, and started checking her gloves were in the pockets of her coat.

"Well you live and learn," Bellman said to the room. Jesus, but even the man's *voice* could swagger. "Our lady pilot might be a dike, but it seems she holds up okay."

Bellman created silence. At her back every movement ceased. She froze with one hand on her locker door, the other in the pocket of her coat. She thought, though, that she could hear their heads turn.

Then the locker closed two along on her right. That was Dwight Pinkett's. In the side of her eye, she saw his hand turn the key in the door. "Where," Pinkett said, "do you get that about Thorndike being a dike?"

"Come on, Pinkie – are you turning into some kind of a libber-lover? Okay, so tell me, you guys. Which one of you ever had his finger in the dike?"

She waited with assassins at her back. By itself in the coat pocket, her hand started tightening on the glove it had found. Another locker banged closed.

She was an object fit for curious attention, but she was excluded from their group and from its internal life. Suddenly, seamlessly, the men had closed ranks against her. The accusation Bellman made was that she might be a sexual and social threat. She might possibly be a non-available woman. They didn't require that she should in fact screw one of them – just so long as they could be sure she would do it with some man some day, and therefore wouldn't subvert what men insisted women should exist for. If she was going to step out of line and challenge their special rights in life – then they had to cut her from their world.

She wasn't even out of line. But in a people's court, in a peer group, an accusation is enough.

Talley, she thought, tell them something. Let them know it isn't true. Please tell them, Talley? I tried to help you, so try to help me. It doesn't have to be the details, just the fact of it. *Please* Talley, tell them?

"Friday night," Talley started to say. "After the party –"

Bellman laughed. "Talley Boy got to drive her home, didn't he? He also wrapped his car around a post. But did he make any impression on the lady pilot? Talley Boy, your wife and you must have some *real* bad problems, if you've gotten as far as trying a hard target like Thorndike."

Talley walked out.

In a graded silence, they all left. She heard them walk
away down the corridor and heard the door bang. She
heard their voices outside. The BMW started up and its
doors slammed. Bellman was taking some of his friends
into the center to eat. They could discuss her at leisure.
Bellman, with exquisite precision, hit Talley on his open
wound. Talley couldn't take it in public. He might have
been going to help, but instead he ran.

The BMW rolled over the ground and its tires crunched
on ice. Then it drove away.

18

February 26th, afternoon

Sleet, silently, was slapping the window. The slippery
lumps of white slithered down the panes and slid unhin-
dered over the shallow dams of the metal window frame.
Inside it was marginally warmer. Along the back of the
shed, beneath the shelving, ran the outward and return
pipes of the heating loop which served the sheds and stores.
By the time gravity had persuaded the water to circulate
all the way across from the crew building on the other side
of the Special Team area, the water was no longer hot.
Those British engineers from the Property Services Agency
had brought the performance of the ancient system back
to what it should be, but that wasn't really a lot.

Illumination came from two glaring bulbs mounted in

metal galleries screwed to the ceiling. Beneath the lights was a work bench, and laid out along the bench was a pair of test set pods, side by side with their plastic cases opened for mirror image surgery. In rows along each edge of the bench were the scalpels – multimeters, probes, pressure gauges, pliers.

"This side," Roy Sellert said. "This is the righthand pod."

Eileen moved around the bench to Sellert's side. Jake Baker attended from across the bench. Master Sergeant Rodeck stood halfway between the bench and the door, and watched.

Sellert waved his hand along the pod. In his hand was a screwdriver, but the gesture belonged to a pathologist in a murder mystery. "Basically we know that the avionics failed on Thorndike's aircraft because of saturation jamming. The effect of the jamming was imported inboard – inside the aircraft's protective shielding – by the Lolite control computer when it freaked out. Lolite's computer freaked when the jamming signals came up through the control line from the pod here. The source of the interference was the ECM equipment Jake switched on when the Raven got the word to commence Dark Shroud. Okay?"

Eileen nodded. The preamble was for her benefit: Baker had been helping Sellert with the work. Rodeck had called her at home after Sellert called him at security. Sunday afternoon she'd been dozing after another late Special Team night. This hadn't been what she expected.

"The first problem is, why did the pod pick up the interference and let it get into the Lolite computer? Every piece of the system is shielded." Sellert tapped with the screwdriver on the edge of the open casing. "Here's how."

Eileen leaned forward so she could see inside the pod. The interior was mostly filled with black-box components. The three with *Aerosensor* painted on them were Iris cameras. The one nearest the tail compartment bore the name *Datadyne* and was screwed to the assembly for

Lolite's pointing mirror. Beneath and behind the boxes ran the cabling. A fat band cable was plugged to the Lolite camera. Like all the other connections, it was sheathed in bright silver.

Except where the sheathing had been stripped from the electrical insulation beneath. An entire stretch between two retaining clips was laid bare.

Sellert's screwdriver poked at the naked cable. "All the separate lines in the Lolite connection are protected by coaxial mesh – basically like any domestic TV cable. But that isn't any use at all against the kind of interference jamming encountered in a battle environment. The main protection is this outer sheathing which has an electrically conducting layer of metal foil. Right here where the foil is stripped away, that's where the jamming got into the system and wiped it out."

Obvious, Eileen thought, once you got around to checking mundane things like cables. "So why did the protection fail?"

"Well, that took some time to figure out. Aside from the mirror, which is cased, there are no moving parts in here. The pod is ventilated, obviously. It has to let out the freon which bleeds from the Iris units, and it has to keep pace with air pressure variations as the carrying aircraft changes altitude. But it's draw ventilation from those vanes at the rear of the pod. There's no draught inside. Finally, though, we did find a hole." He leaned across in front of her and tapped the shaft of the screwdriver against the underside of the cylindrical casing. "Take a look."

Eileen stooped to look. Underneath, in the shadow, was a tiny triangular hole. She wouldn't have seen it at all if it hadn't been ringed with chalk. She straightened up again. "Could that hole make enough of a draught?"

"Make a hurricane," Baker said, "at four hundred knots. Strip the foil away like a knife."

Eileen shrugged, conceding to the experts. "So – the ultimate reason for the Lolite failure and the rest of the problem was a tiny fault in the casing of the pod?"

Roy Sellert shook his head. "This particular test set was being flown for the fourth time when it went on the last mission. If the fault had been there in the casing, it would have done the damage the first time it went in the air."

She thought about that. "Damaged in handling? I don't mean it would be you, Roy. It's technicians from the ground crew who put these things on the aircraft and then take them off again after each mission."

"Feel the hole," Baker said. "Run your finger over it."

Eileen stooped to inspect the hole again. She drew her fingertip across the tiny blemish. All she felt was a slight roughness. "So? This is reinforced plastic, isn't it? You'd expect it to splinter around a hole."

"It's GRP. It deforms away from an impact." Baker shrugged. "The hole was punched from the inside."

She looked at Baker, and then at Sellert. "Punched?"

"By a screwdriver," Sellert said, and looked at the one in his hand. "Just about this size."

"I see." But she didn't see at all. If they weren't going to tell her, she'd just have to nudge. "So how did that happen?"

Sellert nodded across the bench at Baker. "Jake figured it out. It's where the Iris fault fits in." He waved his hand over the pod again. "The crucial components in the Iris imaging units only work when they're cooled by freon. The freon is bled off gradually by the control computer. All seven units failed in this test set because the freon vented clean away. The question is, why? I was assuming it was a control line fault, but that hole gives it away."

"How?"

"Well, these units come from the manufacturer ready to use. We just plug them in the pod, and that's all. Every adjustment is factory set. Okay? Well look at this unit here, right above the hole. See right around here, down on the side?"

She peered into the pod where his screwdriver was pointing. There was the faint gleam of a screw cap.

"That's the adjustment screw controlling the bleed rate

for the freon. Again, it comes to us already factory set. We don't touch it. But when Jake looked into this, we found that the adjustment screw on every single unit is too far open. Each screw is one full turn too far. As a result, when the Iris computer thought it was opening the valve to let out a tiny amount of freon, in fact it had the valve almost wide open. The freon just flew away, and the units failed."

"The manufacturer set them wrong?"

"If so, the units would have failed on the first flight, not the fourth." Sellert had reached the point where he didn't like what came next. So he crept up on it. "These units have never been taken out of the pod since we brought them to Mondrum. I checked my equipment record, and that's an absolute fact. So whatever happened, it happened with the unit mounted in the pod – just like it is now." He leaned over and inserted his screwdriver past the side of the unit. "So if I want to get at this screw, it isn't easy. It's awkward to see, and it's real awkward to get the screwdriver in there. In fact I can't line the shaft up properly. It's off line. And these screws are tough little critters and you have to push real hard to turn them. And if you're going for a full turn, well half the way around your screwdriver is going to slip – "

His wrist was twisting. And then something came free and the screwdriver stabbed down inside the pod.

He didn't hit the inside of the casing, but she could see from the angle of his mime. The tip of the screwdriver would hit where the hole had appeared.

Eileen just stared for a little while, thinking my God, this I don't need. Security at Special Team is *my* responsibility. Every member of Special Team is a dedicated professional, and we're deep in the heart of a defended base. Security should be a piece of cake, so damned routine that they give the job to a dumb black woman with nothing else to do. I didn't even put extra locks on Sellert's store! This I *really* don't need.

"You see what it adds up to?" Sellert asked.

She saw quite clearly what it added up to. She glanced

across at Charlie Rodeck, and he looked as though he also knew. "Let me see if I have this right. It starts with Iris. Someone takes a screwdriver and sets out to change all those adjustment screws so the units will fail. This would be some time before the last mission, right?"

Sellert nodded. "Any time during the week."

"Any time during the week." She took a whole week, they'd tell her, and handed it for free to a saboteur. "And when this person gets to this unit here, the screwdriver slips and hits against the inside of the casing. It punches this little hole, but the person doesn't notice. The person just thinks the Iris units have been successfully sabotaged." What a word, she thought. What a *disaster* for me. "But because of the hole, when the set is flown on the next mission Lolite's shielding is damaged. Because Iris has failed thanks to the sabotage, the pilot is using Lolite – so the jamming from Romulus gets into the computers, and this has such a massive effect that we actually notice. So you and Jake start looking for the cause, and you find the hole, then the change to the screw settings. Right? The Lolite fault was just bad luck. Without it, there'd only have been a failure with Iris."

Roy Sellert nodded again. "We'd never have found the cause. Whoever did it would just have had to sneak in here a second time and turn the adjustment screws back to the correct setting. We'd have gone on assuming it was some kind of computer error. It was a neat trick."

Neat, Eileen thought. Except the saboteur made a mistake and poked that tiny hole in the casing of the pod – and punched her own credibility all to pieces. *Why* did that have to happen? She looked across at the impassive face of Master Sergeant Charlie Rodeck, and hoped he couldn't see how sick she felt inside.

19

February 27th

After lunch on Monday, Eileen sent Charlie Rodeck over
to Special Team to take the MP guard off Sellert's equipment store. The evidence had been photographed, documented, tagged a piece and a part at a time, and carried
away to the safety of the security building's basement. Roy
Sellert still had more than enough test sets and component
spares to keep the unit's Eagles flying.

She didn't want to go over there herself. Lutwidge had
exploded when he heard the news. She wasn't nearer than
a corridor away at the time, and she left as soon as it
started, but she still felt singed. It seemed best to keep out
of the way.

After all, there was enough to do. Suddenly she had an
expanding mess of reports and assessments to prepare and
collate. Aside from everything she was going to have to
write herself, the worst problem was the technical stuff
security needed from Sellert, Heller and Thorndike about
the cause and practical effects of the sabotage. She had no
trouble getting them to do the work, because Lutwidge's
explosion had been echoed as far away as the Pentagon
when the news was phoned through to Famula, the general
who'd brought Operation Blind Date into existence. But
what they produced was specialist stuff for initiated
experts. Reports of that kind were needed, but not by

security. Getting the authors to reformulate in terms accessible to the military police mind wasn't going to be easy.

The knock on the door was an irritation. She didn't answer very politely, and she didn't look up right away.

"Am I disturbing you, Captain Ware?"

It was Kathrin Talley who was closing the door. She wore a long green trench coat with the collar turned up and a scarf draped loose around the outside of it. When she turned, the coat was unfastened. It was a Burberry with a buttoned-in lining. Under it she wore a bottle green sweater and khaki cords tucked into low-heeled ankle boots. She didn't dress like any mere major's wife.

Eileen put her pen aside. "Can I help you, Mrs Talley?"

"I've just collected my car from the motor pool, captain. I gather you're the person who leaned on them about getting the damage costed today, and releasing the vehicle provided I made a booking for the repair. I'd like to express my thanks. Without a car I'm quite isolated out on Dresden. It's a great help to have someone stir up the motor pool administrators."

Eileen shrugged. "That's no problem, Mrs Talley. My routine job is helping out with Special Team personnel."

"All the same, captain, it's particularly nice of you to take the trouble when you have your hands full with this new business."

"Well, it just took a telephone call."

"A favour is a favour, Captain Ware." Kathrin Talley put on something that could have been a tennis club committee smile. "In fact, I called by to ask if I could help in any way. By that I mean – I've heard how certain persons might be inclined to make trouble for you on account of what's happened with the sensor equipment. To do so would be purely vindictive, since you could hardly expect sabotage to occur in the heart of one of our air bases."

"Mrs Talley, I should ask you not to forget that the incident is supposed to be as secret as the whole operation."

"I do know that, captain. The point is, a favour deserves a favour. I'm not quite sure precisely what I might do to help, but if it got to the point where you could use some smoothing influence in the background – well, I could try having a word with one or two people I know."

The offer ended in a nice smile. Slowly Eileen began to feel insulted. What was the assumption – that her own competence, her reliable record and the obvious facts of the case weren't enough to keep her out of unwarranted trouble? That she couldn't handle herself in a straight fight? Or she failed to earn the support of her own department superiors, so they wouldn't do their bit in protecting her against any outburst from Lutwidge? That she couldn't cut it one way or another on her own territory? And what was it made Kathrin Talley feel obliged and empowered to intervene? Innate superiority? White girl's preppie élitism? All her family and her social connections?

Slowly, Eileen began to feel angry. If Talley ran up against this all the time, no wonder the marriage was in evident trouble. Doubtless it took two to tear a relationship apart. Well some of the wife's side was showing. That was how she got her damned car ahead of the waiting list. It might be nice to know if her husband hadn't dented the thing on purpose. While Kathrin Talley waited, Eileen started looking for a strong enough answer.

"I think I can look after myself, Mrs Talley." The politely worded but impolitely intoned rejection didn't wipe the smile away. So she went for something stronger. "By the way, in connection with my responsibility for Special Team's personnel, I have to keep an eye on their general state of mind. Would I be right in noting that you and your husband have some difficulties together?"

That got rid of the smile. It got rid of Kathrin Talley. The woman swept out of the office without another word. She had too much style to slam the door.

Well now, Eileen thought, it seems I'm in a bad mood today. So keep out of my way, world. She picked up the pen again –

Another knock at the door. In walked Colonel Wolford followed by Lieutenant Colonel Charles.

"Sit down, Captain Ware. Sit down." Wolford waved his hand and flagged her back into her chair. His mid-forties face crinkled up into a smile focused on his eyes – but his eyes, in fact, didn't smile at all. "This won't take a moment. Except –" He motioned over his shoulder. "Was Mrs Talley just in here?"

"She was, sir."

"Bad temper?"

"Not when she came in, sir."

Wolford frowned. "She's not a person I'd want to make an enemy of – you never know just how powerful her influence might be."

Eileen folded her hands over the papers on her desk. "Is her influence that powerful?"

"Well, I can quote you one example. Not documented, of course, but these things never are." Wolford, minus smile, folded his arms as he adopted his mood of deliberate seriousness. "Getting on for three years ago, the then *Captain* Talley was pilot of one of those EF-111As at Upper Heyford. He wasn't the most senior pilot, nor the most experienced, and you'd think that an older man with some combat experience from the end of Vietnam might have been a better bet for the escort mission on the Libya raid. But of course, Talley got it. Now I'm not for one moment trying to detract from his brilliant performance on that mission, which proved he was the right choice – but from what I remember hearing, it surprised some people that he got the job. The rumour was that Third Air Force assigned pilots because of influence exerted elsewhere – which came mainly from SAC and the Pentagon." Wolford glanced cautiously at Charles, the Pentagon man. "That's where Kathrin Talley's family ties lead – father in SAC, uncle in Air Force policy development, I believe. Basically, she arranged for her husband to get the mission and the chance to prove himself and make his reputation. She really can pull strings."

"I guess so," Eileen said. "Let's hope she's not vindictive."

"Quite." Wolford half hugged himself with his arms. "Talking of which, I believe I've managed to calm Colonel Lutwidge down somewhat. At least, sufficiently so that I don't have to reassign you and put in a replacement."

That surprised her. "It was that bad?"

Wolford nodded – at her desk, more or less. "I reminded him that the brief you were given for this assignment concerned keeping information from leaking *out* of Special Team, not preventing any form of physical assault being delivered from outside. I really wouldn't say anyone could have dreamed we'd get targeted sabotage. Would you think so, Ernest?"

Lieutenant Colonel Charles shook his head.

"So, that's one marginal part of the mess cleared away."

"Yes sir. Thank you, sir."

"No need, Captain Ware. No need." This time he averted his gaze to the window. Outside, a wind whipped up ripples on pools of water draining from the snow on the parking lot. "The other matter is the pursuit of the saboteurs. Since Special Team moved in, only two outsiders from off the base have gotten into the unit's buildings."

"The heating engineers, sir? The ones from the Property Services Agency?"

"Exactly. The two Brits. We're hauling them back here. We've sent through an urgent request for a further repair on that medieval heating system. They should be here tomorrow. Then we can check them out ourselves."

"Couldn't we put the British authorities on them, sir?"

"And have to explain about Special Team and the task it's engaged in?" Wolford appealed to Charles. "We don't want to go doing that."

Charles shook his head.

"So." Wolford finally got around to looking directly at her again. "I'm putting Bob Villers in charge of that side of things."

Eileen nodded. Major Robert Villers was the man who'd

wanted her to play airman driver when Mrs Kathrin Talley was ready to be brought in for the purpose of inspecting her new car. "And I'm to continue with internal matters at Special Team?"

"On the nail, captain. Okay, now." He turned and started to open the door again. "That was it for the moment. Coming, Ernest?"

Ernest Charles hesitated. "Actually, I have a couple of questions for Captain Ware. I'll be along in a few minutes."

Wolford nodded. "Well, I'll be in my office. Good day, captain."

Wolford went out, and left Charles behind. Charles just stood there, smiling faintly.

"Sir?" Eileen pointed to the empty chair rolled in under Rodeck's desk in the corner. "Would you like a seat?"

Charles just went on smiling gently. "Captain, I'm not all that impressed with this notion the Mondrum team is pursuing – basically that enemy agents, infiltrated into the British Ministry's corps of heating engineers, were sent in to sabotage Special Team's operation. Aside from the plausibility, the sense would have to be that the Soviets *know* about Operation Blind Date in order to want to disrupt it. But if they did in fact know, they'd simply stop flying Red Wraith missions. They'd let us look for Red Wraith until we got bored out of our minds and concluded it doesn't exist."

"I suppose so, sir."

"Unless this whole thing is an elaborate set-up. They let us photograph mock-ups at their airfield, they buzz our aircraft, then they sabotage us so we think they have something to hide – so we're convinced Red Wraith *does* exist, even though it doesn't."

"That sounds overly subtle, sir."

"I agree entirely. So in actual fact, I was hoping you might be considering other possible sources for the sabotage, captain."

"Yes sir." And she wondered what this might be leading to. Why was Charles recruiting her opinion, instead of wielding the weight of the Pentagon to persuade Wolford to widen the case into a proper investigation? "I mean, possible motives do concern me. When I get time away from this paperwork, that is."

"I think you should make time, captain. What alternative motives might you be considering?"

None, she thought. She'd been a little more interested in the consequences it was going to have for her personally. Find some plausible motives fast. "Well, in general terms – a grudge, someone who doesn't like the Air Force any more. Or a personal hate – for example, someone who wanted to spoil things for Colonel Lutwidge, or Sellert, or Thorndike. Or maybe one member of the ground crew thinks another member stole his girlfriend, and figured he could get the guy into trouble. Conceivably, someone just doesn't like me. Then there's the possibility we might be dealing with a minor head case, or at least – "

Charles was looking amused. "You mean a high-tech murderer out to hit one of the pilots, Captain Ware?"

"Oh no, sir. The sabotage was planned to spoil Iris, not to affect the entire aircraft. That's also the final option, I guess – industrial sabotage."

"That's also a little far-fetched, isn't it?"

"Not necessarily. I mean, for a couple of years now there's been this rolling scandal about corruption and fraud in the arms supply industry. There are Congressional committees, the FBI keeps arresting people. All kinds of illegal steps have been taken in the pursuit of contracts. There's always a first time for actual sabotage – although I'm only thinking aloud there, sir."

"I hope so, captain. But keep pushing at those other possible motives. Try and put a profile on them. That's where the answer's most likely to be found."

"I assume so, sir."

"Yes." In slow and diagonal strides, Charles sneaked up on the door. Once there, he stopped. "By the way, don't worry too much about trouble with Colonel Lutwidge."

"Sir?"

"The colonel is under extreme pressure. Do you remember what he said at the unit's first briefing? He said that basically this mission is impossible. Having been on the team that collated the intelligence for this operation and defined the available resources, I can only agree with him. He has to find an aircraft you're not supposed to be able to find, which might not even be flying where we think it's flying, and he has to do it in a very short time. He is, of course, paying the penalty for showing initiative. He's the only person to have managed a photograph of this damned aircraft in the air. As a reward he gets an extremely unenviable job, and because of his past record he might not meet with too much understanding if he fails to pull it off. That is to say, he's supposed to be good enough to beat any odds, so if he doesn't, and if it happened to suit the wrong people, he might conceivably find himself carrying the can. Personally, I hardly consider that likely, but it can't help but have crossed his mind."

"I guess not, sir. I admit I hadn't thought in those terms." The concept of finding sympathy for Lutwidge, a commander who might have been almost the Air Force's number one killer in the air, but who showed none of the finer managerial skills a unit commander ought to possess, sat a little strange. "I suppose you certainly wouldn't be hinting at the possibility, sir, that Colonel Lutwidge might have sabotaged his own unit's equipment to give him a better case if the operation fails?"

"Captain Ware, I consider you to be an under-appreciated but intelligent officer. However, that notion would hardly support my opinion, would it?"

In the evening they were both of them home. She had her car back, dented, but didn't choose to use it. She didn't talk, beyond the communication necessary for her to cook the meal and for him to wash the dishes that didn't fit in the machine. They might have discussed the sabotage, and who could have done it. Instead she read and he watched cable. He kept the volume nice and low so it didn't disturb her, because then she'd have withdrawn to the kitchen, or to bed. That was the way it went over years, ever since the kids had a regular bedtime. The second half of the evening, she used to say, was when her brain got the chance to slip back into uninterrupted gear. When Kye's brain did that nowadays, it drove away and left him standing.

He sipped his whisky, and over the glass he saw her close the book. Fat and un-American, Vidal's *Empire* slapped on the coffee table. Caught in it like a sword blade between a Ninja's palms was her analytic bookmark.

"Better not take a sleeping pill, Clyde, if you're still drinking this late in the evening."

"What do you mean, drinking?" He held the glass out with a half extended arm, presenting a piece of evidence she probably wouldn't want to consider. "It's a drink. It isn't *drinking*."

"I was just reminding, Clyde. Don't say a medical officer who put you on regular sleeping pills didn't tell you that."

Rosen, the MO in question, had told him. It was what he told Rosen that would produce problems. "I've been wondering," he said. "I guess it might have been a better idea to bring the kids."

Kathrin shook her head. "Too much disruption, even if they're both still at grade school. Bringing them over here to study for two months with a bunch of strangers would just upset them."

"If they were here it might have helped *us*."

"No, Clyde. What might have helped us would have been if you'd come here by yourself. You shouldn't have put me down as coming with you. That wasn't fair."

"Fair," he said at the whisky tumbler. "I guess fair is like the way you've behaved since we got here."

"What way I've behaved?"

"Staying out late. Staying out all night. Flirting with other guys. Having other guys like Beamish take you home with them after parties."

She stood up, quite without flurry or fury. In this impasse it was the sheer bitch-powered calmness that killed off every tentative dream. Every time she let him know: no rapprochement would be allowed, no deal would be worked out to hold things together while they tried cutting through the dense and dead thorn hedge which divided their world in two. There was going to be no talking about hopes, beliefs, suspicions or fears. "Wolford and his wife drove Todd Beamish and me home. I've told you before. If you want to maintain this accusative attitude to that – or any other episode – go ahead. But you're not a court, Clyde, and I will not be arraigned by you on any *charges* and obliged to play at defending myself."

Untouchable. She'd chosen to remove herself from the little community called a marriage, and she'd left him floundering inside. "I was just thinking – just because we're going through a bad time at the moment, there's no reason to let it get public."

"Clyde, it's no secret. Believe me, everyone already knows about this. I can't say whether they'd gotten the message before Friday night, but after you had your stupid episode with Thorndike and tied the car to a post – *everyone* knows, Clyde. There's no point in trying to perform for the outside world any more. There's going to be no point in trying to keep it from the kids. They'll get it from their surroundings. If people haven't realised by now at Wright-Patterson, the Air Force's gossip lines will ensure the news follows us back from Mondrum. The kids won't stay protected from the truth, so the sense in going on is over. It hasn't been healthy for years, and ever since Libya it's just gotten worse. Now we've reached the point where we're crucifying ourselves for no reason at all, and I've finally had enough."

The television kept talking quietly in the silence. He looked up at her, slowly, and hit her eyes. "What does that mean?"

Her mouth twitched for a moment as if she might smile. It was a throwaway, a token gesture, goodbye to all that. "I've made up my mind, Clyde. I want a divorce."

Gradually, after she'd passed out of his view and left

him staring at the space where she'd been standing, he could feel the floor of his private universe creak. The roof of the church had already fallen, the walls had tumbled down. Now the floor was going to drop through the crypt and disappear. He'd go down with it, buried in a brutal architecture of broken dreams in stone.

Halted on her way out of the room, Kye's voice hovered behind his chair. "Clyde, it isn't my fault. It isn't my fault that the MiG you shot down wasn't a MiG."

20

February 28th

This time the paint had been scratched less patiently, and the job had turned out messy. But Thorndike's retouching had been erased and the locker door said *The dike* once more. It told a sick little story of some smirking overgrown schoolboy sneaking around and sabotaging name labels when no one else was to be found at Special Team. Or it was witness to the senseless hatred of an adult male. The first alternative made you feel superior. The second was frightening.

Eileen waggled the door on its hinges. It wouldn't even snag. "I guess if we bend it, I can report it damaged and get a new door."

"Forget it. Leave it like it is." Thorndike slammed the door, caught it on the rebound, and banged it closed. "So my reputation is sabotaged for the duration? What do I care? End of March we'll all be out of here." She turned the key and pocketed it. "How about the other sabotage? Has anyone discovered who did it?"

"Not the Russians, that's for sure."

Thorndike shrugged. "I don't know. The idea that the KGB maintain squads of heating engineer commandos all through Nato has a kind of wild plausibility. If you don't buy that, you're stuck with little motives like head cases or hate campaigners. Or someone with a major share holding in the company that makes Lolite. The way Lolite under-performs, the manufacturer could use some help swinging the contract back away from Iris."

Eileen shook her head. "That's a no-no. Sabotage isn't the way it's done. They go more for bribes. What kind of hate campaigners would you be thinking of?"

"What do I know? Someone who hates Lutwidge and wants to hurt his operation. Someone who hates Sellert and wanted to make him look incompetent. Someone who hates the Iris manufacturer because their cousin got fired from the company a decade ago. A grudge or something. Say – this isn't a theory I'm proposing. I was just playing with the idea."

Without anything to go on, play with the idea was the best that anyone could do – like Wolford and Villers and the British angle. Eileen initiated the first step towards the locker room door. It was past noon, and lunch was due. "I'm driving back to the center. Want a ride?"

"No thanks. Erin Heller already offered – she's taking a break in half an hour. I'm helping out with my aircraft, mostly." Sandra Thorndike paused, and let her face display a sour smile. "She can afford the association with me with-out people talking, now she's taking Dwight Pinkett home every night."

"That was something I wanted to ask." Eileen looked away, and found herself looking back from the mirror screwed on the wall above the locker room's washbowl. In a chipped-silver reflection of a dim room, she caught the eye of a black woman in drab field security garb, and the woman looked half as though she might die with embarrassment. Pull yourself together, she thought, you're getting this wrong. "Without wanting to put any names at the top of the list, might there be someone who hated you enough to do it?"

"Sabotage the Iris system in the test set?" Thorndike shook her head. "No. At the time it was done, there'd be no way of knowing which test set would wind up bolted on which aircraft. Believe me, I'd like to hang it on Bellman — or any of these other balls fetishists. But it doesn't fit."

It didn't fit. You got a long, wet British winter as if the previous fall didn't want to go away, then came proper snow, and three days later it had vanished apart from some melted heaps of dirty white wax piled beside the road. The world turned windy, bright and sunny. You drove through working traffic in the middle of the day, pushing your own shadow north on Manhattan — and right here, inside all the bustle and the barriers and the double perimeter fence, with patrol roads and ground microphones and remote TV cameras sealing the base from a surrounding country which was supposed to be friendly anyway, right *here* a saboteur penetrated as far as the secret equipment with a secret unit engaged on a secret mission? It couldn't happen. It didn't fit.

The Mondrum establishment's solution of the moment, squeezed out of their panicky guts by the horrified alarm back home in the Pentagon, was a mere pantomime of instant action. She hadn't needed Lieutenant Colonel Charles to tell her that. If Moscow found out about Blind Date, Moscow would ground any Red Wraith it might be flying, and General Famula and Colonel Lutwidge would discover they'd gone on a duck shoot in the Sahara. She might have needed Charles, though, to remind her that sabotage is serious. Sabotage is the worst — the kind of thing they'd *shoot* people for in a real war.

Eileen made a right and followed the road through the middle of the workshops area towards the center. No trucks allowed here, but that was why cars chose the route at busy times like midday, so the road was choked and slow. She plodded along in a traffic column like a good security officer should. The work, too, would have to be step by step and methodical.

A plausible angle was deliberate industrial sabotage in order to erode the better performance demonstrated by the Iris system. The beneficiary would be Datadyne Avionics, who manufactured Lolite. Unfortunately, desperate defense contractors didn't stoop low in that direction. They went for slick presentations, massaged data, and incredibly glossy brochures of the kind that might otherwise be sent out along with invitations to the auction of Graceland or Buckingham Palace. In a corner they might offer such things as paid vacations to referees from the services and from Congress. Defense industry greed could conceivably motivate sabotage – but who would be their saboteur? To name names, how would Datadyne, afraid of losing the Lolite sale, get two heating engineers from the Property Services Agency to do a little wrecking job on a rival's equipment inside a stores area on a United States Air Force base in Britain? The scenario fell apart.

Which left only plausible and *credible* alternatives. And to pursue those, she'd have to plough through personal data on every man and woman in any way associated with Special Team until she hit upon a combination of motive, access and suitable competence. Then she could start wondering if she'd found her saboteur – someone, maybe, who for some reason wanted the operation cancelled and the unit disbanded, and figured that making Iris look as unreliable as Lolite might do the trick. At a rough estimate, there'd be at least two hundred candidates to eliminate.

She came out on Enola Gay in the middle of the dog's leg, turned south, and then crossed the oncoming traffic and cruised around to the parking lot behind the security building. Standing on the lot was a small van with *Property Services Agency* painted on its door, which meant the heating engineers were here. Last time they brought a Transit.

Interesting. But much more interesting was the blue Land Rover with RAF markings parked right in front of the rear door of the building. It suggested interference which had arrived in a temper.

Huge and impassable, Master Sergeant Charlie Rodeck blocked any attempt to get into her own office. He pointed past her and down the corridor. "Seen what's parked outside?" He let out his little school kid's laugh. "Well wait until you see what's inside."

"Well tell me," she said, backing off while he came out of the door.

"Major Villers pulled the two Brits in from the gate. He was waiting there with an MP squad." Rodeck started all but ushering her along the corridor. "*Waiting* there. He brought them in at gunpoint. I just called the gate. You wouldn't believe. Seems he pointed an M16 through the window at the driver."

"Is that funny?"

"Well the next bit is. Major Villers is standing there with an M16 at his shoulder and its muzzle poked in the collar of one of the Brits, when Squadron Leader Blair drives up, our tame and friendly liaison officer from little England."

"How did he know about this?"

"He didn't. But he has this habit of leaving the base to spend his lunch break at some kind of pub. Cheshire's full of them – real nice pubs. One of the neat things about England. So anyway, Blair sees what's going on, and when the arresting detail heads back here, he comes right after. The colonel's with them now."

They were right around the corner. Major Robert Villers was standing with his back against a closed door and an M16 still tucked under his arm like a hunting rifle. Arguing across his face and the averted rifle barrel were Colonel David Wolford and Squadron Leader Eric Blair.

"Unwarranted!" Blair was saying. "It's downright insulting! You actually have the *nerve* to arrest British government employees going about their legitimate business! In accordance, I might add, with the treaty and leasing agreement which allows you to enjoy the facilities of this base!"

"Eric, we do have our very good reasons –"

"Don't you bloody well try using first names with me, Colonel Wolford! This business throws friendliness right out of the bloody window."

"We *arrested* them," Villers cut in, "as they attempted to enter the base without being in possession of legitimate United States Air Force passes."

"Bloody hell, man – *I* don't have a United States Air Force pass, and you let me go in and out through that gate every day! And you also know damned bloody well that our PSA chaps have proper Ministry of Defence passes which are *accredited*, damn it."

"Today we use Air Force passes for the PSA."

"You pin-brained imbecile with your bloody great pea shooter!" Blair reached out and knocked the barrel of the M16 towards Wolford. "Do they or do they not have Ministry of Defence passes?"

"Look, Bob." Wolford was stepping aside in the uncomfortable constriction of the corridor, trying to remove his groin from the line of accidental fire. "Maybe you should put that thing away again."

Reluctantly, Villers let the muzzle droop towards his CO's knee.

"Major Villers! Would you have the courtesy of a brother officer and answer me! Do those men have Ministry of Defence passes? Yes or no!"

"Eric –" Wolford started. "Squadron Leader Blair. Please? Would you just listen to me? The pass business is a pretext to detain them long enough for questioning."

"I bloody well know that! Major Rambo here blurted *that* out before we even left the gate. A cock and bull story about sabotage – by *British* PSA employees working under the auspices of the Ministry of Defence!"

Villers hitched the M16 up again so it pointed right at the opposite wall. "Dave, colonel, sir – will you tell him his fucking Ministry's been penetrated by the Reds?"

"Now look here, you pin-brained bloody idiot. The Cold War is *over*! Our side won! Your president *said* so –"

"Sir! Excuse me, sir." Eileen marched up and jammed herself in the space between Wolford and Villers. "Colonel Wolford, Squadron Leader Blair, excuse me. You don't mind, Bob?"

Villers blinked at her. She'd caught him in one on the friendship hook. Blair had dodged Wolford's cast, but Bob Villers had been too slow to escape hers. It was the fact of a black female junior jumping a white male superior that trapped him.

"Since I have the Special Team security detail, do you think I could take a look at your saboteurs?"

"Special Team?" Blair said. "What's Special Team?"

"It's –" Wolford wriggled. "Just terminology."

Eileen put her hand on the door handle at Villers' back. "Got them in there, Bob?" She turned the handle as he was starting to twist to see what she was doing. His shoulder came up to her cheek, but she just pushed him and his gun aside.

Inside the room was a mean tableau. Two civilians in overalls were spread against the wall, while four helmeted MPs kept watch over them, clubs drawn and pistols holstered at their hips. The pair of prisoners were leaning with hands on the wall, feet splayed apart, heads down and looking at the floor because they had nothing else to see. They were middle-aged. They had uneven English hair cuts. One was going bald at the back of his head. The KGB agents were obviously masters of disguise.

"What," she said, "are you holding them like that for? If they're allowed to move, are they going to blow up the building with their explosive overalls?"

"Captain Ware," Wolford said from behind, "it doesn't help us if you suddenly start getting witty here."

Eileen stepped into the room. I'm winning this one, she thought – God help me, but I'm winning. "You," she said straight up into the face of the nearest MP. "Those chairs over there – get them over *here*. Get those men sitting on those goddam chairs!"

Villers was pushing in. "Are you trying to countermand my orders or something?"

She put her fists on her hips like Lutwidge might. The MP's got a club, he's got a handgun – well I got a captain's tabs on my shoulders and I got *sense* on my side. "I can't look at them," she said to the face packed under the helmet, "while they're standing with their backs turned to me. So *move it!*"

Her voice squeaked when she yelled an order. She never could cure it. But the MP moved just the same.

He got the chairs. He slammed them down on the floor. He grabbed each prisoner by the shoulder in turn, hauled him around and pushed him into a chair. The other MPs didn't even blink. Hunched up like two rabbits in a trap, the Brits managed to look towards the bunch of crazy American officers jammed in the doorway.

"Sergeant Rodeck!" She didn't even look over her shoulder. "Come in here, please."

Rodeck made apologies and his sheer size made Villers squeeze past her out of the way. The M16 in Villers' hand pointed right at the floor as his command of the situation subsided.

"Sergeant Rodeck, did you ever see these men before today?"

"No, Captain Ware. I can't say I did."

She turned around. She pushed the wall of Rodeck in the chest, and he obligingly backed out through the door, expelling Wolford ahead of him. Charlie Rodeck reversed a couple of more paces down the corridor before he stopped, and at that point Blair managed to pop out from behind him and got ready to rejoin the fight. Right at her back, Villers came out and yanked the door closed.

"What," Wolford said and glared at her, "was that about?"

"Identification," she said. "Basic military police procedure," she added for Villers. She looked at Wolford again, and she had him worried. "They drive a different vehicle. They have different faces. They are of different approximate ages. They are *not* the same engineers we had up here to fix the heating system in the first place."

Wolford's head tried to retreat into his collar. "You're sure?"

"I spent half a day – with Sergeant Rodeck – escorting the engineers around the Special Team area. I really would know if those two in there were the same men."

Wolford's head came back out again as he realised there was no way of avoiding the mess. Instead he folded his arms and hugged himself. "Shit," he muttered, and glanced at Blair, who was inflating himself like a leftover lion suddenly loaned a set of teeth.

"Colonel Wolford," she said, "Major Villers, Squadron Leader Blair – if you'll excuse me, I have some work to do."

Back around the corner in the corridor, Rodeck was a shadow looming behind her shoulder. "Captain Ware, I hardly recognised you there."

"When I'm right, Charlie, I know no fear."

Charlie Rodeck giggled.

21

March 1st, afternoon

Clyde Talley killed time. He didn't want to talk with anyone at Special Team, but he wasn't going to sit around at home immobilised by Kathrin's freezing influence. He took his coat and zipped it closed, and walked out into the wind under a cloud roof that was trailing showers. He walked away from the buildings and the service area. He went out of his aimless way to avoid the ground crew team still working on Thorndike's aircraft. He crossed the end of the road that led from the taxiway, and headed off between the wide rows of dispersal shelters.

It was Kye's influence which put him in the hot seat and got him into this mess. But it was the MiG over Libya that haunted him. In the background looming over everything, in the underground running beneath and undermining everything, was the long drawn out fear – one day it would come back on rushing wings to take its inexorable revenge. It was his fear of that thundering ghost which had wrecked and ruined their marriage, a marriage whose fabric was already unravelling and tearing full of holes before Libya. She put him on the mission to cure some of the imbalance between his insignificance and the weighty splendour of her father and her uncle, starry generals atop the Air Force tree. It was Kathrin's fault he flew to Libya.

But it wasn't her fault he was being eaten up inside, the hero who wasn't any hero, the top-gunning rightest of stuff who in fact was a secret disgrace, the vilest possible fraud. It wasn't her fault he'd eventually gotten so awkward, so difficult, so downright impossible to live with that at last she had to turn against him in her own defense. He could understand how she couldn't take the suffocating private spectacle of a man rolling himself up and then squeezing himself down to some personal vanishing point, some psychological black hole in his internal universe into which he was going to collapse, into which he was going to disappear out of any hope of rescue or recovery. Because even if the MiG never came back, the ceaseless guilty fear would gradually crush him down to nothing at all.

He could understand why she couldn't bear to witness it any more, why she could no longer bring herself to even try to help, why her patience was at last exhausted. She was going to divorce him, and he couldn't beg her not to and couldn't hate her for the fact. Even though it would pull the plug. Even though the last little hopeful fires in the core of Star Talley would go out with the divorce. Even though then Star Talley, after burning far too bright, would silently implode.

He could understand, as the raindrops hit the ground around him and bounced off the nylon shoulders of his coat. But if Kye thought it was too much to bear just looking on – what did she think it was like on the inside?

The raindrops, riding a northwest wind, stencilled his outline on the ground. He stepped on his dry rain-shadow. He looked up and sought shelter among the shelters. Over there, between the grassed banks stretching forward from its flanks, was an aircraft hideaway with its door rolled open. He jumped over his shadow and ran.

On the way, he looked ahead through the pelting rain and saw the numbers painted over the shelter's door, and realised the irony was complete. Romulus waited within.

Under the barrel vault of the bare shelter, the EF-111A, the Raven, pointed its snout at his head. Its wings were folded at full sweep as it waited to come out into another night. A Raven didn't kill. Its mission was to hide other killers under an electronic cloak. But Clyde Talley had done something different with another Raven, and this one looked at him and knew.

There were no technicians in the shelter, but ladders stood each side of the cockpit. The hinged portions of the canopy were folded up like the beetle-wing doors of some airborne sports car. A power umbilical dropped from the underside of the aircraft and trailed to the shelter's single facility point. Slowly, he began to walk down the left side of the Raven, thinking: these I used to fly. One of these flew me to Libya – and into a private nightmare.

There was a movement inside the canopy. Someone leaned over from the seat on the far side. Someone in a coat and the fore-and-aft cap of an aircrew officer stretched to stick his head out past the rim on the pilot's side of the machine.

"Come on up, Clyde." Jake Baker grinned at him. "Come on, take a look inside."

Uneasily, he went up the ladder. On the little platform at the top, he paused. The outer edge of the folded-up canopy hovered like a barrier in front of his chest. He stood up high in the shaded vault, with the outside world and its rain and its wet concrete rollway down to his left. To his right, the rump of the aircraft stretched back between the high shoulder-sleeves and the folded wings to the tailplanes that filled the notch in the rear of the full sweep delta. Over the tail rose the slab of the fin, and on top of the fin balanced the huge electronic warfare pod. Inside that pod was the antenna system that gave the Raven its vital sensing power. It picked up incoming radiation from any source and allowed the computer, under guidance from the electronic warfare officer, to direct the suite of jammers and flood the intrusive electromagnetic feelers with a swamping cacophony of noise. The Raven's mission was to blind and deafen the enemy.

"Clyde?" Baker was still leaning across the cockpit, twisting his head so he could look up from under the spine of the hinged canopy sides. "Climb in, why don't you? Do you good. Bring back a little of the old glory. Anything but this see-nothing operation. Remind you that flying can also add up to achieving something."

Clyde stooped, ready to duck under the canopy wing. "What did we achieve? We took out some aircraft on the ground. But mostly we're remembered for killing Kaddafi's daughter and knocking chunks off the French embassy. The Navy went one better and took out a hospital full of kids."

"You shouldn't knock the success. Libya's kept its hands away from international terrorism ever since − except for supplying weapons to the IRA, which some of Irish-America paid for in the first place. So come on, get in here."

Clyde stepped into the cockpit and slid down into the seat. He kept his feet off the rudder pedals and placed his hands flat on his thighs so he wouldn't touch the throttles, nor the cobra head of the joystick rising between his legs. The seat itself wasn't so tight, being set for Todd Beamish, who was a slightly taller man. The cockpit, though, felt cramped. It was two years since he was stationed at Upper Heyford, and two years of time spent on other aircraft such as the F-15. He'd forgotten how disconcerting it was for a fighter pilot to sit off-center with another human being at his shoulder, a crewman whose head and shoulders blocked a whole piece of his life-saving view. He'd mislaid the sense of trust he used to have towards Jake Baker.

Jake grinned. "Relax. There's no power on anything but the ECM computer." He waved at the digital console between his knees and the big screen dominating the board above it. "I'm just checking through the settings for the jamming system. The bird won't fly away with you."

This Raven wouldn't fly with him. It flew for Beamish. Did Kathrin really fly for Beamish – sliding out of her clothes, lying back and opening her wings, holding tight and bucking underneath him as they went in low? Beamish was older, but he was one rank taller, not quite so far from generals Everett and Uncle Ames. Beamish was also married, and that really wasn't fair.

"Relax, Clyde. Say, what do you think of the sabotage? Some son of a bitch with a grudge?"

"Could be." Outside the open shelter doors, the rain was still trawling spattering curtains across the rollway.

"Well let's hope the guy with the grudge *isn't* one of the other pilots. That could be frightening."

"Why's that, Jake?"

"Because of the mission profile. Just let's say – for the sake of it – the Russians really are flying a secret stealth aircraft into Nato's airspace, exactly the way Lutwidge and Charles believe they are. What might happen if we find Red Wraith? I tell you, it's plausible Red Wraith would turn nasty and shoot the lucky hunter clean out of the sky. I mean, wouldn't they give their pilots orders to stay out of being caught, no matter what?"

"They might. What's that to do with our guy with the grudge?"

"Well imagine what you could do to someone else up there in the middle of a mission. Total darkness, no IFF transmissions to tell people where you are, no radar hitting you because of the jamming. It's as good as being a real stealth aircraft. No one can see what you do."

"So?"

"So — if someone has a grudge against a fellow pilot, or just doesn't want the operation to continue, or hates the CO enough — think what they could do. They have to make sure the gun camera is off and doesn't record what they really shoot at, and then one of us can shoot another one of us to pieces out there. And who gets the blame? Red Wraith. If you want to have some fun, just try mentioning the idea sometime when both Craig Bellman and Thorndike are listening. After you do, Craig's going to fly every mission with his head screwed on backwards. If I was Thorndike, lesbian or not, I might do it to him at that."

Clyde shook his head. It was an amusing piece of daydreaming to suppose there was anything in existence capable of putting Bellman's ego out of joint. He smiled at the parked pointers on the engine monitors in front of him. "That's bullshit, Jake."

"I know it is." Jake poked a key on the panel between his knees, and the big screen's readouts went blank. "Something very different is bothering me, Clyde."

He knew that. He left a drunken Jake Baker in the men's room at the party five days ago. But now a sober Jake Baker had snared him in this private place, this look-alike scene of some crime. "What's that, Jake?"

"It's been worrying me for some time, Clyde. I even dream about it. And the dream never comes through with a neat and clean answer."

Clyde turned his head, and Jake was staring straight back at him.

With the knuckle of his index finger, Jake stroked the

wings of his moustache. "That was a real little piece of scary excitement over Libya, wasn't it?"

It was a moment of terrifying, horrifying excitement. After the penetration flight, the target approach and the bomb laying by the attack aircraft, after the crazily ineffective anti-aircraft fire by the Libyans on the ground – suddenly there was someone locked on their tail, and with a missile and then a burst of gunfire he'd come within a yard of killing them. And if they didn't shake him right then, he'd come around again and kill them for sure in a handful of seconds. So Clyde grabbed at the first opportunity, at the first wild chance that presented itself. Afterwards they called it heroism, but at the crucial time it was pure terror and blind luck.

"When we were on the turn, and I looked up over your head, Clyde. Remember?"

Up over his head now was the open leaf of the canopy, and above it the corrugated sheeting of the shelter. Then, it had been a spinning world of night, balanced on its edge. Now it was rain lashing square yards of metal sheet. Then it had been the headphone sounds clamped on his ears – squawking from the terminal threat warning system, chirps from the ECM self-protector, the alarm buzzer telling him the turn was overloading the outstretched wings. And Jake's voice on the intercom.

"And I called a Flogger. Well – I only got a glimpse of that MiG. And I think I mis-identified it."

He'd tried to look himself. It would have been heading exactly the opposite way as it went past. But he couldn't afford time to search for it as they went around the turn, because that turn was threatening to tip them into the sea, so he had to watch his instruments instead of the blind night. He missed it.

"It's possible, Clyde. Both a MiG-23 and an F-111 have variable sweep wings. They have a similar profile with that big tail fin, and it was just about side on. Sure, the MiG has twin inlets forward of the wings, and a single tailpipe for a single engine. The F-111 has its inlets under the wings, and it has twin pipes for two engines. But you'd lose that distinction with a side view in the dark. What really distinguishes them is size, when you don't see much, but you lose even that when there's no depth perspective."

The identification had been as good as impossible. Jake was right about that.

"It's a positioning problem, Clyde. I guess the MiG who shot at us, he came right up behind us following the noise we were making, but blind to how far away we were. Suddenly we're right on his nose. He was ready for a missile shot, so that's what he lets go. But he's so close, the missile doesn't lock on properly, and that's why it misses when you throw that little jink before we've even started pumping decoy flares. He follows up with his gun, so he can't be more than five hundred yards behind us. And then you threw that tight turn. And if he was right behind us, by the time we'd come halfway around – he'd flown straight on out of sight. Or he'd turned at a different angle, or climbed or something. Either he was just guessing where we went, or he'd gotten shit scared and was bugging right out of there. And that means I couldn't have seen him, Clyde."

He looked through the blank combining glass of the head up display, through the canopy, through the Libyan night. He saw a giant doorway like a movie screen, and the picture was rain easing off on a wet winter's afternoon in England. "So?"

"Well I'm afraid – that maybe I called the aircraft wrong."

"So?"

"Well – when we came around out of the turn and levelled off, I called the MiG out in front of us. I was *hoping* he'd be there where we could see him, and hadn't come around to get behind us again. I saw a tailpipe glow out in front, right where the aircraft would be that went past us. But it was pitch dark, with the distance opening out because we'd dumped so much speed. Maybe it wasn't in fact the single exhaust of a MiG-23, but the twin exhausts of an F-111. The points could have been fused by the distance. And there just wasn't the time, if we wanted to take the one chance and survive. We couldn't see better than next to nothing, and all our aircraft had their radars and transmitters and IFF shut down so the Libyans didn't see us, and when I called it and you fired the Sidewinder, well the Sidewinder doesn't care what it's chasing just so long as it's hot enough to hit."

A wet afternoon in England. Almost, apart from the distance between Mondrum and the Oxfordshire base, right back where he'd landed oh-so-carefully, already fearing what Jake Baker had finally worked out for himself.

"We lost one F-111, didn't we, Clyde? The bodies of the crew were washed up on a Libyan beach. And we were over water at the time of the encounter. So I'm afraid — I'm afraid we shot down one of our own. And we're heroes for it. And I called the target. So it's my mistake."

"It couldn't be your fault, Jake. You weren't in command of the ship. You called the target, but you didn't sight it and release the missile."

"I prompted, Clyde. I gave you the identification."

But Clyde Talley had given the missile machine its suicide and its kill.

In silence they looked at anything but each other. The rain shower had ceased — no drumming on the shelter, no hosing on the ground. Just lonely water dripping from the rail outside the top of the shelter doorway. He sat in the cockpit of someone else's Raven, but he sat beside the man who helped create the catastrophe in the Libyan night. And the cream on the cheesecake irony was that the seat he was sitting in belonged to a man who might have fucked his wife.

The fuck-up was complete. The MiG that was never a MiG had come thundering from the dark inside his head and was going to burst out into daylight for everyone else to see. Jake had realised, Jake knew. Jake thought it was his fault, but that wouldn't be what the court-martial would say. It wouldn't be what the colleagues, the superiors, the papers, the TV, the man and woman and every patriotic America-loving kid on the street would say.

We all mourned those two guys as our martyrs, slain by the enemy while giving it to the ravening monster and proving once and for all that you never, but never, mess with the United States. We all loved those two guys for their sacrifice in our name. And now we learn they were butchered in the mixed-up heat of the horrifying moment by our own incompetent Clyde Lincoln Talley.

Home to roost. The Libyan MiG that was never a MiG is here at last, is circling around and getting ready to land.

"I was so sure, Clyde. I just knew you'd tell me it wasn't true." Jake had tipped his head against the back of the seat, so he could see through the upraised acrylic and the sheeting of the shelter and the clouds – straight up to heaven. "We have to talk this one through. We have to decide what to do about it. I just don't think I can go right ahead and spend the rest of my life lying about what I did. What I think I did." His head turned. His eyes slid sideways, and they hadn't seen God anywhere. "This is what I've been afraid of. We'd meet up again, and you wouldn't be able to tell me I was wrong. What I'm afraid of, Clyde, is that once I know it's really true – I'm going to have to own up to it." He licked his lips. "We have to talk, Clyde."

22

March 1st, evening

Eileen Ware worked late in her office, long after everyone but the night staff had gone home. On her desk was a list of the entire strength of Special Team – she even included herself and Master Sergeant Charlie Rodeck. This list was long enough to start out with. The bigger one, the roll of names of Special Team personnel plus dependants, friends and associates, could wait until she got nowhere with the first approach.

Over on Charlie Rodeck's desk was a stack of records pulled from the personnel department. The information on the unit's visiting specialists was totally inadequate: their files hadn't been transferred to Mondrum, and all that was available were career basics and a personal summary. Each summary was short, and glowed with praise. There were no medical records, psychology profiles, no background data – nothing that told you about the *person* involved. If she wanted more, she'd have to apply for copies of file extracts to be faxed in. And if she needed the data, she would also need persuasive reasons. It would mean putting a good case to Wolford. Right at the moment he was more enthusiastic about encouraging Villers in the search for external saboteurs. The reason was quite simple: it would be bad enough if the Air Force had been penetrated by the enemy, but it was *unthinkable* that one of its own people might have done the deed.

The trick was to trim the list until it reduced to a manageable core of suspects for investigation and elimination. She had four lines of attack, two covering the practicalities and two taking care of the motive.

No one could have done the sabotage without access to the equipment, whether officially allowed or not. The saboteur also needed the right know-how, and either enjoyed it as part of his or her own skills, or had obtained it from someone else who possessed that knowledge. The saboteur might have been driven by a specific and rational grudge against an individual, some unit or echelon, the whole US Air Force, or the manufacturer of Iris. Finally, the saboteur might be suffering from some form of temporary or permanent mental instability – anything from a mid-life crisis through alcoholism to certifiable psychosis.

She started with the practical side: limit your suspects and then look for motivating factors.

The access list included everyone who held, or had the authorised use of, a pass key to the equipment stores. Anyone else might conceivably have stolen or copied the key, but that complication could wait until the simple version had failed to pan out. The access approach listed everyone from Lutwidge down to the NCOs on the ground crew. The tally of those who would definitely possess the know-how came out much shorter. The encouraging result was that everyone with the obvious know-how also figured on the access list. But there was a problem.

Sellert could sabotage Iris. So could Erin Heller, who would have the right kind of skills to be able to figure out how to do it. Then came Bellman, who had experience with the equipment from the Kirtland evaluation program. Baker could cope, as had been demonstrated by the way he helped Sellert diagnose the trouble. Beamish would be able to do it on the basis of his training and experience as a pilot of combat aircraft. The same applied for Luzzi, McGee, Pinkett, Talley and Thorndike. It also put Lutwidge on the list. And for good measure she added Charles, the Pentagon's intelligence expert.

Eileen didn't like that list.

It got worse when she looked at the motive. Thorndike had a clear reason to hate Bellman, who would have exactly the right knowledge to do the job, so Thorndike could have done it in order to frame Bellman. The fact that the test set wound up flying on her own aircraft was irrelevant. That it nearly downed the aircraft and put her life at risk would be the unplanned effect of a careless piece of work. Somehow, though, Thorndike didn't seem to be the kind to make a mess of things.

Eileen didn't like the list at all. It added up to a joke at her own expense. She needed to widen the definition of adequate know-how. She required older and deeper grudges to offer an explanation — someone with some appropriate connection in the past to an operation associ-

ated with Blind Date, or to an individual serving on Special
Team. She would have to comb through the files of all the
personnel, and then start looking for networks of personal
ties. It was going to be a terrible tangle. She joined the
Air Force, and went into military police work, in order to
contribute to national security and the defense of freedom
by helping guard and protect the people and the equipment
that did the up-front work. She didn't join through any
ambition to be a law officer.

Then the phone on her desk buzzed at her.

"Captain Ware? This is Susan Wizer. I tried you at
home." Major Wizer's voice, dissected free from the
unblinking gaze, had the same unsettling steadiness. "I'm
calling from operations. We have what looks to be a potential Red Wraith penetration mission lining up at the
moment. I thought I'd alert you in case we get the go-ahead
and we need to pull the pilots in."

"Fine. Thanks." A mission would give her time to kill,
with nothing to do all night except think around the
sabotage. "How soon will you know?"

"Around an hour. Would you be joining us here for the
mission?" The voice had a still surface but an underswell
of warmth, as if it wanted her there.

But she had the choice between waiting it out at her desk
or her apartment, where she could work – or sitting for
hours in the company of Lutwidge and Charles and the
steady eyes of Susan Wizer. "I guess not. With the Iris
business, I have a lot of work."

"Pity."

Clyde Talley took a quinalbarbitone almost an hour before
he intended to go to bed. He swallowed the tablet and
washed it down with buttermilk. Sleep was necessary for
functional fitness – and sleep would be an escape.

Every time he blinked he saw, off to the side, the flash
and the fireball far away where the AIM-9L Sidewinder
surged up the exhaust pipe of that aircraft and exploded
inside its guts. And on no single occasion could he turn his

head in time, or by some miracle banish the night that haunted the kitchen, and see for certain that it was, after all, a MiG-23. He couldn't reach the controls, couldn't talk to Baker. He couldn't tell him to switch off the jammers and turn on the radar, he couldn't do it himself. There was never a way to obtain that IFF squawk on the screen which would tell him in time it's one of ours, an F-111, and stay his hand before he released the missile.

He gulped more buttermilk.

"What is it, Clyde?"

He found her standing inside the kitchen door, watching him.

"This is something new, not the divorce. You've been like this the whole evening – completely locked up inside. You say you had a talk with Jake Baker?"

Clyde shrugged. Why not tell her, if she was playing at being concerned? "Jake wants to talk with me about the Libya raid. Seems I've been wrong the whole time. I always figured he hadn't really realised what must have happened. But it turns out he knows –" He stopped. He had to use the protective code they employed on those rare occasions when the topic surfaced, the name that didn't fit for the thing that was something else. "About the MiG."

"Oh."

He waited. And while he watched the expression on her face and the tension in her stance, he saw Kye come back to share the space with Kathrin Talley, born an Everett. Kathrin could no longer take the emotionally destructive cost of being with him, and in memory of love he understood her. Kye still sensed his guilt and doubt and misery, and Kye still cared.

She was losing her strength. Her armour of immaculate isolation was peeling away a plate at a time. She was sinking out of her superior dimension and melting back into a world where he could reach her. She was coming down to touch him again.

"The crazy thing," he said, to disguise his new confusion

as the necromancy of the past began to smash the icy magic
of the present. "The crazy thing is, Jake thinks it was his
fault. He thinks he's responsible —"

The telephone rang in the hallway.

"— and he can't handle the guilt."

Kathrin turned and went out into the hallway.

He closed his eyes — and saw the flash. It was the
detonation of failure, of a mistake caused by fatigue and
inattention and momentary overload. It was the appalling
consequence of a night mission that lasted for hours before
culminating in intense and concentrated activity, and then
peaked in a moment of life or death response where there
was no time, no second thoughts, and no forgiveness. It
was the reason he took such special care to keep alert by
increasing his amphetamine dose during night operations,
and why he took sleeping pills so that he stayed refreshed
during the waits between missions. Fatigue provoked
errors, and errors could make corpses.

Kathrin came back into the kitchen. She was brisk and
businesslike again, the professional's wife. "You're to be
at the team area in ten minutes. Lutwidge has called a
mission. I said you'd be driving yourself over. There's no
sense in involving that Captain Ware every time." She was
already turning away. "You finish your drink. I'll get your
clothes together."

Clyde watched her disappear back into the hall. Then he
looked at his half-empty glass. Inside his stomach, the
tablet of quinalbarbitone was dissolving in a sea of curdled
buttermilk.

Sandra Thorndike sat in a chair at the back of the booth,
watching Lutwidge, Charles and Wizer. Nothing out of
line had happened on the mission: McGee reported the
Lolite on his aircraft had crashed, but that was just another
infuriating fault in a fucked-up system. No kind of
sabotage at all.

She wasn't flying because the avionics of her Eagle still
weren't put back together. Erin Heller was hoping to get

the F-15 mission capable by the end of tomorrow. Well that was too late for tonight, so Sandra was sitting in the shadows at the back of the booth, remaining by choice in the presence of a commanding officer she near enough despised. The thing was, she couldn't contemplate going home and sleeping right through it. This was Special Team, this was a mission.

The smudge of Dark Shroud interference on the big wall screen was almost stationary. It wiped out its own source on board Romulus, it obscured the interceptors, the circling hunters, and the bait. If there was to be a secret cat-and-mouse rendezvous with Red Wraith at last, this was when it would be happening. The hunters were a trio — Pinkett paired on Talley's tail, and Bellman all on his own-some. Bellman had no one to make a fool of this time out, but within the confines of Dark Shroud's jamming and with no partner to tell any tales, he could fly around wherever he liked. There were clear advantages to being the apple of Superman's eye.

It was twenty minutes to midnight. Lutwidge and Charles sat at the instrument desk in front of the booth's window, and concentrated with psychic clarity on the invisible event out there over the north Norwegian Sea. Lutwidge, for sure, was riding with his shadow hunters, weaving a net of willpower with which to snare Red Wraith. Lutwidge, as like as not, was the Pentagon's dupe. The only kind of stealth they'd find would be an American machine, staging in the dead of night from Iceland, and testing its undetectability against a bunch of fired up patsies armed with electronic eyes and a Superman's sheer belief.

Susan Wizer eased out of her chair and turned away from the window and the main room and the wall screens. She walked into the shadows and sat down beside Sandra. She was one of those female officers who wore perfume on duty. Chamade.

"I have a question," Wizer said softly. "It's an up-front question, and not an insult, so don't get upset. I've come across an opinion that you might be homosexual. Is this in fact true?"

"No!" she said, and heard it come out like a hiss. "It fucking well is not."

"Don't get upset. I'm just asking. I like either combination. Guys or girls just turn me on." Wizer's eyes were a steady brown inquisition. "I'm sorry if being up front about it upsets you, but I don't give a damn if the fact itself offends."

Sandra was caught by a pass coming clean out of the sun. Wizer won, whichever way she turned. Clear eyes could set up a target perfectly – hook it, or escape unscathed. "Who's offended if you're bisexual? It's just that I definitely am not."

Wizer shrugged. "Well, you never can tell until you get right down to asking. Pity you're not interested. I like girls and guys, and I know how to handle both. You don't mind my saying this?"

Sandra minded. Spending every hour of every day as a potential pick for any predatory male who happened by wasn't exactly fun, but you learned how to deal with it. She wasn't used to it coming from the side where she thought she was safe. At least Wizer was being polite about the turn down. "I don't see why you're pursuing it, seeing as I only like guys, as you'd put it."

"Well, I just thought I'd mention the subject. As they say, from appearances you never can tell." Wizer's gaze still hadn't moved. The woman made a measured map of each specimen she chose. "I hear you've had some trouble over this from Bellman. If it's any interest to you, his motive might be ego compensation."

Sandra had no idea what kind of conversational trade she might be trapped inside. She looked away towards the front of the booth. Charles and Lutwidge were still staring out at the big screen. Something that might be the echo of the bait was emerging from the mush of radar interference. All the repeater clocks said a quarter of midnight.

"Bellman comes on like he's a man among men, doesn't

he? All stud and no stutter. So on the night of the party I took him home, thinking this guy might be too good to miss." Susan Wizer shook her head with intimate emphasis. "But he wasn't. He didn't deliver quite as advertised. I thought it might amuse you to know."

23

March 1st, night

He was mesmerised in the dark, euphoric with additional doses of amphetamine, but hypnotised by the barbiturate still busy in his blood. It was a biochemical balancing act, and it made him feel insane.

If he was following Pinkett he'd have something to see, but instead Pinkett was tied to his tail. The view was a meaningless monotony without moonlight – blank black stratosphere, blossoming black cloud tops a thousand feet below his flight level, and the panel of emptiness dead ahead emphasised in Iris monochrome on the head up display. The same rectangular segment, miniaturised on the control panel's multifunction display, was graded in greys through Lolite's forward eye. It told him nothing at all. The only usable information that came to his eyes was carried by the sparse symbology combined on the HUD, and repeated in the stopped down glows of the instruments in the sightless well above his knees.

There was a flash out on the peripheral right. He turned his head and blinked. Nothing. Just undulating cloud, dark as the abyssal floor under an ocean of night. No fireball, no MiG-23 or F-111. Just a ghost.

There was an F-111, of course – a Raven variant with the call sign Romulus. It was two thousand feet higher and ten miles behind as they gradually pulled out in front of it, hidden under its blanket of electromagnetic noise. On board Romulus, packed side by side, were Beamish who'd obliged his wife, and Jake Baker who searched the nights of his memory but never found a MiG. Jake Baker, who thought it was his own fault, and who couldn't contain the corrosive guilt any longer. Jake, who wanted to talk about it. Who wanted to *talk*.

He nudged the rudder so the scale across the top of the HUD slid sideways and stopped with the 180 mark under the notch. Due south. That was the heading McGee kept reporting to Mondrum control. That was the course Romulus was following. That was the line to hold in order to close up behind the interceptors. Ahead in the night, flying a close pair, were McGee and Luzzi, Lutwidge's ever faithful Bitburg Boys. Behind them, maybe, was a Red Wraith which had slid up on their tails as they circled the bait. If it was there, he was going to come in nice and slow, framing it as an eyeball ebony point, as an infrared signature on Iris, stapled on high in the stratosphere sky. This time it wouldn't be Thorndike, because Thorndike was grounded at Mondrum. No new mix-up, no eager idiocy, no near repeat of Libya as he lined up his gun on a friend. His first attempt to shoot Thorndike came within a second or two of a disastrous success. His second try was a failure on a Friday night. There'd be no third shot.

Somewhere far away on the right, beyond the phantom that flashed when he blinked, Bellman should be trailing in behind the interceptors. Bellman should be, but he was by himself, and as long as Dark Shroud lasted he could do whatever he liked. He could flunk out if it suited him, so long as he moved up to a correct position before the jamming ended and the distant Awacs saw them on its radar.

One way or another, Bellman had gotten to fly three out of the four missions without a partner – because he deliberately lost Thorndike, because her aircraft's avionics failed, and because she was still grounded. Bellman got all the luck.

Clyde was always on the line, with an observer stuck tight to his tail. He was the accredited hero whose record showed he could beat a MiG-23 with an F-111, and for him a little night-time number like this must be a milk run. He couldn't pull back, take it easy, slide aside. He had to face the real risk and responsibility of running in behind Red Wraith, and then coping with the outcome. At that moment he would have to perform up to the limits of the possible, and anything merely outstanding wouldn't do. It was what they expected.

It was also what he wanted, because one real piece of perfection would bring an absolution. It might be enough to exorcise the ghost.

"Mondrum to team," said a voice in his ears, and a channel indicator lit on his communication panel. Romulus was jamming everything but that one single frequency. "Say course and speed, Romulus."

"Romulus," said Beamish's voice. "Course one-eight-zero at angels sixteen, speed four hundred."

"Thank you, Romulus. Say course and speed, McGee or Luzzi."

"McGee. Course one-eight-zero at angels fifteen, speed four hundred."

"Thank you, McGee. Confirm interceptors and Romulus are over the bait's horizon. He won't see anyone if Dark Shroud fails."

"Romulus." Baker's voice this time. "Our systems look fine. Dark Shroud won't fail."

Dark Shroud hid them in its thrall. The overload light of his radar warning receiver burned permanently: all channels flooded and blind. The ECM warning set had every indicator on: nothing but solid interference choking the electromagnetic night. Invisible shadows under a

Raven's cloak, the hunters haunted the sky as stealthily as any Red Wraith.

Another flash out on the sideline right. He ignored it.

In order to help expel his ghost he took the extra tablets, and tried to dance along the cutting edge between alertness and careless ease. At the moment, though, it was the unwanted barbiturate that was causing the trouble.

When he relaxed his hand on stick or throttle, he could feel his fingers trembling slightly against the grip and its retinue of buttons and switches. When he clamped his hand tight to stop the tremor, the muscles of his forearm quivered. There was a giddiness from the quinalbarbitone that made the warning signs of amphetamine euphoria difficult to detect. His head seemed to be sitting slightly loose on his shoulders. It was the last thing you needed while flying in the disorienting dark. He had to concentrate extra hard on the heading and the altitude marker's waterline on the HUD, otherwise he'd make a fool of himself right in front of Pinkett.

Alertness and fatigue were a balancing act perpetuated through time. They were crawling home, with or without a Red Wraith caught in the Draw Play trap. The mission was halfway over. It was 23.55 – five minutes short of midnight.

The channel indicator lit on the UHF panel.

"Romulus." It was Beamish's voice in his ears. "We have a possible IR threat on our tail."

It touched him, like a cold finger, precisely on the back of his neck. Over Libya, the MiG had picked the Raven because of the noise it was making. Now Romulus – ten miles back in trail, all of twelve miles behind the interceptors – was making the noise. The aircraft was a blaring beacon in the night.

They were all looking for a Red Wraith sneaking up behind the interceptors who had come to circle the bait. That was the trap called Draw Play. But a Red Wraith might decide to shadow a different target. And now the infrared seeker mounted in the back of the jamming aircraft's fin pod had picked up something warmer than the sky.

"Romulus. Confirm IR threat on our tail. Six o'clock low. Assume it's an aircraft."

Clyde snapped the stick left, then right, then center. He waggled his wings to alert Pinkett, right behind, that he was going to make a maneuver. He was going to get Red Wraith.

Red Wraith was low on the tail of Romulus, ten miles back. He wanted to be lower still so he'd see the phantom against the sky, just the way the phantom was watching Romulus. And he wanted to turn in order to get there fast, but a lateral turn takes up expanses of time and space . . .

He snapped the stick hard over. Dark stratosphere poured to the right, black cloud tops slopped up left. They arched over his head like a tunnel in night surf –

He centered the stick and hauled it back. The inverted horizon vanished under the F-15's nose. His sense of balance caught up and told him that the HUD symbols weren't lying and he was pointing straight down at the world. He twisted right around and looked over his shoulder to see if Pinkett was following. Pinkett should be fast enough at formation flying to do it.

What he saw, in the single glance he had time for, was the doubled pinpoint of twin afterburners as Pinkett sent his F-15 climbing straight up the sky. Dwight Pinkett had realised a Red Wraith was there behind Romulus, and Dwight Pinkett wanted it too. He'd picked the Immelmann, the upward vertical turn which also used gravity to fly square corners and save time and space. The display fleet pilot had chosen the flamboyant option. But the vertical turn was faster, and it was going to place Clyde ideally low.

He hauled the stick back again and the nose tracked over black clouds. His spine tried to collapse into the seat. Plus-seven gee: near enough the limit. A spectral night horizon dropped down in front of his canopy, and the artificial horizon slotted neatly around the waterline on the HUD.

Gee came off. The altitude scale steadied at thirteen thousand — a thousand feet down from where he started. The heading indicated 000 — due north, right back the way they'd come.

The black horizon had a bulge in it. The bulge got vast. A huge cloud head rushing to swallow him. He was three thousand feet below Romulus's flight level while heading right back to meet the aircraft, and cloud didn't matter. He glanced down at the Lolite view in miniature on the cockpit's multifunction display, just to see what the cloud top looked like. And at that moment it swallowed him and the last light went out.

Everything turned, like a frenetic Ferris wheel. The artificial horizon stuck with the waterline and told him he was straight and level, but everything still turned. A crunch of seven gee squashing the blood out of his barbiturate-giddy brain. It hadn't done him good. Believe the steady instruments, not your swirling senses. Forget the blank little Lolite panel. Ignore the blinded Iris view right ahead on the head up display. Wait the seconds while you settle down, and do a different preparation instead.

Did he want more speed to get there faster? More speed would stretch out the turn when he'd passed under Romulus and wanted to come around behind its shadow. Too complicated until his brain had steadied. Leave the throttles alone and move to the next one.

Weapon. Missile or gun? They weren't supposed to kill Red Wraith except in self-defense. Gun. He clicked the gun safety off. The boresight mark of the weapon appeared in the HUD. At bottom left the arm cue told him he had nine hundred and forty rounds.

Gun camera. It didn't come on automatically with the extra complication of the Iris—Lolite fit. He should switch on the camera and then set Iris to record . . .

Panel lights changed. His left hand went straight back to the throttles. The radar warning receiver's overload was off. The ECM warning set had no lights. The jamming had stopped.

Romulus wasn't making a noise any more.

He came out of the cloud. On the HUD, as monochrome as night, Iris showed him faintly cold cloud waves under freezing space. Dead ahead was a splinter of feeble brightness in the black nothing, like a fault on the HUD. He blinked, and it didn't go away.

It persisted, a faint speck just above the fainter horizon, a fraction above his flight level. Iris could see something warm in the night sky.

Romulus had been three thousand feet higher. Romulus wasn't jamming any more. Red Wraith had been low on its tail, and close enough. It could have fired an anti-radiation missile up at Romulus, and the missile would have homed straight on the electronic noise. It could have fired a heat-seeker, and that missile would have climbed right into the Raven's tailpipe. This time Jake Baker didn't have a pilot fast enough to help him survive.

So the thing he'd seen coming for a whole second was Red Wraith. And it killed.

Then the thing multiplied. It blossomed in a cascade of bright points, flares that scattered like little diamonds on Iris, which loved to see heat. Blazing decoy flares. It had seen him and feared he was an all-aspect Sidewinder, seeking hot blood like a rattlesnake. It wanted him to miss. But he had eyes and a human brain, and he knew which smudge was the aircraft.

They'd pass each other in seconds. Just this one chance, then he'd have to turn – and by then he'd have lost the radar-invisible phantom in the night. Speed in the air is life – but it means a situation recognised has to be a decision already made.

He nudged the stick to bring the boresight mark through the flares and under the target. A head-on gun attack at this kind of closing speed was almost sure to fail –

He squeezed the trigger and felt the gun screaming in the wing root. He pulled the boresight mark up through the target to hang a curtain of shells in the air. He let go the trigger and threw right stick and right rudder, breaking hard to get away from any debris or opposing fire. He was squashed in his seat in a swirl of sideways night –

A little bit of light picked out the bowframe, then faded. It had to come from a fireball, somewhere behind. Light travels a long way in empty night. He couldn't tell whether it came from the Red Wraith he'd fired at, or from Romulus, already hit and set on fire, and finally exploding in mid-air.

He moved the stick across and kicked the rudder around, and reversed into a more gentle leftward turn. Over his shoulder there was nothing more to see except black cloud tops which had clutched at him. He pushed the throttles to add power so that he could climb slightly in the turn. He'd slipped three hundred feet. He finally noticed the buzzing which had started in his ear, and looked at the light on the radar warning receiver. An Awacs band radar was hitting him, weak and from very far away. He let go of the throttles long enough to cancel the alarm.

He looked at the arm cue in the head up display. It tallied seven hundred and thirty rounds, so he'd fired two hundred and ten in fractionally more than two seconds. One of those shells could have hit.

The channel light. "Control. Romulus report. What was the threat on your tail? Why has Dark Shroud ceased? Repeat, Romulus report."

Romulus wasn't going to report. By the time Jake Baker told Beamish what was happening behind them, the missile was already most of its way home.

"McGee to Luzzi. You see anything?"

"Not a thing, Cole. Nothing on Lolite, nothing on Iris. We're right on the reverse heading. Shouldn't we see Romulus up there?"

"McGee. I'm trying radar."

"Control. Romulus report. Repeat, Romulus report. Activate your IFF for McGee's radar and the Awacs."

The radar warning receiver buzzed at him again. Its light announced an X-band radar, which would come from McGee's F-15. Clyde cancelled the alarm.

"McGee. My radar sees no F-111. Does the Awacs see an F-111?"

"Control. The Awacs can't see Romulus. They see you and Luzzi, and three F-15s without IFF, but that's all."

"I also see the F-15s. Nothing else."

Clyde watched the heading scale slide left to right across the top of the head up display, a line of graduated light slipping through an Iris night. When it came to 270 he levelled out and eased off power. He was crossing back a shade north of the place where he'd shot at Red Wraith. He would be just north of Romulus's last position, too. He eased off more power, and nudged the nose up to increase lift from the wings. He wanted to lose speed but not height. The question was – if he'd missed Red Wraith, what would it do? Would the Russian aircraft stay to keep on killing, or would it simply run? Clyde's life might depend on the answer.

"Control to hunters. Break radio silence. Did anyone see anything out there?"

Clyde switched on his IFF transponder. If radio silence was over, he could let McGee and also the distant Awacs see who he was. Then he looked out to his left, at the nothingness where Romulus and Red Wraith had been.

"Pinkett. I saw a fireball north of my position. I don't have a precise direction or altitude on it. I was just coming out the top of an Immelmann."

"Was that before or after Dark Shroud ceased?"

"I didn't see. I was busy with the maneuver. Ask Talley if he saw anything. He went down when I went up. If he was pointing the right way, it would have been up in his sky."

Red Wraith would run. Red Wraith had known about Romulus and about the two talkative interceptors twelve miles ahead. And then another aircraft had flown right at him out of nowhere. If every shell had missed, he'd have time to realise the sky was more crowded than he'd thought. If he was still alive, he'd be down in the clouds and heading for home.

"Bellman. I came around behind when Romulus called a bogey. I saw tailpipe and flares ahead of me at angels thirteen. Couldn't have been Romulus. I loosed a missile right at it. Didn't see a hit. I hit a piece of cloud, and I guess the missile hit a flare. The bogey must have bugged out. He was Red Wraith, you can bet. When he hit Romulus and the jamming ceased, our Awacs lit us up for him. He'll have seen us all around him. That's why he crapped flares, and why he isn't here any more."

"Control. Talley, did you see anything?"

Clyde pushed the transmit button. "I saw an aircraft coming towards me at angels thirteen. I made a gun attack before turning out. Didn't see if I hit."

"And you didn't see Romulus?"

"No." For Romulus to have been there, Beamish would have had to put his aircraft's nose hard down and dive through three thousand feet. The maneuver would have dropped him right in front of the threat on his tail. He wouldn't do that.

"Control. Romulus isn't in the air. Put your radars down on the water. We're looking for the two guys now."

PART 5

Time Out

24

March 2nd, dawn

Outside was a bleak dawn with frost. Inside, the segmented reflections in the windows were dulled by condensation on the glass. Even the metal strips between the panes were cold enough to glisten with beaded moisture. The briefing room wasn't especially warm, despite the revamped heating. Being exhausted after a night without sleep didn't help. And deaths made it worse.

There were more than just two empty chairs, of course. But two of them counted.

Superman wiped his hands on the cloth, and hung it back on the end of the rail below the board. He might be under stress, but he wasn't going to get his uniform powdered with chalk dust. He looked at the aircraft arrows and parameter numbers written all over the board. A muscle was twitching at the side of his jaw. He was, Sandra thought, a man with a mission that turned out tough enough to deserve him. People had gotten killed. That would be proof positive to Oliver Eliot Lutwidge that the Pentagon hadn't been wasting his time when they gave him the task.

Lutwidge turned from the board. "You want to add anything, Ernest?"

Charles shook his head. "Not at this stage."

So Superman came around the table and adopted his at-ease stance in front of it — fists, as always, on his hips.

"I'll summarise. The whole team was flying due south. McGee and Luzzi were together at fifteen thousand feet. Romulus was approximately twelve miles behind and following at sixteen thousand. Talley and Pinkett were at fourteen thousand, two miles behind the interceptors and ten in front of Romulus. Bellman's position would have been level with Talley and Pinkett, but displaced out to the west." He looked at Bellman. "When Dark Shroud ended, you were in a position right back behind Romulus. How?"

Bellman shrugged. "I turned around when Romulus called the threat on their tail. That's their first call, I'm talking about. I headed back on the outside and turned to come in behind any Red Wraith that might be trailing them."

Superman nodded. "You were a long way back. You took it fast?"

"I'll say."

"Hold on, here." Pinkett leaned over towards Bellman and pointed at him with a finger held out like a pistol barrel. Dwight Pinkett could coexist with Bellman, but he hated the man. "Are you *sure* you were up level with me and Talley before you headed back?"

Bellman just folded his hands behind his head, a supremacist so superior he was out of everyone's reach. "I wasn't level. I was around five miles further back than you and Talley."

"Now his story changes a little bit." Pinkett hitched the make-believe firearm in his belt. "Only five miles? Not fifteen? Or twenty-five?"

"I was there, Pinkie. I should know."

"The point is," Lutwidge said, "Bellman placed himself behind the suspected position of the reported bogey. He ended up exactly right." He treated Pinkett to a few seconds of the Superman-has-spoken glare, then relaxed back into his regular hard-nosed posture. "Meanwhile, you and Talley also went to assist Romulus. You turned back immediately after the second call from Romulus. Right?"

Pinkett nodded. Talley folded his arms. Clyde Talley

looked rougher than anyone else, as though he had a half-sized hangover on top of mission fatigue and lack of sleep. He seemed on the point of folding up. Sandra Thorndike had seen him like that as he stood in the snow, first beside the car he'd just smashed, and then in the street in front of the door to her apartment house. First he'd fouled up in front of a witness, then he'd admitted another failure – a marriage on the rocks. Now he looked as though he'd seen how one more rope was fraying on the bridge across his private chasm. The man needed a lifeline. But she wasn't going to try that twice.

"Talley made a vertical dive," Lutwidge said. "He went down to thirteen thousand feet, putting him three thousand below Romulus, and headed back. He'd be hoping to get a look-up view at the oncoming Red Wraith that was closing behind Romulus. Right, major?"

Talley nodded.

"And then the Dark Shroud jamming ceased. You didn't see any fireball? You were facing exactly the right direction."

"No." Talley was looking past Lutwidge at the board. "I had my head down in the cockpit. I also didn't notice any light shine in. I was level with the cloud tops. Maybe that's why."

Lutwidge nodded, and switched to Pinkett. "You threw an Immelmann with the intention of passing right over the top of Romulus and dropping in behind Romulus and their bogey. You went up to eighteen thousand, and you were coming out of the Immelmann when you saw a fireball north of you. Get a fix on it?"

Pinkett shook his head. "I'd pulled over the top of the Immelmann and I was rolling out level. I just saw the flash while my machine was still on its side, and as I rolled level the fireball disappeared under my nose. All I can say is it was north of me and lower. I turned and then reversed back to take a look, but it had faded. One big detonation, and no burning debris after. It was the right direction to be Romulus."

"I figure it was Romulus." Lutwidge frowned at the floor for a while. It might have been a pause to allow objections to be voiced. No objections came. "Blew apart in one big bang. Wasn't even any pieces left over big enough to go down burning. They had enough fuel on board – ninety minute return flight, plus reserve, plus unused mission margin. One big bang, God help them." He looked at Bellman. "You didn't see that?"

"Nope." Hands folded behind his head, Bellman still managed to shrug. "At the time the jamming ceased, I was further back than Romulus and starting to turn in trail. I was down at thirteen thousand, and like Talley Boy I was encountering cloud."

"Okay." Superman got his head up again: one piece of the analysis sealed and delivered. "Red Wraith killed Romulus, presumably with a missile. It's unlikely he used gunfire. He would have had to get in real close without them seeing him, and he couldn't have been where Talley saw him next. Also, gunfire would have set the aircraft's fuel burning before it blew clean apart. Romulus might have had time to report the hit, or one of the hunters could have seen the fire trail before the explosion. A missile would have just taken Romulus to pieces. It won't have been a radar guided missile, because the ECM from Romulus would wipe out its guidance. Right, Talley?"

Talley nodded. He was their only surviving expert on the capabilities of the EF-111A Raven.

"Besides which, if Red Wraith used a radar, he'd give himself clean away. Either he used an anti-radiation missile aimed at the ECM suite on Romulus, or he used a heat-seeker. Ernest, we're safe assuming Red Wraith packs ordnance of that kind?"

Ernest Charles nodded. "I guess we are – though we have no independent evidence of its designed war load."

"So, we assume a missile. And that would mean Red Wraith could have done it from a couple of miles behind Romulus, and also three thousand feet lower. Which is where Talley saw him."

Talley took a moment to wake up to the way Lutwidge had simply dropped the buck in his lap. The summarising, for a moment, was his responsibility. "I had Iris on the HUD," he said. "I came out of cloud, and saw an aircraft dead ahead and just about at my flight level. It was where Red Wraith ought to be, if Romulus had called the threat correctly and if Red Wraith had been positioned to shoot down Romulus. Also, no one else was supposed to be there on a due south heading at thirteen thousand feet."

"Did you see any detail on the aircraft?"

"No. Iris isn't good enough. I just saw the warm smudge of the aircraft, then the hot points of the flares it put out. I guess it fired flares either because it saw me and didn't know if I was a missile coming at it, or it had seen Bellman or Bellman's missile on its tail. I realised Romulus was gone because the jamming had ceased, and there was no way I could pass the aircraft and come around to find it again – not a stealth aircraft in the dark with cloud to disappear in. So I made the head-on attack."

"And that's where you fouled up."

Talley went rigid. Sandra saw him again, hunched up in a tight ball in the chair of her room. Something went wrong, and he collapsed in on himself. Now Lutwidge said he fouled up – and he looked like the end of the world was going to hit him.

"You didn't ready your gun camera and you didn't put Iris or Lolite on record. Otherwise we'd have pictures of what you were shooting at."

Talley was a cliché of relief. He snatched a deep breath before he got control of himself. Superman sniped because of the lack of pictures, and Talley was actually pleased. Nothing about the real live hero made any sense.

"That's a pity for the Pentagon." Lutwidge glanced towards Charles. "But you only have a second up there to react right – sometimes less. I know it because I've been there, over Vietnam. Fortunately it was always the other guy who took a fraction too long to make up his mind what to do, by which time I was doing it to him. When it's about killing, you shoot first every time, and you do it the instant you have the guy on your boresight. Never mind niceties like pictures. The head-on attack is exactly the split-second accurate response I'd expect from Clyde Talley, because that's how he got his MiG over Libya."

Talley was folding again. If it had been Bellman, he'd have applauded himself for the praise. Talley shrank in his chair. Nothing about him made sense.

"Talley held for approximately two seconds before breaking, and got off two hundred and ten rounds of twenty millimetre. If none of those hit Red Wraith, they'll sure have scared him good. Before turning out, did you see any evidence you hit him?"

Talley shook his head.

"You didn't see a flash? Any light on the clouds?"

"No."

Superman was disappointed: an equalising kill couldn't be claimed. "And when you came around again, there was no sign of him. Either he'd gone down, or he'd dipped into the cloud and turned away. So that means the last piece is what Bellman saw. Major, did you see any part of Talley's gun attack?"

"Nope. I was just coming off the turn to put me behind Romulus and the Red Wraith. Ahead of me I saw the pattern of IR flares and the center point that looked like a tailpipe. I didn't see Talley Boy, but I guess by then he'd turned out wide."

"That's the way I interpret it." Lutwidge looked over his shoulder at the board.

"When Major Wizer has finished analysing the Awacs plot," Charles said, "we'll have precise timings on the encounter from when the jamming ceased."

"It should fit." Superman turned back to his crew. "I figure the following situation. Red Wraith knew he'd taken Romulus out, and right then several things happened to him. He'll have seen McGee and Luzzi by secondary illumination from the Awacs as soon as the jamming cleared — that he'll have expected. But thanks to the Awacs, he'll also have seen Pinkett coming towards him up high. Conceivably he even picked up Bellman the same way a few miles on his tail. Being a stealthed aircraft, he knows he can't outrun or outmaneuver F-15s, so he needs to self-protect. He puts out flares to cope with direct threats, and intends to dive into cloud and bug out before anyone gets tight on his tail. Then he sees Talley coming right at him, and next thing he's flying into shells. And if that wasn't enough, his terminal threat receiver will have told him Bellman's missile was coming in on his tail. At what range did you fire the missile, major?"

"Hard to say without radar ranging. Maybe three miles." Bellman uncoupled his hands and stretched them up towards the ceiling. "Then I flew right into cloud and lost sight of him. Like Talley Boy, I have no pictures."

"Can't be helped. We have to accept there was time for the Red Wraith to turn sharp away or else dive, which would mask his tailpipe glow from the missile. There's a high probability the missile locked on to a flare and achieved nothing. That's a real pity. Two correctly taken opportunities – both of them long shots – to hit Red Wraith, and both of them missed. Or if in fact either of them hit him and he went down, there's no way we can know it short of dredging the bottom of the ocean out there." Lutwidge shook his head. "We have to assume he's gotten clean away with murdering Todd Beamish and Jake Baker. There was no call for that – no rhyme or reason, except he's a Russian and he had the drop on us. Ernest, I guess there's still no word from the search aircraft? No sign of those two guys?"

"I'm afraid not." Charles adopted a look of serene sadness. "Up until half an hour ago, they hadn't found the escape module on the water. Nor any sign of the distress beacon."

Lutwidge chose to study the floor. "Any other questions right now?"

"I have a question." Sandra watched while Lutwidge's eyes swung up to look at her. He didn't want a contribution from his non-flying female pilot. Or maybe in fact he expected it. Maybe he knew damned well she wasn't going to sit as a passenger through the entire debriefing. "How does the operation proceed from here?"

Superman pulled his head up again. He looked *down* at her. "I guess right now we're taking a time out." Then he extended his attention to include the rest of them. "Okay, that wraps it up for now. Go home and get some sleep. We'll run a check briefing at fifteen hundred, and by then we might even have some response from the Pentagon. For the moment just let me point out we've proved the existence of Red Wraith."

We've done it the hardest way, Sandra thought. With deaths. And all the time she'd been so sure – there was no Red Wraith. She even thought it might have been the Air Force's own ultra-secret airplane, making fools of Special Team in a blind test.

"Unfortunately, we've also proved he's dangerous." Lutwidge was nodding at his truth. "He kills people. If I have anything to do with it, the next move is we go back out there, and we get him."

25

March 2nd, morning

Sleet was slanting through the air and slapping the windshield. The wipers shovelled aside pieces the size of crystallised bird shit. Someone had to take the detail, and Eileen

Ware was the nearest Special Team had to an adjutant, aide or personnel officer. Lesser things like sabotage cases could wait for an extra hour. There was more immediate work to do. She brought Charlie Rodeck along to Arlington to lend a hand.

"Am I up-to-date?" Rodeck asked. He sat in the passenger seat, a huge amount of human being on her left. A Sierra isn't quite the smallest of cars, but he filled it. "The search is negative?"

"That's right." She slowed and pulled around into one of the lanes between rows of trailers. "There's some of our aircraft, some British, some Norwegian. No one's been told it's anything to do with any unit called Special Team — they're just looking for the crew of an F-111 that crashed on a training flight."

"The F-111 has an escape capsule, doesn't it? I guess it should float. If it was intact." He stared ahead through the sleet whirling between the trailers. "If the two guys themselves went into the water, it's bodies they're going to find. This is winter, that's the Norwegian Sea, and it's cold."

Eileen slowed some more as the car rolled towards the end of the row. "The search will be suspended at dusk."

"No point in it. Did you get to know either of them?"

"I hardly spoke with Beamish." She brought the car to a halt beside the gap between the last two trailers on the left. Hand brake on, motor off. Silence, with slip-slap sleet. "Baker seemed a nice guy."

Baker's trailer was easy. It didn't take them much more than half an hour to pack the man's possessions into his suitcase and valise, and to have table, shelves, furniture, closet and drawers swept clean of everything that didn't have the Mondrum stamp stuck, stitched or etched on it. It was no effort at all. Even Baker's laundry was neatly gathered in one drawer. Bachelors, especially service bachelors in individual accommodation, couldn't afford to match up to the cliché of disorder and dirt. Untidiness is a luxury which depends on having someone else to rummage through it for you and find things. Baker's effects were limited to clothing. There were no family snapshots, no magazines — nothing superfluous for a professional man who expected to be at Mondrum for a month at the most. Maybe there'd be a picture of his parents or home town in his wallet. It would be waiting with the last of his clothes in the locker inside the Special Team building. Eileen wrote out two collection labels: Capt Jacob Baker USAF, 42nd ECS 20th TFW, Upper Heyford AB. She tied one to the valise and one to the suitcase. Then they turned the heating down low, and left the trailer for the accommodation service staff.

Sleet worried them on the way between the trailers, hitting their faces and trying to glue up their eyes. Eileen walked in the wind shadow of Master Sergeant Rodeck, but not even he was big enough to afford shelter. She kept her head down and looked at the ground. Their boots splashed over wet asphalt awash with icy meringue.

Standing on the trailer steps, she unlocked the door. Getting in anywhere is easy if you have a key. Getting in unobserved is a matter of timing. She went inside, let Rodeck squeeze past her, then closed the door. Staying inside unnoticed is as simple as keeping the door closed, and not using lights. Provided, of course, you picked a time when no one else was there. It wouldn't do just to be around when the store was open — someone might happen by. So the saboteur visited the equipment store in the dead of night — some night when there was no mission, no training flight and no work to be done — and he or she would need the use of a key. It was a deed done in darkness, and it was back to that uncomfortable list combining access and the necessary know-how.

Charlie Rodeck had moved down the trailer and was through in the end room, stripping the bed. He folded the sheets and put them in a neat pile — a domesticated family man. Beamish, in contrast, had created chaos. He'd managed to distribute both clean and dirty clothes just about everywhere. Married, with a full-time wife back home at

Upper Heyford, he'd obviously benefited too long from someone keeping house for him. His bachelor skills had been forgotten. Possibly he'd had an interest in reviving them. On the night of the party he'd been circulating for a time with Bellman, until Bellman and Wizer snapped each other up. But this wouldn't be the disorder you'd want to bring a date home to enjoy.

Rodeck, blocking segments of light, came back through from the bedroom. He held out something in his hand, a little picture in a frame. "This was beside the bed. I guess we should pack it nice and carefully."

The picture showed a smiling wife and three beaming kids. It was a lost moment from the lives of people who'd just become a devastated widow and three wailing half-orphans. Eileen held it by the frame. For a moment she wanted to stroke the glass, but that would be an intrusion, like hugging strangers. Did they know yet? Had they been told? Were the kids at school and Mrs Beamish out shopping, still blissfully unaware of the chasm waiting for them? "I suppose," she said, "in a war this happens so often you just about get used to it."

"I guess you can get used to anything. Captain Ware, can I ask you straight out? Is it true what I heard – they ran into the Russian stealth on the last mission, and it shot them down?"

What would the people in the picture be told – that the father of the family had died in a flying accident, or that he'd been killed by enemy fire? Honourable mention or Purple Heart? "That seems to be what Lutwidge has decided." She looked up at Rodeck. A tall man under the ceiling of a trailer home, his face was shadowed from below by the cold light outside the windows. "Charlie, don't contribute to that rumour. The possibility that they were shot down is supposed to be as secret as the fact that they're searching for any kind of stealth aircraft. You're supposed to be helping me keep the truth from getting out. When you hear a rumour like that, squash it."

"Oh I did. But half the ground crew know about Red

Wraith by now." He shrugged. "I know they shouldn't. I know I shouldn't. But we all of us do."

"Surprise," she said. Oh shit, she thought.

They started sorting things, folding them, putting them in piles. No one but Baker had known anything about Beamish: the man must have had a patient wife, if he habitually generated such a jumble when left to himself. Baker was different. Baker had previously flown with Talley. Baker and Talley shared a piece of common past. Talley's marriage was in a mess. Baker and Mrs Talley would have known each other well at Upper Heyford.

The problem with that little list of Special Team officers was that every name was unthinkable. They were the wrong kind of people to go committing acts of sabotage. And when was the one and only time between the second and the third mission when the coast was completely clear – when no mission or maintenance work was being done at the unit area, and there was no risk at all that a dedicated and work-overloaded officer, sleepless through achievement worries, might happen by to catch up on some outstanding task? The one and only time was when all the officers were at the party. Which gave every one of them an obvious alibi. So it stayed at the far less unthinkable prospect of sifting through years of personal records for all the scores of people attached to Special Team, matching past postings and looking for some crossover, some occasion for a grudge, some reason to want to wreck the unit's operation.

The Talleys had a wreck of a marriage, by all accounts. Jacob Baker had said as much when Eileen asked him direct. But he also said the marriage had healed. Why say so? Did he have something to do with the problem? Were there grounds for a grudge, or a hate? The Talleys might be as far as routine adultery, and conceivably it started back at Upper Heyford. That it was continuing certainly seemed plausible. Talley could have been intending something with Thorndike when they left the party – Thorndike, after all, was the one who'd voiced concern about Talley.

It didn't end on target. It ended with Talley wrapping his wife's car backwards around a fence post. His wife, meanwhile, was where?

His wife left with Beamish. Wolford drove them home. Later, Eileen herself drove Baker over to Arlington. Beamish's car, covered in snow, had been parked outside Beamish's trailer, and the lights in the trailer were out. That didn't mean a thing. Kathrin Talley *could* have been inside. Beamish could have driven her back home later in the night. Talley could have found out about it. He might even have been home sooner than they'd expected, and been there when they arrived. It was a scenario that held together.

It was nothing better than lurid speculation. It might provide reasons for Talley to try something against Beamish or Baker, but not for any of the three to resort to sabotaging an Iris test set. Unless there was a nasty little scene, and either Beamish or Baker ended up hating Talley's guts. Or one of the alleged trio of rivals just couldn't take the situation, and wanted the operation to fall apart so Special Team would be disbanded. All she was doing with notions like that was inventing dirty laundry out of thin air.

"I'll take that." Rodeck's hand lifted the crumpled undershirt out of Eileen's grasp. He looked at the pile she'd separated on the table. "The guy's dead, captain. I mean, you don't need to sort his dirty laundry."

"I think we should sort it. When his wife receives this stuff, at least it should look as though someone here cared enough not to just throw everything together."

Charlie Rodeck considered the jumble of undershirts, shorts and socks. "I guess that's right, now you mention it. But I'll do this. You pick something else."

There wasn't so much left by now, except for packing the stuff in the bags. Eileen turned away to see what the weather was doing. Sleet was still swarming down like thickened tears, and the ground outside was covered in a white sorbet made from distilled winter. Only the slightest

signs remained of the footsteps they'd left on the way to
the trailer door, and there was no trace at all of any tire
tracks her car had made when they arrived. The Sierra was
acquiring a coat of inconstant icing. Little slabs of water-ice
kept sliding over the edges of the roof and skiing down the
windows. The ones that escaped at the sides collapsed like
sand pies into the sorbet on the ground. Underneath the
car, the asphalt was dark and wet with sleet that had
melted.

Tracks in the sleet, tracks in the snow. Tracks that half-
melted and were covered within minutes. Tracks that lasted
for hours, until they were driven over and finally ploughed
aside. She'd seen tracks after the party, a record of a single
vehicle's passage printed for a while in the middle of a
wintry night. The tracks had been heading towards Special
Team.

It wasn't Beamish. That was one suspect struck off the
list. His Chevrolet had been parked outside his trailer,
almost exactly where the Sierra stood now. The Chevrolet
had been covered with snow and obviously hadn't moved
all evening. Eileen drove straight from Arlington along
Manhattan until she encountered the road block. She
turned aside into the service area – and she saw the trail
of a single vehicle leaving towards Special Team. The trail
had looked fresh – it must have been made in the snow
after the snowfall ceased. It hadn't been a truck, nor had
it looked like the heavy tires of an MP patrol.

If she'd been less tired and more curious, she might have
found herself a saboteur.

It was a deceptively neat notion. It didn't move her one
step of the way towards any kind of a motive which would
make sense of the sabotage. Sense was the key. There are
endless occurrences of insane crimes, but there are none
without their own sense, their own internal logic. All she
was doing with this daydreaming was trying to conjure up
shortcuts to avoid the inevitable work. Dig into the past,
sift biographies, search for motives.

Meanwhile, finish this job. After clearing out the trailer,

they still had to go over to Special Team. There were two lockers full of clothes to be emptied, there was Beamish's ancient Chevrolet to be driven across to security, where it would wait until someone could organise a driver to take it back to its inherited owner, Mrs Beamish at Upper Heyford. There were collection labels to be tied to the dead man's baggage. Lt Col Todd Beamish USAF, she wrote, 42nd ECS 20th TFW, Upper Heyford.

Not any more.

Back at security, Eileen set Charlie Rodeck on the task of correlating past histories. He had files stacked on his desk, but he could do the job more efficiently by going over to personnel and working with their computer. What she wanted was a cross-referenced list of every posting of every Special Team member over the previous five years; for those who hadn't been in the Air Force that long, she wanted the towns they'd lived in. Some paths must have crossed in the past.

Alone in the office, Eileen took a handful of files to her own desk and sat down to read through personal profiles and medical histories. The work was going to take a very long time. It was worsened by the temptation to chase up on that shortcut. When she asked who had a car, or access to a car, the sweet little shortlist got seductively shorter.

Beamish owned a car and Baker certainly had access to it: but Kathrin Talley might be Beamish's alibi, and Eileen herself could prove Baker didn't drive to Special Team on the night of the party. Erin Heller leased a car from Mondrum. Talley had the use of his wife's leased car. Sellert didn't have one, but he might have had the use of Rosen's that night – in fact, if he was so good at bluffing that he could even investigate and discover his own sabotage after the mission, he might have let Rosen drive him direct to the unit area on the excuse of finishing off some test he'd been running. The insidious and corrosive thrill of a little bit of police work was the way it made you so *suspicious* of everyone. Bellman joined the shortened shortlist. Bellman drove his own car, which meant he'd had it flown in for this short-stay posting – generals did that kind of thing when it suited them, but on a major's salary? Finally, Lutwidge and Charles still dangled at the foot of the list, each of them with a Mondrum vehicle.

The list was just as ludicrous. Time to break for lunch.

But Colonel Wolford interrupted her. He closed the door while waving her back into her seat. She noticed smudges of melting sleet around the soles of his shoes. He'd come in from outside, but he hadn't been far: one advantage of having a window that looked direct onto the parking lot was the way you saw who was arriving or leaving by car. Wolford hadn't been further than one of the other administration buildings.

"How's the investigation proceeding, captain?"

"I'm getting some strategies in place, sir." Then she thought, since he raised the subject she could make use of the moment. "I wanted to ask, sir. On the night of the party, last Friday, you drove Beamish and Mrs Talley home. What time was that, exactly?"

Wolford shrugged. "Eleven thirty, eleven forty-five. Why?"

"I'm just eliminating some coincidences, sir. Did you drive them home directly?"

"Yes. I drove Beamish down to Arlington, then Mrs Talley up to Dresden. Mrs Talley invited us in for coffee, but my wife was feeling tired so we said no. We only live a couple of corners further away on Tokyo Avenue. I guess we left the party nearer to eleven forty-five, in fact. We got home just a couple of minutes after midnight." Wolford surfaced out of the serious business of memory, and produced his crinkled smile. "That any use?"

"Yes, I think so." Beamish had just lost Kathrin Talley as an alibi for the night in question, but if you put it together with the fact that his car had been frozen to the ground outside his trailer since long before eleven forty-five that evening . . . She crossed Beamish and Baker off the list. Now it was so short, it was tantalising.

"I've just been meeting with General Dodgson."

Eileen looked up and saw the smile had vanished. Never take your eyes off an insecure colonel. "Yes, sir?"

"He agreed I should keep Bob Villers chasing the external sabotage angle – though I feel, basically, it's probably a no-no we unfortunately just have to cover. Meanwhile, your responsibility remains the internal investigation. However, there's a new complication." Wolford's gaze had wandered as usual to the window: he wasn't too good at managing eye contact in a conversation. "The situation is, Special Team have lost one aircraft and are claiming it was shot down by this Red Wraith. Unless someone ever decides to mount the most amazing operation to locate and raise the wreckage, that claim will never be confirmed or refuted, I imagine. I mean, the sea's thousands of feet deep where it happened."

"So I believe, sir."

"Anyway, Lutwidge has reported confirmation of the existence of this Red Wraith – and I'll bet he's pleased as punch under that Ollie North exterior, dead men yes or no. Well, the response just came through from Famula in the Pentagon. It isn't praise nor congratulations, no way. Anything but. It's clear the last thing the Pentagon types wanted was a shooting match. There's the extreme seriousness of United States aircraft being obliged to open fire on Soviet aircraft. There's the diplomatic consequences. There's the gravest implications of the possibility that a Soviet aircraft shot down one of our machines – killing the crew – without any due cause. I mean, the politicians keep telling us the Cold War is as good as over, so what would the Russians be *doing*? The whole thing has to be checked, double-checked and then checked again."

Eileen nodded. It filled in time while she tried to anticipate the relevance of the Pentagon's reaction to her own work.

"Lutwidge will be hearing this from Dodgson right about now. If you open the window you'll probably hear the explosion. Instead of a pat on the back, he's getting something that's halfway to a reprimand for what happened, and damned near a suggestion that he's gotten his interpretation entirely wrong."

"I don't follow, sir."

"Well —" Wolford resorted to folding his arms and hugging himself. "The idea of some invisible Russian shooting the aircraft down could be a misinterpretation. Could be it was an accident — a pilot error, or a fault on the aircraft, or something like that. In the end, that would come down to human error — someone on the aircrew or the ground crew made a mistake. It could be a disciplinary matter, it could be *serious*, and it might have unpleasant consequences among the personnel. From someone junior, right up through the tiers to Lutwidge. You see what I mean?"

"I don't see where I fit in, sir. I don't have the expertise. I'd be useless on something like a crash investigation. If that's what's called for, they'll have to send us a full-scale team to do the job. Security and such is my specialty."

"That's the point, Captain Ware." Finally Wolford decided to look at her again. "We already had one act of sabotage."

She blinked at him. She looked down at that ludicrous list on her desk.

"We're in a corner on this. For obvious reasons, we need to know as quickly as possible whether it is — or whether it is not — the Russians killing our aircrew. I mean, is the Cold War in fact still on, are they still the same enemy? Now I realise we don't have the resources for something this big. Believe me, I do. But we're the people on the spot, and right now it's up to us. I'll back you with anything you reasonably need. Your job is to pursue this angle, no matter how crazy it looks." Wolford seemed as unhappy as Eileen had started to feel. "And, ah, the Pentagon wants everything done yesterday."

26

March 2nd, evening

The breeze was falling asleep in the east, the world was darkening under cloud, and the Special Team area had become paddies of thin water dammed by barriers of sleet turned to slush. Feet splashed and car tires surged through the mush as people started to head for home. No mission in prospect tonight.

Roy Sellert had the lights burning in his shed. A test set pod lay opened up on the bench, and he was probing its interior with an assembly of instruments. The examination was merely a routine autopsy: this was the Lolite that chose to die during the mission of the previous night.

"Who do I think might have done the sabotage?" He looked at the water draining on the cement floor from the soles of Eileen's boots, as if that water might worsen the state of his temperamental toys. "I think no one here did it. But I only know for sure that I didn't do it, and Jake Baker didn't either. I was looking at the stripped cable on the Lolite set and he was looking at Iris for me, and *he* found the hole in the pod and noticed the coolant bleed screws were set false. Apart from that, how should I know who did it? That's your job."

"That's why I'm asking bothersome questions," Eileen said. Sellert didn't outrank her, nor did he intimidate her — she should take care not to snap at him merely because other people made her feel useless and in the way. "What do you think? Was the sabotage the work of a skilled operator, or was it just a piece of damage done by someone out to make trouble?"

"The trick pulled on Iris?" He reached out and switched off a multimeter that had been clicking patiently. "To tell the truth, I think it was a piece of very clever work."

"Why?"

"Well, turning those bleed screws around so they were set false and caused the coolant to leak from every imaging unit – that was a near enough invisible adjustment. Let's say the guy's screwdriver hadn't slipped, there was no hole in the shell of the pod and no wind through the thing, so there was no catastrophe with Lolite and we didn't know why Iris failed. Okay? I'd do some initial checks on Iris, I'd find the coolant was vented but nothing seemed damaged. The next thing is, the saboteur would come back and turn those screws to the correct setting before I got around to taking the Iris system completely apart. We'd never find out what was wrong. The only possible conclusion left would be that some glitch in the control software caused the error with the coolant. No one would ever find a physical fault, and no one would get the software fault to repeat itself and surface. That would really throw the manufacturer back on his heels. Nothing is worse than an insoluble problem. It could cost Iris the procurement contract."

"The end effect could have been that bad?"

"I'm sure it could. Whoever thought up the job must have one hell of a grudge, and my guess is that Aerosensor – the Iris manufacturer – is the target."

That, she thought, is valuable. I most desperately need logical grounds for inferring a possible motive. I need suggestions that fit. "If it was clever work," she said, "why was it botched enough to take Lolite out, draw attention to the cause, and give the sabotage away?"

Roy Sellert lifted his head for a moment to look towards heaven. It would be the deliberately impossible *why* which made the question infuriating. How could he know the motive, as opposed to the mechanism, for a mistake by someone else? His gaze came down again, and as it did so one of the lights reflected off his glasses and flashed blank impatience at her. "A clever guy thought up the plan, but had to rely on some numbskull to do the actual work. Or the clever guy did it himself, but he wasn't handy enough to stop his screwdriver slipping. And when it slipped, he didn't think to check for any hole it might have made, or didn't realise what the hole could do. He might have been in a hurry before someone else came by. Or he was sneaking around here in the middle of the night with nothing but a flashlight. How on earth am I supposed to know why the job ended up a mess?"

A saboteur sneaking around in the middle of the night. On the night after the party, in the snow, the saboteur might not have worried about tire tracks that would be driven to invisibility shortly after dawn. "So it was a piece of sabotage cleverly conceived but badly executed. So why do you think it was done?"

"What?" Roy Sellert's patience was running out. Ever since the sabotage he'd been working extra hours under intense pressure to check and safeguard the rest of the equipment, and to complete detailed reports for the equipment evaluators at Kirtland, the Blind Date overseers in the Pentagon, and the security administration here at Mondrum. "How the hell should I know? A grudge, obviously. The only other explanation is that the head of Datadyne Avionics came over here in person, and tried to spoil Iris's record to even up the score for his own baby, Lolite. Ever since the first test sets were delivered to us at Kirtland, Lolite has been a *pain*, if you want to know the truth. Ask Craig Bellman. He's one of the victims who've been flying the stupid equipment for us. Ask *him*."

"Bellman isn't very helpful, I find."

"Well then." Sellert turned to the shelves lining the wall at the back of the shed. "*Well* then." In among the stored equipment, he pushed aside a stack of report files and hauled out a fat folder. "Here!" He waved it at her. "This is the interim summary of the results from Kirtland. I'm supposed to be reading that right now. I'm supposed to approve it like everyone else on the program. I brought it with me on this damned posting – and I haven't had the time to even *look* at it since I arrived. I mean, they didn't provide one single technician to help me out. *You* read it!" He stepped towards her and pushed the folder into her arms. "You read it if you're trying to find a reason for the sabotage. For all I know, it might even help!"

Eileen took the folder and wrapped it in her arms. It might protect her – mild Roy Sellert was losing his temper, and calm people out of control could get vicious. She moved towards the door before deciding to loose the parting shot. "Incidentally, Roy, your reasoning is flawed. You say it wasn't anyone here. But you think the perpetrator might have intended to come back after the mission and reset those screws. That means it would be someone right here on Special Team. One of your suppositions has to be false."

He didn't answer. He had his head down and was poking around inside the pod.

Down at the far end of the corridor, someone switched off the lights in the briefing room. If it was Lutwidge, beset by sabotage, the loss of an aircraft and mistrust from on high, she'd better turn back to the locker room and hide.

"So how do you know," said Pinkett's voice, "the Red Wraith didn't drop right down on the deck to run out of there?"

"Because you all turned your radars on the water to look for the escape capsule from Romulus." Thorndike's voice sounded patient but assertive. "If Red Wraith was down on the water, you'd have seen him."

Pinkett said something obscured by the sound of the briefing room door closing.

"Dwight, your radars would have seen him. Lookdown mode is pulse-Doppler mode, right? It responds to the *movement* of objects. It would blank out the movement of the water surface relative to the aircraft using the radar, because the Doppler shift on all the waves would be the same."

"I *know* how my own radar works."

"But a fully stealthed aircraft doesn't send back a radar echo. It sends back a hole. A regular radar can't see *nothing*, its computer doesn't register *nothing*. But a pulse-Doppler radar in lookdown mode looks for *differences* in Doppler shift. Where the stealth aircraft was looking like a hole, it would see an infinite difference, so long as the aircraft was down so low it threw a shadow on the water or the ground. The radar would see the difference, the computer would register it, and up would pop your Red Wraith on your radar display. A stealth can't fly down on the deck when there's a lookdown radar about."

"So who says?"

"We say, at Nellis. But the people flying the F-117A – also at Nellis – won't lend us one of their aircraft to try it with. Their invisible airplane is so fucking secret we're not even allowed to find out if we can in fact see it. Must be all the money tied up in the thing. Better no use than not bought."

"Like Lolite," Pinkett said. Then he stopped walking, and Thorndike stopped, too.

They didn't look pleased to see her, Eileen thought.

"Want us for questioning?" Pinkett asked. "If so, where are the MPs to escort us to your office?"

Two captains against one, she thought, and no lower ranks around to impress with commissioned solidarity. They could be as outright rude as they liked. "Why?"

"News travels fast," Thorndike said. "Everyone but Talley knew even before Superman told us this afternoon. Some broad-assed general back in the Pentagon suddenly doesn't want to know about any Red Wraith. He wants us to check those guys didn't do something dumb and kill themselves, or their aircraft didn't just drop out of the air from a maintenance fault. The pilots are accused of imagining things and the ground crew of incompetence."

"And someone, maybe, of sabotaging Romulus." Pinkett stabbed loosely at her with his index finger. "Which is why *you're* here. So we're just leaving. We have reports to write."

"Hey, wait a minute," Eileen said. She was between them and the corner to the outside door, so at least she could slow their move to push past. "I didn't dream up the sabotage notion. Nor did I do the piece of real sabotage to Iris. On *your* aircraft," she said to Sandra Thorndike. "Which nearly killed you. So doesn't either of you have ten minutes to explain to me what actually happened out there last night? Show me how you know it was Red Wraith, so I can stop thinking my way up blind alleys for my own boss and the people in the Pentagon? I mean, I also have a report to write on this. It might as well be accurate and well-informed, and not a mishmash of desk-pilot nonsense."

Pinkett looked at Thorndike. She was on the outside on account of smears about her sexual preferences – but she was back on the inside when it was pilots versus service bureaucrats.

Sandra Thorndike shrugged. "Why not?"

In the briefing room, they cleaned the chalk board and then drew her a big, clear plan with symbols and altitude figures and course lines for the Special Team aircraft, and a dotted line for the movements of Red Wraith. It looked persuasively simple – all straight lines and hairpin loops for the doubling-back maneuvers of Pinkett, Talley and Bellman. The only complications were the sharp curve of Talley's turn out, and the guesswork about which way the Red Wraith would have gone after he dipped into the cloud for safety. Most of it, though, was without any confirmation from positional plots. Until the last phase of the encounter, their own radars had been turned off and the jamming from Romulus had blocked the radar of the Awacs aircraft patrolling the area. And of course, there was no radar track at all of the Red Wraith.

Eileen copied the diagram in her own little notebook. Cramped on the page, the altitude figures maneuvered around each other in close combat. "You're certain Romulus was shot down by a Red Wraith. You're certain both Talley and Bellman saw the Red Wraith. But you're more or less convinced neither of them shot it down. How do you make that judgement?" She paused with her sketch and looked at Pinkett. "After all, you saw an explosion in the air, and it was in the right direction for where they shot at the Red Wraith, wasn't it? And the timings are imprecise in terms of seconds — of what happened exactly when."

Pinkett shook his head. "The analysis is easy. I saw one explosion, and Romulus disappeared at just about the same time, and never appeared again. It couldn't have gone down into the sea so fast — intact, that is — that it wasn't still there to show on the Awacs radar a few seconds later. But it can't have come to pieces without an explosion to blow it apart. So the explosion I saw was Romulus. There was an explosion from Red Wraith blowing up only if there was a second explosion. I didn't see one. Talley didn't see one, but he should have done if his shells hit — he'd be turning away and banked steep over, but it would have lit the cloud. And Bellman didn't see one. So there was no other explosion. So no one hit Red Wraith."

Eileen started to put in the broken line of Red Wraith's phantom flight. It moved ahead of Bellman, it ran right into Talley. The dogfighting altitude figures were all identical. "You have no pictures of what Talley and Bellman saw. How do you know they didn't both make a mistake? How do you know a Red Wraith really was there, and it wasn't some kind of explosion on board Romulus?"

"What's your alternative?" Thorndike asked. "Romulus blows up because someone put a bomb on board? Why, for Christ's sake?" Her finger poked into the middle of Eileen's sketch. "Then what do Talley and Bellman shoot at? Each other? I wouldn't call them the best of friends, but they don't hate each other that much."

Eileen finished drawing her invisible Red Wraith. If

people want you to believe in an aircraft no one can see, they shouldn't complain when you adopt the stance of a devil's advocate. "They were flying towards each other at the same altitude. Total darkness, no radar, and at least one piece of equipment, namely Lolite, that isn't reliable. Why shouldn't they make a mistake?"

"One of them, maybe. But both?" Thorndike circled her shoe on the wooden floor, searching for a simple enough argument to convince a non-specialist. She looked up, argument found. "Okay. Both Talley and Bellman believe there's a Red Wraith because Romulus has just gone. Talley sees Bellman coming towards him, thinks it's Red Wraith, shoots and turns out wide. He misses, of course – which is highly likely in a head-on gun attack – and Bellman lives to come home. Bellman sees Talley coming right at him, and thinks it's Red Wraith turning back after attacking Romulus. He fires a missile, but a head-on shot is an uncertain thing, even with the all-aspect capability of the Sidewinder type he was using. The missile misses when Talley turns out hard. Plausible, isn't it?"

Eileen nodded. "That's why I asked."

"Sure. But it means they must have realised their mistakes, because they lied about it at the debriefing."

"They wouldn't have to lie. If they believed they saw Red Wraith, they'd report it just the way they believed it."

"But your scenario isn't what they reported. Talley reported meeting Red Wraith head-on, and Bellman reported closing on it from behind. If they shot at each other, they'd see each other head-on. There isn't room for confusion here. The front view of an aircraft doesn't have a tailpipe with exhaust gases burning inside. The tail view does. If Talley and Bellman shot at each other, they'd have to lie at the briefing. They'd have to tell stories which supported each other." Sandra Thorndike shook her head. "Can you honestly – can you *honestly* – see those two doing anything at all to help each other out?"

Eileen drew a ring around her Red Wraith that was or

wasn't there. She couldn't imagine Talley and Bellman making any kind of allies.

"Besides," Pinkett said, "Romulus called an aircraft on their tail. They called it twice. Something was there."

On her cramped little sketch, the ring around Red Wraith included the symbol for Romulus. The big diagram on the chalk board was clearer: the last position of Romulus was up high, and the Red Wraith had moved forward under that last position and just out ahead to where Talley ran into it. With the altitude figures, on the chalk board you could see the separation. On her tiny sketch, figures entangled and Red Wraith and Romulus merged. "What would they have done once they saw a threat coming in behind them? Romulus, I mean."

"We don't know what they started to do," Pinkett said. "They didn't come back to tell us."

"I'd have switched off the ECM – the jamming – and dived," Thorndike said. "They saw an aircraft low on their tail, and assumed it was a Red Wraith because the hunters would be up ahead by then. Their ECM was acting like a beacon, and their position higher than the Red Wraith put them in an ideal line-up for it to attack, most likely with a missile homing on their ECM noise, or on the heat of their tailpipe. Maybe they intended to sit it out, letting the Red Wraith trail in on them while the hunters got around behind and took the Red Wraith. But I wouldn't have felt happy about that. An F-111 can't protect itself the way an F-15 can. I'd have switched off my ECM so he couldn't see me that way, then dived to get down out of the sky where I was a sitting duck. Ask Talley what they should have done. He knows the training they go through."

Eileen nodded. She simply didn't have the expertise. She couldn't go on asking questions about air situations without eventually making a fool of herself. With a little intelligence she might be able to compare different assessments, but she couldn't provide those assessments herself.

"We have to go." Pinkett started moving towards the door. "We have those reports."

"Sure." Eileen closed her notebook. "Just one last question. At the party last Friday, you left with Erin Heller. Would you mind telling me *where* you went?"

Dwight Pinkett lost any trace of friendliness again. "Her place. I stayed the whole night. If it's the Iris sabotage you're thinking of, Erin and I have an alibi."

"I'm just trying to chip away at the list and remove everyone I can." Eileen turned to Sandra Thorndike. "How about you and Talley?"

Thorndike hesitated. She tried to look away, but Pinkett was waiting and she didn't want to look at him either. "Talley didn't do any sabotage. Not that night. Not any night, okay? Look, can I talk with you some other time about that?"

"Sure." Eileen shrugged. "No problem." So, she thought, something happened between the two of them that night – a tumble in bed, a fight, a sob-sister conversation. Something occurred after Talley wrecked his wife's car. Two more names provisionally off the Friday night list.

Thorndike and Pinkett left. Eileen stared at the diagram on the chalk board. Who said it wasn't a Red Wraith Pinkett saw exploding, while Romulus went down unseen – hit by the Red Wraith, or sabotage, or just a straightforward accident? Who said there really was a Red Wraith? Who said Bellman or any one of them really flew around the way they claimed? She could check up on things like the whereabouts of pilots during a snowy Mondrum night after a late party. But who could tell her where their aircraft really were at the critical moment when Beamish and Baker died?

Charlie Rodeck had left her a note. Almost no people from Special Team had been together anywhere but Mondrum in the last five years. The exceptions were Sellert and Bellman at Kirtland, and Talley and Baker at Upper Heyford more than two years ago. So out the window went one approach to divining personal grudges.

Eileen sat at her desk and worried about how to get another rational handle on the problem. The only starting point was the deliberate damage done to the Iris system: wild notions about any possible sabotaging of Romulus were useless, unless someone could tell her what that sabotage was supposed to be. At nine thirty her mind finally refused to fight it any more. Go home, she thought, get something to eat, then get some sleep. She'd gotten as far as her feet when a solution to a different problem presented itself. She picked up the phone and called operations.

Major Susan Wizer was working late. An aircraft had gone down into the sea, so the Air Force required a full report on the mission it was flying. General Famula required duplicate details because of the grave diplomatic implications – and Lutwidge wanted a record of the facts that should bear him out. So Wizer had been working through the mission log since the mission itself came home. She hadn't slept, she said, for forty hours.

The endless details in the written draft of the report weren't what Eileen wanted. So Wizer led the way to the booth overlooking the main floor of the control center. The booth had been set aside for Special Team's requirements: no one else would be there.

They sat side by side at the desk in front of the window, and Wizer played her the tape of the radar plot on one of the inset TV screens. What Eileen wanted to see was the sequence from the first threat call by Romulus to the point where the surviving aircraft started to search the water with their own radars. What she wanted to know was the timing of each separate event.

The radar plot was a recording of the view obtained by the Awacs aircraft which had been on station halfway to Iceland. The plot began with the relevant area blanked out by interference. Thirty seconds in, the obscuration suddenly gave way to a speckled snowstorm. It cleared after another fifteen seconds to reveal contacts with altitude numbers and firm identifications as F-15s. The delay between the interference ending and the picture clearing was because the computers on board the Awacs needed time to recover from the saturation jamming. By then, most of what Eileen wanted to see had already happened.

On the screen was a radar repeat of the diagram she'd copied in her notebook – minus extended course arrows, minus the last known position of Romulus, and minus any suspicion of a Red Wraith. All that happened on the rest of the plot was the pilots moving around to start searching the sky and the sea.

Red Wraith wouldn't show on radar, so that omission she could forget. But Romulus was worth a question. "Romulus was flying at sixteen thousand feet, wasn't it? But when the screen clears, there's no Romulus. Could Romulus have had time to dive down so low it was below the horizon as seen from the Awacs, so that's why it isn't on the plot?"

"I doubt it. The Awacs radar could see down to three thousand feet off the water." Wizer swung her chair as she considered the situation. "I don't think there was time for Romulus to lose altitude so fast they'd get too low to be seen. Romulus isn't on the plot when it clears because the aircraft had already blown to pieces."

"So what did Pinkett see?"

"I don't follow."

Eileen tapped the screen over the glowing symbol representing Pinkett's aircraft. "This is Pinkett, just as the plot clears, and you tell me he's right at the top of his climb."

"That's right. He has no vertical and no lateral velocity. He's just starting to pull out of the climb."

"And it's as he's doing that – pulling out – that he sees an explosion. In other words, just as the plot clears. If Romulus had already blown to pieces, what did he see explode?"

Wizer shrugged. "Red Wraith? You know, Lutwidge is probably going to hug you for this. He can use an argument that good."

"If it was Red Wraith – if they're right, and it was Red

Wraith they shot at — why did neither Talley nor Bellman see the explosion? This is Talley here, isn't it?"

"Yes. He's turning out east. He's about halfway through a hard turn. If we run it forward a few seconds, he comes out heading east before he turns again to cross back."

"But if he's just turning out here, it means he's just finished firing his gun at the Red Wraith, doesn't it? And this is exactly the same moment that Pinkett saw the explosion. Wouldn't you think, with a time coincidence so tight, that maybe Talley hit the Red Wraith and Pinkett saw it explode?"

"Lutwidge is going to marry you for this. I guarantee it."

"But why didn't Talley report the explosion? He'd be facing the wrong way, but in pitch darkness he should have noticed the flash. And Bellman's here, about three miles away and flying straight towards it. Why didn't he see it?"

"Cloud? Maybe cloud got in the way. They were at thirteen thousand feet, and some of the cloud tops were higher. Or maybe Pinkett did in fact see Romulus explode. Maybe Romulus switched off the jamming, but was hit a few seconds later by an infrared homing missile — coincidentally at the same time Pinkett came out of his climb and Talley turned away from his gun attack." Susan Wizer shook her head. "Now I'm arguing against a kill on Red Wraith. I'm glad it isn't my problem. In the end they're going to have to go out there and dredge the ocean."

Eileen stared at the stubbornly unhelpful screen. What else could she check? "How about Bellman? He's supposed to have been around five miles in front of Romulus. Then he turned back to take up position here, right where we see him, about three miles behind where Romulus was. He moved back eight miles. Could he do that?"

"When did he turn back?"

"When Romulus made the first call."

"Couldn't be right. An F-15 is fast enough to cover the distance, but he needs time for the turn at each end. If he turned back that late, he'd still be heading due north when the screen clears, not due south."

A liar, Eileen thought. I've found myself a liar. But that was only what she'd expect about Bellman. It didn't tell her what to do with him. "On a slightly different subject – the party last Friday night. You left with Bellman, didn't you?"

Wizer nodded. With the dark booth behind her, in the upward light of the screen, her face looked particularly tired. But her eyes stared steadily back at Eileen.

"Do you mind if I ask what happened next? It's just part of the investigation – just checking on people's movements."

"We went back to my place. For obvious reasons."

"Did he stay the night?"

"No. I don't demand a man should be a star performer, you understand, but I've no time for men who claim to be, but aren't. He was just a mechanic. I like a little feeling. Do you?"

Eileen blinked. "Um – Bellman. What time did he leave? Did he have his car?"

"He had his car. He left a few minutes after two." Wizer's eyes didn't shift, her face didn't change – but something happened as softly as an owl swooping at its prey. "I'm tired, but black and white look really nice together. Is there any point if I invite you back home with me?"

Eileen's hands started to fidget, and didn't stop until she clamped them together. "No." She felt her face folding itself into an embarrassed smile. Life went and threw something new at her she couldn't handle. "Thanks, but – no. I'm not like that."

"Pity." For a moment, Susan Wizer closed her eyes.

27

March 3rd, morning

Kathrin sat across the table, sipping coffee. Clyde processed his way carefully through breakfast. His first attempt to start the day had ended in the toilet. After a pause for his stomach to settle, he began a second and sombre effort, as gloomy as the world outside the kitchen window. Eight thirty and still not properly light, with a miserable drizzle trickling on top of yesterday's shreds of puddled sleet.

Kathrin was staring at morose and windy England beyond the window pane. She should have said she didn't want to be here in the first place, instead of giving in when he told the Air Force his wife would be coming to Mondrum. It would have saved so much resentment. She hated it, and he hated the way his plan had failed. A few weeks away from the kids and the social pressures. He should have realised the kids were the calming influence – or the clamps that kept the lid on things – and that his social pressures were her social pleasures. Always had been.

What did she say about England, after they'd been at Upper Heyford half a year? Little people with little cars and little houses in little towns – like living in *Gulliver's Travels*. She'd approved of the career switch away from fighters to F-111s for a few years. But she'd thought of strategic bombers with Strategic Air Command, stationed

in the continental United States, loaded with prestige, and
perfectly placed for making connections with the right
people — paving the way for major advancements that
would one day take him at least as far as Daddy had
achieved. But he didn't want to be in Daddy's SAC. He
went for F-111s in the tactical attack role, and wound up
in England. He landed himself the highly specialised Raven
assigned to escort missions, as prestigious as you could
get from a pilot's point of view. The training, the mission
preparation, the *flying* was more exciting and involving —
and that was what he wanted.

In the end it paid off. Even Kathrin could see that. In
1986 up came the one and only real mission the Air Force
had gotten a shot at in years, and Kathrin Talley had made
sure it was her Clyde who flew on the team. He came back
to be proclaimed a hero.

But he was a hero sick inside. The golden chance — and
that one split-second mistake. What had been left of the
habitual affection between them was all traded in during
the months that followed, and afterwards there wasn't
enough left to buy their way through the trouble. It curled
and curdled and cursed him inside. It wasn't until New
Year's Day 1987, drunk and halfway to dawn in the new
home at Wright-Patterson — in the States again at last —
that he was finally able to tell her about his heroism, about
the truth, about the MiG, about the mistake. She didn't
believe it. She came back and back at it for weeks, attacking
from every angle with every conceivable and every incon-
ceivable argument. It took a long time before she finally
gave in to his inescapable doubt about what he'd done.

Of course, it kept coming up in conversations with everyone he met, and not wanting to talk about it just branded
him as all the more heroic. No escape, no peace, and no
undisturbed retreat into guilt and sackcloth and ashes. No
cleansing, no purging, nor any kind of punishment to ease
his conscience. Kathrin had never accused him or judged
him, had never permitted him the luxury of rallying to
his own defense. Nowadays she left him entombed in his

personal dungeon, communing with his private torturer. She never once had said a word about it to anyone else at all.

He'd kept the lid on so long, but the pressure had been building all the while. Then came this sudden posting back to England. He'd wanted her with him for the public show of personal success, and in the hope of releasing the tension and giving themselves one last throw at repairing the relationship before it was too late. But she hated being brought back to Lilliput land in its washout winter.

And then came another mistake. He misidentified Thorndike's aircraft and rushed right in like an instinctive killer ace – the backfired assassin of the air seeking that sudden chance to prove his worth to *himself*. He tailed right in on Thorndike's evading machine – an F-15, for Christ's sake, and he didn't register it any more. He wrapped his finger around the trigger and was set to blow her out of the air.

Then up came Baker like a piece of the sunken past suddenly bobbing on the surface. And Jake Baker *knew* and he wanted to *talk* – to Clyde, and then to anyone else in order to exorcise his own little load of misplaced guilt.

And the night before last, Red Wraith finally turned up – and turned the tables by sneaking in behind Romulus instead of the pair of interceptors. Romulus should have switched off its jamming beacon and dived to get away. Red Wraith would have seen the other aircraft light up one after the other in the secondary radar illumination from the distant Awacs, so Red Wraith would have turned aside and slipped away. And meanwhile Clyde was heading directly back, while Romulus had disappeared into electro-magnetic silence and would have traded altitude for speed . . .

"It's getting worse, isn't it, Clyde?"

She put down her cup, silently, on its saucer.

"It's getting worse, Clyde. Every time I think you either have to unwind at last or explode, you wind up even more. You take a sleeping pill every night now. You came back yesterday morning looking worse than I've ever seen. I helped you to bed, and you were asleep before I'd finished getting your shoes off. And then an hour later you were awake. An hour after that you were pouring coffee down yourself to keep us both from seeing how you were drunk with fatigue. You're too *agitated* to rest. Then you come back in the evening, and you won't talk. You put away half a bottle of whisky, and I know you took at least one sleeping pill with the alcohol. This isn't going to do any good at all, Clyde."

She moved the cup, shunting it half an inch across the table.

"Now here you are. You've had one breakfast, lost it all again, and now you're tiptoeing through another. Next you have to go over to Special Team, and how you're going to get away with it I don't know. You've always been an expert at self-control and wearing masks – I've never really been able to see what goes on inside. But this is going to *ruin* you as a pilot. How do you get the barbiturates, Clyde? I didn't realise you had so many. What kind of story do you spin, and how long do you think it can last until people start asking questions?"

She moved the cup again, half of a manicured inch.

"And *why* are you like this? I know Jake Baker used to be a friend, and I know his death has to shake you. I know that for any of you, losing Jake and losing Todd Beamish has to be a shock. But why are you *this* bad, Clyde? Is there any way I can help? Isn't there *something* I can do?"

Hold me, he thought. Touch me. Kiss me on my forehead, with your breath for a moment on my hair. Kiss me – lusciously – on my mouth. Come around the table. Turn my chair. Stand between my legs. Put my hands on the buttons of your blouse. Lean forward. Let me kiss you with my tongue. Make love with me.

But it wouldn't work. They'd learned that by now. With no emotional conduits left open, it was just mechanical dolls. But each knew the person who lived inside the doll, so they couldn't either of them stand making an object, a gratificational puppet, of the other. It didn't work. They couldn't make love. Kye had found that sex still worked with a stranger, where the absence of emotion wasn't in the way. Good luck to Kye. He tried it too, with Thorndike. And blew it. So none of this worked.

"Do you want the car?" he said. "Give me a ride as far as Manhattan, then you take the car for the rest of the day. Get off the base for a while, why not?"

Kathrin shrugged. He watched as she accepted her placement on the safe outside of his mask. He watched her rally for one last little protest. "Isn't there anything I can do?"

"Take the car. This is England. We must be surrounded by neat little towns you could go and see." He tried a smile. "You take the car. I'll be fine."

28

March 3rd, midday

Superman turned his back on the sketch of the fatal encounter that flew through the dusty smears on the chalk board. His number two, Lieutenant Colonel Charles, might still have time to contemplate the past, but Superman was looking to the future. Sandra could see it reflected as points of fire in his can-do eyes.

"The good news, gentlemen, is that Captain Thorndike's aircraft is mission capable as of this morning. Our hunters are back up to operational strength. Captain, have you satisfied yourself the machine is ready to go?"

Sandra nodded. "I spent the morning checking it over with Captain Heller."

"Good." Lutwidge's eyes lingered a moment, as if he was trying to decide whether Sandra herself was fit to fly. The coincidence that it was his female pilot who completed only half the Blind Date missions seemed to confirm something in his view of the world. Then he moved to his genuine boys. "The bad news is that we won't be getting a replacement for Romulus. The Air Force doesn't feel it can afford to lose another EF-111A. That means Dark Shroud is over and we're back to the original concept of Quiet Sky. Well, now we've had some more mission practice, we should be able to run Draw Play with perfection."

"Does that mean," McGee asked, "that Special Team is still in business, and Blind Date stays in the order board?"

"It does." Superman squared up as if he'd won a small war against fate. "We've proved we can do the impossible, gentlemen. We don't stop now. The warriors in the Pentagon are understandably upset that we've lost an aircraft and two good men. Equally understandably, they're not going to retaliate with anything that could risk launching a fullscale war. Hell, not so many years ago the Russians shot down a United States senator on board a Korean Airlines plane, but we didn't declare war on the Soviet Union. We're in the business of defending the Free World, not plunging it into destruction."

A surprise, Sandra thought: a little piece of political peptalk from their all-action Colonel Superman. McGee and Luzzi, the loyal Bitburg Boys, lapped it up. Pinkett had his sceptical look, Bellman wore his regular unimpressibility, Talley just sat like a sack in his chair. The interesting one was Charles. He was their local representative of those desk warriors back home. If he began to look unhappy with anything Lutwidge produced, it would be a sure sign of a split in the little hierarchy of Special Team.

"However," Superman said, "those desk warriors we're working for seem to be career theorists. They don't want to recognise the implications of a secretly operating and

near enough invisible Russian warplane deliberately shooting one of us down. Their theory is that we've spent the
Russians into the ground. Moscow can't afford to build a
stealth – in fact, Moscow is so broke they've surrendered
the Cold War and want to make peace. That means our
theorists won't believe what happened unless they absolutely have to. Instead, they want a stack of reports so they
can bury the issue. But out here, we're realists. We know
we're fighting a very deadly war, every hour of every day
– a contest of probe and counter-probe against an enemy
who has *not* surrendered. And now the Russians have
proved their Red Wraith can do its mission, can penetrate
defended airspace and kill alerted and supported air targets
– and get clean away. The Russians know it and we know
it. The career theorists want some reports about it."

Charles shifted uneasily in his seat.

"At this point the rules of our own little part in the big
game change." Lutwidge moved his gaze along his line of
pilots, looking for commitment, or signs of doubt. He
missed out Sandra, as though the examination of a moment
ago had told him enough. He looked at Talley a long time,
and eventually Talley lifted his head and looked back. The
man's eyes were sore from exhaustion, but they stared
straight at Superman. So Superman nodded. "We know
how dangerous Red Wraith can be. The next move is to
prove he can't get away with it. We want the Russians
thinking twice about what they can do with their secret
weapon. That means we keep flying our Draw Play missions every time the other side puts up a bait. The absolute
minimum we have to do now is find Red Wraith next time
he comes, photograph every last detail of him, and let him
know he's been found and photographed."

Charles nodded his head. Superman was back in line.

"First consideration is self-defense. You shoot without a
pause for thought if Red Wraith gets unpleasant. But we'd
prefer not to shoot the Russian down. That would mean
he might disintegrate in the air, and he'd go down at an
unspecified location over open ocean. The pieces would be

hard to find, and they might not tell us much. Our primary objective remains the intelligence and photographic mission. But what we're going to do, when we find Red Wraith, is box in what is necessarily a less agile aircraft. With six F-15s to take turns using up fuel on air maneuvers, we're going to harry him and harass him. We're going to keep him from turning for home. We're going to stop him flying smooth and straight to conserve his fuel – until he's clean out of fuel and goes peacefully down in the sea. He'll stay in one piece until he hits the water, and we'll know exactly where he's lying on the bottom of the ocean. Then we let the theorists send in the Navy to dredge up the wreckage, and get the greatest intelligence coup of the decade."

Lutwidge looked around at Charles. After due consideration, Charles nodded – he wasn't going to back off publicly from what Superman did with Special Team. But it would be nice to know what Charles had to say when he talked on the line to his chiefs in the Pentagon. It wouldn't do to commit himself to something they didn't necessarily like.

"The operational target," Lutwidge reminded them, "is to obtain maximum possible information on Red Wraith. Obtaining Red Wraith – even in pieces, if we know where those pieces are – is obtaining that maximum possible information. But we also have a couple of targets of our own. First, Red Wraith killed Todd Beamish and Jake Baker. We want to do it to the guys who did that to us. If we can, we're going to fly them slap into the sea. Second, there are people sitting right now in the Pentagon who don't think it was Red Wraith at all." He shook his head, eyes averted at the floor. Those people told him he was wrong, but Superman knew better. It was what a fire-eater met at every turn.

Lutwidge looked up again, with a cynical smile. "They think Beamish and Baker just fell out of the sky, they were so dumb. Or they fell out of the sky because someone here on our ground crew – who in fact have been giving us one hundred percent support — was dumb and fouled up the maintenance. Or even that one of them *deliberately* fixed something on Romulus so it fell out of the air. All of this just coincidentally hit Romulus right at the moment when Red Wraith was sneaking up on the aircraft's tail." Lutwidge shook his head again, shocked at the stupidity of those desk warrior theorists. "There are even some people in the Pentagon who figure there never was any Red Wraith. The Russians are the good guys. We're all idiots. You didn't know what you were doing. Clyde Talley and Craig Bellman are either incompetents or head cases or just plain liars."

He paused. He didn't check on Charles. The intelligence officer, maybe, was too closely associated with the critics.

"That's what it comes down to, gentlemen. That's what a bunch of theorists are saying. After all, what do we know? All *we* can do is get in real aircraft and fly them for real in the most demanding kind of real conditions. So we wouldn't be expected to have the faintest idea what we were doing when one of our aircraft went down. But get out there and get Red Wraith — get pictures, or better still get a piece of him — and that's going to show them what's *really* going on. That's going to show them Moscow is still making war, Red Wraith is real — and we're the guys who're good enough to handle him."

Eileen Ware wore a rain cape and waited by the door. Lurking in the spur of corridor leading to the entrance, wearing an olive cape and Air Force soldier's camouflage drab, she was staging an ambush — or was ready to run from any sudden appearance of Lutwidge. Action Man wouldn't want to see her. She was a symbol saying sabotage and slip-up and suggesting he was wrong.

Unfortunately the cape was dripping on the floor, and soon the spreading pool would give her away. She could wipe some of the water off the cape by leaning against the wall, but the grime of decades might smear on the wet fabric.

Shoes walked along the corridor. Talley, fastening his coat, came around the corner. It had to be Talley who came out first, since he seemed to have least to say to anyone. Ambush perfectly placed, and unobserved. With the width of the cape spreading out from her shoulders, she had no trouble getting in his way.

"Breaking for lunch, major?"

"Yes." He tried to get past without having to look at her.

"I was just over talking to Erin Heller. Routine stuff, checking on people's movements last Friday night. I couldn't help noticing you don't have your car here. Can I give you a ride back to the center? On foot you'll get awful wet."

He gave in. The price of the ride would be questions, but she had the right to ask questions anyhow. The ride was a sweetener to give a face-saving semblance of trade.

They walked across the puddles on the apron. At the car, she put him in the passenger seat and then shook some of the water off her rain cape and threw it in the back. She got in the Sierra beside him and started the motor. They left Special Team before anyone else came out of the crew building. Neat. She didn't want a certain person seeing her have private talks with Talley.

They cruised between hangars and the wipers worked louder than the motor. No point in even expecting to be in a hurry when the midday traffic began. "Is the center okay, or should I drive you home? It's no trouble either way."

"Center's okay."

Before they reached Manhattan the windows started to steam up from damp clothes and a wet cape. She turned on the demister and the fan. The car got louder and Talley stayed silent. At Manhattan she had to wait for a gap in the traffic. Looking left from the rightside, wrong side British seat at the trucks rolling up, she was looking past her passenger's face. He was washed out and worn thin. He showed the results of sleep-disrupting mission demands, a marriage in a mess and the death of a friend. Didn't Lutwidge take any notice at all of the mental state of his pilots? Maybe Action Man just liked to have them strung up tight.

A gap came by and she turned out on Manhattan. The gap put her behind a ten-wheel truck grinding along slowly but kicking up cartwheels of spray. She put the wipers on double speed. Traffic and rain and noise and condensation – enough going on without juggling fancy questions. "This one might be indiscreet, for which I apologise. Can you confirm that you drove Thorndike directly back to her apartment after the party last Friday?"

"You know I did. I wrecked the car."

"I just want to confirm there were no detours along the way."

"I tied up the car. The MP patrol took it away from me. I walked Thorndike to her apartment, then I walked all the way home. Okay?"

Let him get angry. If he didn't want her intruding in whatever he and Thorndike might have been up to, he shouldn't have made such an exhibition of himself with the car. On the other hand, it helped her a lot. She knew when the two of them left the officers' club, and the MP's log told her when he parked his car in a fence at the junction on Yokohama. There was no way they could have made a detour as far as Special Team. Checking that alibi with the people on the suspects list was just a security woman's reflex.

They came to the big intersection with Gateway Boulevard. She wanted to go left on Gateway, and so did the truck in front. In the little wait for the traffic, with its tire spray subsided, Eileen saw the truck had Alconbury plates. It was heading home where she should be – except there'd been a shortage of trivial assignments at Alconbury at the same time as a spare place turned up at Mondrum. Well, the trivial assignment had turned into a serious problem, and in a few hours it was going to land her in a little crisis. The pieces of the puzzle were falling together, like it or not. Pity it couldn't be someone else who had to show people the finished picture.

The truck hauled itself around the curve and rolled away through the rain on Gateway. She followed across Manhattan's traffic, and caught up with the spray behind the truck's tailgate. Time she got the answers from Talley.

"I assume you know I've landed this crazy job of eliminating the Pentagon's idea that Romulus might have been sabotaged. Well, one of the things that could help would be to clarify where exactly Romulus would be when it was shot down. Did they hold the course they were flying, or did they take evasive action."

"When?"

"When they realised an aircraft was closing on their tail. I mean, they'd know it couldn't be friendly, because they'd know where everyone else was supposed to be – up ahead, following the interceptors. I'm told the aircraft they called was low on their tail, in an ideal position to shoot them down. Is it plausible they'd take evasive action?"

"It's plausible." When she glanced around, he was staring away through the condensation on the side window.

"So," she said. "What would they do? Switch off all the jamming noise, then immediately change their position and altitude?"

"Maybe."

"Would that be the right kind of thing to do? I mean, you used to fly that type of F-111."

"Might be. Depends on the situation."

He wasn't going to volunteer an analysis. He wasn't going to cooperate, either because of his own sullen state of mind, or because she was lined up on the side of Special Team's critics. So she'd have to supply the ideas and see what he thought of them. "In the situation they were in, wouldn't the best thing be to dive steeply? That should turn their exhaust pipes pretty much away from an attacker low on their tail, it would get them down out of an exposed position up in the sky, and they'd be able to put on speed so fast they'd gain a good chance of outrunning the attacker.

That's the suggestion I have on good authority. Would you have done that?''

"Maybe."

Why was Talley so hostile? He hadn't been flying Romulus, so no one was examining the appropriateness or otherwise of his actions. It had been Beamish, and Beamish was dead. "The thing is, if Romulus had dived, it still wouldn't have descended fast enough to be out of sight of the Awacs radar once the view cleared, would it? But Romulus isn't there on the plot. That would suggest it blew up before then, wouldn't it? Either on the way down in the dive, or while it was still flying straight and level. If Romulus was hit while flying straight and level, we're back with the idea that Red Wraith hit it with a missile right out, and that the jamming wasn't switched off — it went out when Romulus blew. Right? So, the question is — is that the best analysis? Take the only possible alternative of a hit during the dive. From what's known of where the attacker was, am I right in thinking a hit on Romulus would be least likely while Romulus was diving steeply a mile or two in front of the attacker?"

There was a little thump. Eileen heard it through the wipers and fan and wet-road tire noise. When she turned, Talley had tipped his head back against the head restraint. His eyes were closed.

"I don't like to bother you with thinking about what happened to your friend." The truck in front was slowing for the intersection with Enola Gay Avenue. No indicator, of course. It wanted to go straight ahead on Gateway. "But am I right?"

"Yes." His voice came up from deep inside. "Way out of gun range. Too much angle-off for most heat-seeking missiles. Red Wraith wouldn't use a radar homing missile."

"I know." She made the left across oncoming traffic and into the end of Enola Gay. "Its guidance radar would give it clean away." Without a wall of spray from any truck, she switched the wipers back to half speed again. The noise level in the car went down and the harassment from the busy wipers reduced. "But if they were hit before they had the chance to take evasive action, the question has to be how much warning they had. How far away the attacker might have been when they saw it. So, how much range does the backward-looking infrared scanner on the Raven have? How far can it see?"

Talley's head was upright again. He was wiggling his shoulders to relax them. He'd been terribly tense, from hostility or from personal stress. Now he needed to stretch, but he didn't want her to know. "The fit Romulus carried would see a bright IR source at several miles, in clear conditions against a cold background. With a missile you need all the miles and all the seconds warning you can get. But a missile isn't all that bright, and it comes in at Mach three or more."

"Right. But we're not talking missiles here – at least, not just missiles. We're talking aircraft. How many miles?"

"I guess it could see an aircraft tailpipe at ten miles."

"But that's a tail view. They had an aircraft following low behind them, so they'd see it from in front. How many miles?"

"What you see best in infrared are the warmest parts. Head on, that's inlet turbine blades, nose tip, leading edges of the wings and fin. Maybe five or six miles. Looking downwards you'd lose the turbine blades, but you'd see the parts of the fuselage warmed by the engines inside, as well as the exhaust stream. Again, up to six miles in ideal conditions."

"So, if the aircraft below their tail wasn't right down in the cloud – there was cloud up to thirteen thousand feet, wasn't there?" Ahead she saw the residential blocks coming to an end and shopping starting on the left, administration on the right. Three cars in front, the first pedestrian tried to kill herself crossing the traffic in the rain. Touch of brake, shift down a gear, back on the gas. "If the aircraft wasn't down in the clouds, they could have seen it five or six miles behind them?"

"A regular aircraft. Red Wraith is a stealth aircraft. It

should have configurations and materials to reduce its infrared signature. It would have to be a lot closer."

"So close it could hit them before they could take any kind of evasive action?"

"If the design was good enough."

Eileen nodded. She didn't in fact care where any Red Wraith might have been. She had the information she was after without letting Talley know why she was asking for it. Even Talley might talk now and then, and she didn't want someone else learning what she thought. They were passing the officers' club, with Thunderbolt Drive half a block ahead. "Do you want to get out anywhere special, Major Talley?"

"Here's just fine." He pointed vaguely across the wheel.

She pulled over to the kerb short of Thunderbolt, just opposite the medical center. Sitting on the dangerous side of the car, he had to wait for a gap in the traffic before he could get out, and then came around the front to get to the kerb. He waved thank you at her, without a smile. Must have been the effect of the weather. She drove off again and passed Thunderbolt, going the short distance to security at the beginning of the dog's leg. Checking traffic in the mirror, she saw Talley crossing Enola Gay. He was a hunched up man in a hurry in the rain.

29

March 3rd, evening

Wolford had time to see her at six. By a quarter of six the light was fading outside under solid cloud, so she sent Charlie Rodeck home. She didn't want him to know how nervous she was. This wasn't the least bit like routine criminality and security misdemeanours under Air Force jurisdiction. This was a serious crime.

Eileen arranged the evidence on her desk. Off to the side she put the key piece around which everything else had fallen into place – the Kirtland report Sellert had shoved at her. The other parts of the puzzle were single sheets. That's all it was, cryptic marks and innocent data printed or sketched on bits of paper. Out of it she pretended to divine motive, method and opportunity, and the name of the person who did it. So she had the shakes, a shivering fit coming on as the time ticked towards six o'clock. She stood up and started to pace.

There was the knock on the door, and Wolford came in. "You have something for me, Captain Ware?" He started closing the door at his back. "Progress?"

"Yes sir. I'd like you to look at this." She ushered him across to her desk and maneuvered him around it. "Sit down, sir."

Wolford sat in her chair, a little reluctantly, a man well aware of personal territories. He eyed the array of papers.

Eileen looked at Wolford sitting there, and at herself standing in front of her own desk, and realised she'd put herself at a ridiculous disadvantage. Now *he* could interview *her*. Too late. Get right on with it. "I believe I've figured out the sabotage of the Iris unit. I have the culprit, sir."

Wolford's eyebrows went up. He looked directly at her, which he generally found so difficult to do. "Well then, Captain Ware – let's get to it, eh?" He was pleased. He had no idea how unhappy it would make him. "My wife's expecting me home right now. We planned a private little supper, you know. It's our wedding anniversary. But since this is going to be worth it, I don't mind being a little late." He smiled at her, then looked again at the sheets of paper on the desk.

His wedding anniversary, with his wife putting on a special supper at home. Why – oh *why* – did that have to be? Nothing to do but get on. "The ideal time to conduct sabotage would be during the night, when there was no mission in progress nor any maintenance overrun, so no one would be about. There'd be the risk of a patrol passing by, but if the perpetrator didn't use any more light than a flashlight, and stayed alert for the noise of a motor, that should be a manageable risk. After all, we know the perpetrator must have had a key, since there was no evidence of a forced entry, so getting in and getting out would be quick and would leave no signs. Now, in a hurry and with minimal light – that's the most likely way the saboteur could have a screwdriver slip and punch that little hole in the pod, but never notice. I'm assuming you're familiar with the details of the sabotage itself, sir?"

"I'm familiar with the details."

"Yes sir." She stepped up to the desk and shunted the shortlist in front of him. "The sabotage called for specialist knowledge, plus ease of access through possession of a team area pass key. That cuts the initial list down to this size."

"These people?" Wolford's pleasure had already evaporated. "But these are the *officers* on Special Team."

"That's right, sir. The next step pins down the time when the saboteur would have a guaranteed opportunity to work undisturbed. I'm sure you're aware Colonel Lutwidge is driving a pretty punishing schedule. Up until the occasion when the Iris sabotage affected Thorndike's aircraft, Special Team had flown two fullscale missions plus intensive training flights. Also, they're without any spare aircraft and so need to maintain one hundred percent mission capability, which means they've been working continuously with maintenance overruns — working past midnight and starting again at dawn. In fact, the only night between the second and the third mission — the one when the sabotage came to light — when the saboteur could be *absolutely* confident the team area would be deserted was last Friday night, the night of the party."

"Your list stays crazy, captain. These people were all present at the party, dammit."

"I know, sir. It snowed during the evening, and the snow didn't ease off until after two. I drove McGee, Luzzi and Baker home myself, sir, then headed north along Manhattan. There was an aircraft being rolled across to the workshop areas, so I cut through the service area. I saw a set of tire tracks heading down to Special Team. This was within a few minutes of two thirty. I'm sorry to say I didn't think anything of it, and drove home."

"I'm sorry to say I don't think anything of it, captain. Why would the saboteur drive there in *snow*, for God's sake? Someone clever enough to do the sabotage would be clever enough to know about tire tracks."

"The tire tracks wouldn't matter, sir. A patrol wouldn't think them suspicious, since there's plenty of vehicle traffic during the night. The sabotage certainly wasn't of the kind that would be noticed right away — in fact, without the effect it had on Lolite and the aircraft avionics, it wouldn't have been noticed as a case of sabotage at all. And as soon as people turned up for work the next morning, the saboteur's tire tracks would be totally erased, so there'd be no incriminating evidence. But the use of a car narrows down the list dramatically. I've checked the movements of all those people after they left the party, sir. One way or another everyone has an alibi – except I haven't in fact checked the case of Captain Sellert. I believe he stayed over with Captain Rosen, the MO, but I still have to interview her about that. However, I consider that a formality since Sellert doesn't have a car here at Mondrum. The point is, everyone has an alibi. Except Major Bellman."

David Wolford shook his head. A test pilot, a star in the US Air Force's firmament. He wouldn't be able to accept that. "From what I heard, Bellman left with Major Wizer. You're new at Mondrum, Captain Ware, so you won't know Mondrum people yet. But believe me, Wizer means he had an absolutely classic alibi. No doubt of it."

"He left Wizer's place at a few minutes after two, sir. He was driving. He had time to get across to Special Team so the tracks were there for me to see at two thirty, but there wouldn't have been enough snow still falling to fill them in. The timing is right."

"No. I'm sorry. Nothing points to Bellman that doesn't also point to at least half of the ground crew. They'd know the place would be deserted. This evidence is junk."

"No, sir. It isn't. Have you noticed Bellman's car, sir? It's a BMW, a seven-three-five in fact. It's his own private car, sir – it doesn't carry Kirtland plates, nor any other Air Force lease. I checked this afternoon with the freight depot. He had the car *flown* over from Kirtland, sir. Look." She pushed two more sheets of paper in front of Wolford. "This is a photocopy of the air freight schedule, and this is a price quote. The actual invoice will still be at Kirtland. Bellman owns a top series BMW, and he air-freights it across the Atlantic. How does he do that on a major's salary, even with all the increments he'll be entitled to?"

"So the man has money." Wolford pushed the papers away. The price list turned itself into an aerofoil and skimmed across the desk. He reached out and slapped the paper flat before it went over the edge –

Eileen couldn't stop her own hand in time. She thumped her fist on the back of Wolford's fingers. She managed to cancel some of the force. "Sorry, sir. Sorry."

Wolford retrieved his hand and wiggled its fingers. None of them fell off. The scepticism on his face was directed back at the scattered papers. "So Bellman has more money than you or I will ever see? Maybe he has rich parents. Or a few months back he took a weekend pass and had the win of a lifetime in Las Vegas."

"No, sir. He has a motive. When you think about the sabotage on Iris, the motive is out and out the hardest part. It wasn't sufficiently well targeted to be a personal grudge – except maybe at the Air Force as a whole – and it wasn't intended to be sufficiently damaging to endanger even the mission, never mind the entire operation. Iris was supposed to fail, is all."

"Motive." Wolford was testing his fingers with his other hand.

"Take a look at this, sir." Eileen moved the Kirtland interim report in front of him. "These are the results so far on the Iris and Lolite evaluation program."

Wolford's hands stood still in mid-air. He stared at the title and subtitle on the cover of the report. He looked up at her. "How did you get hold of this? Should you be looking at this? Should *I* be looking at it?"

"Captain Sellert gave it to me yesterday. I guess my questions about Iris were getting up his nose a little. The point is, Bellman is one of the senior pilots on the program. As I understand it, the aim is to evaluate the two systems in competition with each other – and I guess Special Team's requirement has provided an ideal field trial to supplement the program. The results from the program will go to the Pentagon, and then the Air Force and the Navy will decide which system they want. Then they have to go to Congress with the evidence in order to get the money."

"Obviously. It's a procurement evaluation."

"Yes sir. The company that wins the contract stands to make close on a billion dollars over the next decade. The loser writes off the millions spent on the development work. The point is, defense contracting is extremely competitive, especially with the new budget cutbacks. A manufacturer needs every contract he can get. Sometimes things get a little underhand in such circumstances. The temptation is there, and sometimes people fall for it. We have to accept this in view of the scandals that have been coming to light over the past year or so – they're even starting to secure convictions against people. Corruption is a real phenomenon in the defense procurement business."

"I know that – manufacturers, lobbyists, advisers. But we're dealing with sabotage in an operational unit here."

"Only by coincidence." Eileen reached across the desk, rotated the report away from him, and started turning the pages towards the back. She found the start of the summary section and spun the report around again so he could read it. "See this, sir? As the Special Team pilots would tell you themselves, Iris performs consistently and well, whereas the much more ambitious Lolite system repeatedly breaks down for one reason or another." She turned a couple of pages. "The interim conclusions from the pilots on the program. Look at the way they award points for the aspect-by-aspect table. Everyone agrees but Bellman. He rates Iris consistently lower, and reports unexplained and self-correcting failures in flight. He justifies the untypical results on the basis that he's flying closer to the limit than the other pilots, so Iris gets more vibration and gee stresses on his aircraft. It's plausible, too. It fits his image, you might say. But see the way he reports performances for Lolite which the others actually deny it can attain? He's way out of line."

"But that wouldn't mean anything worse than a bias. Wishful thinking. Or better pilot performance."

"I know, sir. But then along comes the deployment of the two systems with Special Team. It provides just about the ultimate test. Once again, Iris does fine and Lolite keeps falling down – until there's a totally unexplained coolant failure on one of the Iris sets. It never would have been explained if he hadn't made that mistake and punched that hole without noticing – if instead he'd been able to sneak around later, and turn the adjustment screws back to the proper setting before the thing was taken entirely apart. It might have been enough to balance Iris down against Lolite to the point where Lolite was no longer beaten. Lolite would have an awful lot of faults, but at least they'd be explicable and amenable to correction. It was very cleverly conceived sabotage. Bellman is the common factor with both the means and the time opportunity. Bellman is the one who did it."

Wolford peered at the pages for a while. He flicked back and looked at the general summary. He turned forward again to the individual pilot assessments. Finally he shrugged. "If Bellman really did it – *why* did he do it?"

"Because that's what the manufacturers of the Lolite system pay him for, sir. That's where he gets the surplus money. I guess he goes and spends it ostentatiously because he's no trained espionage agent or saboteur, industrial or otherwise, and because he's a natural show-off. He just can't hide how rich he is."

Wolford put his elbows on the desk and rested his head in his hands. Eileen waited. She backed off a pace from her desk: there's something inappropriate about staring down on the top of a superior officer's head. Wolford had the beginnings of a bald patch right at his crown. His hat would be upstairs in his office, along with his coat. His car was outside in the deepening dusk. His wife would be waiting at home and beginning to wonder about holding the cooking of that anniversary supper. I'm sorry, Eileen thought. I'm sorry to do this on a Friday evening, and a personal celebration, too. But the pressure to act comes all the way from Washington.

Wolford lifted his head and folded his arms on the desk. "All speculative," he said. "Circumstantial. Doesn't amount to a case to answer. And there sure as hell won't

be any fingerprints that wouldn't have been overlaid by
other people's by the time the sabotaged Iris was fitted to
Thorndike's aircraft." He glanced at his watch, aware of
what had started to happen to his evening. "What would
you need to sew this up, make a case that had to be
answered?"

"Information, sir. Personal data on Bellman. We have to
confirm that he has innocent sources of private wealth,
or eliminate innocent sources. Also records of his recent
movements – at least for the time he's been at Kirtland.
Also his recreational expenditures – what he spent where,
what trips he made. He'd have to inform the base of his
movements so they'd be able to contact him if maybe an
accident happened to one of the other pilots on an evaluation flight. They'd want to get everyone working on the
cause right away, since new equipment was involved. It's
all data that will be on file at Kirtland, or sitting around
in gate and personnel and program office records at Kirtland. We need all of that, sir. I don't have the authority.
You'd have to do it, sir, or persuade someone with enough
pull to do it for us."

Wolford's elbows came off the desk. He sat upright in
the chair and hugged himself. "Captain, do you have the
faintest idea how many people from here to Kirtland and
back – and in Washington – would go up the wall and
clean across the ceiling if we did in fact do that?"

"Yes sir."

"I cannot, on a flimsy suspicion, justify it."

"I know, sir. But there's something else." She stepped
forward and moved two sketches on top of the report in
front of him.

"What's this?"

"This is the air situation as analysed by Special Team.
This one is what the radar plot showed at the moment the
interference cleared. The difference is that the plot doesn't
give any hint of where a Red Wraith might have been, of
course, and it also doesn't show where aircraft had moved
from. It only shows where they were at the beginning of

the time during which their movements were observed and are verifiable."

"So?"

"The analysis shows that Bellman was five miles in front of Romulus, and turned back to take up position three miles behind. We only have his word for that, because he was flying unaccompanied."

"And here he is on the plot." Wolford's finger landed on the symbol she'd labelled as Bellman. "Isn't that the right place? Is that three miles behind?"

"Yes. But in the time from when he said he turned, to the fixed time when he shows up here on the radar – he couldn't have done it, sir. An F-15 can't fly that fast. He's lying about it."

"Lying?"

"He didn't start out in front of Romulus. He should have been out in front at that stage in the mission, but he wasn't. He was three miles behind Romulus's position right as the radar plot cleared, and he must have been there already, or maybe even further back. He couldn't have been in front."

"You're sure of this?"

"I've seen the recording of the plot. It also shows he was three thousand feet below the level Romulus was last known to be flying. Low on Romulus's tail, just like the threat they reported before they were hit. I've checked that the infrared scanner on board Romulus – the one watching the sky behind the aircraft – could expect to see something the size of an F-15 in that position as far away as five miles or more. There was some cloud at Bellman's flight level, so I guess three or four miles is more like it. That's just where Bellman was – low on their tail and three miles out."

"They'd be able to see it was an F-15."

"No sir. They'd only know there was something warm following them. They'd assume it was a Red Wraith."

"Are you saying –" Wolford stopped and stared at the two sketches. The one of the air situation was the tangled little diagram from her notebook. It contained a circle enclosing Romulus and the assumed Red Wraith. She'd drawn a clue for herself by accident. "Are you saying Romulus might in fact have been spooked by seeing Bellman's aircraft behind them?"

"I'm saying it could have happened, yes."

"And why hasn't anyone else noticed this?"

"No one looked, sir. Colonel Lutwidge reckons Bellman's perfect, and that's that. Possibly Colonel Lutwidge is right. For all I know, Bellman was trailing Romulus because he had a hunch Red Wraith would turn up there. If he had the hunch during the mission he wouldn't be able to tell anyone else, because they had to keep radio silence. But there's another possibility."

"What?"

Here goes, she thought. This is the last thing anyone will want to hear. But it's a plausible scenario, so it has to be said. "It was Baker who in fact discovered how Iris was sabotaged, sir. He was helping Sellert check over the equipment. Otherwise the sabotage might have been missed — Sellert had missed it up until then. Without Baker, Bellman might still have had the chance to go back and return the adjustment screws to the correct setting. It's possible Bellman was afraid Baker knew too much. He might have perceived Baker as a threat."

Wolford gaped at her. "Are you trying to suggest — trying to suggest — Bellman *shot down* Romulus?"

"No. I don't know if he did. Or if he would have, or anything like that." But she'd said it. Now it was too late. There was no way to get the notion back out of sight. Persevere, make the point that has to be made — and make sure you don't go down in the case file as actually claiming the unprovable and unthinkable. "The only fact is that he came back with one of his Sidewinder missiles used, and a Sidewinder is perfectly capable of shooting down an aircraft flying at the speed Romulus was making, when launched from three or four miles behind and a little lower. Otherwise it's speculation. There *is* a possible motive. If

Bellman was afraid he risked discovery as a man guilty of sabotage and corruption, he might have acted either out of self-protection or revenge."

"Shot them down?" Wolford shook his head. "*Killed* two men?"

"Murders can happen for ludicrously trivial motives, sir. In this case the motive would be altogether respectable. The sabotage would put Bellman in prison for years, and he'd also lose a fortune in bribes. But I'm really *not* saying that's what actually happened. It's plausible – and I'd prefer it – if a Red Wraith really was there, if it shot down Romulus, and if Bellman in fact fired his missile at the Red Wraith. Bellman might not have felt in the least threatened by Baker. But we have to consider the fuss being made about the consequences if a Russian stealth aircraft really does exist and has shot down one of our planes. The mere possibility of this – of a murder – has to be followed up with the utmost urgency." She paused, thinking: now I sound like I'm telling him what to do. I have to back out of that. "It would be the perfect murder, sir. Instead of having to hide the crime, you pin it on an invisible aircraft from the other side."

Slowly, Wolford nodded. He had to hate the idea – but he had to act on it. The pressure to come up with alternatives for the loss of Romulus was too intense, and the picture framing Bellman as the saboteur was too persuasive to ignore. Bellman was, she knew, the man who did it to Iris. She didn't dare believe he also did it, deliberately, to Beamish and Baker.

"What do you suggest we should do?"

"It's early in the morning at Kirtland, sir. They'll have all day to get on this. Kirtland has to start compiling and sending the data we need right now. They have to do it today, sir – Friday. Tomorrow's the weekend, and some of the people won't be there. It's an emergency investigation we need, sir. It might be an idea to get authorisation from General Famula in the Pentagon, the one who set up Blind Date and who's called this panic investigation. It might be an idea to pull General Dodgson in on this as well, sir." Eileen paused, and Wolford wasn't moving. "Can we get on that right away, sir? It's going to take all night."

30

March 4th, morning

It would make a restful Saturday, still a little cold, but dry, bright and breezy under light cloud. Superman, however, had other plans. Shit was coming his way from the Pentagon, but he was holding himself up under the strain with the force of righteous indignation. There was no way you could feel any sympathy for Superman, but he didn't deserve insinuations of over-active imaginativeness and near-as-dammit incompetence. They'd given him an operation which was as good as impossible – and he'd turned up a Red Wraith after all. So what did they do? They got scared and tried every trick so they didn't have to believe it.

"We're changing the mission configuration," he said. He had his blouse open, his fists on his hips, his hat folded in his right fist. He was the former fighter ace firing up a frontline unit. It was an act he had under perfect control. "We return to Quiet Sky as cover for the Draw Play concept – two interceptors and two pairs of hunters. The interceptors will take the bait and we'll call Quiet Sky, then the hunters will come up from zero altitude, circle the bait wide, then trail in behind the interceptors as they leave the bait. But there are differences. We know Red Wraith is a killer who strikes without provocation, and we've fired back at him once so he'll be twice as aggressive. We're going to have to be twice as careful." He turned to Charles. His smile was grim, like a man who'd started watching his back. "Right, Ernest?"

Ernest Charles nodded. He seemed barely embarrassed. "As Colonel Lutwidge said yesterday, the primary objective is to gather intelligence. But we want to preserve aircrew safety at all costs. There's no denying that opinions currently vary in the Pentagon as to the advisability of continuing this operation, but concern to avoid further losses is common to all views, I can safely say."

He can safely say, Sandra thought. He can safely sit there on his self-preserving fence, while some generals want to risk *our* lives to get follow-up pictures of Red Wraith, some generals don't want us to tangle, and some don't believe there's a Russian stealth airplane anyway. Our intelligence officer, intelligent enough not to go anywhere he might get shot at, intelligently withholds his own opinion. Lutwidge was leading all alone.

Lutwidge obviously knew it. His reputation could be on the line, and he wanted the proof that would protect him. So the fire-eater went for flying more missions. "The interceptors will at all times fly a *close* pair so they can monitor each other's tail and underside zones adequately. As a safety move the interceptors will fly with their lights on. This will also help draw Red Wraith, and should advertise the complete innocence of their intentions. It will look like an absolutely routine intercept mission, not like a follow-up on last time."

Follow-up on last time or not, she thought, Red Wraith won't be there. Not if he wants to stay secret. Whether deliberate murderer or nervous and trigger-happy pilot — spooked, say, when Bellman suddenly dropped in on his tail while he was shadowing Romulus — last time out he had a close call.

"*One* pair of hunters will come up when Quiet Sky is

called, circle the bait, then trail in behind the interceptors to close the Draw Play trap. The *second* pair will stay low when Quiet Sky is called. They will only come up from low level once the interceptors report they have left the bait and are returning. They will close up more slowly, and will remain significantly lower than the interceptors and the first pair of hunters. The second pair are flying safety. Their task is to be in a position to bring them up on the tail of any Red Wraith who by chance has seen the first pair of hunters at the bait, and who thinks he can lock on to them and then get away with anything he likes. That's the modification to the mission. It gives us two pockets in the trap, but the motivation is safety. We don't want Red Wraith making fools of us a second time. And if there's going to be any more shooting, he's the one who's going to get hit. Any questions?"

He didn't want any questions. He gave them his Superman stare with a double charge of kryptonite.

"There'll be position changes," he said. "From now, the two interceptors will be Thorndike and Luzzi."

Bastard, Sandra thought. He *demoted* me. He doesn't think I can cut it, flying the silent hunters and managing to come out in the right place — after the navigation I did to bring me back home the last time I flew! And he doesn't think I can handle a Red Wraith, except by sitting pretty in front of it until help comes along. Male chauvinist bastard.

"The first pair of hunters, with the task of closing the Draw Play trap, will be McGee and Pinkett. McGee will lead."

Sandra watched Dwight Pinkett's face. It must have been a mirror of her own. Pinkett had flown four missions in the hunter role, and McGee none. Pinkett was a maneuver and position specialist, McGee was a good pilot with no additional skills. But Pinkett was black, and McGee was white. At equal rank, black men don't get to go first.

"The second pair of hunters, obviously, will be Bellman and Talley. They have the hardest task. They have to fly safety, and they have to close up their position from a

greater distance with the aim of protecting McGee and
Pinkett, who they won't even see directly and who won't
be reporting where they are. It's the most demanding role,
so that's why our two highest rankers get it."

"Who leads?" Bellman asked.

Superman smiled. "I'll leave that to the two of you."

Bellman grinned at Talley.

Talley stared back.

"Right," Lutwidge said. "That's the new mission configuration. I recommend you start exchanging ideas and
experience on how to fly the positions immediately. We're
back on standby as of this evening. The moon is good for
the next seven nights, giving us total darkness for periods
up to eleven hours. Red Wraith will be coming back. And
we'll be ready."

Talley left and Bellman swaggered right after him: they
didn't say a word to each other. Pinkett obviously decided
to swallow his anger down, and moved over to sit with
McGee: they started a private briefing all of their own right
there and then. Sandra went out into the corridor and
caught up with Donald Luzzi. Ground rules, she thought.
Get them fixed in his head right away.

"Don, let's figure out a survival strategy for if Red
Wraith sneaks up on our tails ahead of the cavalry behind
us."

"Sure." He was four years younger and a rank lower,
he was a little bit taller but a lot less self-assured. Impress
hard facts on him now, and it's going to pay off later.

"You haven't done any Aggressor training, right?"

"No." He fell into step beside her. "I'm due for a spell
with the Five-Twenty-Seventh at Alconbury in the summer.
June, I guess."

"Fine," she said. "That's when I'll probably be there."
They were coming up to the pool of brightness from the
side corridor, where the entrance door let in light through
its glass pane and draught around its edges.

"I guess we'll be training together, then."

"I expect so. I'll be one of your instructors." Sandra looked down the side corridor towards the door. Outside, a bunch of people were approaching, blue uniforms with Eileen Ware's combat dress in the middle. People looking for more acceptable reasons why Romulus went down. People firmly on the sabotage side, to be avoided. She concentrated on Luzzi as they headed towards the locker room. "I did Aggressor training at Nellis. I scored so high they had to make me an instructor. I would have been posted to the Five-Twenty-Seventh *last* summer, but up came this need to develop a training program for eyeballs-only flying against stealthed opponents. My lead experience on that is why I'm here. Okay?"

"Sure," he said.

Craig Bellman came out of the locker room. He let the door bang behind him. To hell with Bellman. "In case you're thinking Red Wraith is going to be easy once we've found him – in case you're thinking he's a stealth aircraft so he won't have the agility or the speed or the acceleration, so you'll have the edge – don't. You won't."

Bellman was starting to pass them, and she was keeping a straight line and letting Luzzi make room. "Stay alert, Don." Bellman said. "Watch your new wingman. If she goes for your balls, it's only because she wants them as worry beads."

She kept straight on and tried to pretend Bellman hadn't even existed. "Don't underestimate the problem involved in a night-time tangle with an aircraft you can *only* see with the unaided eye and *only* while you keep at spitting distance. One blink and you've lost him. But there is no way at all you can know whether he's also lost you. And if he hasn't –" Sandra put her hand out and pushed open the locker room door. "Next thing you know you might be dead."

"I guess it won't be easy." As they went into the room Luzzi caught the door, then let it swing peacefully closed.

"It won't. In fact it's so difficult, so incredibly fucking difficult, that *all* of us on the program – not just our guinea

pig trainees – tried to cheat out of pure frustration. In the
end they had to remove the cables that powered our radars
so we couldn't sneak a few seconds seeing each other the
easy way. Doing that was just learning how to kill ourselves. The radar would never have seen a real stealth
opponent, but it would light you up for him to shoot at."

Talley came out of the toilet and turned to the bowl to
wash his hands. No routine moment of eye contact. No
anything from him any more. Talley and Bellman flying a
pair would be the ultimate disaster. Lutwidge couldn't have
gotten it any better.

"You understand what I'm saying, Don? When it comes
to the crunch, you're going to do anything I tell you –
exactly that, and nothing more nor nothing less – if you
want to survive. If I'm no longer in a position to tell you
– *then* you get to make up your own mind. Understand?"

Luzzi understood. Sandra was surprised, when she
looked at his face, to see just how much she'd impressed
him.

And then people started shouting in the corridor.

Charles was waiting by the door to the CO's office. Pinkett
and McGee had moved up behind him to take a look. Right
down at the other end, more of Special Team emerged
from the locker room. In the middle of the corridor stood
Lutwidge. He was rocking with fury and getting ready to
commit murder. It wasn't fair, because it was Eileen he
was going to kill.

Wolford was unarmed. Even Villers was unarmed. The
two MPs had pistols and clubs slung from their belts. They
wouldn't be needing their weapons. They stood each side
of their man, and he wasn't going to make any trouble.
Bellman was quivering, but he didn't intend to fight or run.

Eileen wanted to run. It was the way Lutwidge's hands
were flexing before he finally reached for her throat.

Then Wolford, awkward and contact shy Wolford,
amazed her. He reached out and grabbed Lutwidge by the
arm. "Easy, colonel." He hung on while Lutwidge tried to

shake him free. "Take it easy, now. General Dodgson doesn't just expect, he *requires* that you call him at his office right away. The arrest order has been issued here at Mondrum. General Dodgson has countersigned it himself. And this regrettable – this *deeply* regrettable course of action – has the approval of General Famula in the Pentagon. There's no sense in protesting or making a scene."

Lutwidge swung his free hand up with a finger aimed at her, like an old recruitment poster. And it was blood he wanted. Eileen's name was on the arrest order as investigating officer. "You put this *crap* together, Ware! You're off my team! Don't let me ever see you here again!"

"At the latest since September of last year," Wolford said, "Bellman has been in receipt of illegal payments by the Datadyne Avionics corporation. He is suspected of falsifying data on the evaluation program currently running at Kirtland AFB. He is suspected of being responsible for the sabotage of an Iris system here at Special Team. He will be the subject of a further enquiry into the possibility that he was directly involved –" Wolford balked at uttering the unthinkable charge. He swallowed, then tried again. "Directly involved in the deaths of Lieutenant Colonel Beamish and Captain Baker, and the loss of their aircraft."

Lutwidge stalled with his mouth wide open. That last one got him cold. He managed to swivel his eyes around to Wolford.

"It's a horrible business," Wolford said. "I know. It's a horrible business."

Lutwidge got his mouth to close. "Dodgson," he said. Then he turned on his heel. Wolford went after him, Charles backed away in front of him. All three disappeared into Lutwidge's office, and the door slammed.

Major Villers stepped into the breach. "Major Craig James Bellman, it is my duty to inform you that you will be placed under close arrest pending removal to the United

States. You will be denied all mobility on the base, and you will be under guard at all times. Are you prepared to accompany me in a peaceful and civilised manner, or will you oblige me to employ restraint?" He already had one hand in the pocket where he was holding the handcuffs. Robert Villers was a keen security officer.

"Forget it," Bellman said, and took his first step under detention. The MPs moved with him as if they were wired to his flanks.

Then he stopped, and the MPs stopped, just as Eileen was moving aside. One of them started to take hold of his arm. He'd sucked his cheeks in hollow, and his head tipped back –

She barely closed her eyes in time. Saliva slapped in her face.

"Stinking nigger bitch!"

She'd barely closed her eyes in time. The saliva hit in the corner of her left eye. It felt as though some was shut inside the lid. She kept her eyes clamped tight. A slither of cooling fluid slid down the side of her nose, around the crease of her nostril, onto her upper lip. It trickled over the edge. She pressed her lips together. Sickeningly, his saliva ran sideways between her lips and out at the corner. Her whole face felt filthied. The venom from his mouth sought to seep inside her own. She didn't dare to move her lips or unclamp her jaw for fear it might succeed. She stood in a darkness coloured pink with sick disgust.

Something was pushed into her hand. A tissue. She crumpled it together and then scoured away at her lips. Air got in, cold – as if it was cold saliva. She opened her right eye and blinked with it at the corridor.

They'd gone. They left her there, unwanted, shunned as the agency of everyone's disgrace. They'd all gone except Thorndike.

Sandra Thorndike took away the wet tissue and offered a fresh one. Eileen worked at her left eye until it felt dry enough to open. She wiped her nose and her cheek while the corridor went back out of focus. Her eyes were turning hot, goddam it. The stickiness left by the cold fluid was filth, poison, disease.

Sandra Thorndike took her by the arm and pulled her all the way along the corridor and inside the locker room. Sandra Thorndike stood her in front of the washbowl and turned the tap. Cold water splashed and gurgled in the bowl. In the chipped-silver mirror, a shadowy reflection with a quivering face blinked back at her. Captain Eileen Ware, sharpest sleuth in Uncle Sam's Air Force, gets ready to cry.

She threw water up in her face. She rubbed and rinsed her skin. She scooped water to her mouth, sucked it in, rolled it around, and spat it out. Slowly the white man's insult washed away. In the process, her eyes cooled down again. Gradually the water from the tap added up to sufficient substitute tears.

Thorndike had a towel for her. It felt dry, it smelled fresh. When her own face emerged over the top of the towel in the mirror, it belonged to a woman who'd regained her self-control.

Thorndike was leaning against her locker, the one with the defaced name. Bellman's bile etched everything.

"Well," Thorndike said. "Guess that good and fixes our favourite test pilot. Did *you* put all of that together?"

Eileen nodded.

"Neat. So what's all this about him being involved in the loss of Romulus?"

"That just emerged." She got on with drying her hands. "From the circumstances. From the fact that he lied about his position at the time Romulus spotted something on their tail. He must have been several miles behind them all the while."

"Oh," Thorndike said, and nodded slowly. "I guess I should have figured that out. He did that once before. At least once. Coming in last, he let the rest of us make the mistakes and then let himself look real clever. So what's he supposed to have done to Romulus?"

"Nothing. I mean, I hope it was a Red Wraith. I hope

he just happened to be in the wrong position, and was even too far back to see the Red Wraith in time before it shot down Romulus. He'd have to lie about making a total mess like that." Eileen started moving around the locker room's bench in order to return the towel. "I don't feel very comfortable with the idea of murder. The very worst I can think is that Romulus saw Bellman behind them and called it as a threat. Bellman would think a Red Wraith was between him and Romulus, so when he moved up and saw the exhaust pipes of Romulus, he might think it was the Red Wraith about to attack them, and fired his missile. The worst I can think is that if he did kill them, it was an accident." She held out the towel.

Thorndike took the towel and turned to put it in her locker. "Well that's bad enough, believe me. I hate the motherfucker, but I'd have gone for a Red Wraith sneaking up on Romulus, with Bellman blundering in behind the Red Wraith and spooking it so it got scared and shot down Romulus. That would also be bad enough."

"Really I just used the possibility to get Wolford to believe me about Bellman being the saboteur. It got him moving – and then I've never seen so much happen so fast in my life. We had stuff coming in by phone and telex all night. Don't ask me what investigatory powers or organisation they used. It really started to come after our first results from Kirtland got back to Famula. He must have set something in motion. Bellman had been taking weekend passes at Kirtland and going to the Bahamas, to Hawaii – and to this little town near Cincinnati where Datadyne have a subsidiary which in fact *doesn't* make anything to do with Lolite. Then we got his financial details. No rich relatives, no real estate, no share capital – nothing. Just a major's salary with test pilot supplements. But an awful lot of cash going through a couple of accounts. He must be a total amateur. He didn't take the most basic precautions to hide it all."

"You got all of that *overnight*?"

"I guess it went so fast because of Romulus, and the

relevance for the operation. I guess I should get some sleep. I'm really tired."

"You look it." Thorndike took her coat out of the locker and closed the door. "So you nailed Bellman's ass to the floor. And he did the sabotage on behalf of Lolite? That's going to put him in jail a few years. Put the manufacturer in with him, too." She locked the door and pocketed the key. "Since all those questions you were asking have gotten Bellman off my back, I should supply that answer I owe you."

"What answer?"

"About the night of the party. After Talley wrecked his wife's car, he looked so miserable I invited him in. Well, we started making out. Then he lost a little control, you know?"

Eileen shrugged. She didn't want to know. Other people's privacies, the ones they preferred to hide, were usually upsetting little things.

"But I've never seen anything like it. He just collapsed. Broke down. Then — well, I kind of threw him out. I didn't know what to do. I mean, I felt sorry for him. I still do. His head's all in a mess. It's as though he doesn't believe in himself any more. He can't cope with emotional pressures, his marriage is a wreck, his wife is cheating on him. She even stayed away overnight while he was on a mission, would you believe that? So I invited him in and tried to do my little helper act. But then it went slightly wrong — and it was like watching him tip over the edge of a cliff or something." She turned her coat and started to pull it on. "But I guess it doesn't matter any more."

Eileen shook her head. Sleep mattered, and then the huge amount of evidence she was going to have to prepare.

Sandra Thorndike tugged her coat up on her shoulders. "Oh well. Talley's life is falling apart. Everyone believes I'm a lesbian. Bellman's in the worst kind of a mess. Lutwidge has lost the apple of his probably repressed homosexual eye. Two guys are dead. There's no Red Wraith. The operation is wrecked. And you are the most unfavour-

ite flavour of the week around here. Oh well, that's the
way it goes. You win a couple, you lose plenty, and the
rest you can just about hold to a draw. Ain't life a scream?"

Clyde Talley got home to find Kathrin wasn't there, nor
the car. He just couldn't believe it – Bellman *arrested* for
sabotaging Iris, for faking test results. And incredibly, they
thought Bellman did it, they thought he shot down Romulus! The upsurge of relief was like a fountain wanting to
burst out in smiles, giggles, gales of hysterical laughter.

No way. Self-control. You got across the chasm and
you're back on solid ground. You're safe. Any more missions are off. Blind Date is over. The impossible doesn't
have to happen any more. Unsustainable perfection no
longer has to clash head on with an unperformable task.
You got away with it. You survived. You got through to
the end!

The stress emptied like a parachute landing in a windless
field and caving in on itself before enveloping its passenger.
It settled over his head and shoulders and wove him softly
with silk to the floor. Without its translucent protection,
the swirl of unleashed tension would have spun him into
pieces.

By noon he had an appetite for the first time in days, he
was shaking with excitement, and the parachute had let go
of him at the top of a lightless shaft that went down for
ever. He had to eat, and then sleep. Otherwise he'd dance
around the house until he dropped. He took a barbiturate.
He fixed a mishmash lunch and was halfway down a cup
of coffee before he realised coffee was dumb. He looked
for beer in the fridge but there wasn't any. So he took a
cue from his ecstatic mood and filled a tumbler with whisky
instead. Then to seal the lid on sleep, he took a second pill.

With the curtains drawn, he crawled into bed. He shut
his eyes and slid on swooping waves between the luxurious
sheets. Breakers of personal night curled up and flooded
over him with a bubbling surf of exhaustion. And riding
in the shadow in front of each breaker was an aircraft, tiny

in black, heading right his way. Sometimes it was Red Wraith, sometimes it was a MiG-23, but every other single time it wasn't either of those. It wasn't, it hadn't been, and it never would be.

PART 6

Blind Date

31

March 4th, 1900 hours

First it was a voice. The voice was Kye's and started kind. Then it turned insistent, it turned harsh, it turned into Kathrin come to torment him. A warm glow was seeping through his eyelids from the lamp on the bedside table. It was a close and cosy cocoon, like a subsiding fever without pain.

Then the room light came on like lightning, and he blinked.

"It's almost seven, Clyde. Time to get up. You're wanted."

"Wanted?" He wanted to find himself. He was still in there somewhere, where the sleep had been.

"They want you. It's seven in the evening." She loomed beside the bed. Under the sloping ceiling at the end of the room, she had to stoop a little, the better to study him. "My God, you look terrible. Are you that tired, or are you ill?"

The whisky, he thought. And the thought dropped out of sight into the dry vacuum inside his skull. With lunch, a glass full almost to the brim. And two quinalbarbitone. "I guess I took a sleeping pill."

"A *sleeping* pill? But you just had a call from Charles. A possible Red Wraith configuration is starting to show. You're going on mission readiness."

"What?" It tugged him from his private darkness and out towards the light. "No. That can't be."

"I'll say. You can't fly if you took a sleeping pill."

"No. It can't be that Lutwidge intends to fly a mission."
He started to roll on his side, and the bed tipped over like
something slung on gimbals. "We lost another pilot."

"What?"

"Bellman. He was arrested this morning." Wedged on
his side, he waited while the seesaw spin of the bed stilled
itself. "He's been working for Datadyne. Fixing results on
the Kirtland program. He fixed Iris so it failed. And the
best of it is, they think he shot down Baker and Beamish."

"*What?*"

"They think *he* might have done it. If it wasn't Red
Wraith, that is." He smiled at the bright lamp on his bedside table, and it smiled happily back at him. "No chance
they'll ever think it was me who did it."

"Clyde? You're talking nonsense."

Wish I was, he thought. Wish I was. Didn't even realise
until halfway home, an hour after we knew Jake Baker and
Todd Beamish were dead and the sea search was going to
be a waste of time, because the beacon on their escape
capsule wasn't to be heard. Didn't even realise until then.
I *saw* the explosion. Saw the flash light up my bowframe
and the clouds outside. Thought I'd killed the Red Wraith
that must have killed them. Being a fool is so easy.

"Clyde? What are you smiling at?"

Only one thing they could have done, when you had a
few spare minutes to think it through. Nose hard down and
dive. That turned your tailpipes away from any oncoming
missile, and made you a target crossing transversely
through the attacker's sights – the hardest kind of target
to hit. Going transverse down the vertical plane didn't
make much difference – a crossing target is a crossing
target – except that a dive helped you pile on speed. *Speed*
made you hard to hit, and speed meant that when you
came out of that dive, you could run like hell. All you had
to remember was to switch off your entire jamming suite,
so you didn't light your own progress with a brilliant
beacon of radio noise. Obvious. Even Ware, the down on

the ground security woman, figured it out. But she had a couple of days to do it. She had the advantage of time.

"Clyde, this is impossible. I don't think you can fly in this state."

Impossible, she said. The lamp smiled happily back. It knew better. It couldn't go poking its light around inside his sleeping eyelids without knowing a thought or two. Ware knew it, but she'd tipped the wrong guy. Why? Easy, when your mind was working well. If Bellman did the little job on Iris, and if Jake helped find out how it was done, Bellman had a reason to take advantage of a sudden situation. Or alternatively, if Bellman could make a mess of sabotaging Iris, he could shoot at the wrong thing in a crisis, couldn't he? Not like Clyde Talley. Good old Talley Boy was the fired up, right-shooting, medal-wearing real live hero who always hit his man.

Always hit his man.

"You have to report sick or something. If Lutwidge actually calls a mission tonight – what are you going to do?"

Get up on my elbow, he thought. So up he went – and the ceiling, for a moment, sloped every available way. So did the bed. Be smooth, be easy, and wait while the world settled down. Good old Talley Boy had figured it, too, by the time he was halfway home from the kill. An hour is long enough for the truth to surface, if you're the topmost pilot in the entire goddam Air Force. Pity he couldn't have figured it in those two or three seconds that mattered, when he came out of that itsy bit of cloud and saw an infrared smudge of something flying right at him – exactly where Red Wraith would have been. If Red Wraith had been there. If Red Wraith even existed at all.

She reached down and shook the shoulder he'd raised. "Clyde, you *can't* fly a mission like this. You'd kill yourself."

Not me. I wouldn't kill me. Just friends. Just like Libya, just like I nearly did to Thorndike. Good old Killer Clyde. Why didn't Beamish go all the way into the cloud, instead of levelling after diving just three thousand feet? Because he was so close to the cloud he could dip into it easy if danger threatened again, but if he stayed above it he could still see backwards and try to keep track of what the Red Wraith on his tail was doing. Because he was working for the mission, and the mission was to find and trap Red Wraith.

Jake had called an aircraft down behind, and they knew who it had to be. They wouldn't know it was Bellman, yellow-bellied Bellman hanging back from the heat. Bellman spooked them, they turned off the jamming and dived, they levelled out — and had Killer Clyde coming right at them. Clyde Talley, who knew the jamming was out and thought it was the two of them blowing up when the Red Wraith they'd called actually hit them. Clyde Talley, who wanted the Red Wraith so he could believe in himself again. Who only had a second or so to react, who thought he knew the situation, but who was guessing on the basis of wrong information which they themselves had given him.

Clyde Talley, who blew them and his hopes clean away.

Except for two little lingering orphans bereft of belief. It might have been Bellman who hit them with his missile, while all of his own shells missed. Bellman wouldn't say. He'd be intelligent enough to realise what he'd done, he wouldn't go swaggering into the limelight to claim his kill. But the timing was too tight for it to have been Bellman. So the only alternative left was Red Wraith.

"Clyde — what are you going to do? *Clyde?*"

"Fly the mission." He pushed his free hand back until it managed to find the sheet. "I'll be fine."

"Fine? My God — *look* at yourself!"

"I'll be fine. Help me. Get me some *coffee.*" With one elbow and one hand on the sheet, he started to lever himself upright. So long as he took it slow, the gyroscope whirling in his head wouldn't tumble. "I took the pills hours ago. Hours. By the time I get over to the briefing I'll be fine. I'm just goddam *tired*, is all."

She hesitated. She hovered. She wasted seconds while she dithered. "I don't think you should —"

"Help me." He hauled himself into a sitting position and hung in there. He nodded past her towards the door to the stairs. "Kye, please? Fix me some coffee."

She had to go with the inevitable flow. He couldn't call in sick, and she knew it. This wasn't school. It was flying against a real enemy. "Okay. Coffee. And eggs. What would you like with your eggs? Ham?"

"Yes. And some bread. My stomach's kind of uneasy."

"Right." She was backing towards the door. "A plate heaped with ham and eggs." She got to the door. "In exactly ten minutes. The briefing is in thirty minutes. I'll drive you over. That should help you a little. I'll leave the car for you there. I'll walk home. It's miles, but it won't hurt me. Okay?"

He nodded at her. "Thanks, Kye. Ware's no longer available to ferry us, anyway."

"Good. We don't want Ware poking her nose in our business." Kathrin disappeared through the door and hurried down the stairs.

He kicked off the covers and went over the foot of the bed. It was supposed to be smooth and quick and graceful. He felt himself tumbling like someone seriously drunk, and rolling *so* softly on his back on the carpet. He pulled and he pushed and came up on hands and knees, at the focus of a room doing a sedate rotation through two directions, like a slow-motion two-axis tail spin during an advanced flying lesson. The task was to correct the spin with both hands on the chest of drawers. He did it perfectly, and got the room to come out straight and level.

With enough motive, you can do anything. Even fly a mission that drains senses and muscles and psychology in endless pitch darkness, even with alcohol and barbiturate in your blood.

Because he had to help them find a real Red Wraith. This might be the final chance, Lutwidge's last throw before the people in the Pentagon digested the mess with Bellman and cancelled the operation. He had to go along on the mission and maximise the prospect of success. He *needed* Red

Wraith. If they found Red Wraith was real, then the possibility became equally real that Bellman hadn't spooked Romulus. He could believe it had been Red Wraith after all. He could *know* it. And that would mean Baker and Beamish were killed by the Russian – and it was the Russian aircraft he hit.

In the back corner of the bottom drawer were the tablets. Snapping the lids off the containers, he spilled the things and had tablets all over the drawer under his clothes. He scooped them together with clumsy fingers, half out of sight and half in his shadow, grabbed a little handful –

Kathrin's footsteps again on the stairs. Naked, he had no pockets. He pushed the drawer closed. He went up and over like a diver leaving water, got himself upright at the closet door, got the door open so he could lean on it. He pushed his fist in the pocket of his uniform blouse, opened his fingers, and let the tablets trickle to the bottom. He was going to need the amphetamines, but if Kathrin realised –

"Clyde?" There was something ice cold about her voice as she came up the stairs. "What did you mean – there's no chance they'll think it was you?"

32

March 4th, evening

Eileen Ware had managed no more than three hours of sleep. Out on Starfighter Drive West, she was too close to the end of the runways. Too many aircraft were thundering around all day and screaming up and down in the sky. Once she woke up, she stayed that way.

But once she was awake, she couldn't rest. The magnitude of what she'd precipitated caught up with her. She should go to the office, where a mountain of urgent reports and evidence summaries was waiting. That would keep her from worrying about what she'd done. Except that she didn't want to go to the office. People would still be busy sorting out all the consequences, Wolford would be searching for someone to replace her at Special Team – unless he'd already given the job to Villers. Probably he'd transfer Charlie Rodeck to Villers, too, so she wouldn't even have an assistant to help with the reports. Eileen didn't want to go back to the office. She'd go tomorrow: on a Sunday there'd be no one about to point at the freak who'd fingered a test pilot for sabotage.

But while she sat around at home, all she could do was go over the chain of reasoning again and again. It made sense, but the loose ends bothered her. Those missing little pieces had to be put in place for the reports. Tying them up would be a blessing for her peace of mind.

By eight Eileen was getting ready to leave. At the officers' club she was sure to track down someone she could ask about some of those final details. And it would get her out of the apartment's single room for a while. So go to it.

She was most of the way to the club. She was heading south out of the dog's leg on Enola Gay. The medical center, with its lights still burning, was coming up on the righthand side. She pulled in at the kerb. She ignored the parking restriction.

Captain Jessica Rosen had drawn the short straw for the Saturday night surgery this week. The last patient had left, the nurse was tidying the waiting area, and Rosen was clearing the top of her desk. Bull's-eye.

"You're lucky you caught me." Rosen finished straightening her hat in the consulting room mirror. "Saturday night's a bummer. The customers seem to think there's no hurry to get here, since tomorrow's Sunday anyway. They just trickle in as late as they like. But we don't usually get as many stragglers as we had tonight." She unhitched her coat from the hook beside the door. "I assume it's something to do with the arrest this morning?"

Eileen nodded. News, of course, travelled fast. "Just some loose ends about people's movements on the night the sabotage was done. I need to fill in a few gaps."

"Confirming alibis?" Rosen started pulling on her coat. "On the night of the party, Roy Sellert came home with me." She smoothed the coat over the shoulders of her tunic. "He stayed all night. But you already know that. I mean, we're still seeing each other, and you chased him up at my place on the night the sabotage was discovered, didn't you?"

"The night it hit Thorndike's aircraft, yes. It's just that I have to ask formally on account of the reports."

"I understand." Rosen crossed back to the desk to collect her briefcase. "I also understand, incidentally, that Roy is married. But when you meet a nice one, you hang on while he's available. Don't you agree?"

Eileen shrugged. "I guess so. I'm not trying to pry into personal matters. I just have to confirm the alibis of the other people who would have known how to do it. That means everyone, including all the pilots from Luzzi up to Talley."

"I do understand. But if that's all, we might as well leave." Rosen lifted her briefcase off the desk with one hand, waved her keys with the other. "Talley isn't one of the pilots, by the way."

Eileen had already started moving towards the door. "Pardon?"

"Talley. He's their tactical adviser. I'd have thought you knew, captain."

Eileen stared at the other woman, who was still smiling at her with a trace of breezy superiority – the look of a person who's unearthed a piece of someone else's ignorance. Eileen shook her head. "Talley's a pilot, Doctor Rosen. He's flown every mission with Special Team." The smile was starting to wilt. Secure the point, she thought. "I've watched him climb in his aircraft to take off, and climb out of it again when he landed. He's no tactical adviser."

Rosen's hand let go of the briefcase, and it slammed flat on the desk. Her hand, a very neat little hand, went up and covered her mouth. Muffled, behind the hand, she said, "Are you sure?"

"Of course I'm sure." Rosen's reaction was ridiculous. "Why?"

Rosen dropped her keys on top of her briefcase. Her freed hand went up to meet the other coming down. Neat fingers locked together. They squeezed each other red and white.

"Doctor Rosen, what's the matter?"

"He told me he wasn't flying missions." She was staring past Eileen at the door. "He said he was the team's tactical adviser. He said he had to monitor their missions during the night. He was having difficulty sleeping regularly, and difficulty staying alert during missions. I mean, I know he's a *pilot*, so I knew I could trust him to handle the medication. He's a very experienced pilot. But he said he didn't have a flying role with the unit. His main work is on stress evaluation at Wright-Patterson."

"I know that. I don't follow. Talley told you he *wasn't* flying with Special Team?"

"Yes. He said he has sleep disruption and attendant fall-off in his work performance. He explained the unit is under intense time pressure, so he doesn't have the opportunity to adapt." Rosen closed her eyes for a moment. When she opened them again, she was looking at Eileen. "I prescribed sleeping pills and stimulants."

Eileen stared back. She stared at a small woman with short dark hair, who'd lost every trace of intellectual self-assurance, who was wringing her hands and whose face had turned pale. "*What?*"

"I prescribed sleeping pills and stimulants. Oh my God."

"But he's flying *missions*. He's on active flying! You mean you put him on regular uppers and downers? That's not possible! You can't put a pilot on a regime like that when he's flying regular *missions*, for God's sake."

"I *know*." Rosen unclasped her hands. "Captain, I *know* that." She put her hands on the desk and leaned forward, pressing hard on the desk's support. "Psychopharmaceuticals are used to assist pilots under rigorously controlled conditions. The control is very important. Normally you'd advise people against either driving or operating machinery while using barbiturate or amphetamine preparations. Barbiturate is a soporific. Amphetamine induces a euphoric state which can affect mental concentration."

"I know. My background is police work. We know about drug abuse. You just *prescribed* the things for him? Didn't you read his record? He's receiving mission medication from Major Dyson at the hospital. *All* the pilots are."

Rosen shook her head. "It's not on his record. He has no medical record at Mondrum. They're here on a temporary posting, aren't they? Their main records won't have been transferred."

"But – didn't you think to check the hospital?"

"Of course I checked!" Rosen pushed herself upright again. She slapped the top of the computer monitor on her desk. "What do you think this thing is for? We're on-line to personnel and to the hospital. There are no medical records transferred to Mondrum, and no medical records being kept on the pilots at Arlington Hospital!"

Eileen shook her head. "But Dyson can't prescribe mission medication without keeping a record. It's in the regulations!"

"Of course he'll be keeping a record! He'll have a record card. Do you think he'd go through the hassle of opening a computer file, cross-referencing it, instituting a full medical record repository address at personnel – just for people on a temporary posting? He's a busy man! Can't you grasp that? If he was doing mission medication for those people – people like Talley – he'd know he could trust them not to abuse the stuff. I mean, they're top pilots, aren't they? You can *trust* them to exercise self-control."

You could trust them.

Eileen stared at Rosen, and Rosen stared back. You could trust them. Talley lied to Rosen in order to obtain drugs. But you could trust him. Eileen had watched Talley leave the briefing room in order to dispose of the surplus tablets Dyson sent over. She'd watched him do it every single mission. Not once had she checked on *how* he disposed of them. Because you could trust him. A top-rated and highly motivated pilot like Major Clyde Lincoln Talley just didn't do that kind of thing.

Slowly, Eileen dispelled the image of Talley leaving the briefing room, drugs in his hand – ready to disappear into his pocket, or his locker. So he kept it from her, from his fellow pilots and his CO, probably from his wife, certainly from medical officers Dyson and Rosen? Someone sliding into drug abuse develops a repertoire of little tricks and stories and subterfuges. He even fools himself. Until a visible physical and behavioural decline sets in, an addict keeps his secret.

"A record," Eileen said. "Do you have a prescribing record?"

"Yes." Rosen picked up her keys and stooped to unlock one of the drawers in her desk. "I started a record card. I've given him two prescriptions so far – just over a week ago, and yesterday."

"Yesterday?" Eileen could see Talley in her driving mirror again. She gave him a ride from Special Team, let him out on Enola Gay – and he crossed towards the medical center.

"Yesterday. He was here at midday surgery." Rosen produced the record card and held it out towards Eileen. "See? Two prescriptions for quinalbarbitone sodium and two for dexamphetamine sulphate."

Eileen took the card. She could read Talley's name, she could just about recognise the descriptions of the drugs. Every doctor in the world writes with the same vaguely undulating line. "I'd better keep this. I don't see any way around confronting Talley. Before I do anything, though, I think I'd better talk with Dyson. Do you know if he's likely to be home?"

"I doubt it. He and his wife are culture lovers. They go off base for the evening almost every weekend. I believe there's a Mahler symphony somewhere in Manchester tonight. Mahler's long, and Manchester's quite a way from here. They probably won't be back until the early hours."

Eileen nodded. Culture freaks. Dyson had time for the finer things in life, but he sent tablets over for the pilots at Special Team without ever checking their state of health. Once again, because you knew you could trust people like Talley. She put the card in the breast pocket of her blouse and buttoned it closed. "Guess I'll wait until tomorrow. It's only fair to warn him first. At least there's no danger they'll be flying any more missions."

"That's what Roy said this afternoon. He's sure the arrest means the operation is over. Is it true, by the way, that they're looking for a Russian stealth aircraft?"

"What?" A sieve. Special Team was as watertight as the *Titanic*. "Did Sellert tell you that?"

"No. It's the rumour going the rounds."

"Is it?" Well it wasn't her worry any more. Lutwidge had kicked her off the team, and thank God for that at last. "Talking of Sellert, didn't he tell you that Talley was a pilot?"

"I never mentioned Talley to him. It's known as medical confidentiality."

"Sure. Well, keep *this* confidential. Until I've talked with Dyson, that is. We don't know yet what kind of a mess Talley is in, nor if there's going to be a criminal charge. Unless there's a charge, we can't go branding him as a drug abuser. Think what that would do to his career."

Rosen nodded. "Talking of — consequences. What about me? And Major Dyson?"

And me, Eileen thought. And me.

Eileen went home. She fixed herself a TV dinner and tried to put her brain into neutral. It didn't work, the new mess with Talley kept frothing up into the focus of her attention. The only consolation was the way she'd be sharing the blame with a trio of people whose responsibilities put them way ahead of her in the queue for trouble — Rosen, Dyson, and above all Lutwidge. He'd hate her for this, too.

At nine thirty she tried Dyson's home number. No answer. So she checked with the gate. Dyson and his wife had left at seven forty-five, Dyson in a tuxedo and his wife all dressed up with earrings and necklace. They left in a hurry, not only to judge from the way the car zoomed up to the barrier and then revved away into England, but because Dyson still had his name badge pinned to his tux. He must have been called back to the hospital for some kind of problem, and that would have made him late setting out. Most Saturdays the Dysons left earlier in the evening.

So Eileen sat around, isolated in the company of new knowledge she didn't want but couldn't yet share. It was the uncertainty of having to decide where to jump, and then having to wait to see if you'd landed safely — like the business with Bellman. She couldn't cope with the emotional upset of this kind of thing. Should have taken mom and dad's advice and gone into the housewife and mother profession in downtown Detroit.

At ten thirty she called the gate. Dyson wasn't back, of course. Slowly she decided to do something just the same. If she went along to the officers' club, she was sure to get into conversation with someone for a while. With a little luck she might even run into one of the people from Special Team who were still speaking to her — Thorndike, maybe — and get a chance to ask some more about Talley. She wondered about changing out of her field security dress and maybe putting on civilian clothes, but then decided what the hell, and pulled on her boots instead. All kinds of uniforms turned up at the club. She went out to her car at a quarter of eleven.

It was chilly, with drizzle. The wipers calmly swept the way clear for her as she cruised towards the center of the base. She went down Sabre, along a piece of Nagasaki, and turned into the north end of Enola Gay. The new thing with Talley wasn't like Bellman. She got to Bellman when she realised he lied, and she found *that* out because the entire business lay outside her own field of expertise. Unlike the flying specialists, she hadn't known where it wasn't supposed to be necessary to ask questions and check answers. Sometimes a little ignorance – and no fixation on ghostly stealth aircraft – goes a long way. Bellman had in fact been out of position behind Romulus. Well then, the simplest hypothesis was that Romulus had seen Bellman. Bellman fired a missile at something, Romulus disappeared, and Pinkett had seen a fireball ahead of where the radar showed Bellman to be. Again, the simplest hypothesis was that Bellman hit Romulus. With Talley it was entirely different, because her military policework past told her exactly what to look for, but her awareness of élite status fooled her into paying no attention . . .

What was Talley shooting at?

The Sierra rolled to a halt all by itself. She'd taken her foot off the gas. She reacted in time to avoid stalling the motor. She sat there in the middle of Mondrum's main street, well south of Yokohama and right in the heart of the deserted shopping zone.

Bellman did the sabotage. No doubt of that – the Kirtland evidence had nailed him in a box. It made sense that he spooked Romulus by sneaking up on the aircraft's tail. And he fired a missile at something – conceivably a real Red Wraith, if a Russian stealth had in fact been there. He couldn't hide it, because he came back with one missile missing and had reported firing at a target minutes after Romulus went down. Same with Talley, except in Talley's case it was shells. Talley shot at something.

The radar plot had cleared to show Pinkett rolling out at the top of his turn, and Talley veering sharply away after what that chalk board diagram indicated as a gun attack. No evidence of a kill, or any kind of a hit. But it was right then that Pinkett was looking down towards Talley's position – and saw a flash as something exploded. Talley *must* have seen it, too. Why didn't he report it?

If Pinkett saw Romulus go, then Talley was shooting at a target right at that instant. *What* target?

If a Red Wraith – or Bellman – shot down Romulus, what did Pinkett see explode at the same instant Talley was firing shells at something? If he saw a Red Wraith explode as Talley hit it, *why didn't Talley report the kill?*

Headlights flared in her mirrors. A car surged past and blew its horn. In the illumination of streetlights and shop fronts, she could see the driver wave a fist at her as the car entered the first curve of the dog's leg. The vehicle left shadow-gleam tire tracks on the wet road surface, a fading trail like the one that took Bellman through the snow on his way to Special Team, like dying tracer pointing at something no longer there . . .

Talley himself had said a dive by Romulus would be a plausible evasive maneuver: if that was the case, he couldn't say otherwise without arousing suspicion. Thorndike had said it was exactly what she would do, if a missile didn't get her first. Thorndike was an Aggressor squadron instructor, an air combat specialist. If Beamish had been good enough to put his aircraft into a dive, Romulus could have gotten exactly as far as where Talley ran into something . . .

And then disintegrated in time not to appear on the radar plot.

Eileen shifted the car into gear. She looked behind to check the street was clear, then she wrenched the Sierra around in a tight turn and headed back the way she'd come. It was late, just on ten of eleven. But it was time to talk with Talley.

33

This time the bait was a Badger, a Tupolev Tu-16. It rode the night on long, swept-back wings. All of its lights were burning to make sure it looked friendly. It was a Badger-D, a maritime reconnaissance variant, with a bulbous radome under its nose. But its own radars were shut down as the Badger listened to Nato during its intelligence mission. Nato, though, was silent because Superman had called for Quiet Sky. If the Russian decided to turn on a radar, he'd light up the shadowy hunters and blow the trap wide open.

Quiet Sky. With its engine scream and slipstream rush, an F-15 was a noisy machine, even inside a helmet and its built-in earphones. But those were constant sounds. After a while you only heard them every time they changed. Otherwise you waited for instrument alerts in a self-censored silence.

They had their own navigation lights burning. Luzzi was a sparse constellation, with a red wingtip star, slightly low on her right. Beyond him was the Badger, lit up like some high powered Santa on a rehearsal run in a sub-Arctic night. Otherwise it was darkness with stars, with long pancake veils of stratospheric ice above, and the faint tops of a weather cloud blanket spread below like milky chiffon. It was a layered world painted parsimoniously in monochrome, brushed as an infinitely thin wash on black paper. The unaided eye was lost in the depths of distant night.

They'd paced the bait for fifteen minutes. McGee and Pinkett would have climbed up from below those weather clouds, and would be circling in a secret follow-my-leader duet at half a dozen miles. Down there still, somewhere near the ocean, Talley was all alone, waiting to bring up the rear.

When Talley turned up for the mission briefing he looked like a stunned drunk. He hadn't believed Lutwidge could call a mission. No one had. But Lutwidge gave them another fiery pep talk about finding Red Wraith and proving to those Pentagon theorists how the frontline realists mattered and knew what was what. By the time they got down to the position details Talley was transformed, bright and alert and ready to go. In part, it might have been the way he was beating Bellman. They didn't need big mouth for the mission, because Talley could take the safety role all by himself, and Superman knew it.

Talley, the man with a real kill to his name, was good news. Otherwise, if a Red Wraith tied himself to her tail, Sandra Thorndike wasn't happy. The problem was the first protection at her back. Pinkett was having to follow McGee, go where he went – but McGee had never flown hunter before, and had displayed no other outstanding talent aside from a loving loyalty towards Lutwidge. If she ever saw a Red Wraith behind her, she wasn't proposing to tell McGee via control, and then wait to see how long he took to turn up. She was going to take care of her own protection, with whatever help Luzzi could provide.

But there wasn't going to be any Red Wraith. Superman's final throw was certain to be another zero. If Red Wraith had been there last time, then whether or not he did anything to Beamish and Baker, he got himself both seen and shot at. He'd have more sense than to come back into another trap. Most likely Red Wraith didn't even exist, the shambles of the loss of Romulus stayed unthinkable, and the crazy notion that Bellman shot them down began to make sense. Either way, Lutwidge had sent them fishing in a desert.

Sixteen minutes with the bait. She thumbed the transmit switch. "Thorndike. How about we leave our friend here and head for home?"

While she was waiting, she took her hand off the stick and poked buttons on the test set control board. Iris reported no faults. Lolite reported no faults. Just the same, Lolite could go to hell.

"Control," said Wizer's voice. "Concur it's time to leave. Your initial heading is one-seven-five degrees. Leave when ready."

Transmit. "Guess we'll be on our way. Luzzi, flash your lights at our friend."

Luzzi flashed his lights off then on again. Sandra flashed her own lights twice. The Badger winked back three times, escalating like any friendly rival should.

Transmit. "Okay, Luzzi, we'll peel out left nice and easy. Just in case anyone else is listening, please take note we're turning for home on one-seven-five. Luzzi, here we go now."

She tipped her Eagle ten degrees, with a little left rudder but no extra throttle. The night banked upwards on the left, in harmony with the artificial horizon as it adjusted around the waterline symbol in the center of the head up display. The HUD's heading scale slid sideways. The altitude scale slipped down one slow graduation after another as she shed a little height in the turn. She looked over her right shoulder. Luzzi had joined the turn and was keeping pace at her four o'clock. When she twisted further around, the bait's lights were winking one by one behind her right fin. They shrank into the night exactly over her tail.

The heading slid to 175 degrees. She levelled out, checked how the rate of descent stabilised, and hitched the nose up a shade to bring it to zero. Outside in the encircling night, Luzzi's pattern of lights came level on her wing.

"Luzzi," said his voice in her ears. "What's our spread?"

Transmit. "Go to five hundred feet and level."

"Five hundred feet and level."

At no more than five hundred feet, if he put his lights out she'd have no trouble seeing the black silhouette of his F-15. But at five hundred feet, they would be just far enough apart to oblige any stealthy prowler who trailed in on them to pick one or the other from the pair. Then they'd have a maneuver option for turning the tables on Red Wraith. Who wasn't going to be there.

But if in fact he was, she intended to get pictures. She put the Iris forward view on the head down multifunction display. She set Lolite on its forward camera, but didn't call the view on any screen. The Mark Two eyeball, the trained pilot's eye, was what she would need. Neither Iris nor Lolite would be able to follow an opponent as he pitched and turned around the sky.

Keep talking, so McGee and Pinkett and Talley, too, would have a constant voice to follow. Transmit. "Thorndike. Course one-seven-five, angels eighteen, speed four hundred. The bait went on his way. We got the sky to ourselves up here."

You hope, she thought. You hope. There isn't going to be any Red Wraith. Either he was there last time and he was seen, or he doesn't even exist. But last time, if it was him, he shot down Beamish and Baker. So not only will a Red Wraith have a near invisible advantage. He'll also be dangerous.

Stealth. You can't see him. But he can kill you.

Clyde Talley had his F-15 at five thousand feet, with the nose pitched slightly high and the throttle adjusted so he was climbing gently. He was deep inside the cloud layer, in a darkness so intense that all the angels of hell and heaven could be fluttering around his machine, and he wouldn't see a single one of them.

Thorndike and Luzzi were twenty miles ahead, flying at eighteen thousand feet and reporting regularly to Mondrum control. Ten miles behind them, and trailing slowly in at around two thousand feet lower, should be McGee and

Pinkett. They covered the backs of the interceptors, he covered their backs — and no one protected him at all. His only insurance was his position. Any Red Wraith would have picked up the interceptors at the bait, or it might have seen the two hunters circling out in the wide sky. It wouldn't have seen Clyde when he was loitering down below the weather clouds.

In his head up display, the heading scale read 192. He'd pulled off course. He eased the rudder and brought the marker back on 175. His rate of climb had dropped to zero, while airspeed had increased a shade. He touched on the stick to lift the nose again. Rate of climb went up, airspeed went down.

In this total blackness, the symbols and scales stencilled in nothing at all on the HUD were going blurred. It had started at his holding position short of the bait, five hundred feet off the ocean and simply circling around and around. He had a can full of coffee right after Kye woke him — and after the little revelation that caught her completely by surprise. He took an amphetamine from the boxful Dyson had sent over to Special Team, and by the end of the briefing he'd felt so good he was shining. No need to palm the surplus this time, because he had a handful in the pocket of his flying suit, brought along from home. For a couple of hours it had beaten back the fatigue, the emotional reaction, the dullness from the whisky and the slow hypnosis from the two quinalbarbitones he took with his lunch.

But at the holding position he could feel the curtain closing. He'd been watching the repetitive circles of the heading scale without any remnant of an idea what it might mean. So he popped another pill and swallowed it smartly down. By now it should have transformed him into a wide awake and bright eyed hero.

The rate of climb had dropped to zero, the heading scale said 161. Bad. He had it bad. Something should be done. He eased the stick and touched the rudder, and watched the heading creep back to 175. Then it continued a degree at a time further around. That had to be corrected, too. If he ran into a Red Wraith in this state, he wouldn't even notice when it blew him out of the air.

He unstrapped his oxygen mask. He pulled off his left glove and tucked it safely in his lap. He unzipped the pocket of his suit, fiddled his fingers inside under his harness, pincered a pill between his fingertips, pulled it out and popped it in his mouth.

The heading had drifted to 190. He tickled the stick and the pedals and nudged it back to 175. The tablet still sat on his tongue. One thing at a time. The rate of climb had gone negative and indicated two hundred feet per minute down. He eased the stick so the nose came up and the artificial horizon on the HUD slipped below the waterline symbol again. Back on line, back on climb. He rolled the tablet free against the roof of his mouth . . .

It came away sweet, then turned instantly and acutely bitter.

He froze with his tongue immobile in his mouth. A tablet of dexamphetamine, if you accidentally took too long to swallow it, tasted slightly bitter, but it was salty more than anything else.

The barbiturates were the ones so bitter they came with a sugar coating.

He flipped on the map light, a tiny shielded glow beside his knee. To hell with wiping out his night vision. He spat the tablet into his palm and held his hand under the map light. White, saliva soaked and formless, the tablet was far too big to be a mere five milligrammes of dexamphetamine sulphate.

It was quinalbarbitone. He almost swallowed quinal-barbitone – in the middle of a mission and at least two hours from home.

Instead, he swallowed its taste from his tongue. Then he smeared the sodden tablet on the thigh of his suit. Only place to wipe it. Don't forget to brush off the dried remnants once you land. The heading said 160, the artificial horizon was over the waterline and the rate of climb was three hundred per minute down. He corrected line and climb. He was flying a roller coaster course. He came out here to find a Red Wraith and prove to himself he didn't do wrong. Instead of that, he was falling asleep.

He fumbled in his pocket and brought out the rest of the tablets.

They were all too big. All quinalbarbitone!

He clenched his fist. He'd mixed up the tablets. In a dazed hurry, he picked the wrong ones out of the drawer.

He mixed them up. The tablet he swallowed twenty minutes ago – it was also quinalbarbitone! He swallowed it too fast to notice the taste, too quick and neat and perfect, no thinking or checking. He did it just the way he took targets of sudden opportunity with missile or gun – *always too soon*, as if the sticky mess with Thorndike had been a metaphor for it all. Too sudden, too soon, and never right.

Heading 164. Rate of climb four hundred per minute down. He corrected back to the blurred-edged figures he should hold. Already doped up and half drunk with exhaustion, he'd taken another sleeping pill. His naked fist, palm upwards, was quivering on his knee. Inside it, sticking together with sweat, all the tablets were wrong.

He forced his fist open, slipped the tablets back in his pocket and zipped the pocket closed. He strapped his mask in place and then pulled on his glove. This is going to test you, Clyde Lincoln Talley. If you get away with this, there's nothing is ever going to beat you again.

34

March 4th, 2315

Kathrin Talley finally closed the door on the cold night. She stood in the hallway and held the record card in both hands. She was wearing stay-at-home casuals — checked cotton shirt, long navy cardigan, stonewashed jeans, Timberland shoes — but she looked like a lifestyle picture from the pages of a quality magazine. Whatever that elusive something might be, Kathrin Talley lived it. Eileen waited in her field uniform and her boots, out of place, out of her depth, slightly out of her mind. On a mission! Talley was out flying a *mission*. Action Man called one after all, and they took off at eight forty-five. Round about then she was still talking with Rosen at the medical center.

It took a while to register that Kathrin Talley was still staring at the record card, but couldn't see it any more.

"Mrs Talley? You really didn't know about this?"

Kathrin Talley shuddered slightly, an image coming back to life. "Not the amphetamines. I knew about the sleeping pills. I didn't know he got them from this Captain Rosen. The unit MO is Major Dyson, isn't it? I also didn't know he'd received a second prescription. What was Rosen *doing*?"

The card was shaking in her hands. Eileen took it away from her before it got crumpled or torn. "Mrs Talley, do

you know if he's in fact been using the tablets? May I see
how many are left?"

Kathrin Talley just turned and started up the stairs.

Eileen followed, boots thumping on the treads. Talley
was on a mission! If this checked out, she couldn't possibly
wait until Dyson came home in the middle of the night,
any more than she could wait until the pilots returned.
They'd all be back together, Dyson from his concert and
the pilots from their latest blind date. That was why Dyson
left in a hurry, with his name badge pinned to his tuxedo
– he must have been about to leave with his wife, when
Action Man called a mission and obliged him to stop by
at the hospital long enough to release medication for the
team. Now Dyson was out of reach while the aircrew under
his supervision were actually flying, and Eileen had to tell
Lutwidge, and the scandal would probably ruin Dyson.
She *had* to tell Lutwidge and pass the buck. From this
moment, if any accident involving Talley occurred and she
hadn't already sounded the alarm, her own career would
be over.

She tried not to look around the bedroom. It was tidy,
with half-sloping ceilings. It was a private place. Her boots
crunched the carpet.

Talley's wife was squatting in front of a chest of drawers.
She'd pulled open the bottom drawer. From the back
corner she lifted out a tracksuit and a pair of swimming
shorts. Slowly, without looking, she laid the shorts on the
tracksuit, folded the suit over twice, and squeezed it tight.
She shook her head.

Eileen moved up and crouched so she could see inside
the drawer. Right in the back corner were two little medication pots with their lids lying open beside them, plus a
couple of plastic containers for thirty-five millimetre film.
Spilled across the base of the drawer were tablets, at least
two dozen. She reached inside and tipped the pots. More
tablets rolled out. She gave the film containers a little shake.
There was a buckshot rattle from each of them: both about
half full.

"I had no idea there were so many." Kathrin Talley put the folded tracksuit on the floor and wiped her cheeks, quickly, with the palms of her hands. "All these years. I never spied on my husband before."

Eileen looked around at the bed, tidied without fold or fault. On each side was a night table complete with shallow drawer. "But you knew they were here?"

"He said it avoided temptation to put the supply out of immediate reach – if he just woke up for a while in the night, or something."

Eileen scooped up a few of the tablets and rolled them in her palm. The big ones contained fifty milligrammes of quinalbarbitone sodium, the little ones five milligrammes of dexamphetamine sulphate. Standard tablets she'd seen countless times before. Mixed together like that, it looked at though he'd grabbed some in a hurry. "What was your husband doing when the mission call came through?"

"He was asleep. Where did he get so many? Where did he *get* them from?"

"Dyson prescribed excess tablets every time." Eileen started sweeping pills together and pushing them into the pots. Sorting the things could wait. "I guess he pocketed the excess. I thought he put them down the toilet. I should have checked." She lifted the edges of clothing in the drawer in order to sweep her fingers underneath, then paused. "I'm sorry about this, Mrs Talley, but it's serious. He's concealed it from his CO and the unit MO, and he's fabricated a story to obtain a supply from another medical officer. I have to impound these."

"Obviously." The woman stood up, high above Eileen's head, while Eileen scrabbled around in a corner of her life. "I'll be downstairs."

From under the clothing she rounded up three more tablets. She put them in the pots, snapped on the lids, put all the containers in the pocket of her blouse. Then she put the folded tracksuit back in its place and closed the drawer.

She started towards the stairs. From the mixed up mess there was no way to tell how many tablets Talley had used, nor whether he went on the mission doped with barbiturates or high on speed. When she reported this it was going to destroy Talley, ruin Dyson because he didn't check his charges, damage Lutwidge because he didn't note the behaviour of his pilot, hurt Rosen because she didn't check properly before she prescribed – and probably hurt Eileen herself. First fix Bellman, and now break a hero and a bunch of careless bystanders. Before she took that step, she wanted some idea of how much of a mess Talley might be stuck inside.

Talley's wife sat in the middle of the sofa, hands folded on her knees. The posture, hunched a little forward, was the only sign of distress. The woman commanded such self-control. General's daughter, general's niece, major's wife. Her style and her self-certain superiority enforced the icy refusal to cry. It meant her distress was real. She hadn't known.

On the coffee table, right in front of her, lay Gorbachov's *Perestroika* with a bookmark trapped inside. Strange reading for a general's daughter.

"Mrs Talley? I'm afraid I have to ask you about your husband's emotional stability."

Kathrin Talley looked up at her and waited. She didn't invite her to sit. She was going to hold court.

"Emotional stress can affect a pilot's performance, Mrs Talley. That could be exceedingly dangerous. I believe you and your husband might be having personal problems. Is that so?"

"I'm aware of the danger, captain." She pulled herself upright and let her back settle against the sofa. Her folded hands slid from her knees into her lap. "I'm filing for a divorce."

"Oh. I see."

"Do you indeed, Captain Ware? Do you indeed see? Do you think divorce is a thing a person simply *does*, like throwing something in the garbage can, or giving an old suit to charity? It's the end of a long process that lasts for years. It's a bereavement where the mourning comes before the death, as well as after. It started years ago. We repaired it every time, but it always surfaced again and it was always worse."

"Mrs Talley, I don't need to know –"

"If you ask a question you can suffer the answer!" Kathrin Talley took a deep breath – then let it out slowly. "We were really in love once, I do believe. But it cooled off. Then along came Merryl and we were a family, and it seemed worth making the effort. Then there was Stevie, and we were stuck fast in the roles and the social expectations. Instead of giving up on something that's broken, you find yourself always taping it back together again. Until one day you find there's just a collection of fragments wrapped up in bandages. It's a slow, inexorable, senseless little process. You see, we're what's known as a mésalliance. I have a Harvard education and a higher degree –"

"I guess I don't need –"

"And my husband has an engineering degree, but that isn't as cashable in company. Try talking vortex shedding or band gap manipulation at a top people's party in Washington. They fly in and out of Washington thanks to aerodynamics and electronics, but their cultivated brains don't give a damn about science. That's what I so liked about Clyde – he's concerned with the way and the how of things, right where they happen. But we're a mésalliance. I'm from a rich family loaded with social and political connections, I know who the right people are, and even more to the point they know who I am. Clyde comes from the archetypal wrong side of the tracks. He's done it all himself – earned an Air Force scholarship on merit, become a top pilot, landed a well-connected wife. But unfortunately the marriage no longer works. We've been keeping it up for the sake of the kids, but in the end it's going to damage them even more than a divorce will do. Can you understand that?"

Eileen waited to be sure the confession she didn't want had stalled. Most of the human race probably had long

drawn out problems they could barely contain. What she
needed was an insight into Talley's momentary state of
mind — would he have been right now, today, off balance
or under control? "Mrs Talley, it's important for me to
know how upset your husband might be. I don't want to
cause any more trouble than I have to. But I know about
the tablets now — and I just can't ignore it."

"What is it you want to say, captain?"

"I'm told by someone your husband confided in — that
he believes you've been unfaithful to him. That is to say
adultery. That is to say —"

"Screwing around. I can't tell you if he really believes
that, captain. I can't tell you if he really believes I'd cheat
on him and humiliate him. If he does, it's his problem."

"I believe you stayed away a couple of nights while he
was on a mission."

"Do you indeed? Get your damned facts right before
you make your accusations!"

"Mrs Talley — please? I'm not making accusations.
Please, don't you understand? I just got hit with information that's going to destroy your husband's career. I
can't just do that. Just do that to him. Unless I'm sure."

Kathrin Talley closed her eyes. "Peace of mind. You're
not the only one who'll be looking for that, Captain Ware."

You will, Eileen thought. And Dyson, Lutwidge and
Rosen.

Kathrin Talley opened her eyes and sighed. "I went to
London. You can drive to London from here in not much
more than three hours, in case you didn't know."

"I know it, Mrs Talley."

"I had lunch in London. I spent the afternoon at the
British Museum. I went window shopping. In fact I bought
a raincoat — you might have seen it. I ate dinner in the
evening and then I drove back. I started back late, I arrived
back late. We had a fight about it. Fights are stupid things.
My husband wouldn't say what he believed, and I wasn't
going to disabuse him. That means persuade him he was
wrong."

"I know the word, Mrs Talley."

"A few days later, I took myself off to Wales. God knows why I wanted to see the Welsh hills in the middle of winter, but Mondrum doesn't have much to offer, does it? On the way back I came through Shrewsbury. Before I got to the next real town – Whitchurch, if you want to check – I ran out of gas. The nearest village had a gas station, but it wasn't open. Fortunately it had a pub with a decent room, so that's where I stayed. They were very nice people. They helped me get my car to the gas station before breakfast. It opened early, you understand, because the whole region is a commuter area for management types from the big cities. Shall I go on? Do you want the name of the village? The pub? The landlord?"

"No, Mrs Talley. I didn't want to pry like that."

"I thought you'd be used to it. Isn't your background police work?"

"It doesn't make me inhuman, Mrs Talley."

"Doesn't it?"

Eileen folded her arms. The tablets rattled in her pocket. She unfolded her arms and pushed back her cuff to check the time. Just coming up to eleven thirty. Ticking away all the while, and she wasn't finding out anything of use. She parked her hands on her hips. The tablets rattled.

Kathrin Talley shivered, like the façade of a building when the roof caves in. Slowly, she looked up at Eileen again. "I apologise for my temper. This isn't your fault, after all."

"It's no one's fault, Mrs Talley." Unless something happens while I'm still hunting my own courage, she thought. Then the entire disaster's going to be mine.

"How could this happen, Captain Ware? The tablets, I mean. How could this happen without my realising in time to stop it?"

Eileen shrugged. "Trust. Like the rest of us, you've always known you can trust your husband not to do anything so dumb. I mean dangerous for himself."

"You mean dumb." Kathrin Talley looked at her own

hands in her lap. "My God. I've helped him lose the thing he needs the most."

Time ticking away. Lutwidge wasn't going to believe her. He was in the middle of running a mission, and she was going to come bursting through the door and tell him his senior pilot was a drug addict. He'd throw a fit and throw her out. But hauling a senior officer out of his house and persuading him to go with her to Lutwidge would waste an hour or more. She needed an expert opinion to back her up – one already alerted. "Mrs Talley, I have to go to Lutwidge with this. Before I go, is there anything else – anything at all – I ought to know?"

Kathrin Talley lifted her head. She stared at Eileen for a long, motionless moment. "My husband has no other secrets."

Eileen nodded. "May I use your phone? I have to get hold of Captain Rosen."

35

March 4th, 2330

She had the Iris forward field out of the way on the head down display. She had Lolite's forward field selected but wasn't going to use it. If anything happened it would be her eyes she'd need. Bright images right in front of her on the head up display would wreck her ability to see the rest of the night. To hell with technology. Stay with technique.

The drop tanks were empty and thrown away. The

conformal tanks were empty. She was on internal fuel, she had two Sidewinders and a cannon with a full magazine. Her F-15 was clean, light and lethal. No one was going to take her out of the air.

The night was an infinite canopy draped with milky scarves of stratosphere ice. Below, between the ocean's weather world and her empty heaven, was a vast layer of lenticular cloud like endless ranks of freshly made marshmallows, glued together on a celestial baking sheet and left out to cool in the starlight.

Out to her right was Luzzi's little constellation of red wing and tail lights. She looked high, twisting back over her shoulder to see the tip of her own right fin. Then she swept her eyes steadily around the night: past her canopy's midframe, over the top of Luzzi, past the bowframe and through the top of the HUD, past the bowframe again, high over the wing, past the midframe, clean around to the top of the left fin. Nothing at all but night with distant ice veils under stars, the same emptiness she'd seen ever since they left the bait. No Red Wraith was going to show.

She swept the sky low: over the left wingtip, down in front of the leading edge, past the midframe and over the air intake, down towards the endless marshmallow sea, past the bowframe and through the head up display, bowframe again with marshmallow distance, under Luzzi's lit-up silhouette, air intake, midframe, right wing's leading edge. So much exercise – no fighter pilot ever lived long with a stiff neck. Back to the leading edge to check –

It was larger and closer than a speck. It sat barely in front of the wing. It hardly had a shape, just a dark little patch with long fins on its tail. Beyond it, milky marshmallows blended smoothly into a veiled distance a hundred miles away.

It didn't look much like any aircraft type she knew. It certainly wasn't an F-15.

She checked her heading, horizon, nose angle. Hadn't wavered a hair. She turned back to the tiny thing over her shoulder. Her left hand thumbed the transmit switch on

the throttles. Tell it to Luzzi and everyone will hear. Let's
see if Superman has the sense to keep his mouth shut while
this starts going on.

"Thorndike to Luzzi. Don't do anything at all until I
say. Stay straight and level and keep your lights on. We
have company. The bogey is here. He's closing on your tail
at around two thousand out. He's slightly low at my four
o'clock. He'll be at your five o'clock and hidden under
your wing. Stay straight and level and don't try looking for
him."

She checked fuel state, checked there were no lit alarms
on the caution panel, checked the Eagle was ready. So he
turned up after all! She switched Iris and Lolite to record.
The bogey would be crossing in and out of the forward
fields. He really existed – and she was going to get him
good. People might tell it to Talley and Bellman, but no
one was going to tell *her* he wasn't there. Where was
Luzzi's answer? Was he going to freeze?

"Luzzi. Understood bogey on my tail at five o'clock. Do
we turn and fight?"

If they started with an aggressive turn, the Red Wraith
would dive straight into the cloud and disappear. Transmit.
"We try to lock him up and hold him while the others
arrive. Hear that, you guys? Okay now, Luzzi, you ready?
We can't just sit tight until they get here. He might turn
aside and we lose him." Over her shoulder, the little black
shape was still there, just forward of her wingtip and growing slightly larger. Over-confident, he was creeping too
close on a line a shade too far out to the side. "Also, he
might be aggressive, if we killed one of his friends last time.
So we don't just wait. We try to get him in the sandwich."
She released the gun and checked the armed cue came up
on the HUD, just so she knew she could use it. Then she
locked the gun again. When she squeezed the trigger, only
the camera would fire. Where was Luzzi's response?

"Guess I break right and pull him in."

Transmit. "By the book, Luzzi. He's still at your five
o'clock, maybe one thousand five hundred back. Your

move is to break right and stay level and don't throttle through. Maintain speed so he can come in close behind you. Don't put out your lights until you start the break. We want him to see which way you go. Be ready to start a dive when I call, and start it *slowly* so he follows. We want to catch him in the sandwich and then take him down to the deck where he has less sky to fly around in. Down on the sea we can ride his tail and shut him anywhere we want. He won't have the power to outrun or outclimb us. Okay?"

"Okay. When do we go?"

She stared over her shoulder at the guesswork object. She could see two tail fins, but no other details. Transmit. "I'm calling the break after three. Here we go. One. Two. Three. Break!"

Luzzi's little constellation banked away, slipped slightly down and slid back. His lights went out –

She banked left with left rudder, pushed the throttle through to maintain her height. Opening the sandwich let Red Wraith know they'd seen him and were separating. He'd go for Luzzi, the one who broke across in front of him. She put out her lights.

Then she snapped over the stick and rolled out right against the turn, kicked hard right rudder and pushed the throttle. The gee force tried to fold her head down inside the cockpit. She forced her head up, looking high and right along the canted horizon. Sliding down came the F-15's tail silhouette with two tailpipe flares, and another shape, nearer, with two fainter glows.

She centered rudder and stick so the world tipped level and gee came off. She triggered the camera and eased the throttle. Red Wraith in the sandwich. Now take him down before he has time to react. Transmit. "Luzzi, slow dive now!"

The silhouette of the F-15 out in front pitched nose down and dropped. Too abruptly. Too obviously. Red Wraith didn't follow. He knew she was on his tail –

He tipped on his side and broke hard left. She banked

left, kicked the rudder, and followed him around. The horizon came steeply down through her head up display. Red Wraith was high over her bowframe at eleven o'clock. Delta planform with nose strakes. The gee force grew and the horizon started to stand on its side, stars right, marshmallows left and rotating. He was pulling the turn tighter. He was going to reverse and start scissoring back and forth, forcing her out in front, making her vulnerable. He was coming closer and her overshoot was beginning.

She eased off bank and rudder, opening the radius of her turn. If she couldn't shed speed as fast as Red Wraith, she had to get outside his turn and stay there. His silhouette came closer and climbed higher at eleven o'clock. She slid into position for a lag pursuit, tucked under his tail, outside his turn and matching it exactly. No risk of overshooting, no risk of losing him. He was a foreshortened black fuselage with long twin tailpipes, smooth delta planform wings, long forebody strakes. The fins didn't look tall and were canted outboard. No tailplane. So *close* but too damned high to photograph. His engine exhausts showed no glow at all at this angle. Good heat suppression.

The carousel horizon moved out right and clouds came across her nose. She'd foiled his scissors and was pacing him, he couldn't see her but he knew where she was. He was tightening the turn still more, letting his nose drop and entering a spiral dive. The gee force increased. He wanted her off his tail. He wanted her to overshoot and come out in front so he'd get a shot at her – or he wanted to keep her from getting a shot at him until he could spiral down into the cloud and vanish.

He was keeping his speed, going for the cloud. She had to close right up to have any chance of sticking on his tail inside the cloud. To hell with safe separation. The heading indicator spun right around twice in a row. He was coming closer over her head, a bigger silhouette. He was too close! He'd eased off throttle and she was going to overshoot and he'd have her in front and dead –

She relaxed the angle of bank, hauled on the stick and

pulled the nose high. The horizon went left past her wing and started to tip clean over. Symbols slewed all over the head up display. Airspeed came off as she went up in the climb and began to roll over left. At the top of a loop drawn through two planes, she was upside down with clouds over her head and a clear sight of her opponent's profile through the roof of her canopy. She could aim her descent out of the yoyo to drop down neatly right on his tail —

Against the cloudtops, his tight turning profile flipped into a plan view as he rolled inverted — then foreshortened abruptly as he put his nose down and turned into a tail silhouette. Straight for the clouds.

She didn't pull through to complete the descending half of the yoyo. She rolled out and stayed with the turn. Out there, down there, he was disappearing over her left shoulder as he stood on his nose and dived. Then he met the clouds and vanished. Too far away to chase.

She threw the yoyo just as he decided to change his turn into a Split S and dive away. Lost him.

She settled the F-15 into a wide circle. Down in the cloud he would make an aileron turn while still descending vertically, then he'd pull out and head who knew which way. Lost him!

She switched Iris and Lolite off record. She pressed the transmit button. "Thorndike. I just lost Red Wraith. He dived into cloud at twelve thousand. Luzzi, get down on the deck and bug out. He might be intending to follow up on you if he can find you. What's your heading and angels?"

"Luzzi. I'm on one-three-five at angels two hundred." Running southeast, down on the deck where he was supposed to take Red Wraith. "Cloud base is at one thousand and no rain. Guess he might see me at that."

Someone should support Luzzi. Talley was too far back, so either Pinkett or McGee had to go after him. Let it be the guy she didn't trust. Transmit. "Luzzi, keep your heading and act as a draw. Okay, you hunters. Listen to this and don't acknowledge. McGee and Pinkett split your pair.

McGee, go after Luzzi fast and back him up. Pinkett, you come right on towards me in case Red Wraith picks me again after all. Talley, you come in on me as well." Self-interest every single time.

"McGee to control," she heard in her ears. The fool was transmitting and giving his presence away! "Request confirmation on that one."

"Control." That was Lutwidge's voice. "Thorndike knows the situation. Do it and keep quiet. Thorndike, do you have any description of Red Wraith for us?"

She eased her aircraft into a gentler curve around the sky. Transmit. "I got Iris, Lolite and camera pictures for a couple of seconds. He's around the same size as an F-15. Black camouflage. Underside looks clean with no weapons slung. Broad delta plan with long forward strakes. Rear view suggests he's got wing to body blending like an F-16. Two long tailpipes, well separated. Double fins, long fore and aft but not very tall, canted outboard at around thirty degrees. No tailplane. He's at least semi-stealthed for sure. He's more maneuverable than I expected but his delta will limit that. He isn't fast and he sheds speed easily – shit difficult not to overshoot. And he thinks real quick."

She should think fast herself. She lost him because she gave Luzzi something to do that was outside his competence and the steadiness of his nerves – with a possible killer on his tail, she expected Luzzi to go down slow and easy. So she lost Red Wraith, and he wouldn't be coming back. At least she proved he existed. She'd believed she could outfly anyone else in the air – then a slow and clumsy stealthed opponent kicked her loose like a sack.

She *lost* him.

Well, there was nothing else to throw away, so one final trick was worth the try. She switched on the F-15's radar and selected lookdown mode.

The screen at top left of her control panel showed nothing at all except the mode and the range scale – a forward-looking fan reaching out to one hundred and sixty nautical miles. On pulsed-Doppler discrimination the sea simply wasn't there. All the waves were travelling at the same velocity relative to the radar in the nose of her machine, so the computer ignored them. There might be ships, but they wouldn't be moving fast enough with respect to the marching sea surface – anything slower than fast freeway traffic fell below the mode's velocity gate. Lookdown was designed to search for aircraft skimming low over ground or sea. It sought fast objects, and nothing else.

As her heading swung from south towards southeast, a symbol representing Luzzi's aircraft appeared on the left of the radar scan. It had his altitude and his velocity vector. Luzzi's IFF was on, and her reply evaluator flashed a confirmation of his identity. Nothing that showed up on radar was chasing him.

As she came around from southeast towards east a second contact moved across her screen, down low and almost supersonic. It showed no IFF, but it was McGee going after Luzzi at speed.

Swinging past northeast, she switched off her radar. Both Pinkett and Talley, coming in from the north, should be too high to show on lookdown mode, but she didn't want to catch either of them in her radar floodlight and risk telling Red Wraith they were there. It meant she couldn't look northward, the direction the Russian would have to go to get home.

She waited until she was pointed northwest before switching the radar on again.

Over in the right of the scan was a fuzzy little ring with a hole in it. No altitude, no velocity vector. The computer couldn't do anything with it except offer a true bearing from her own position – 335 degrees, near enough north-northwest. It vanished off the side of her scan as the slow turn swung her nose around the horizon. She switched the radar off.

What was going to make a mess like that? A hole. Something that didn't send any signal back, so the radar had neither a different Doppler from a speeding contact, nor the reassuringly constant Doppler from the sea surface below. A speeding radar hole, a little nothingness close over the water and casting its own shadow. Red Wraith, down low and leaving.

She reversed the turn and pulled back towards north. If she tried to keep the radar on him he'd get suspicious. His radar warning receiver would tell him someone was looking steadily his way and was locked on. He'd realise he could be seen, he'd climb up off the sea so his radar shadow faded – and he'd disappear. She would have to sweep across him repeatedly and regularly so he'd be sure she was circling and searching in vain. Don't spook him now. But send someone to catch him.

Transmit. "Thorndike to Pinkett. Red Wraith is down on the deck heading approximately three-three-five. He's around ten miles out to your northwest. Go right down where I can see you and go fast, and I'll vector you in on him. Do not use your IFF, do not acknowledge." Now hope, she thought. Hope and pray that Pinkett is alert enough to answer for himself the question, how does she know where Red Wraith is? Hope he doesn't do like McGee – transmit a dumb question and give himself away.

"Control to Thorndike." That was Superman again. "How in hell do you see Red Wraith?"

Transmit. "Pulsed-Doppler lookdown mode." She'd swung far enough around to the north. She reversed into a leftward turn again and switched on the radar. There was the impossible little hole with its fringe, swinging slowly across her screen. "It's what our own people with the stealth at Nellis wouldn't let us try. He's down low, he throws back no signal at all, so his Doppler doesn't conform to the wave background. So he shows up nice and clear." The fuzzy ghost was crossing out of the scan again. "I'll track him. Pinkett can get on his tail while he's down low and can't maneuver. Talley should stay high and move in to back him up."

The radar screen was blank once more. She switched off and reversed the turn, swinging slowly back around the sky. Luzzi and McGee were too far south, too fast, and out of it. Superman's favourite Bitburg Boys wouldn't have the fuel to join the chase in time to make the target, and still get home afterwards. It was herself and Pinkett and Talley who got to be the heroes – and *she* was the one who pulled Red Wraith back out of the hat.

"Control to Pinkett. Follow Thorndike's vectoring. Get right down on the deck so Red Wraith doesn't see you by secondary illumination until you're up close. Talley goes high to get above Red Wraith. Both of you keep quiet until you're on him."

She reversed into a lefthand turn again, and switched the radar on. There was the hard contact of Pinkett's F-15, no identifying IFF showing, already down on the deck and making better than supersonic with the speed gained from his dive. Very low and very fast, he'd be shaking his head off his shoulders with the vibration in turbulent air. His course looked a little too far west. On the left of her screen the fringed ghost appeared again, higher up the range scale and further away. Transmit. "Pinkett, turn thirty degrees right. He's eighteen miles from you."

She watched the velocity vector on Pinkett's contact swing around. If he stayed low and stayed quiet, she'd be able to take him right up to Red Wraith's tailpipes. Pinkett would catch him.

Not bad, for a woman.

36

March 4th, 2345

Lutwidge sat between Charles and Wizer at the desk in front of the window. Beyond the window, across the other side of the control center, the screen covering Nato's north flank showed a gap where radar coverage of the Norwegian Sea had been shut down. Quiet Sky was still in effect, the mission still locked in its critical phase. So Lutwidge was going to like this even less.

All three of them wore headphones – sets with a single earphone and a microphone boom on one side, and a pad on the other side which left the ear free. Charles, however, also held a telephone receiver in his hand. "He's on his way," Charles said. He put the receiver back on the desk hook. "In a hell of a hurry."

Lutwidge turned to Charles. From behind, Eileen saw a smile which creased Lutwidge's cheek and bared his teeth. Action Man sensing some kind of blood, the savage thrill of victory. "If Dodgson gets here fast enough to see the fun, we've nailed our first ass to the floor. Every one of them who's looking for it to be anything but Red Wraith – we got them all."

"That's for sure." Charles nodded happily. "Blind Date panned out. This settles the whole intelligence argument, and an awful lot besides."

"Must be the most fun Mondrum's seen," Lutwidge said, "since the last war."

Eileen was pulling Captain Jessica Rosen through the door so she could close it properly and let the blackout curtain fall into place again. Oh no, she thought – did they *find* their phantom aircraft? She let go of Rosen's arm. Turn around, get out of here, come back later. Don't try it now. Not *now*.

But Rosen had too much momentum and went forward another step, so the door and the curtain stayed open while Eileen tried to catch Rosen's sleeve again. Like a predator wary of new light, Susan Wizer turned her head. It was an undignified entrance she saw, but her eyes showed no expression at all. Eileen pulled the door closed and let the curtain fall across it.

"Jessica?" Wizer said. "Are you supposed to be in here?"

Jessica Rosen just pointed at Eileen.

"Captain Ware?" Wizer asked. "I thought you were no longer with Special Team?"

Lutwidge turned to stare over his shoulder. Charles swung his chair around. Ernest Charles looked faintly amused. Lutwidge, as he glared at the shadow haunting the back of his booth, looked hostile.

"Come for the fun?" Charles asked. "Captain Rosen, isn't it? What are you doing here?"

Rosen pointed again. "Captain Ware brought me over."

Because of Talley, Eileen thought. Because of what you and Dyson helped Talley do to himself. So *say* something. Rosen couldn't claim she was still surprised at the speed of events. When Eileen tried calling her, Rosen wasn't home. So Eileen immediately tried Sellert. He told her Rosen had been upset for some reason since meeting him and learning that a mission had been called. Rosen had been trying to reach Eileen, had given up, and had gone looking for her at the officers' club. That was where Eileen found Rosen five minutes later. Then she drove from the officers' club to the control center a lot faster than Mondrum's speed limit allowed. On the way over in the car, Rosen got to see how many of Dyson's over-prescribed tablets Talley had been hoarding.

Colonel Oliver Lutwidge, man of action with a hot mission on his hands, had turned his back again. "Next problem will be Pinkett's fuel state," he said to Wizer. "He's going away from home, so he's short on pursuit time. Set up alternative airfields for him and Talley."

Wizer nodded, pushed buttons, and started talking into her microphone.

Eileen pushed Jessica Rosen forward. Charles was the only one still looking at them. He still seemed amused.

"It's about one of the pilots," Rosen said to him. "Talley. Major Talley."

Lutwidge was jotting mission notes on a pad. "We're busy, Ernest." He didn't look up. "Get them out of here."

"We have a Red Wraith," Charles said to Eileen. "A *real* one. We're trying to tie him up. We really don't have time right now."

"Major Talley," Rosen repeated.

"Ernest, get them *out* of here."

"Drugs," Eileen said. "He has a serious drugs problem. He pockets the excess tablets Dyson prescribes. He's also obtained two prescriptions for quinalbarbitone sodium and dexamphetamine sulphate from Captain Rosen. He did this by lying to her about his work on Special Team."

"I wouldn't have prescribed for a *pilot* —"

"His wife tells me he takes quinalbarbitone regularly as a sleeping aid. Before this mission he might have taken —"

"I have someone working on alternate fields," Wizer said. "I guess Norway is out for security reasons. RAF Leuchars won't be any use if he chases Red Wraith much further north. We should work on the assumption it's going to be Keflavik."

"Right." Lutwidge started to turn around again.

"Also," Wizer said, "I suggest the minute Pinkett locks up the Red Wraith we should let the Awacs illuminate the area with radar. That way we'll see exactly where everyone is."

"Right. Set it up." Lutwidge completed the turn, swinging his chair away from the desk. He pointed at Eileen like a recruiting poster again, still thirsting for blood. "Get out of here!"

From left to right and right to left, high, level and low, she swept the sky with her eyes. Nothing but night with milky smears and star-dark marshmallow cloud. She'd started to circle again, slow and easy to conserve fuel. If she continued reversing back and forth, her F-15 would snake steadily northwards and further away from home. Fuel didn't last forever.

She switched the radar on as the heading swung through due north and counted down towards the west. On the screen she got the same bare fan of overlooked sea, with Pinkett's aircraft picked out clearly – and just in front of it, that flimsy ghost of the fleeing stealth machine. Red Wraith had settled on a new course, ten degrees east of north. He was set on making the long haul home around Norway, or he was aiming for an airborne tanker waiting to feed him somewhere deep inside the Arctic Circle. Soon he'd want to come up off the sea. The higher the altitude, the more efficient the use of fuel. Staying low, like running fast, is an extravagant way to fly. If Red Wraith lifted off the sea, he'd vanish.

But Pinkett just about had him.

Transmit. "Thorndike to Pinkett. He's three miles away, dead on your nose. I guess if it isn't snowing down there, you can already see his tailpipes on Iris." And if Red Wraith had a really good rearward looking infrared receiver, he should be able to see an F-15 closing from behind. In fact, if his radar warning receiver was sensitive enough on his tail sector, he should see Pinkett by secondary illumination from her radar. But if he knew Pinkett was there, he'd already be on his way up to the cloud where he could get into concealment, make a turn – and never be found again.

Pinkett was going to catch Red Wraith – and once he

got over Red Wraith's tail, he wouldn't let him go. If not even Bellman, God incarnate in an F-15, had been able to shake formation-trained Pinkett, a slow Russian stealth, down on the deck and with only a hemisphere of sky to play with, sure as hell wouldn't do it.

Her heading was northwest, 315 degrees, and they were gone from the radar screen. Maybe Red Wraith hadn't seen the aircraft on his tail because his self-protection sensors weren't discriminating enough. Or because it was snowing down there, in which case Pinkett couldn't see him yet, either. Don't let it go wrong now. Get another look with the radar without waiting to circle around.

She switched off the radar so its constant caress wouldn't warn Red Wraith. Then she reversed, banking right and pushing right rudder. Automatically, she checked over her right shoulder to get a look at the sky at her back —

The silhouette of a wingtip, outlined against starlit cloud, slipped out of sight behind the base of her right fin.

Someone was there.

She'd been circling for almost eight minutes, all alone in an empty heaven, round and forlornly around like God's last little angel, no one else near. She thought.

Someone was there. Right under her tail, where she was totally blind. He'd been pacing her perfectly, until for a moment he was caught when she changed the direction of her perpetual turn.

Someone had come in, probably slow, and probably low enough to be down among the clouds. He'd homed on her radio transmissions as she steadily vectored Pinkett towards his own target. He was probably helped by her radar floodlight — but the radar hadn't shown her he was coming. Eventually he must have seen her, warm and infra-red bright, against the freezing upper sky. And then he paced her in ascending circles until he'd tucked right under her tail. It was a textbook exercise in stealthy precision.

He didn't want to kill her. He could have done that long ago.

He was sitting right under her ass, photographing,

recording, and making a monkey out of her. He was some second Bellman, some think-alike, act-alike absolute asshole who'd gotten his cocksure self into the cockpit of the most macho-making secretive toy the Russians had to play with. She'd been watching the other one speeding for home all these minutes, and sometime in the middle of it, this second shadow had slipped in underneath her tail and stuck there.

Red Wraiths come in pairs.

Wizer was busy watching the wide Atlantic plot with its creeping bustle of air traffic, while listening to the mission out over the Norwegian Sea. Charles and Lutwidge were both hunched over the console beside her.

Then Lutwidge punched Charles on the shoulder. "Got the fucker!" He threw a comm switch on the console. "Control to Pinkett. Good man. Lock him up. Photograph and record. Watch for aggressive defense. If he gets dangerous, kill him. Control to Talley. Descend and make close support on Pinkett. Pinkett will talk you in. The two of you can box up the Red Wraith on the deck. Then one of you tumbles him with your slipstream and you fly him in one piece into the sea. Acknowledge, Talley."

"I'm not sure —" Charles hesitated. "We don't need to down him. Pictures will do."

Eileen stared at Jessica Rosen, but the medical officer had given up. She'd parked herself in one of the chairs at the back of the booth. Up to me, Eileen thought. Why is it always up to me?

"Talley," Lutwidge was saying. "Descend and make close support on Pinkett. Acknowledge."

Eileen stepped up behind his shoulder. Charles looked up at her, Wizer did. Lutwidge didn't. "Sir! It's the problem with Talley. He can't be relied on. He —"

Lutwidge's fist hit the rim of the console. "Shut your mouth! This is no game! We don't need —" Then he ripped off his headset and dumped it on the console. He started to climb out of his seat, twisting into Eileen. "Ernest, take it for a moment. Get Talley to answer. And as for *you*!"

Eileen tried to back off as he stood up. His hand grabbed the neck of her uniform blouse. Going backwards became a lightfooted balancing act.

"You and your *theories* tripping me up the whole time! Do I have to throw you out with my bare hands!"

Rosen had come to life again. Rosen was trying to get her arm across Lutwidge's chest. "Colonel, there's going to be an investigation as it is. Don't make it any *worse*."

"Investigation! Sabotage and investigations and my best pilot arrested! And now a proven combat veteran is supposed to be some kind of an – an *addict*!" His grip on the front of her blouse lifted her up on her toes. His knuckles tipped her chin back. "What in the name of Jesus is he supposed to have done wrong!"

"Colonel!" Rosen shook his shoulder. "Colonel Lutwidge!"

Lutwidge let go. He glared at his unclenched fist, and then whipped it out of sight. He took a single step backwards. But with the disengagement and token retreat, he'd done his bit for contrition. He was back at the edge he lived on, back under rigid and vicious control. "*What* is he supposed to have done?"

Eileen tugged her blouse in order around her waist. Under it, her shirt front was half out of her pants. She still wanted to leap for the door and run. But if Action Man wasn't going to budge more than a single step backwards – she wasn't going to damned well move an inch. "On the last mission he made a mistake. I think he might have shot down Romulus."

Lutwidge shook his head, as if the gods had made everyone else mad. "You people were muttering the same about Bellman. Now it's Talley. What do you hate my pilots for, woman?"

"I *know* he hit something. It's on the tape of the radar plot. He hit *something*. So why didn't he say?"

"Trouble!" Wizer was out of her seat, too, but she was

leaning across Lutwidge's vacated position. "Thorndike has another Red Wraith on her tail! She's calling Talley to back her up."

Lutwidge turned instantly.

"Talley doesn't answer her." Wizer held out Lutwidge's headset as he slid into his chair. "Let me use the Awacs to find where Talley is. Pinkett already has his Red Wraith locked up. If the Awacs illumination alerts the new Red Wraith to Talley's presence and spooks him, we don't lose that much."

"Do it." Lutwidge pulled his headset into place. "Pinkett can handle his end. We need Talley to go help Thorndike before she gets in a mess."

Jessica Rosen was reaching out to Eileen, as if to put a hand on her shoulder, as if Eileen looked as shaken as she felt. But a black woman can't go white in the face. It's her only advantage in life.

Rosen, though, stopped. She turned to the back of the booth.

Major General Elias Dodgson released the curtain and let it fall across the door behind him. He was in uniform — except that he had no hat, he had no tie, and the neck of his shirt was unbuttoned. But he looked amazingly awake. He ignored the frenzy at the control console, he ignored Rosen who shouldn't even be there. He stepped right up to Eileen. "Ware, do you realise what you're *saying*?"

"It's on the radar plot. And in the mission reports, sir. And what Talley reported doesn't tie in. He said he never saw a hit on his target, but Pinkett saw an explosion right at the moment —"

"You and Wolford already came to me with your concoction about Bellman, and his possible motive for taking out that aircraft. The sabotage was clear cut, but the rest sounded like crap to me. Now you dream up Talley. For Christ's sake —" Dodgson stopped himself, as if he wasn't prepared to let his voice rise in anger. He must have heard some of the previous yelling. "For *pity's* sake — tell me what state of mind the man would have to be in to go making a mess like that?"

Eileen couldn't answer. The universe was coming down on her head. Everyone would round on her for uttering the incomprehensible accusation. *All-American heroes don't make mistakes.*

"Drugs, sir," Rosen said.

Dodgson turned his head and looked at her.

"Talley." She had to pause long enough to assemble her courage. Everyone in the world was taller than Rosen, and now it was a general who was glaring down at her. "It seems he's been dosing himself regularly with psychotropic drugs, sir. That might induce judgemental errors. Under stress, that is."

He wasn't really flying the F-15. The aircraft was flying itself and he was just about keeping a check on where it was going. They gave him problems he didn't need, because under Quiet Sky with no radar and no IFF beacons, moving between aircraft positions was a game of blind man's buff where the targets themselves were travelling. That was bad enough, with the giddiness whirling in his head. But then they sent him back and forth as if they were doing their best to disorient him. First, he should close up to help Thorndike and Luzzi with their Red Wraith. Then control wanted him to turn around so he could help Pinkett trap the Red Wraith as it tried to escape. Now he had to run all the way back to Thorndike to help her with a second opponent.

Because Red Wraith turned up, like any other combat aircraft, with a friend.

His course was about right. So was his height. The nose kept dropping and he had to correct. The heading scale slipped repeatedly out to one side or the other, and he could hardly read the error any more. He kept his speed at five hundred knots because he wasn't sure he could cope with slowing down when he got to Thorndike's position. Things had gotten that bad.

He knew exactly what was wrong. He was up high in smooth air, but every symbol and instrument reading was blurred and quivering, just like the way it jarred and dithered when you were down low and flying at speed. But it wasn't vibration as turbulent air buffeted his machine. It was nystagmus, a quivering of the eyeball that made perception difficult and all but wiped out acute vision. It was one of the things a little too much barbiturate could do.

You didn't need nystagmus when flying – least of all flying at night with no moon on what was going to turn any minute into a tight maneuvering mission, and maybe a deadly one at that.

His mind was clawing to hold on at the sloping edge of sleep. He was at the edge, he was hanging over it. And so *slow*, his mind was so incredibly *slow*. And his hands were trembling when he let them. He had to clamp his fingers around the throttles and the stick, lock them so hard his forearms were starting to burn with the muscle tension. Every time he dared to relax, his hands shook and the aircraft wobbled. Do not drive or operate machinery when taking amphetamine or barbiturate: that was the routine medical advice. The joke hovered behind the Air Force's use of the things to boost both concentration and postmission relaxation for pilots flying solo at night. But it wasn't any joke at all.

They kept calling for an acknowledgement, for his course and height and speed. He wasn't going to transmit and warn Red Wraith that he was there.

It *must* have been Red Wraith on the previous mission. Red Wraith killed Romulus, and then Clyde killed Red Wraith. When their aircraft failed to return to its home base on the Kola Peninsula, the Russians would come looking. Angry, and nervous, and wanting to play safe – obviously they'd come in pairs. So if two had turned up this time around, it must have been a Red Wraith on the last mission. It just had to have been.

It was possible. It was plausible. It gave him the benefit of the doubt.

Time he started getting ready. He wasn't even going to switch Lolite on, the thing had made such a mess for him before now. But he could use the bright image of Iris combined on his head up display. It would give him a chance to see what he was shooting at. No repeat of nearly killing Thorndike.

He had to stare for a long time at the test set control panel, and then he had to aim his index finger carefully at the buttons. His arm didn't much want to move his hand around. Iris on. Aim again. Forward field selected. Aim again. HUD selected.

The radar alarm buzzed in his ear. Gradually he got his eyes to point at the radar warning panel and to decipher what they saw. It was an Awacs aircraft hitting him with its surveillance radar, lighting up the night for anyone with a receiver to see. He managed to check his IFF was off, and wasn't squawking back and alerting the Red Wraith as it kept Thorndike company on her journey through heaven.

37

March 4th–5th, midnight

Sandra Thorndike checked her radar warning receiver. She was being swept by the Faeroes station Awacs, and Quiet Sky was over. The Awacs would also light up Talley as he headed in from the north. If the shadow under her tail happened to see him by that secondary illumination, it might decide to cut and run. The risk of spooking the

Russian pilot could explain why Talley was answering neither her nor control. Maybe he was a stubborn genius.

Genius or not, her shadow might still see Talley and run. If the Red Wraith dived direct from his hidden position under her tail, she wouldn't even know about it until he was out of reach, in or near the cloud layer. She wouldn't catch him, the only way left to find him would be with a radar search, and then *only* if he was right down on the deck. That much luck didn't happen twice.

She pressed transmit. "Thorndike to control. I'm going to give my friend here something to think about so he doesn't have time to notice Talley. I'm going to try and get on his tail."

She didn't wait for, nor expect, any countermand from Lutwidge. In his terminology, right at the moment she was the realist, and he was just the desk theorist. She was the one who could feel this situation second by second. She could feel the fear of it. If the Red Wraith saw Talley coming and got really spooked, he might shoot her down to be sure she didn't chase him in close pursuit when he bugged out.

With him so tight under her tail, she would have no trouble throwing him off by using a two-plane maneuver – climb and turn or dive and turn. But if she tried that, he'd flee and disappear into the dark before she could get in behind him. A slow turn into a spiral dive might pull him with her, thinking he could stay tucked away in lag pursuit. But then he might turn out or dive down in a Split S, and she'd lose him just the same. So something different was called for. Something faster.

She checked her missiles and her gun, just in case. She released the gun camera. She put Iris and Lolite on record.

Flying straight in lag pursuit, they were starting with zero relative speed along exactly the same vector. She only had to shed a little velocity and force his airspeed up a fraction, and he'd be out in front. She started a gentle bank to the right with a touch of right rudder. No added throttle. He would have to give a little extra throttle to stay outside her turn and tucked under her tail: the wider radius required greater speed. The ice-smear sky and marshmallow-cloud flatness tipped lazily down towards the left, and the sloped horizon crossed the nose of the F-15. If he was playing lag pursuit she could play lag pursuit roll, unorthodox but unexpected –

She throttled back to provoke an overshoot. She pulled on the stick and the F-15's nose came up into the turn. She put the stick across hard left and rolled upside down against the turn –

There he was, right outside the top of her canopy and not two hundred feet away, trapped in a plan view against a floor of clouds. Broad black delta, forebody strakes, snub nose, long tailpipes with shallow outboard-canted fins. Up front the barely discernible outline of a long canopy with two sets of faint instrument glows inside it. And one behind the other, lit by starlight and brighter than the aircraft and the helmets and oxygen masks, two little pairs of cheekbones and eyes looking back at her.

The high gee roll took her up and over and outside his turn. She was dropping into plane and pulling her nose up hard to get full gee and lose more speed to force him out ahead of her –

Then he stood on his wingtip, presented his full delta again, and slid crabwise up the sky and across her canopy. He was rolling clean over her and whipping out of sight. She kept rolling, kicked the rudder harder right against the roll, let the nose down a shade and followed him over and around. She lost so much forward velocity with the double roll that she dropped in tight behind him. She *caught* him. She was riding just outside the curve of his slipstream in a turn, could see into his tailpipes and spot the fire deep inside.

He started jinking left and right and up and down. He looked too clumsy to jink that effectively, but he never once crossed the gunsight she wasn't going to use anyway.

Airspeed was coming off so fast she was going to stall if she had to throttle back much more. Maybe his wide delta could fly slower than an F-15. He would be wondering now if she was going to kill him. He was dancing too neatly to line up the gun, but if she dropped back to a thousand feet off his tail so the missile would have time to lock on, she could split his insides with a Sidewinder. He should use reheat and try to scram – except his engines wouldn't have reheat or they'd incinerate those long heat suppressing tailpipes.

One of his jinks stuck as a turn to the left. She followed, but the angle-off got uncomfortable as he climbed over her nose –

He pulled the turn suddenly tighter and broke hard left. She started to overshoot and he went sliding up and back at eleven o'clock high. His underside silhouette flattened as he banked hard and reversed right, crossing over the top of her canopy. She threw the stick right and kicked right rudder to follow – but he'd already crossed over her head and they were scissoring at spitting range.

At three o'clock his cut-out silhouette on the stars flattened and flipped as he reversed again. She reversed left with hard rudder but he'd already flashed up over her head because she couldn't fly any slower, but he could. As she started to come around left she found him high at eight o'clock over her left shoulder. One more reverse and he'd be on her tail to kill her, or just dive and disappear. He *could* fly slower and she needed a maneuver to avoid an overshoot *after* she'd already overshot!

He reversed again and started to come in behind her, unless she could delay the end with another scissoring reverse to the right –

Instead she pulled the nose up hard. She rammed the throttle through, then pulled it back and instantly rolled over inverted as she went up a forty-five degree climb, stick still back, turning it into the top of a loop – So that suddenly she was halfway through a miniature yoyo. She was upside down and looking through her canopy at his black profile against cloud, as he stood on his right wing, as he realised what she'd done and tried to turn out to his right —

She let the roll continue and then put the nose down hard as stars slewed over her head again. She dived, with him high on her nose against the cloud layer. She throttled back and zigzagged sickeningly left and right at crushing gee while dropping down the dive, throwing her airspeed away to each side and keeping her forward velocity vector low. She pulled out of the dive and dropped in behind his tail on a gentle right turn. Got him again — but the overshoot is still there. He'll break and start the scissors, which he can win again, and this time he'll be expecting the faked yoyo counter —

He broke hard right. She yanked her machine right to follow. Two reverses and he'd have her out in front again. He should make his first reverse now —

His end silhouette rotated left as he barrel rolled against the turn. A *mistake*. He thought she was overtaking faster after the dive than she really was. A barrel roll is wrong with a slow opponent on your tail.

She threw the stick left against the turn and barrel rolled with him. The gee force tried to fold her into the seat. Stars and cloud cartwheeled but she stayed on his tail with wings aligned. He rolled out level and started jinking. She levelled with him and pulled up the nose to trim high, dragging her wings through the air. She added flaps as if it was a landing approach. She dumped some more of her unwanted speed advantage —

She stayed back on his tail. She'd dumped enough speed. Her F-15 was more maneuverable than that radar-absorbing, clumsy but so luxuriously slow delta. For a moment she'd killed the overtake problem and could follow him anywhere. Anything he tried now, she could do at the same speed. He'd have to pick a straight dive into cloud. If she was still tight on his tail when he tried a hard turn out of the dive to lose her — if she stayed on his tail then, she'd have him trapped all the way to the deck. Down there, his delta would be a huge liability and she could hold him the way Pinkett was tying up his friend. And she'd have flown so much fuel out of him with the maneuvers that if only Talley would show with fresh reserves, they could fly him to exhaustion.

So where was Talley?

The Iris forward field was combined on his head up display, and right at the top of the field against its dark sky was a pair of bright specks. After Thorndike said she was going to tangle, he opened up the throttle to come in faster. Now his airspeed was going past Mach 1.2 at the same time as he was thinking his way through molasses. He didn't know any more how fast he was closing. Radar could tell him, but it would scream at Red Wraith that he was coming. What he was coming towards were two nose-to-tail targets crossing in front of him from left to right. Impossible. He should shed speed and turn in behind – but he couldn't remember how in heaven or hell the trick was pulled.

He only had seconds left to decide. He couldn't use a missile, not from any angle. Red Wraith would have heat suppression, so the Sidewinder would lock on to the nice hot F-15 right next to the Russian – and then fly clean up Thorndike's ass. So it was a gun option. But he couldn't use radar to help his aim. He didn't know how to handle a slowing down maneuver and come in for an easier tail shot. He was going to zip past at near enough Mach 1.3, at supersonic and a third. He was going to fly right on by, and he was too giddy and numb to think through the turn he'd need to come back for a second pass. A lateral turn would take too much space and too much time anyway, and he simply couldn't *cope* with the space and time saving vertical climb and turn-out of an Immelmann, not with hands that shook and arms that wouldn't work properly.

The two hot little targets were coming closer at top left in his head up display. He was rising steadily to take them. He fumbled the gun release and tried again. Something

unreadable for his blurred eyes lit in the bottom corner of
the display where the gun armed cue should be. The boresight cross appeared at upper center, just beneath the useless heading scale. It was going to be a crossing target, the
hardest shot of all, with no aiming radar or computer
assist, no working brain of his own and almost useless eyes.
He had no idea how much lead to allow, how far to aim
off, so the shells would shoot out ahead of the target and
it and they would fly into each other.

And which was the target anyway? Which one was
Thorndike?

She had Red Wraith on her tail. But she was going to
try forcing him out in front. Which of those fuzzy little
things in the infrared view was Thorndike and which was
the target? Think! It's about stopping Red Wraith and stopping him good. Catch him at all costs and clear your name
in the court of your own conscience. But don't get it wrong,
don't hit one of your own. Not the same horror for a third
time. So *think*. No time. No chance to call Thorndike and
ask. A zombie can't fly, talk and point a gun all at once.
So *think*!

They were much closer, crossing center. He pulled his
nose up towards their shallow underbellies. His useless eyes
couldn't make out any difference between them.

The lead aircraft was dancing in his sight even more than
the other. His eyes couldn't create the difference. It was
jinking. It didn't want to be killed by the one behind.

So he put the boresight on the second aircraft and closed
his finger around the trigger. Must be entering range —

Jinking? Would Thorndike be jinking?

She wouldn't jink. She'd want to swap positions, but she
wouldn't jink. She wouldn't want to escape. Red Wraith
would want to run, once an F-15 had forced itself in on
his tail.

They were coming right at him as he nudged the stick
and put the boresight on the jinking target, the leader. As
he squeezed the trigger and the gun screamed, he could see
it was no F-15.

He let go the trigger and put his nose down a shade. The delta of the Red Wraith went out right and up –

He forgot the lead. He forgot to aim off. He forgot the computer wasn't doing it for him. He had the fastest possible crossing target, and like a kid on his first flight he put the boresight slap *on* the target to fire. Every shell would pass behind Red Wraith –

The second aircraft, the F-15, flashed towards him, out of infrared and over the head up display, a silhouette against stars high on his nose. He saw it stagger –

Sandra Thorndike had never expected she'd feel it, if it ever happened. But the huge F-15 Eagle jolted in the air.

There was a bloom of light behind her.

As she turned her head left, for a fraction of a second, she saw the twin points of two tailpipes passing below.

Then she'd twisted all the way around, and was looking at white fire that torched out of her left wing and enveloped the tailplane behind it.

She shut her eyes and turned forward.

She opened her eyes again. Night vision ruined and she couldn't see a trace of Red Wraith, and she didn't give a damn. The shadow of her head and seat and shoulders was plastered on the instrument panel and the bowframe, and she couldn't even read her night illuminated instruments in the glare.

She could feel the machine slewing by itself around the sky, but she couldn't see any symbols on the HUD or the backup dials. She took her hand off the throttles to turn up the brightness of her instruments. She had to go right to daylight setting.

On the HUD the waterline sat below the artificial horizon – nose pitched down. The heading was turning steadily left. Altitude was winding off, rate of descent eight hundred feet per minute. Down in the cockpit, the fire warn panel told her both tanks in the left wing were ablaze. The caution panel said the control actuators for left flaps, left

aileron and left tailplane were out. Her Eagle was starting
to die.

But there shouldn't be more than dregs of fuel remaining
in the wing. If only it would burn out before the fire got
to the left engine in the back of the fuselage – or the huge
bags full of fuel a few feet behind her.

She pressed transmit. "Thorndike. I'm disengaging. I'm
hit. Left wing burning. I don't know if it's going to go out,
or if I'm going to blow. Point me at a ship if I have to
eject."

"Control to Thorndike. Understood."

If she had to eject. Nothing down there but cold winter
water. It would kill her in minutes. If she went in right
beside a ship that knew she was there, it would still kill
her. Only a helicopter hovering right overhead as her parachute hit the sea could pull her out in time. A miracle too
many.

"Control to Thorndike. We'll get you a heading. Did
Red Wraith fight? Did Red Wraith hit you?"

Fuck their intelligence requests. *She was on fire.* The bird
would blow up in her back!

Instead of panicking, do something. Find the right thing,
and do it fast!

If it's only dregs of fuel, a few score pounds, put it
out before it breaks through to the fuselage. *Blow* it
out.

She pushed the stick forward to drop the nose into a
dive. As the Eagle pitched over the top, it started to roll
left and slew against the roll – right tailplane working to
cause both pitch and drag, and the left tailplane doing
nothing at all. She countered with left rudder and right
bank. The aileron on the left wing wasn't working, and the
recovery was sluggish.

She got enough stability to stay in the dive. Then she
pushed the throttles through to pile on speed. She made
her own meteor trail, streaking down the sky. Framed in
the hoop of glare around her canopy, she could just see
those beautiful marshmallow clouds as they came up close.

Then she punched into the cloud layer and flared inside her own reflected light.

He saw the flash of fire – just a glimpse departing – over his right shoulder. He heard Thorndike call she was hit.

It didn't even shock him any more. There was a clear and simple inevitability, looking back. A hit-and-run driver must know the same slow motion state of mind. He picked the right target, but he forgot to aim off ahead of the target as it crossed. He forgot because his brain was as good as asleep. So all his shells passed clear behind the target. If it was being followed in a tight tail chase, well the following aircraft had to fly through his stream of shells. If Thorndike was flying that second aircraft, then Thorndike got hit. Simple.

So what should he do?

Over the Libyan coast, neither he nor Jake Baker knew what they'd done, if they'd really done it, until the mission was over and one F-111 was missing, and they each had time to think it slowly through. He still wasn't certain he had to believe it, until the Libyans showed the two bodies washed up on their shore. When Romulus disappeared, and the aircraft he fired at exploded as he was turning out, he didn't realise until they'd failed to find any escape capsule on the sea and were more than halfway home. By the time he worked it out he'd already helped do what little was possible. There was no capsule and there were no survivors.

Now he'd shot up Thorndike. No doubt about it. No time yet for guilt. At the moment she still wasn't dead. Get his mind turned around in its blind molasses and start doing something to help. If she had to eject over the Norwegian Sea, she'd need assistance immediately she hit the water or the cold would kill her. She'd need someone to spot where she fell.

He was the only someone anywhere near. But he was racing away to the south, more or less, and opening up the distance. Which meant he had to turn.

At speed, a turn would take forever, and if Thorndike ejected he'd never find her.

You need help to turn a speeding aircraft quickly. Gravity helps. How does it help?

He should be able to do this automatically – in his sleep, he would have said. But he was so far on the wrong side of the edge that his brain couldn't react, and he was going to have to work it out as good as from first principles. Gravity will pull you down, like it was going to pull Thorndike down. Gravity adds energy in a vertical direction. So gravity subtracts energy if you're trying to climb. Energy translates as speed.

The Immelmann. Half loop with a phase of vertical climb, so gravity can slow you down before you come out at the top. In plan form – viewed on a map – you can fly a square corner with an Immelmann, because you use the vertical dimension for the space the maneuver requires, and that space is even smaller because gravity drains energy and speed away and tightens the curve you can fly. On the way up you twist with your ailerons to take the new direction you want.

He wanted nothing more than back the way he'd come – just up and over the top in a half loop with a roll out level. Easy.

He tried pulling on the stick, but his right arm seemed hardly able to move it. By feel he knew the nose had pitched slightly upwards. He couldn't see the artificial horizon nor read the rate of climb figures in front of him. He took his left hand from the throttles and added it to the stick, then with both arms together he hauled the stick back into his guts –

Pulling gee. Pulling masses of crushing gee.

Taking the blood out of his brain, ramming his bones through each other. Just the HUD in front of him, and nothing else at all. Vertical yet? Pulling too much gee. Just the fuzzy center of the HUD, fading. So much gee. Must get over the top any moment. And then what? Fading. Doesn't even hurt much –

All the last lights had gone out in a deserted heaven where there's no God, no hope, no belief and no relief, where the altar of perfection is broken and dark . . .

Never blacked out since back in graduate pilot training. Long time ago. There's a problem with blacking out. There's a memory of the effects – the senses recover in seconds, but the mind doesn't work right for minutes.

Situation? With unconscious arms and no force on the stick, the aircraft should have gone over the top of the loop and settled out with its nose straight down in a vertical dive. That hadn't been the idea.

Isn't there something a pilot should do now?

38

March 5th

Sandra Thorndike fought the nose of her aircraft up again. With only the right tailplane working, the drag from the control surface was so asymmetrical that the F-15 wanted to slew around and tumble under its left wing into its direction of flight – out of control, breaking apart, killing her. She had to push the stick hard over to pitch the right aileron down, so it counteracted the tendency to roll caused by the single tailplane. The clockwise slewing force was worse: rudder countered it, but now the rudder on the left fin was dead and she only had the one on the right – more asymmetrical drag causing more slew.

It took a long time and a lot of height to pull out of the

dive. She finally levelled below the lowest clouds at six hundred feet, much lower than she wanted to be. Another two thousand feet of maneuvering room would have been nice, in case the machine started to sag away if more of the wing came off.

But beneath the layers of cloud she was in total darkness. Her dive had blown the fire out. She wasn't burning!

She shut down the left engine, cutting its fuel pump just in case something was still quietly on fire inside the rear fuselage. With the right engine only, she had asymmetrical thrust. The single rudder corrected it at the expense of asymmetrical drag.

With the stick centered, the Eagle wanted to bank and roll over to its left. The left wing had lost so much of its surface that it wasn't producing enough lift to balance the machine. She needed a steady touch of right stick to counter the roll. Yet more asymmetrical drag, since the left aileron wasn't working. She could reduce drag and reduce structural stress by losing speed. But as the speed bled away she had to trim the nose higher to increase lift and maintain altitude. The higher the angle of attack and the more violent the parking of air under the wings, the greater the vibrational stress on the damaged structure.

It was a trade, one way of shaking the machine to pieces against an alternative way. The trick of staying in the air as long as possible meant finding the safest compromise. The problem was, the margin for error had disappeared.

Well, she was flying the crippled machine. Next thing, she needed some direction to fly it in. Transmit. "Thorndike to control. Fire is out. I'm holding at angels six hundred, repeat six hundred. Did you find me a ship?"

"Control." It was Wizer's voice. Superman must be busy with important little things. "Can you fly home? We advise against ejecting over the sea."

Transmit. "I can fly the thing, just about. Eventually the structure's going to break. And I'm never going to get this bird down in one piece. I'll have to eject."

"Understood. Your nearest land is Shetland at one-six-zero miles. Can you make it that far?"

One hundred and sixty miles. She looked at her airspeed, steady at three hundred knots. Any faster and she'd be shaking the Eagle too much and shortening what was left of its life. How long would it take to cover a hundred and sixty miles? Around twenty-eight minutes. Transmit. "I guess I can try. Give me a course."

"Course coming right up in a moment. Did you get into combat with Red Wraith?"

Transmit. "No. I got into aerobatics, and I won. Then someone came from the side and hit me with a gun, I guess. I took one or two shells in the wing tank."

"Can you confirm it was not the Red Wraith you were tangling with who did the shooting? This is important right at the moment."

Was it, now? Holding a crippled aircraft in the air over the middle of nowhere ocean wasn't, maybe? Transmit. "It was not the Red Wraith I was tangling with. And I have my hands full here! Where's the course for Shetland?"

"Okay, we have the course. Turn on heading one-eight-one."

Transmit. "Heading one-eight-one. Okay."

The wing fire had taken out all her leftside control surfaces, and she was holding the F-15 in the air against unbalanced thrust, lift and drag. To accomplish the turn meant taking off a touch of the compensating rudder, and letting the stick come back towards the center so the right wing could rise and the left wing drop. Be smooth – be as smooth as possible through the maneuver. A trace too much roll or rudder and the machine will cartwheel and come apart.

The turn was lousy. But she got the heading around.

Transmit. "I'm on one-eight-one at angels six hundred, speed three-zero-zero. What happens next?"

"We watch you all the way. We're alerting emergency and rescue facilities on Shetland right now. By the time you arrive they'll have a helicopter in the air. Once you're nearer we'll give you a course to take you over land, then

we'll call your eject point so you come down nice and
dry where the helicopter can collect you. How does that
sound?"

Transmit. "Nice." The F-15 juddered for her. She had
too much nose-up for the crippled Eagle. She eased off a
little. "Hope I see you guys again. Who was it shot at me?"

No immediate answer. She was all by herself in invisible
night. With a single engine and wrecked control surfaces,
she was keeping an F-15 airborne on something less than
one and a half wings. She was almost half an hour from
safety, and that haven involved coming down on a parachute after flinging herself out the canopy on a rocket. The
process usually broke bits of a pilot. She was all by herself,
and it was a long wait for Wizer's answer.

"We think there was a mistake. We think Talley hit
you."

She stared at the symbols in the head up display. Heading
correct, altitude steady, horizon level on the waterline. She
decided quite deliberately: I can't handle both problems.
It's handling *this* problem which is keeping me alive. So
that other one will have to wait. She pressed transmit. "Tell
me later. Right now I'm busy."

The F-15 juddered again.

Major General Elias Abrams Dodgson had pulled a chair
forward into the middle of the booth. From there he could
see what Lutwidge, Charles and Wizer were doing at the
desk. He could also see the recessed screen where Wizer
had run the sequence from the radar plot recorded during
the previous mission. Frozen on the screen was the moment
when the plot cleared after Romulus had stopped jamming
every radar frequency.

Dodgson was in his shirt sleeves, with his tunic dumped
over the back of the chair. Slowly he leaned back, crushing
the tunic. He stared at the blank wall of the booth, and
sighed.

Charles unhitched his headset and rubbed the side of his
skull where the pad had pressed his hair flat. He turned

around, looking past Dodgson to where Eileen sat at the back of the booth. He didn't have an expression for her.

"Pinkett," Wizer said. "It's time to bring him back while he still has a fuel reserve at Keflavik."

Dodgson didn't move. Lutwidge nodded.

Susan Wizer flipped the communication switch. "Control to Pinkett. Confirm your alternative field is Keflavik, Iceland. Come on heading two-four-zero, repeat two-four-zero. You have seven-one-zero miles to Keflavik." She listened, then she looked at Lutwidge. "Pinkett wants to know whether he should disengage, or if he should shoot down his Red Wraith first."

Lutwidge turned towards Dodgson. He flexed his armature of oiled steel: Action Man acting in cold blood. "We can see exactly where Pinkett is. He's so low, if he puts his Red Wraith into the sea, it's going to hit right in front of him. We'll know exactly where the wreckage is sitting on the bottom. The Navy can go out there and get it. We'll have the highest intelligence return possible, short of bringing back an intact aircraft. Right, Ernest?"

"That's correct," Charles said carefully. "Although Pinkett has an entire film of pictures, plus his recordings on Iris and Lolite. That already fulfils the operational target."

"With bits of the aircraft we get a whole lot more."

Dodgson shook his head. "You might be happy to risk starting a war on your own responsibility, Colonel Lutwidge. But I'm here in this room, and that makes whatever you do *my* responsibility. And I am not prepared to risk starting a war."

Lutwidge waited for an argument from Charles. But Charles was busy checking the wire from his headset hadn't tangled. He wasn't going to vote against intelligence return, but he wasn't going to support any drastic action, either.

"The Cold War, some politicians say, is coming to an end." Dodgson shook his head again. "I don't know if that's true, Colonel Lutwidge. But I'm not going to go down in history as the man who prevented the peace."

Lutwidge still waited, taut and wanting to pounce. Charles stayed busy with the wire of his headset.

Dodgson waited for Lutwidge.

Lutwidge, robbed of his prey, finally nodded. "Disengage."

"Control to Pinkett," Wizer said. "Disengage and do not shoot. Repeat, do not shoot. Acknowledge." She listened for a moment longer. "Okay, Pinkett let his Red Wraith go."

Lutwidge took off his headset. Halfway towards putting it down on the desk he paused, and took hold of the hoop of the headset with both hands. His hands tightened. Eileen watched his hands, waiting for them to twist the hoop and snap it in two. My neck, she thought, or Talley's, or whose?

"Where's Rosen?"

Eileen switched her attention to Dodgson. His question was for her. "She went out, sir." Eileen waved vaguely at the blackout curtain over the door. "I told her not to leave the building."

Dodgson didn't even nod. He turned around to Wizer. "You checked direct with the Awacs. Are they sure?"

Susan Wizer had the same blank gaze for a general as for anyone else. "They're sure. They checked the recording of their plot. An F-15 — in other words Talley's aircraft — crossed right below Thorndike immediately after she stopped making tight maneuvers, and immediately before she called the hit. Talley made the pass, flew on for eleven miles, then threw a loop. He went over the top, and then he dived straight into the sea."

They made a silent little tableau, Charles, Lutwidge, Dodgson and Wizer, not one of them looking at anyone else. Then Lutwidge turned his eyes on Eileen.

She looked away. She found what Dodgson was staring at. On the recessed monitor screen was that frozen moment from the previous mission, the instant when Pinkett saw a fireball and Talley turned away from his gun attack. Wizer ran it for Dodgson. Eileen explained it. By the time he'd believed it, Thorndike was on fire.

Dodgson sighed. "Captain Ware, you said Major Dyson is expected back most any time now."

"Sometime after midnight, sir."

"Place a message with the gate that he reports to me the minute he arrives. Some of this is his mess. He's going to be the one to decide in writing – with reasons and the *whole* medical background – whether it was suicide, or Talley blacking out, or falling asleep, or what. *He's* going to be the one who writes that report, believe me. And Rosen is going to help him."

Lutwidge was still looking at her with the expression of a murderer thwarted at the moment of his pounce. His hands quivered as he held the headset. Eileen couldn't tell whether he hated her personally, or just hated her for being the messenger who brought the news. "I'm sorry," she said. "I'm sorry I didn't spot it sooner. I'm sorry I didn't see it in time to get them recalled, or stop the mission going out. I'm *sorry*."

Nothing but a stare.

"No one else spotted it at all," Dodgson said. "Right, colonel?"

Lutwidge turned away.

Dodgson sat upright again, hands on his knees and back stretched. His tunic slipped in a pile on the seat behind him. "Autopsies on all of this can wait. So can the other side's motive. Maybe they were just playing with their airplane, maybe they were trying to provoke something, maybe their leadership doesn't even know they were flying these missions. Main thing is, they weren't intending to shoot us up tonight, just trying to take us for fools. We spoiled that for them good – but we managed not to start a war. Right, colonel?"

Lutwidge, staring out of the booth into the main room, nodded.

"As they say in Strategic Air Command, peace is our business." Dodgson reached around and retrieved his tunic. He held it in front of him and started trying to organise it into orderly folds. "Major Wizer – you go down there and make goddam sure that when Thorndike jumps out over the Shetland Islands, she comes down dry and she gets helicoptered to a hospital in *minutes*. Ejection most always produces fractures and sometimes internal injuries, and it's a mighty cold night to be lying on a hillside."

Wizer took off her headset and stood up.

"And send someone up here as assistant for Colonel Lutwidge. He still has half his boys to bring home. Right, colonel?"

Lutwidge nodded.

Major Susan Wizer walked between Dodgson and Eileen to get to the door. As she was passing, as she was busy lifting the blackout curtain aside, she touched Eileen's shoulder. Just a brief pressure with firm fingertips. Someone doesn't hate you. Someone, at least, doesn't think you did wrong.

Dodgson held his tunic out in front of him by its folded collar while he straightened the sleeves. Even in the shadows, the material was visibly creased. He tugged at a cuff, and then he turned to look at Eileen. "Now I have a real bummer for you, Captain Ware. But someone has to do it."

"Sir?"

"You're the one officer here at Mondrum who seems to know Mrs Talley at all. After you call the gate about Dyson, go right over and tell Mrs Talley her husband is dead."

PART 7

Exorcism

39

March 8th

Outside the window, even the parking lot glistened where the sun peered in. An overnight frost had coated Mondrum with a white rime, and as the morning warmed under a faultless vault of English blue, the rime had melted. Mondrum had turned into an unreal world tiled and paved with glass, a fantasy landscape made from dazzling lakes of light and blind reefs of shadow. But the forecast for the afternoon said clouds were coming, with rain.

Sandra Thorndike was in Arlington Hospital with a broken ankle, a dislocated elbow, a broken collar bone and three cracked ribs — not too bad for an ejector seat ride followed by a parachute landing in a Shetland glen in pitch darkness. Another week and she'd be back in the States. Dwight Pinkett was already there, having been ordered by Famula to ferry his F-15 direct home from Keflavik. Charles was back in the Pentagon, Lutwidge was there to give his own briefings on Blind Date, Sellert was in Kirtland with his precious test sets, McGee and Luzzi were back at Bitburg. Special Team had only two assigned personnel to its name — Eileen Ware and Master Sergeant Rodeck. Tomorrow, Charlie Rodeck resumed his regular duties. Eileen was going to have to wait until her reports were done. It would be interesting to see if United States Air Force Europe could finally find a routine duty for her to do.

Operation Blind Date had turned up its Red Wraith. Lutwidge's final mission came in with Iris and Lolite recordings and a film full of pictures shot by Pinkett, together with Thorndike's debriefing information on the aircraft's performance. The Russians wouldn't be flying any more Red Wraiths around Nato's north flank, not after the buzzing they got when they were caught in their own trap, and not after they let their best kept aviation secret blunder in front of the eyes and cameras of a bunch of F-15s. If Moscow was looking to cut funds for new defense projects, the stealth aircraft was probably dead. Red Wraith was caught, Lutwidge and his pilots were vindicated, everyone should be happy.

Except that Major Craig Bellman was in prison awaiting trial, some people from Datadyne Avionics were answering questions for the FBI – and quite a few more people, including Eileen, would be working for a very long time before they were through with all the case related reports. Colonel Oliver Eliot Lutwidge found his success at running a longshot operation marred by doubts as to his suitability for further promotion into positions which demanded ever more personnel management skills. There was a disciplinary investigation lining up for Major Dyson and Captain Rosen: Rosen might survive it undamaged, but Dyson wouldn't. The Air Force was short one EF-111A Raven and two F-15 Eagles. Todd Beamish and Jake Baker had been killed in the line of duty, with Beamish leaving a widow and three fatherless children. And Major Clyde Lincoln Talley was dead.

If the Pentagon wanted to clear up the loss of Romulus, one day the Navy would go fishing for the remains of Beamish and Baker and enough bits of their aircraft to show what brought it down. The same wouldn't ever be done for Talley. His machine had dived vertically into the water at something close to one thousand miles per hour. Both F-15 and pilot would be nothing more than tiny pieces at the bottom of the Norwegian Sea.

"Break for lunch, captain?"

Charlie Rodeck was smiling at her, catching her dreaming instead of working. It was nightmares she was dreaming, not glistening parking lots outside office windows. She passed a hand over the papers spread on her desk. "You go, Charlie. I don't have time right now."

He stood up, buttoning his tunic closed. "Okay. Back in under an hour. By the way." He lifted his coat off the hook. "Seeing as today's my last day on Special Team, Jolene and me thought we'd like to invite you over for supper again. I mean – well, it's been nice working with you and all." He shrugged. "So how about it?"

Eileen shook her head. "I have too much to do just to meet today's deadline. I'm going to be here until midnight."

"Well – tomorrow. Or the day after. The kids would like to see you again. You impressed them. Can't you make time tomorrow?"

Time, she thought. All you ever really trade is time – for work, for rest, for people who seem to like you. "Okay," she said. "That's a nice idea, Charlie. Tomorrow's fine."

He grinned. "Six thirty. But it's just a family supper, you understand. No dinner party stuff." He started to open the door.

Outside the door, hand halfway raised to knock, stood Kathrin Talley.

Charlie Rodeck stepped aside and let her in. She was wearing the green Burberry coat with a scarf around the outside of its collar. Under the coat she wore a checked blazer, unbuttoned, over a white blouse, and then denim jeans and those low-heeled ankle boots. She looked ready for a walk on a day warming up at the end of winter. It was a world of brilliant sunshine outside – and she wore sunglasses.

"Be less than an hour," Charlie said. Then he went out and closed the door.

Eileen checked the papers spread over her desk were in a retrievable order, then pointed towards Charlie Rodeck's vacated chair. "Sit down, Mrs Talley."

Kathrin Talley rotated the chair and sat down, legs

crossed, coat falling aside to the floor. In the drab little office she made a pose of excellent taste. The lenses of her glasses grew paler. They never quite became transparent enough to show whether she'd been crying, or was concealing the fact that she hadn't. "My flight leaves in an hour. I came by to say thank you, Captain Ware."

"What for, Mrs Talley?"

"For trying to get my husband back on the ground before it was too late. No one else realised what was going on. Even I didn't see it. I wanted to divorce my husband and get away from –" She paused, then managed a twitch of a smile. "From the stress we were putting ourselves under. In part, that made me less attentive to the state he was in. I believe that gives me a large measure of guilt in his death."

"I don't think you should feel guilty about not recognising what he was beginning to do, Mrs Talley. He probably didn't recognise it himself. Drug dependence is a socially unacceptable behaviour, and the sufferer knows it. An intelligent victim of such behaviour can be amazingly skilled at concealment. It's much the same as alcohol abuse. Think how many people have a worsening drink problem that no one notices until it's far too late." Think how many people, she thought, start talking to brand new widows like a junior military police officer giving a lecture to service personnel as part of a social education program.

Kathrin Talley shook her head. "I'll decide to what extent I was wrong, Captain Ware. What would interest me, however, is what the conclusions are going to be in my husband's case."

Eileen didn't want to walk those waters. The final conclusions weren't hers to make, although most of the crucial information had passed through her hands. The end result of the official enquiry was probably predictable, but it was the unpalatable possibilities the enquiry would try to avoid that made the waters murky and cold. Navigating them would have to be confined to a quick little sprint across the surface. "Obviously, your husband was under more stress than he could handle. Unfortunately, he appears to have been very good at concealing his personal problems from his colleagues and superiors —"

"The Air Force takes care to supply specialist monitoring skills, in this case the unit commander and medical officer. They are supposed to pay particular attention to signs of stress in their pilots."

So Talley's widow was going to trip her before she got halfway across. "It's cumulative stress that's the most difficult to identify, Mrs Talley. A frontline pilot is trained specifically in resisting stress, and is selected on the basis of an ability to perform under stress. In a sense, a pilot is conditioned to suppress and conceal stress rather than externalise it and deal with it. Cumulative psychological stress just isn't going to show if the victim is motivated never to display weakness. Trouble can brew without the victim or the victim's associates being aware of it until things are ready to explode."

"Which is why stress evaluation and performance monitoring is supposed to be built into the system, captain. When it goes wrong, people have to respond in a manner designed to prevent, as far as is possible, further failures. What's going to happen to Colonel Lutwidge and Major Dyson?"

Kathrin Yvonne Talley, born Everett, Air Force daughter and Air Force wife, cut straight to the nerve of the Air Force's sensitive self-protection. And dumped Eileen in the murky depths. "I can only repeat some unofficial opinions I heard concerning Colonel Lutwidge, Mrs Talley. The assumption is he's probably going to stay a colonel until he retires. Major Dyson will have to answer to an investigation, and I guess he'll find himself on some kind of a disciplinary charge — but I'm not competent to judge on medical matters. I don't know what will happen there."

"And who will get the blame for the losses?"

Deep down in the dirty depths, Eileen thought. It would have to be the least uncomfortable set of culprits that still accommodated the unavoidable facts — convenient villains where available, and as few undesirable inadequates or wrongdoers as possible. The Air Force establishment wouldn't want scandals, internal or otherwise. "There's no way around the fact that your husband made a serious error and hit Thorndike's aircraft. I assume the error will go down as being motivated by fatigue, personal stress, and possible complications induced by self-administration of drugs. It's believed he was intending to return and render assistance by marking the point where Thorndike ejected or went into the sea, should that have happened. As I understand it he tried to make a turn in the vertical plane –"

"An Immelmann, Captain Ware."

"An Immelmann, yes. And then lost control of his aircraft, probably through blacking out."

"And the deaths of Beamish and Baker? You are the one who suggested he might have been directly involved."

And suggested Bellman might have been. She'd used both unthinkable notions as levers to get attention for what she knew to be fact – Talley's unfitness to fly, Bellman's sabotage. She still hadn't asked herself if she believed either suggestion to be true.

"The intelligence opinion is that there must have been a Red Wraith tailing Romulus, and that it shot them down. No one has an answer as to whether the infrared sighting they called was a missile, the Red Wraith, or Bellman's aircraft following even further back. The Russians didn't act aggressively on their second appearance, so the view is that the Red Wraith panicked and shot down Romulus when it saw Bellman closing on its tail. I believe that's Bellman's own explanation of what he was trying to do, incidentally – catch out any Red Wraith that was being too clever. It would fit with his personality that he didn't tell anyone else so he wouldn't have to share the glory. And then immediately after it shot down Romulus, the Red Wraith was engaged by both Bellman and your husband. No one knows whether or not either of them hit the target."

"So that's going to be the official version." Kathrin Talley smoothed a crease in the denim over her knee. "What's your opinion, Captain Ware? You spotted the inconsistency in the mission reports. What do you believe?"

"I don't know, Mrs Talley. I mean, the evidence for any answer is missing. Even in the case of Thorndike, I've heard the view that your husband might not in fact have shot up her aircraft. There could conceivably have been a *third* Red Wraith that remained undetected. It might have seen how Thorndike got on the tail of the second, might have been afraid she was going to kill the Red Wraith, so it attacked her. Your husband might have coincidentally made his gun attack at the same time, aiming at what he believed was the correct target, then heard Thorndike was hit and assumed he must have done it. I mean, with a near enough invisible aircraft involved, anything is possible." Like putting a Red Wraith on the tail of Romulus — a plausible and convenient villain whose presence or absence at the scene of the crime could never be proved.

Kathrin Talley shook her head. "That would be far too many coincidences. I'd prefer it, but I can't believe it's true. No one ever knows what's true."

"I'm sorry?"

"There's a film, captain. An extremely famous film by a famous Japanese director. It tells the story of a murder. There's the victim, the killer, and two witnesses. We hear all four testimonies — even the dead man gets to tell his story through a medium. We hear everything there is to say about what happened. But we still don't know the truth."

Eileen nodded. "I guess you don't see many Japanese films in the parts of Detroit where I grew up."

"I don't suppose you do. Shall I tell you what killed my husband, Captain Ware? Perfection did."

"I don't follow, Mrs Talley."

"Perfection killed him. There's no such thing as perfection. Nothing and no one is, or can be, perfect. But there's an all-pervasive myth of perfection. It's embedded in our culture as the belief that you can attain anything if you just try hard enough. It's the fictional legacy of an actual pioneer past. It denies circumstance and makes failure nothing else but the consequence of personal inadequacy. My husband was terrified of failure, of making an error, of not being perfect. He pushed too hard in his attempt to attain the impossible – the absence of error. He pushed himself over the edge and lost control. Our myth of perfection killed him."

"I don't think –" I don't like what you're saying, Eileen thought, it makes me uneasy and I'm sure you're wrong. "Isn't that an awful heavy answer just to explain a hit on a mistaken target when he was in – well, an impaired mental state?"

Kathrin Talley sighed. "I'm going to tell you something, Captain Ware. I'm going to tell you because as far as I'm aware, you're the only person connected with Special Team who in any way concerned yourself with my husband. In fact, you're the only person I'm aware of who actually realised how much of a mess he was in. So I'm going to tell you. I'm afraid it won't be of any use for all those reports you're writing, but I'd like you to know. I'm the only one in the world who knows this, you see, and at the moment I'm finding it a rather intolerable burden."

"What, Mrs Talley?"

"It's about the incident that established my husband as one of the best pilots in the entire Air Force."

The MiG, Eileen thought, the thing he didn't seem at all happy to talk about. "The Libya mission?"

"The MiG he was credited with as an unconfirmed kill. He never believed it was a MiG. He was convinced he in fact shot down one of the F-111s he was escorting."

"No." Eileen shook her head. A brand new widow, much less self-possessed than she's acting, might come out with all kinds of things.

"Whether or not it's plausible isn't for me to judge. My husband, however, was a pilot and an expert in such judgements, you'll agree. What *matters* is that he believed it was so. He never really came to terms with his fear about what he thought he'd done, and then it all surfaced again with this operation. It got worse when Jake Baker, his electronic warfare officer on the Libya mission, turned up on the crew of *Romulus*. And then *Romulus* was lost."

The connection closed all by itself. Talley must have seen the explosion. He didn't report it. Why?

"My husband believed he'd repeated the same error. The details of his reasons don't matter. He believed he might have shot down *Romulus* and killed Beamish and Baker."

Terrified of failure, of making an error, she said. He pushed himself too hard – pushed himself over the edge and lost control.

"He didn't actually tell me until just before he left on the last mission. We weren't exactly talking much by then. The point is, you see, I knew he wasn't in any state to fly. I didn't know the extent of his drug dependence, and at that stage I still thought he was using the things under medical supervision. But I did know he was exhausted and quite distraught. I only let him fly the mission because he was desperate to find Red Wraith. He seemed to think that if he could be certain it really existed, then he could also believe it shot down *Romulus* and he didn't. I know it isn't rational. He only believed he *might* have shot down *Romulus*, just the same as he only *believed* he shot down an F-111 over Libya. But he was terrified it might be true, and he was convinced the existence of a Red Wraith would alleviate that terror. Is this making any sense to you, Captain Ware?"

Eileen opened her mouth, she started to shake her head – but then she didn't do anything at all.

"It makes sense to me, after a fashion. It helps me understand where my own part of the blame lies. It also provides an explanation of what happened at the end of my husband's life, I think. Red Wraith turned out to be real. But Clyde wasn't fit to fly. He made a final mistake and hit Thorndike's aircraft, and all the Red Wraiths the Russians might possess couldn't protect him from it. I honestly don't know whether or not that was the only genuine mistake he made. But it meant he ran right into the ghosts that were haunting him. Now they're exorcised. Do you see?"

Eileen looked down at her desk. Interview transcripts, mission protocols, draft reports of her own actions, discoveries and conclusions — a shield of words being assembled that systematically screened out unpalatable possible truths, and the speculative privacy of a dead man's mind. Her own little piece of a cover-up, a soft deceit sanctioned by good intention and sealed by inaccessible facts.

Kathrin Talley stood up. "I have to be getting over to the airfield. The hardest part starts now, I think." She moved towards the door. "I have to face the children."

Eileen nodded. "Do they know — that he's dead?"

"Yes. But I have to decide whether I'll ever tell them anything more." She opened the door wide. "Well, have a nice day, Captain Ware."

"Sure. Thanks, Mrs Talley."

Eileen stared for a long time at the door after Kathrin Talley had gone. It all made its own kind of sense. It also matched up with whatever that was about hearing every angle on the truth without knowing what happened. Too many things turn out like that. Uncertainties always remain to haunt you.

Exorcism. It meant expelling a ghost from the place or person it was busy tormenting. Logically, the ghost would then have to find somewhere else to hide. That would be why Kathrin Talley told her — to spread the load. Eileen could feel a shadow moving in. It was going to be there for a while.

DAVID MACE

CHASING THE SUN

Michael Tranter was going to fly round the world. Solo. Non-stop. In a very special plane built to his own design.

The flight would raise millions in sponsorship for worldwide charities. And be worth millions in publicity for his computers-to-airlines business empire.

The empire that, beneath the bold, bright surface, was beginning to fall apart.

His back-up pilot, strictly for PR purposes, was Ruth Clifford. Not that she'd ever get her hands on the controls. That wasn't part of his plan.

But then the surprises began ...

HODDER AND STOUGHTON PAPERBACKS

ROBERT D. BALLARD and TONY CHIU

BRIGHT SHARK

A wrecked Israeli submarine is disturbed from its twenty-year grave off the coast of Crete by an American geological research ship.

A submarine with a secret cargo that still has the power to explode the entire Middle Eastern balance-of-power.

The Israelis are prepared to go to extreme lengths to destroy all evidence of its existence. And the Russians are prepared to use their latest underwater technology to stop the Americans from solving a long-buried enigma.

Dr Robert Ballard is best known for his discovery of the wrecks of the *Titanic* and the *Bismarck*. Now, with bestselling author Tony Chiu, he has used his unique expertise to tell a breathtaking story of underwater adventure and international intrigue.

'Compulsive reading' *The Oxford Times*

HODDER AND STOUGHTON PAPERBACKS

STEPHEN GALLAGHER

FOLLOWER

First she saw the tracks, clear but beginning to blur as the wind whipped up the powder-dry snow.

Wolf tracks. Ahead of her.

Then, out of the corner of her eye – a shape, outlined against the tree line. Behind her. Now out to one side, driving her like a sheep dog. Stumbling, panting, she struggled down towards the village and safety.

She sensed it closing in, huge and silent. Terrified, she looked around. And saw it rearing up, reaching out at her with its forepaws, lurching and determined . . .

Not a wolf. A Follower. A half-beast, half-human nightmare out of Scandinavian folklore. A creature come not just to kill, but to steal a new shape.

'Gallagher is a master of abnormal psychology and he just gets better and better' *Mystery Scene*

HODDER AND STOUGHTON PAPERBACKS

OTHER TITLES AVAILABLE FROM
HODDER AND STOUGHTON PAPERBACKS

DAVID MACE
☐ 58782 2 Chasing the Sun   £4.99

ROBERT D. BALLARD and TONY CHIU
☐ 58037 2 Bright Shark   £5.99

STEPHEN GALLAGHER
☐ 54062 6 Follower   £4.99

All these books are available at your local bookshop or newsagent, or can be ordered direct from the publisher. Just tick the titles you want and fill in the form below.

Prices and availability subject to change without notice.

Hodder & Stoughton Paperbacks, P.O. Box 11, Falmouth, Cornwall.

Please send cheque or postal order for the value of the book, and add the following for postage and packing:

U.K. including B.F.P.O. £1.00 for one book, plus 50p for the second book, and 30p for each additional book ordered up to a £3.00 maximum.

OVERSEAS INCLUDING EIRE – £2.00 for the first book, plus £1.00 for the second book, and 50p for each additional book ordered.

OR Please debit this amount from my Access/Visa Card (delete as appropriate).

Card Number ☐☐☐☐☐☐☐☐☐☐☐☐☐☐☐☐☐☐

Amount £ ....

Expiry Date ....

Signed ....

Name ....

Address ....